Caught in the Maelstroms

He's not part of the plan, but I wish he was.

Hanna Grace

To my younger self; the girl who was never anyone's first choice and always wanted what she could never have.

And to Joseph.
Also to Maddog.

ISBN: 979-8-9929988-2-5

One

Briar

The universe has a funny way of ruining your life. I try to think of it more as a redirection, but that's hard to do when everything is falling apart.

Just this morning, everything was perfect. Now, after condensing my entire life into two suitcases, I'm practically fleeing the country.

"Ladies and Gentlemen, this is the final boarding call for flight A239 to New York JFK International Airport. All remaining passengers, please proceed to gate twenty-five immediately. The gate will close in five minutes, and the aircraft will depart shortly there after. Once the gates are closed, they will not be reopened for any passenger."

The announcement plays over the intercom at London Heathrow Airport and forces me to move faster. I rush to keep up with my mom and try desperately to locate the gate before the plane leaves us.

We weave through the horde of people blocking the path until gate twenty-five looms over me. I catch my mother's side-eye, still radiating disappointment.

Her scowl vanishes as she offers the gate attendant a gracious smile. Handing over the boarding passes, my mother apologizes profusely for our delayed arrival as if the attendant cares. The tight-lipped woman barely looks at our documents before ushering us onto the loading bridge.

"Goodness, Briar. First, you're expelled from your university, and now we've nearly missed our flight home. Is there no peace with you these days?" My mother's voice sounds strained, but a touch of relief slips through as we hear the gate close behind us. Rolling my eyes, I follow her onto the plane.

The slight smile I offer the flight attendant who greets us feels forced. Nothing about today is going well, so why should I pretend otherwise?

My fake smile disappears as I glare at the back of my mom's head. "Mom, I told you I'm sorry. How many times do I have to apologize? I didn't mean for any of this to happen, and you act like I'm happy about getting expelled. I think you're forgetting this sucks for me, too. This is going on my permanent record. Law schools will see this."

"Briar, please," she begs, holding up a hand to silence me. She doesn't have to look at me for me to feel the annoyance and exhaustion radiating from her. "Just sit down. Let's get through this flight, and we can discuss this with your father when we land."

I sink into the seat I'll be trapped in for the next nine hours, exhausted. Disappointment still radiates from my mother across the aisle, but I do my best to ignore it.

I stash my bag under the seat in front of me and buckle the seatbelt. Relaxing back into the seat, I put in my headphones, drowning out the sound of the safety briefing and ignoring the animated demonstration by the flight attendants.

Eventually, I feel the plane pull away from the gate and begin to taxi to the runway. Moments later, we're airborne, and everything finally starts to sink in.

I'm going home.

This time, not just for a long weekend. Not just for the holidays. Not for an event. For real.

It's been six years since I moved to London with my mom. Back then, it felt like a new start, like something exciting. Now, I realize we were just running. Running from Montauk, from my parents' problems, from my problems. My stomach churns at the thought.

My brother and I, we used to be inseparable. Nate and I were practically attached at the hip. I can't help the longing that tears at my mind, remembering how we would wake early in the mornings to catch the sunrise, or how we'd spend hours building sandcastles, collecting seashells, or sneaking off to our favorite fishing spot.

The memories disappear in an instant as we hit a patch of turbulence. I grip onto my seat as the plane rattles, and the familiar pang of guilt washes over me.

My mom quickly moved the two of us from Montauk to London after my parents' separation, and we rarely come back to visit anymore. Now that the dust has settled, I get to be in Montauk four or five days a year, typically around Christmas. But not last year. We missed Christmas because I was sick and Mom deemed me too ill to travel.

But now I'm going home.

And none of the past matters anymore.

And I get to see everyone again.

I'll get to reconnect with my best friend Harper, and maybe I'll even have a cute summer fling like I've always wanted. *Maybe.* It's unlikely, seeing as I'll probably be spending most of my time with Harper and family. Although my brother is the only family member I can stand right now.

Throughout everything these past few years, Nate has always been my constant. Always just a call or text away. We'd do anything for each other. Without question.

The downside is dealing with my parents.

My mother was less than enthused about the unexpected invitation to meet with the headmistress this morning. Being stuck in Headmistress Feller's office is unpleasant on a typical day. With her lack of humor and her choice to forego certain personal care items, like deodorant, today, an unusually warm spring day, was not a good day to be trapped in a confined space with her.

According to the school, I was a model student. *Was.* Until today. Now, apparently, I'm the ringleader of the biggest cheating scandal in the school's history.

I thought it was a joke.

Throughout my educational career, I've always been referred to as "academically gifted" and praised for my high marks. The truth is that I have a near-photographic memory to thank for my academic success. I never needed to cheat.

However, according to their supposed trusted source, I am the mastermind responsible for half the class cheating on their exams. I balked at the idea, honored but unwilling to accept the undeserved title.

Nevertheless, the headmistress wouldn't listen to reason. Instead, she believed the "anonymous student" who overheard me crafting plans to cheat on our exams.

What the informer forgot to mention was that these "plans" weren't mine. And that they were made in good, a way to blow off steam from the impending week of hell.

The second year is the hardest, and no one felt remotely prepared for the end of term exams. So, a handful of my friends, well, we did what any student would do. We went for a drink to revel in our misery. And one drink led to another, and before long, we started to feel better. Sort of. It even made Kent, my roommate's boyfriend, loosen up enough to crack a joke about being desperate enough to cheat on his exams.

But that was all it was. A joke. To the best of my knowledge, none of us chose to cheat on our exams. We all know better than that. But for the school, it was of no importance that I had no part in leading or participating in the alleged cheating scandal.

There was no investigation. No looking into the matter. Nothing. The university was happy to enact swift justice. And that "justice" was my untimely departure from the ever-prestigious London School of Economics with a now tarnished academic reputation.

Within the hour, the school informed my mother of my immediate suspension, and the headmistress summoned us to her office for a conversation, as she liked to call it.

After lengthy negotiations and a generous donation to the school, the headmistress agreed to finally investigate the matter. For now, I have completed the semester with an incomplete, and pending the final results of the investigation, I could be up for expulsion.

To say that my mother isn't very pleased with me would be the understatement of the century. But I can't blame her, especially after spending four hours locked away with Headmistress Feller. After only an hour, the woman could make even the sanest individuals mad. And after four hours, clinically insane doesn't begin to cover it.

But now here I am, wilting under my mother's scrutinizing glare as I try to figure out what I'm supposed to do now.

Because being expelled was never part of the plan.

The plan was law school.

The plan was Yale.

But right now, I can feel that plan slipping right through my fingers.

Two

Rowan

"Let's go, Nate. You got this."

Darian's words are encouraging, but I doubt Nate hears them over the sound of his own grunting.

"Bro, how many reps of this are we doing?" Nate huffs. His arms are shaking, and he's struggling more than he should with the weight, but he doesn't stop.

"Only eight reps. Not that hard, but I guess there's no shame in dropping some weight." I joke, "Unless you're trying to impress someone."

He takes a sharp inhale and pushes through the reps before dropping the weights with a grunt. He's red-faced as he stands from the bench, pushing back his shoulders to look bigger than he is. But even at his full height, I still have a few inches on him. And we both know it.

"Why don't you shut up? We all know you're out here falling all over some girl who won't even look at you for more than two seconds." Nate's tone is sharp but laced with sarcasm. He moves over to the old, rickety oscillating fan in the corner and lets it cool him. But the stench of his sweat permeates the air. Darian chuckles, shaking his head. They love that I'm finally having girl trouble.

"Damn. That's tough, Rowan." Darian continues to laugh as he walks over to pick up the weights Nate dropped. He flops back onto the bench and powers through his reps like they're nothing. He's not even breathing heavily when he's finished. Not even sweating.

"You have no idea what you're talking about. I could have Calista in two seconds if I wanted. I'm Rowan fucking

Callahan. I mean, look at me. I'm a perfect specimen—a Greek God." I gesture to my body, making sure to flex every muscle. Darian and Nate both stifle their laughter and roll their eyes like they aren't having any girl trouble.

"He's got no shot." Darian elbows Nate, his words almost too quiet to hear. *Almost.* I level him with a glare as Nate slaps my back.

"No, man, really, what's happening with you and Calista? You taking her to the party tomorrow night or what?"

I shift my gaze to Nate as he waits eagerly for a response. They both wait. But there's nothing to tell.

"Yeah, about that." I run my fingers through my sweaty hair. "She keeps telling me I don't have what it takes to date her. I don't even know what that's supposed to mean. She walks around, thinking she's the hottest girl on the island. But she'll come around."

At least I hope she will. She's having me chase my tail for nothing. And I'm starting to think she gets some sick kind of enjoyment out of playing these games.

Darian bursts into laughter with Nate, ripping me out of my thoughts. "She is the hottest girl on the island, dude. You're an idiot!"

"She has every guy out here chasing her, begging for a date. At this point, what makes you any different?" Nate chimes in between his heaving breaths.

I'm different because I'm better than the other guys. But I keep the thought to myself and snatch the weights from their spot and start on my set.

"See, people say stuff like that, and it just feeds her ego." My words are more grunts and pants than anything else as I start in on my set.

And I'm starting to think that maybe I shouldn't have given Nate so much shit. The weights are actually heavy. Heavier than I thought they'd be.

"I told her I was taking someone else." I force the words out before letting the weights clank to the ground, echoing through the nearly empty gym.

"Yeah, bro?" Darian leans over, giving me a pat on the back. "Who are you taking instead of Calista?"

I breathe deeply. This is the part I was hoping to avoid. But the pair have their full attention locked on me.

"See, that would be the problem. I don't know yet." My admission hangs in the air for a split second before the boys double over in more laughter. They're sucking in ragged breaths, and yet somehow manage to continue to laugh between it all. I ignore them and put the weights away while they continue to cackle to themselves. After a full minute, they finally calm down enough to speak again.

"You're an idiot," Darian says, wiping a tear from the corner of his eye.

"Yeah, yeah." I brush him off. "Anyways, Nate, are you taking Melissa? I mean, hell, are you guys hooking up yet?"

"Yeah, we'll meet at the party, but I'm trying to take things slow with her. It just feels different with her, man. I don't want to get ahead of myself and ruin anything," Nate chuckles, rubbing the back of his neck as a flush comes to his cheeks.

"Look at you! My man!" Darian is far too excited, but I can tell Nate likes her. It's hard to miss, especially when you've been friends with someone since primary school. He talks about her every chance he gets, and he's cut off every other girl in his life. He's practically in love. It's almost disgusting.

With an unspoken flow, we move to the next exercise as Nate prattles on about Melissa. Again. I don't pay much attention to what he says; it's nothing I haven't heard before. She's so pretty. And so smart. And she's practically perfect in every way. Blah. Blah. Blah.

Instead, I try to focus on my set. But I can't focus, and my mind drifts to tonight. I rack the weights and give the boys a sly grin.

"You guys still in for the poker night I'm hosting at The Lounge tonight?"

"Hell yeah, man!" Darian responds excitedly while Nate shakes his head.

If there's one thing about Darian, he's always in—no question. I knew he'd be there.

It's Nate that I'm really questioning. He's been so wrapped up with Melissa lately and learning to take over his father's business. He's the one who always bails, which is new for him.

"I wish, but my dad called me earlier and said dinner tonight is mandatory. I don't know what that means, but I hope it's not another business lesson disguised as a meal. I can try to make it after dinner."

"I'm sure the Russian twins who are flying in tonight will miss you," I taunt Nate.

"God, I love when Nadia and Yelena come to visit. You know I wouldn't miss that." Darian looks at me knowingly, nearly drooling at the thought. He's a horrible gambler but loves blackjack. But he mostly loves the girls who work at the club. And I'm happy to take his money any day of the week.

"What time is this dinner, Nate?"

"Not until seven," he says, trailing off as he searches for his phone. A glance at my watch lets me know he's cutting it close. Really close. And his old man won't like that.

"It's already after six," I tell him as Darian, and I move on to what I hope is the last set for the night. Every muscle of mine is sore, and I still have hours of work ahead of me tonight.

It takes more than just showing up to get The Lounge ready for the poker game tonight. And Kai, my business partner, is the least valuable player when it comes to running the business. He couldn't tell you anything about our bar, although he might correct you and tell you it's *his* bar.

Which it isn't.

And if tonight's game of blackjack is going to be another success, I have to be on my A-game.

"Great," Nate groans, grabs his water bottle, and rushes to the door. "I've got to go. Let me know how the game goes…and say hi to the twins for me." He throws us a smirk over his shoulder as he heads out the door to his car.

"You're not telling those girls Nate said anything, are you?"

I shake my head. "Absolutely not."

Three
Briar

The drive home is silent. Painfully silent. The only words spoken come from my mother, delivering directions as if our driver doesn't already know the way. He's got the GPS pulled up, but he hums along to my mom's suggestions. As we near the place I've longed for, I take in the familiar scenery of the island. The heat is there, too, but it's a welcomed warmth—a feeling of home. Aside from a new shop and a few new houses littering the landscape, not much has changed.

After what feels like the shortest and longest hour of my life, we pull up to the gate that separates the island from the mainland. Seeing the looming wrought iron, my eagerness to be home fades. Now, it is an even mixture of excitement and dread. The gates open, welcoming us in, and I suck in a breath as I prepare to face what's to come.

I brace myself as my father's disappointed face swims in my mind. Disappointing him is worse than being subjected to Headmistress Feller's stench. His disappointment lingers much longer than her acrid scent.

There was a time when I'd have been described as a daddy's girl. Tall and broad-shouldered, Jamison Abbott is the biggest name in international finance. He's unquestionably the best, and his travel schedule keeps him busy. Just busy enough not to visit.

As we pass the rows of houses, I settle into my seat and try to relax. If I know my parents, the consequences won't be severe. Things will be tense, and then we'll all try to forget what happened and move on as planned. That's how it always goes.

And forgetting, that's what we Abbotts do best. WE love to pretend the problems in our lives don't exist.

As long as nothing impedes my plans for my future, no one bats an eye.

As long as we don't tarnish the family name, we're in the clear.

Nate and my futures have been carefully mapped out since birth. Maybe even since conception. We know what's expected of us. Nate is expected to follow in my father's footsteps. And they expect me to do what I supposedly do best: argue with people. They've built this family in the exact image of their dreams, anything for us to look like the perfect family.

Before long, we pull into the driveway, and the nerves settle back in. The house feels bigger than I remembered and looks a little lonelier, but otherwise, it's the same. As I slide out of the car, the setting sun paints the house with beautiful hues of pink and orange. It almost doesn't look real, like it's a painting of a house that's home to a happy family. Not the shell of a broken home that it is now.

The front door opens to a disappointingly empty foyer. The only sign of life is the heavenly aroma that fills the house. Everything looks just as it did the day we left two Christmases ago, the same furniture and décor, all neatly tucked in the same places. It is as if this place were frozen in time, waiting for us to come home.

For *me* to come home.

For a minute, I almost expect to hear the rowdy laughter flitting through the house. But we haven't had that here in years. Not since we left.

I drop my bag on the console table and follow the voices coming from the kitchen. The sound of my mom announcing our arrival makes me jump, her voice louder than usual.

"Hello, we're here!"

The kitchen conversation abruptly ends, and my father and Nate turn the corner to greet us. The pair is a sight for sore eyes and makes my heart swell. I'm really home.

My father's face is kind as he opens his arms for a hug. "Ah, Briar! It's good to see you!"

He rubs small circles on my back in a comforting way. I hug him back and inhale his familiar cedarwood and rosemary scent.

He pulls away and greets my mother with a polite, rehearsed smile. "Marie, you look lovely." She returns the gesture with a slight nod.

But my brother remains in his spot, frozen and dumbfounded as he looks me over. In an instant, he regains control of his body, shouting, "B, I can't believe you didn't tell me you were coming for a visit! Get over here!"

He pulls me in for a hug, and I can't help but smile through his bone-crushing embrace. "It was more of an impromptu trip," I mumble against his shoulder.

Nate releases his hold on me and turns to our dad. "So, this is why dinner was mandatory tonight?"

Dad nods. "Well, it's one of the reasons. We can get into the rest after we sit and catch up."

Before I can stop it, I snicker at Dad's response. I've always been impressed with how artfully he can sidestep questions. He could be a politician with how careful he is with his words. His non-response placates Nate as we move toward the pre-set dining table.

As dinner begins, we fall into easy conversation. Dad shares his most exciting acquisitions and recent travels, which include an upcoming trip to Milan. Nate regales us with his fraternity event antics from his semester at Columbia. Mom glows while talking about the new celebrity clients she's signed, and I can't help feeling proud of her and all the work she's poured into her PR agency.

I'm proud of all of them. Proud of how they're all doing exactly what they set out to do. And here I am, trying to salvage my reputation.

Finally, it's my turn to share, which feels less exciting considering the circumstances. I can feel the tension in my parents' shoulders as Nate leans forward and rests his elbows on the table.

"What about you, B?" Nate eagerly awaits my answer, blissfully unaware of our parents' mood shift.

"Well… it's been an interesting semester." I laugh nervously, glancing between my parents' stern looks and my brother's curiosity. "To make a long story short, I'm taking some time away from London and its 'poor influences' after getting suspended."

My mother rolls her eyes at my use of air quotes, but I'm not focused on her reaction. I keep my eyes locked on my father, searching his face for any sign of what he's thinking. But he's stone-faced and gives nothing away. The four of us sit quietly around the table in the uncomfortable and nearly deafening silence.

Nate is the first to break the quiet, barely containing his amusement. "You've got to be joking. Expelled?"

I shake my head. "Just suspended. For now."

Nate's booming laughter fills the kitchen, but my eyes don't leave my dad's. We're locked in what feels like the most high-stakes staring contest. I'm trying to silently convince him of my innocence, and he's searching for any trace of guilt.

"Care to explain yourself, Briar?" My dad's voice is calm, almost too steady. To anyone else, it might seem like he's genuinely interested in hearing my side. But I know better. It's not curiosity. It's a warning.

I give him a curt nod and choose my next words carefully. I don't want to show how worried I am, afraid it might read as guilt.

"I'm being wrongly accused of masterminding a cheating scandal." My words hang in the air.

Dad shakes his head and looks at me disapprovingly as Nate erupts into more laughter. "That is hilarious, B." Nate's comment earns him a stern look from both of our parents, which quiets him quickly. Then all eyes are back on me. And now I'm in full-on defense attorney mode.

"I was kindly graced with the title of ringleader by an undisclosed source. There's no evidence I was involved. The school acted on hearsay. It's defamation, really. The argument wouldn't hold water in a court of law, so I don't see how this is grounds for suspension, let alone expulsion."

I do everything I can to keep my tone level, but I can feel my voice shaking. My dad responds best to facts and reasoning, so that's what I'm trying to give him. We're a lot alike in that way. So I have to present my case, just like I would for a judge.

The tension in the room is palpable. My dad sits across from me, dissecting every word and silently assessing me.

Dad clasps his hands and rests them on the table. "I cannot believe we have to have this conversation again. While Nate may find this amusing, I can assure you neither your mother nor I find this to be comical in the slightest. What on earth were you thinking?"

I have to fight the urge to roll my eyes.

"I didn't cheat. I didn't tell anyone to cheat. I had nothing to do with this." I feel my composure slipping as desperation seeps into my voice. I can't keep fighting to prove this isn't my fault. My dad must sense the frustration radiating off me, and he gestures for me to continue speaking. I finally let my gaze drift across the table and see my mom, arms crossed with her glare trained on me.

"I didn't cheat. And the school didn't even plan to investigate."

I sit silently, waiting for my parents to say something. Anything.

"I didn't cheat," I repeat, praying that hearing it a second time will somehow make them believe me.

Silence. Again.

Finally, my mother sucks in a forceful breath. "We'll speak with the school and the board of directors on your behalf to hopefully sway their decision not to expel you."

I feel the pressure in my chest loosen slightly. Only a bit, but it's enough to let me breathe again. "Thank you."

"But," my dad interjects, "you're to spend the rest of the summer here in Montauk, where I can keep a close eye on you. That includes a ten o'clock curfew and no more trouble. Even a hint of trouble, and expulsion will be the least of your concerns."

I nod along and try to hold back my smile. This may be his attempt at punishment, but it feels like I've won the lottery. A whole summer back home. Rules or not, this is better than I could have hoped for.

"Of course."

Their brows raise with my quick agreement, but they don't question it. If anything, they look relieved to be done with the conversation. And neither parent spares me another glance as they get up from the table and go their separate ways.

As soon as they're both out of earshot, I exhale a long breath. That went better than expected. No argument. The truth is out. I survived dinner.

Two seconds later, Nate erupts into laughter beside me. "A cheating scandal, B? I swear, I don't even know who you are anymore," he mocks me as I shoot him a dirty look.

"You got expelled? That's hilarious." I can barely make out the words as he forces them out between heaving breaths.

"I didn't cheat, and I'm not expelled," I push back, my brows raised in as much of a pointed look as I can muster. "Yet."

"I know. I know. But seriously, it's good to see you again," he says, leaning back so far that the front legs of his chair lift off the ground. "I can't believe I get you for the whole summer. We're going to have one hell of a time. Plus, I get my workout buddy back."

"I'm excited to be back," I agree, but my mind is already drifting to thoughts of days by the pool with Harper, and nights avoiding our brothers. It will be just like it used to be, except maybe this time things will be different.

Maybe this time I'll be brave enough to actually go after the things I want.

The person I want.

I might have survived dinner, but now I have to survive the summer.

Four
Briar

Nothing compares to a good night's sleep in your own bed. Well, maybe a slow morning and a croissant from the café around the corner from my university flat. That's a close second.

Sunlight spills across my childhood bedroom. Everything here seems so peaceful and still. Everything is just as it's always been. And the thought makes me laugh because everything is exactly as it was when I left, it's like no time has passed. Everything has stayed the same.

Everything except me.

I inhale deeply and can nearly smell the ocean that crashes against the sand outside my windows. Getting out of bed, I pull back the curtains to reveal the beautiful water reflecting the morning sun at me. The waves stretch out to the horizon, tempting me to disappear into them. I can't do that, but I can go out to re-explore the island I get to call home for the summer. Before the peace evaporates.

Downstairs, I find Nate sitting on the couch, lacing his own running shoes. His fingers fumble with the laces as he yawns. He barely notices me with his eyes closed under the brim of a hat that I can only assume covers his bedhead.

"Well, good morning, brother, who I love dearly," I greet him with an overly enthusiastic smile. "Are you also running on this fine and beautiful morning?"

He levels me with an I-hate-how-peppy-you-are-in-the-mornings glare. "Yes."

I opt to ignore his death stare. "Do you mind if I join you?"

"That depends. How many miles are you doing today?"

"Just the usual route." I trace a circle in the air beside my head as if to signal the path I plan on taking. Nate doesn't need the visual. He knows the route I'm talking about. We ran it every single day in middle school. The one that goes down by the water and back up to our favorite breakfast spot. The route I know will be empty because no one else likes the hills.

"That works." His voice is still rough. I chuckle as I head outside with Nate and his lack of enthusiasm. Maybe after a mile, he'll be able to string together an actual sentence that consists of more than one or two words. After a quick stretch, we start with a slow jog. I let the warm morning air relax my muscles as we follow the gentle turns of the pavement.

Nate doesn't take longer than a minute to find his voice. "How was it sleeping in your bed again last night?"

A grin spreads across my face. "Nice… and amazing to wake up to that view," I say, pointing toward the ocean only a block over. "But it's weird that nothing was out of place. And I mean nothing. I think the trash was exactly as I left it."

He chuckles, beginning to pick up the pace. "That's fair. Dad and I never go in there. Hey, the bonfire's tomorrow night. You going?"

I light up at the mention of it. The bonfire is the official start to all things summer. Everyone comes out, and the parents turn a blind eye to it. "I forgot about that!"

"Good times," Nate muses.

"There's no way I'd miss it." I kick our pace up a notch and take the familiar turn that leads us toward the café.

"Last year, a couple of parents showed up to the thing. Safe to say it was a buzz kill." Nate's laughter sounds strained, but I give him a wide-eyed look. I cringe at the thought of our parents attending a bonfire for rowdy teenagers. A shudder runs through me.

"I'd be so embarrassed if it was Mom and Dad," I tell him.

"I think their heads would explode." His voice is soft, but there's a slight accusation in his tone.

I nod in agreement, hearing the words Nate didn't say. If they stopped arguing long enough to notice they were out of place. We drop the subject and take a few minutes to focus on our breathing as the hills start.

In the silence, I find myself questioning who I might run into at the bonfire. And who I *want* to run into. Rowan's face flashes through my mind, but I quickly push it aside. He's off limits. He's Harper's brother and Nate's friend. That's too messy and has trouble written all over it. And this summer is all about staying out of trouble.

At least until I can get back on track.

I'm pulled out of my daydream and laugh as I hear Nate practically wheezing beside me.

"You okay over there? Not getting tired, are you?" I tease him, but he smiles at me.

"Who, me? I'm fine. I didn't remember the Sunrise Café being this far away, or the hills being this steep. I think you're taking the long way."

"Right." I drag out the word, not believing his lie for a second. I push myself to run faster and watch Nate struggle out of the corner of my eye. After another mile, the Sunrise Café comes into view, and I start to slow my pace.

"Oh, don't slow down on me now, B. Final sprint. Finish strong." He's gasping for breath now, and suddenly I'm not sure he's run at all since I left.

"I'll race you," I offer, grinning mischievously, anticipating the easy win. He's sluggish and already panting, but I watch Nate mentally weigh the challenge.

"You're on. The last one there has to pay for breakfast."

"Deal," I tell him as I pick up my pace to a full-out sprint. My legs burn, but I keep the pace and cross the entrance into the parking lot two steps ahead of him.

"I win, Nate! You've gotten slow, I see. Practically an old man now."

"Don't call me old. You're old," he snips back, a lazy smile on his face as he leans over, trying to catch his breath.

"Wow. Slow and bad at comebacks. You've seriously declined." I wipe a few beads of sweat from my forehead and start toward the front door.

It swings open with a chime, and we sit at our usual table in the back corner. A young-looking waitress approaches us, ready to take our order. She's cute, and her gaze lingers on Nate, but I don't miss how my brother's eyes skip over the girl altogether. He barely spares her a glance as we order our breakfast, and Nate's three sides of bacon.

"No way you need three sides of bacon," I laugh as the waitress walks away. No, she saunters. And he doesn't even glance her way, which only confirms my suspicions. Something's got to be up, and it smells suspiciously like a crush.

"Protein!" He nods along and gives me two thumbs up in response.

I don't even have a chance to question Nate's dismissal of the girl before our food is in front of us. And all conversation stops when our plates hit the table. Nate all but inhales his meal, three sides of bacon included, before I've even made a dent in mine.

"Gotta make a stop on the way home. See somebody." Nate tosses some cash on the table and leans back in a way that screams he's trying to look composed.

"Ooh la la," I sing. "A girl?"

He gives me a pointed look.

"Why so secretive, Nathaniel?"

"I'm not being secretive," he says, ignoring my question and the use of his full name.

"She must be serious if you ignored our waitress for her."

He laughs off my comment, but I don't miss the blush that colors his cheeks as he stands up. "See you at home later?"

"I'm right! I know it!" I call out after him, but he walks out the door as quickly as he ate.

Left alone in the booth, I smugly finish my breakfast and enjoy people-watching as people begin to filter into the café. As I sit, I feel a pair of eyes on me and find the waitress watching me. She doesn't avert her gaze when I catch her. Instead, she tilts her head curiously, like she's asking me a silent question: *He just left you here?*

I flash her a polite smile to hide my discomfort and slip out of the booth.

Suddenly, the island feels too small, and it feels like everyone knows how badly I screwed things up. Like they know that I'm out of my depth. So, like always, I head out and run home to hide from the truth of it all.

Five
Rowan

I'm still dateless for the party tonight. And Darian and Nate still find that fact absolutely hilarious as we pull into the driveway at Nate's house.

"Bro, you're screwed. You still have no date, and Calista won't want a spot no one else is fighting for." Darian taunts. I shove him as we head up the stairs toward the front door. "What are you going to do? Just not show up to the party?"

Darian is already struggling to contain his amusement, but this sends him and Nate into more howling laughter. They are nearly in stitches by the time we make it inside.

"Can you guys just shut up? I'm going to figure something out. I have backup plans, trust me." I roll my eyes, but that is a total lie. I have no backup plan, and I'm getting desperate at this point. I'm even considering Darian's idea of ditching the party altogether.

"You're pathetic, dude." I ignore Nate as he reaches for me, trying to stay upright. He's wheezing now, which only adds to my growing annoyance. That is until I see what's on Nate's back patio. Or more like *who* is on the back patio.

My eyes trace her figure, and I can't force myself to look away. She's long, lean, and exactly my type. The girl actually has some muscle to her instead of looking like she hasn't had a meal in days.

"Nate. Are you already out here cheating on Melissa?" I taunt him, pulling my eyes away from the girl for just a second. "I mean, you're just out here keeping a blonde bombshell in the backyard. I mean, God, look at her, those legs and ass—"

"That's my sister. She got back into town yesterday." As he cuts me off, Nate's tone has lost all sense of humor, and a rush of guilt consumes me. I stand there, too stunned to speak for a moment. I glance back at the girl on the lounge chair, but I am still unconvinced that it's Briar.

Briar didn't look like *that*.

The Briar I know is gangly and self-conscious. And this girl isn't anything like it. I can't put my finger on it, but there's an air of confidence that radiates off her, even from a distance. Darian whistles in agreement.

"That's Briar?" I look at Nate for confirmation, eyebrows raised. "She did not look like that the last time I saw her."

"Well, considering she was only fourteen the last time you saw her, I hope not." There's a bite in Nate's voice now. He's always been protective of his sister, and now I see why. She's *stunning*. And she's grown out of what used to be lanky limbs and an awkward height. There's nothing awkward about her now, and it feels a little wrong for me to be looking at her like this. A strained silence falls over us as Nate watches me watch Briar.

And then it clicks.

"Bro. Let me take Briar with me to the party tonight." The words come out of my mouth before I can stop them.

"No." I stare at Nate in disbelief, and he continues as I open my mouth to protest. "Absolutely not. Not in a million years. Not in your wildest dreams. No." Nate smiles at me, but it's a humorless one. He brushes past me and moves into the kitchen, signaling the end of this discussion. But I'm not dissuaded that easily.

"I mean, think about it, man. She'd be the perfect date. If she goes with me, that'd take her off the market. You wouldn't have to worry about anyone trying to get with her."

It's a piss-poor argument, but it's the only one I can come up with. Nate takes a few deep breaths, glaring daggers at me as I continue to glance at his sister over my shoulder. She's lying in the sun, completely oblivious to me, like she's always been.

But this is my shot to change that.

"Do you need to hear it in Spanish? No. In French? Non. In German? Nein. In Russian? Nyet." He pauses, eying me. "It's not going to happen."

Darian claps me on the back in silent support.

"C'mon. It's a win-win for both of us. I get to make Calista jealous, and every guy on the island doesn't hit on your sister. Those idiots my sister hangs out with wouldn't even be stupid enough to go near her."

Nate stills, and I finally have his attention. He crosses his arms across his chest, and I see the wheels turning in his head. He dislikes my sister's friends as much as I do and I rack my brain, trying to find something else to help convince him that this is a good idea. But I've got nothing.

Because suddenly the stakes have changed. This isn't just about Calista anymore. This is about Briar.

"I hate to say it, man, but he's got a point, Nate. If she looks like that, she will draw some interest. Being there on Rowan's arm, with you and me in tow, she instantly becomes off the market."

And there's the Darian I know and love. The voice of reason. My wingman and backup in every bad decision.

I smile and try not to look too eager. But I'd do anything for a shot with Briar. Anything.

Nate drags his hands down his face with a frustrated sigh. "You can take her if you can convince her to go with you. You know she's stubborn, and as I recall, she's still mad at you for the pool thing."

I know he's trying to deter me from doing this, but all I heard was him agreeing. All I heard is that I'm finally getting my shot.

I glance over my shoulder at Briar, lying on the pool chair. For a second, I feel a little guilty for using her like this. But I'm not using her. If anything, I'm using Calista to get Briar.

She just doesn't know it yet.

Six
Briar

The sunlight washes over me, loosening every muscle as I stretch across the lounge chair. A gentle breeze blows across my skin, keeping me from being too warm as I bask in the glow of the midday sun and fight the urge to fall asleep.

As I feel myself drifting off again, the sliding glass doors open and close to my right. I don't open my eyes, praying Nate won't bother me as he passes. But to my dismay, a shadow blocks the sun, interrupting my perfect afternoon.

I keep my eyes closed, but a smile spreads across my face. "What do you want, Nate? Can't you see I'm asleep?"

"I hate to burst your bubble, Sweetheart, but I'm not Nate."

The smooth voice isn't Nate's, and it's not one I was hoping to hear. I have to wonder if I am dreaming, but as I open my eyes, he's there. My heart does that stupid thing it always does when he looks at me, but I force a frown.

"Ah, Rowan. To what do I owe this displeasure?"

"I need a favor, Briar."

"Good to see some things never change. You always need something." I try to dismiss him, but he doesn't move. I squint into the light and level him with a stern look. "Would you at least mind stepping out of my sun? Wouldn't want an uneven tan now, would we?"

He laughs but steps aside and sits on the other side of my lounge chair. "C'mon, Briar. I need your help with something. Please?" He sounds more serious now, even a touch desperate. As much as I want to fight it, he's piqued my interest. Propping myself up on my elbows, I give him a pointed look.

"No one calls me Briar anymore. It's Bri." He smirks, tilting his head as I speak. "What do you even need?"

"There's this party tonight."

"There's always a party."

He smiles at me, almost like he's amused. "There's this party tonight, and there's a girl I'm interested in who will be there."

"Good for you, but how's that my problem?" I pick up my phone, needing to look anywhere but at Rowan. I still feel that stupid palpitation in my chest, and I want to ignore it. I want to ignore *him*. As I scroll through my notifications, I pray he gets the hint and leaves me alone.

But he doesn't.

Instead, he reaches over and plucks the phone out of my hands. "She told me she was going with someone else, so I want to bring a date," he continues like he didn't just snatch my phone. "I was hoping you'd go with me. Nate and Darian are going, too. It's not like you'd just be with me." He pauses again, his eyes tracing the contours of my face. "Please?"

I take a moment to contemplate the idea. It's an enticing offer, especially since I've had a crush on him since I was eight. But I'm not eight anymore. And I know how Rowan is. He's a player, and he's got a reputation for playing with girls' hearts. And that's a game I can't afford to play right now, let alone lose. I know going with him will only end poorly for me.

But the way he's looking at me, like he finally *sees* me, I almost don't care how poorly this ends. Almost.

"And I was hoping to be married to a prince by now, but I guess we don't always get what we want, do we, Rowan?"

My reply catches him off guard, giving me just enough time to seize my phone from his hands. His face drops a little, but he recovers quickly, and it makes me wonder if anyone's ever told him no before.

"Please? I wouldn't be here if I had another option. You know that, B." The hint of desperation seeps through his voice again, but I can only think about that little nickname.

"Don't call me B. Only Nate does that. It's Bri or nothing at all."

"Sorry, Bri. Will you help me out?" he asks again, not missing a beat.

"I think I'll pass, Rowan. But thanks for the offer," I say as I get up from the chair. I strut toward the pool, keenly aware of Rowan's eyes tracking my movements, and add a little hip sway as I walk. Leaning forward, I dive into the pool and let the water cool my skin. I don't know if it's from the sun or Rowan, but I'm suddenly sweating.

The water glides across my skin as I swim to the opposite side of the pool, and when I come up for air, Rowan's there. He waits for me at the end, arms crossed and watching me intently. He's practically undressing me with his eyes, and it brings a flush to my cheeks.

"C'mon, Bri, please?"

It's funny to see how frustrated he is over this. And it does something to my stomach to hear him begging me like this. I gesture for him to sit on one of the lounge chairs and cross my arms over the pool's edge.

"So, what's her name then?"

Rowan runs a hand through his hair, giving him a tousled look. "Her name is Calista."

I click my tongue, trying to pretend like there isn't a pang of jealousy that's made its home in my stomach. "Wow. Calista. What a fun name. Where'd you meet her?"

"C'mon, Bri. Are you going to go with me or not?" His words are short, and I can't help but smile, knowing I'm getting under his skin.

"I'm just curious," I tell him, trying to sound innocent and genuinely curious. I'm not. I don't want to know anything about this girl he's so enamored with. But I just want to be half as annoying as he's been through the years.

And maybe it will serve as a good reminder that Rowan won't ever look at me that way.

"Yeah, right. I don't need this," Rowan huffs, standing back up and turning back toward the house.

"Then have fun impressing no one tonight," I call out after him. I'm not sure what makes me do it, but it's like I couldn't help myself. I guess I'm just a glutton for punishment when it comes to Rowan.

He stops dead in his tracks, turning slowly to face me again. "What was that?" The corner of his lips tips up, and humor plays at his words.

"You heard me," I tell him, knowing I might have shown my hand. The way his eyes scan my face tells me he knows I *want* to go with him. But now I have to keep up this act.

"You either want a date tonight and you'll sit back down, or you walk away and enjoy having whatever her name is laugh at you." I stand my ground and watch him contemplate his options as I float around in the pool.

He takes his time, pretending to evaluate me, but I can't focus on that. I want him to come sit back down and give me another ten minutes of his time, and that's the only real option here, and we both know it. But we'll play this little game of cat and mouse until one of us breaks.

And it won't be me. I know better than to fall into his trap.

He reluctantly returns to the lounge chair and gives me an amused smile. "Continue," he says, leaning back and resting his weight on his palms.

I can see his muscles bulging, and I have to tear my eyes away. He's good-looking. He's always been good-looking. But now, he's somehow more. It's more than just how he can make my heart sputter with just one look.

But this is his game.

He does this with every girl. I've seen it plenty of times.

And besides, he's not part of my five-year plan.

But he could be, just for a night.

I take a few slow laps around the pool, trying to feign disinterest, meanwhile my brain is busy doing cartwheels, trying to find a way to rationalize this to myself.

"So Rowan, if I agree to go with you, and that's a big if… I want to know who I'm making jealous," I pause, then add, "And there would be some ground rules."

"Yeah?" His expression softens, still watching me like it's physically painful for him to look away.

"Where did you meet this girl?"

"We met a week or so ago on the beach."

"A week ago?" I taunt him, but feel some relief. They're not that serious. He's just after another girl who will end up as another notch on his bedpost. And like that, my heart deflates.

Because he really is the same.

The same player he's always been. The same player who would break my heart if I let him.

The same player who's not worth risking my future over.

But I can't tell him no. I never have been able to. And I suspect he knows that and is playing into it. So I might as well say yes, get him out of my system, and then when I wake up, I can go back to being his best friend's little sister, and it will be like none of this ever happened.

"Fine. I'll do it, but you'll treat me like a princess. Do you understand, Rowan?" He looks stunned by my sudden agreement.

"Sure," he nods.

"No, no," I shake my head. "That wasn't very enthusiastic. I want you to make me believe it."

Rowan smiles, amused by this whole thing now that he's getting what he wants. "Anything, Bri, I'll do anything," he agrees, and my heart skips a beat with those words. I've always known that he's smooth, but there's something different about experiencing it in person. I try to recover, creating a list of silly demands to breeze past whatever just happened.

"You'll open all my doors. And I mean every single one. I won't touch a single doorknob. And you're not going to leave me alone at this party. I won't know anyone there. You'll be genuinely stuck with me."

"You don't know anyone and I'm stuck with you." He gives me another dazzling smile as he repeats my words back to me, and my stomach flips.

I squint, trying to come up with something else. Something that could be any kind of deterrent from the perfect night.

"And I'm not going to drink cheap beer. If they don't have tequila, I'll hold you personally responsible for—"

"Bri, I'll take care of you. I think you know that. I'll be an absolute gentleman. I'll open your doors. I'll bring you a bottle of tequila. I'll make your drinks. Whatever you want."

I raise my hand to block the sun and give him a questioning look because this all feels too easy.

"I swear."

He doubles down, and I'm stumped. I don't know what else I could ask for, or should ask for.

I huff, swimming back to the side of the pool. "Fine. I'll go with you. But let the record reflect: I'm only going because I have no other plans tonight, and you were begging."

And because it's Rowan.

"I was begging," he agrees in his annoyingly smooth voice.

"I wouldn't admit to that if I were you," I tease, but I can feel the flush on my cheeks.

Rowan smiles and walks over to stand on the edge right in front of me. He holds out his hand for me to shake, and I know this is my opportunity to get him back for the polar plunge of '09.

I try to hide my growing smile as I reach up and shake his hand. One quick shake, and I tighten my grip, pulling to drag him into the pool.

But he doesn't fall in.

In fact, he doesn't budge.

He stands his ground, barely moving an inch before pulling back and lifting me out of the pool effortlessly. He helps to steady me on the ground and places his hand on the small of my back to keep us face-to-face.

"Nice try, Princess."

He smirks, but there's something else behind his eyes, something that doesn't quite match his charming façade.

I try to convince myself I imagined it.

But as he turns to walk away, my heart stumbles over itself as a new question fills my mind.

What did I just get myself into?

Seven
Briar

I'm running late. You'd think it wouldn't be that hard to get ready for a fake date with your brother's best friend. But you'd be wrong.

"C'mon, B, hurry up! We don't have all night to wait on you!" Nate shouts from downstairs. One last look, and I turn the corner to descend into the living room and see the boys with their backs to me, watching some game on TV. With how they're engrossed in the screen, it looks like I'm doing them a favor.

I laugh, seeing that they are wearing nearly identical outfits: boat shoes, khaki shorts, and a polo shirt. The outfit of every frat boy ever.

"Well, don't you three stooges look lovely this evening."

They turn around to greet me with three wide-eyed stares, and Nate's face immediately turns to an exaggerated look of disgust.

"Gosh, I want to make this girl jealous. Not make her want to kill herself," Rowan says, looking me up and down. Twice. Darian smiles at me, giving two thumbs up, while Nate is still rocking the lip-curled face of disgust.

"There is no way you are leaving the house dressed like that, Briar. Go change, now."

I knew the dress was short when I put it on, and that's *why* I put it on. But I opt to play dumb. "Nate, it's just a sundress. Why would I need to change?"

"Wh-why would you need to change? Are you kidding? That is the shortest and tightest sundress I've ever seen. Please just go change."

I crack a smile while he tries to usher me back upstairs. I knew he'd be upset with my choice of dress, but I also knew it would get Rowan's attention. And I was right on both counts.

"I don't have anything else to wear. And besides, you just told me we are late, so I don't have time to change."

"You sure?"

His question sounds innocent enough, but it's more of a check-in. He knows I know what I'm doing in this dress. He's giving me an out, and I'm not going to take it.

"I'm sure."

"Nothing else to wear," Nate grumbles in annoyance, going to find his keys.

Darian snickers beside me. He also knows exactly what I'm doing. It's pretty transparent. But it's also clear that he's in full support. And Darian's always been the fun one when Nate has his panties in a twist. Nate gives me a death glare as I turn to walk out the door, but he pauses, and he grabs Rowan.

"You better keep your eye on her tonight, Rowan," Nate warns him, but it sounds more like a threat from where I am. "And keep your hands off her." His voice is softer with that final warning, like he knows how bad this idea is.

Rowan catches up to me just as I approach Nate's car and opens my door. My stomach flips for a second, but then I remember. This is what I asked for.

He's not being a gentleman.

I had to ask him to do this.

I suck in a breath and slide into the car, reminding myself this isn't real. Rowan doesn't actually want me to be his date. It's all for show.

He pauses a moment, and I scan his face, taking in his freckled skin and piercing blue eyes.

"Thanks."

"Anything for you." The corners of Rowan's lips tip up before he closes the door and jogs around to the other side. I have to hide the blush creeping up my cheeks as he slides into the backseat next to me. He is a few feet away from me, but this car is starting to feel a bit too small for both of us.

Nate sends daggers at Rowan through the rearview mirror, but I pretend not to notice. I'm too busy trying to keep my imagination in check.

The drive is short, and I feel a hand on mine as we approach an unfamiliar house.

"You good?"

The way his eyes scan my face makes me less sure of this idea. I was already nervous, but now it's tenfold.

"I'm fine," I say, trying to sound convincing. I should be fine, but it feels weird to be back and partying again, like nothing happened.

And to have a curfew.

And to be here with Rowan of all people.

I thought I knew anxiety before, but this is another level.

Rowan leans closer, trying to keep my attention like he knows my mind is spinning, "Hey, I got you, okay? Just have a good time tonight."

Before I can give him another unconvincing response, he slides out of the backseat and rounds the car to me. He helps me out of the car and moves around to the trunk. To my surprise, he pulls a bottle of tequila from a cooler, displaying it to me like a sommelier.

"In case the beverages here aren't to your liking."

I raise my brows in amusement as he mixes a tequila soda in an insulated cup. "You've thought of everything," I joke with him, taking a tentative sip.

It's good. Though it's also hard to mess up a tequila soda.

"I didn't want you to drink from a red cup like the peasants, Princess." His easy smile puts me at ease, and I hate that.

"Thank you."

"Of course." Rowan quickly stores the bottle back in Nate's trunk, and that's when I'm aware of Nate's steady gaze on me. His glare doesn't seem to faze Rowan, who lets his eyes rake up and down my body. Again.

But I'm suddenly very aware of what I've gotten myself into. Being here, with Rowan, sends a signal. It says I'm just like every other girl he's been with. I'm just a notch on his bedpost.

I want to back out, to go home, but before I can, Rowan tucks a strand of hair behind my ear and wraps his arm around my shoulder, leading me toward the house.

I can feel the vibrations from the music radiating through my body the second he opens the front door. We push further into the house, and everyone we pass greets the boys. They're like some local celebrity. Rowan keeps me close, his palm resting comfortably on my hip as I pretend not to be screaming inside. Instead, I scan the room, searching for any sign of a familiar face.

But there's no one.

Rowan grazes his fingers across my back and leaves a trail of goosebumps in his wake. "Let's find somewhere quiet, yeah?" Rowan's breath fans across my neck when he talks, making me even more nervous than before. I swallow hard and nod, scared my words might fail me.

With our hands interlocked, I follow him as he makes his way through the house. He's effortless in how he moves, and people are drawn to him like he's magnetic. As we walk, people nearly trip over themselves to get out of his way. It's almost comical. I'd laugh myself if I weren't so worried about how sweaty my palm currently is—hoping that Rowan doesn't notice.

He exchanges a few more hellos but doesn't stop to chat with anyone. And I'm grateful for that. We stop briefly in the kitchen for him to pull a beer out of the sink, which has become a makeshift cooler now packed with ice.

"Wow, well, aren't you just Mr. Popular?" I try to laugh off the uncomfortable feeling of twenty pairs of eyes glued to the back of my head, but I can't. Not with how Rowan's watching me.

"That's what happens when you don't run away to boarding school."

"I didn't run away." I correct him quickly.

"I know, I know. I'm just giving you a hard time," Rowan assures me, dragging his hand down my arm. "But try to remember, I need you to at least pretend like you want to be here with me."

I don't need him to remind me why I'm at this party with him. I know what we're here to do, but my heart wants to believe it, too. And that's the worst part. I can feel myself forgetting that this means nothing to him.

But that reminder is enough to make me want to keep my distance. Leaning against the counter, I give him a quick nod.

"I know. It's just hard to pretend when I think you love yourself enough for both of us."

Rowan smirks at me, stepping forward to trap me between him and the counter. "Let's head out to the back. Find somewhere to sit and relax." His voice is loud enough to hear, and I playfully push him back like he's said something suggestive. Just in case anyone's watching. And definitely not because I was looking for another reason to touch him.

"Sure." His hand finds mine again as he leads me toward the back door through the horde of bodies.

I look around with casual interest, tugging Rowan behind me before I settle on a nice corner with a plush-looking couch, I plop down.

Rowan chuckles, joining me and watching the tension leave my shoulders. "Is this what you expected from your first day back home?"

"You mean pretending to be interested in you? Not at all," I smirk and sip my drink.

He places a hand over his heart. "Ouch. Even boys have feelings, Bri. But you know that's not what I meant." Rowan wears an amused smile as I look around and see almost everyone's eyes on us.

"I know. I honestly was hoping to keep a low profile. But with the number of witnesses, I feel like that's just gone out the window." My eyes meet Rowan's again.

I move closer to him as he rests his arm behind me on the back of the couch. I drop my voice, asking, "So, which one is Chelsea?" It's a poor attempt to change the topic, but I don't care. I can't take another second of feeling like whatever is going on between us might be real.

He furrows his brows in confusion; then I watch it dawn on him. "Her name is Calista," he says, correcting me.

I nod along, not sharing that I do in fact know her name. But if pretending I don't helps keep Rowan at arm's length, then so be it.

"Right. So, where is she then?" I gesture around the backyard at the clusters of girls, all pretending they're not watching us.

His eyes leave mine for only a few seconds to scan the yard. "I don't think she's here." There's a slight pause before his eyes find mind again. "But what about you? I heard you're only here because you got expelled. What's all that about?" He taps my knee lightly. "The Briar I knew would never get into trouble."

"Well, you must not have known me very well," I taunt him. "But good to know Nate is out here filling everyone in about what goes on in my personal life. Besides, I'm only suspended, not expelled." I take another sip of my drink, needing a distraction and certainly needing to feel the effects of what's in my cup.

"All he told us was you came home to 'get some distance' after being expelled."

Rowan's use of air quotes makes me want to punch Nate in his throat.

"Suspended," I correct him again with a pointed look. "Only suspended."

"Are you going to tell me what happened or leave me hanging?" Rowan's tone is teasing, but the stupid smirk on his face as he leans in makes me uneasy. "Because I'm happy to let my mind fill in the blanks. I've been told I have quite the imagination."

I slap his chest, pushing him away. "You wish. But the truth isn't nearly as interesting as you would imagine."

"Doubtful." Rowan's jaw ticks, and his eyes dart to something over my left shoulder. Before I can get a good look at the flash of brunette hair, Rowan grabs my chin, gently pulling my gaze back to him.

"So I guess the famous Calista must have arrived," I laugh, trying to cover the blush of my cheeks by taking another sip.

"That would be correct." He's still calm and collected, but his gaze shifts from me to her, then me, then her. Now, it's my turn to lean in closer to him.

"How jealous do you want to make her?" I whisper as his gaze snaps back to meet mine. I didn't intend my question to sound so suggestive, but I can't take it back now.

His smile grows as the words leave my mouth. "What are you up to?"

"Nothing! I just think you'll have to up your game and fake flirt with me like your life depends on it." I crack a sly smile, trying to lighten the mood. "I mean, I've heard of your charm, but I'm embarrassed for you if this is all you have."

Rowan leans away from me just an inch and gives me a wild smile. "You must just hate me, coming for my ego like that. I can't believe you're questioning if I have game."

"Just really go for it. Do whatever you have to do to get your girl."

The words hurt coming out of my mouth, but it's more for me than him. I need to remember why we're here, so I twist the knife even further.

"We can even pretend you've always been in love with me, but you're just now getting the nerve to act on it."

His expression quickly morphs into one of shock and what looks like embarrassment. "What?"

"I'm joking," I laugh, touching his shoulder. "I mean, come on. You can't tell me this cliché isn't hilarious. If I didn't know you're a terrible person, this might be cute."

Rowan's shoulders visibly relax as he moves barely an inch closer to me. "Oh, now I'm a terrible person?"

"That's what I said," I nod.

"Well, would a terrible person be willing to follow all your little rules tonight?"

"Rowan, the night is still young. Plenty of time for you to fumble the ball here."

Eight
Briar

The party is in full swing now, and so are my nerves. Jessica is dancing on the living room table, per usual, and Matty had to be carried out twenty minutes ago. So everything is right on schedule, and the drinks are doing nothing to get me through the night.

Rowan and I haven't moved from our spot on the couch in nearly an hour. We're flirting. We're chatting. And now I can't tell what's real or for show.

Somewhere along the way, we started touching. Not in a weird way. More in a hesitant, flirty way. At least, that's what I'm telling myself.

But it's making this night feel less like a fake date and more like a real one. And I don't know how to stop that.

Rowan reaches out, putting his hand on my knee. I don't even know if he recognizes that he's done it. My eyes flick down to his hand, then back to his face. My skin is on fire where his hand lies, and I don't want him to move it, but he should.

"Sorry." He pulls his hand away as soon as my eyes meet his again.

"It's all part of the plan: Operation Make Her Jealous," I tell him.

He laughs. "I'm just a touchy person in general, and—"

I grab his hand and put it back on my knee. "No worries. We need this to look as real as possible, right?"

"In that case," he trails off, reaching for me. He grabs my waist and pulls me closer, draping my leg across his lap in one swift movement. Relaxing back onto the couch, he looks proud of himself, and I realize this may be more than I signed up for. This makes me want more, and I can't want more. Not with Rowan.

He does this with everyone, and I refuse to just be another one of Rowan's conquests.

"A little bold there, Callahan," I say. He ignores my comment, resting his arm on the back of the couch. His hand hovers just a hair above my shoulder, drawing light circles on my arm. And I hate the way he looks more comfortable than he has all night.

"Anyways, back to this suspension topic you keep trying to avoid," he says. "See, as I remember it, you were always a goody two-shoes. I've never seen you in an ounce of trouble."

"Isn't that what I'm supposed to be? The good girl who never gets into any trouble?" I ask, feigning innocence. A mischievous glint dances through his eyes.

"I'm sure you could be whatever you wanted to be."

I hold his gaze and refuse to continue to play his little game. Even though I started it. I can't play this game, not with Rowan, because I'll lose. He'll pull back once I've taken the bait, and my heart will be left as wreckage.

He drops his smug look, studying me. I can feel the shift that happens before he even speaks. He looks softer than before, like he's really seeing me for the first time tonight.

"I know Nate doesn't talk about it much, but how are you doing with your parents?" he asks lowly. His sudden change of topic catches me off guard. Of everything I thought he might ask, this wasn't it. I shift in my seat and stare into the empty cup in my hands.

"It happened years ago. The move was an adjustment, but I'm fine," I repeat the practiced line. I've delivered it countless times, and I'm almost starting to believe it myself. I look up, my turn to scan his face, and I can't tell if he believes me. "You know, I could ask you the same thing, Rowan. How's it been with everything that happened with your dad?"

He physically recoils.

Only an inch, but I still notice it. Then his mask is back up. This time, I hold eye contact, refusing to back down. Two can play this game. If he wants to try and make me uncomfortable by bringing up my family history, I'll bring up his. He's the first to give in, looking away.

There's a moment where he sits there just opening and closing his mouth, and he looks truly lost.

Then he surprises me.

"Like you said, it's been an adjustment."

I nod, hoping he'll keep speaking if I stay silent. They normally do, but he doesn't.

Rowan sits just as silently as I do.

We're just alike. Both too stubborn for our own good.

After a long pause, he finally meets my eyes again, and I smirk. "So where's your friend?"

"Don't know. And I don't care," Rowan answers quickly. Too quickly.

"Liar," I say, pointing an accusing finger at him. "You know exactly where she is. You've probably been watching her all night."

He chuckles at my comment but doesn't break eye contact with me. It's unnerving and makes my stomach flip. "She may have noticed us a few times, but I've been a little pre-occupied."

"Right," I laugh, drawing out the syllables.

"She's watching now. So, let's ramp things up a bit, yeah?" Rowan asks, looking smug.

Leaning close to him, I smirk, "And what exactly did you have in mind? And please, at least try to remember that my brother is at this party with us, so we should behave." I tap his chest lightly with my pointer finger, and I *swear* I feel Rowan flex his pec as I do.

"Nate is always getting in the way of my fun." My mouth falls open in surprise. I didn't expect Rowan to take the bait. "I guess I'll have to settle for getting you another drink." His eyes drop to the empty cup in my hands before lingering on my lips.

"Sure." I pull away from him, a little too caught up in this. I quickly remind myself that this isn't real. It's all for show. Moving my legs from his lap, I put some much-needed space between us. "I'll follow you."

Rowan winks at me before standing and extending his hand to help me. I reluctantly take his hand, and he pulls me into his chest. He holds me close, and I start to feel dizzy.

I can't tell if it's the drink or our proximity. Or both. Either way, I'm liking it more than I should.

"Let's go." His voice is just a whisper, and his hand finds the small of my back. I shiver involuntarily. Leading me back through the crowd, I can feel everyone's eyes glued to us. And I don't blame them. I'd be curious, too, if I saw Rowan like this with another girl.

I still can't believe he's like this with me.

I let out a breath of relief as Rowan takes the cup from my hands and moves back to Nate's car. Wordlessly, he starts mixing up another drink for me, making quick work of the whole thing. I lean against the car, watching him as he works. And it's a sight to behold.

"You make an excellent bartender, Rowan. Maybe you should look into—"

"Rowan, what the hell are you doing?" A shrill voice behind me cuts my sentence short.

Rowan and I turn around to see a brunette standing on the porch. She looks angry. Angry like she could tear my throat out. With her bare teeth.

And I don't blame her.

I'd be angry, too.

But she's undeniably gorgeous. From the corner of my eye, I see Rowan trying to hide his amused smile. Rowan slings his arm around my shoulder, pulling me into his side. As much as I'm reveling in being this close to him, I feel bad for Calista.

"Hi, Calista. How are you? Have you met Briar?" Rowan asks, gesturing to me. I stay silent, offering her a quick wave.

She completely ignores me, but that's what I want. I take a sip from my drink and take in her appearance. She has silky hair that falls perfectly into place at her shoulders. Everything about her is perfect—her nails, her skin, her makeup. Everything. I can't find anything to dislike about her besides her attitude. Even her dress is cute. And her shoes.

Her shoes are really fucking cute.

"Rowan, I need to speak with you. Alone."

He lets out a breathy laugh beside me. "Uh, sure. If you want to call me tomorrow, we can talk. I'm a little busy at the moment."

I can feel my cheeks flush. Not from the attention, or the closeness, or the flattery, but from embarrassment. Because I've been reduced to nothing more than an accessory for Rowan. Something for him to show off to his friends at a party.

"No, Rowan. Now. We need to talk now." Calista's voice is shaking with anger.

"Yeah. Unfortunately, I can't talk right now." He gives me another dazzling smile. "I think we're needed inside. Right, Bri?"

"Yeah, I think so." I agree quickly, ready to be done with this conversation. Ready to go back to our little bubble, where I can convince myself that this might mean something.

"Well, we better go then," Rowan nods as he walks us back into the party, brushing past her. We make it inside and leave Calista shell-shocked on the front porch.

But I still feel bad for her.

She doesn't deserve this.

The music is loud enough inside that I can barely hear myself think, but it's not loud enough to cover the sudden rush of guilt or my best friend's squeal of excitement.

I'd know her voice anywhere.

"Bri! Oh my gosh! Why didn't you tell me you were coming back?" Harper borderline screams while engulfing me in a massive hug, coming out of nowhere.

"It was a last-minute decision, and I didn't have much time to let anyone know, not even Nate." I pull away from her, beaming, but a light touch on my shoulder brings me back.

I don't have to look to know it's Rowan. Harper's face says it all. Her shock. Her disgust. Her *disappointment*.

"I'll be right back, okay? Just stay here."

"Yeah," I agree as he walks away, and now it's Harper's turn to look shocked.

"You're with Rowan?" Her tone is accusatory, and Harper's shock turns to confusion and hurt.

"It's a long story, but it's nothing to worry about. We're not, like, together or anything," I try to explain to her, but there's no easy way to explain what I'm doing here with her brother. Because I don't even know what I'm doing here.

She gives me a look like she doesn't quite believe me. "We'll have to catch up sometime."

"Yes! I want to hear everything about school in London, and I have so many things to tell you about what's been happening here!" She agrees excitedly, all thoughts of her brother gone.

"Let's do breakfast after my run tomorrow," I suggest, and her eyes light up.

"I'll do you one better! I'll meet you at Old Man Grover's house at nine, and we can run together."

I nod as Rowan comes back with a fresh drink, and his hand finds my waist again. Harper scowls at her brother and shoots him the finger before turning to walk off. "Well, have fun with him," her face goes sour with the words, "and I'll see you tomorrow."

As she backs her way into the crowd, I don't miss her tell-me-everything-later face she pins me with before disappearing.

"Come on," Rowan nods toward the living room, where a few couples dance around like idiots. But at least Jessica has been removed from the table.

"You want to dance?"

"I don't dance, Briar," he whispers, and the flutter in my stomach comes back full force. I force myself to ignore the feeling and follow him. It takes all my focus not to trip over the cups littering the floor.

We find a semi-quiet corner, and I relax against the wall.

Just when I think I'm going to get a momentary reprieve, Rowan leans beside me, so close I can feel the heat radiating from him. His face is maybe six inches away from mine, and I try to regulate my breathing while reminding myself that dating isn't part of my plan right now. And dating Rowan is definitely not part of the plan. It shouldn't even be on my radar.

But here he is.

"So, what have you been up to lately, Mr. Player?" I ask, trying to find anything to talk about.

A playful scowl falls on his face. "I'm not a player."

"Mm-hmm, right. So, all these rumors I hear just get started on their own, yes?"

"I don't think I know what rumors you're referring to." He takes a casual sip of his beer, trying to play dumb. "Why? What kind of things do you hear?"

"Oh, Rowan, come on now. I'm sure there isn't a girl in this room that you haven't tried to flirt with," I shove his shoulder playfully.

A cheeky smile spreads across his face.

"Well, I haven't flirted with you," he counters, a sarcastic edge to his voice.

I let out an exaggerated sigh of relief. "I'm glad you noticed. Your lack of game tonight has thrown me off. But I didn't want to hurt your feelings since this is such a big night for you."

He laughs. "I've been trying to take it easy on you tonight, Bri. I didn't want you to fall in love with me or anything. But I'd be happy to step it up and—"

Rowan pauses mid-sentence as my brother puts a hand on his shoulder, more forcefully than necessary. He gives Rowan a pointed look.

One I recognize too well.

It's his what-in-fresh-hell-are-you-doing look. He's perfected it over the years.

"Well, don't you two look extra cozy right now."

I laugh and watch Rowan take a measured step back.

"Are you drunk?" Nate asks me.

"No."

It's not a complete lie. I'm not drunk. I'm a little tipsy and have barely touched my new drink.

He turns to Rowan. "How drunk is she?" Rowan shrugs and rolls his eyes. "Do I need to remind you that she's only twenty? You can't let her—"

"She's fine. Calm down," he tells Nate, raising his hands in surrender.

"I'm fine," I say, echoing Rowan's assurances.

Nate reluctantly gives in and nods toward the door. Rowan gives a slight nod in silent agreement before he turns his attention back to me.

"Okay, Princess, it's time for us to go," Rowan says, grabbing my hand.

Without a second thought, I let him lead me back toward the front of the house. I am again keenly aware of the number of eyes on me, but I don't care anymore.

I don't care that this is stupid. And I don't care if I look stupid.

Because this summer I'm going after what I want.

And that's Rowan.

No matter what damage that brings.

Nine
Briar

If I were a betting woman, I'd bet Harper has never been late to anything. And today is no exception.

As I turn onto Old Man Grover's street, Harper's waiting for me at the end of his driveway. She's doing a few light stretches, and her face lights up when she sees me.

"Morning!" Her chipper voice cuts through the early morning air.

"Hey, hey!" I smile back. I point to the road, and she quickly nods before matching my pace. "So, did you have fun at the party last night?"

"Oh, no, no." She waves her finger at me. "You first. What were you doing there with my brother?" Harper manages to level me with a stern look while keeping pace. And that's impressive.

"He asked me to go with him to make some girl jealous. It was fun, surprisingly. You know I love to cause problems."

"Ugh, Calista," Harper makes a gagging sound. "She's the worst. She always has a bad attitude and talks to me like I'm an idiot."

I can't help but laugh at Harper, who has her nose turned up at the thought of Calista.

"You took the words right out of my mouth. She was kind of rude to me."

"Maybe that's why Rowan likes her," Harper laughs. "He's annoying. She's annoying. They're just alike."

This is a trap, but I fall into it anyway. "I don't think Rowan is all bad, Harper. He may be a player and annoying, but he seems… I don't know… decent."

"Why are you defending my brother?" She asks this as she picks up the pace.

"I'm just saying he wasn't awful last night," I try to explain, without sounding defensive. Though I am. "He was a total gentleman, which is more than I expected from him."

Harper snorts. "First of all, Rowan isn't stupid. He knows Nate would kill him if he wasn't a gentleman. Second, he's proven time and time again to be a terrible person."

"How?"

"He's different now. He changed after everything with my dad. He's done terrible things, Bri. Maybe you don't know what he's capable of, but you may be the only person on this island who thinks he's decent."

I'm speechless. My mind runs wild with the possibilities of what he could have done. I know a shame spiral when I see one, and Rowan doesn't seem like he's spiraling. Even when I brought up his dad last night, he seemed calm. I'd even go so far as to say he appeared to have things under control.

Harper interrupts my thoughts, "Things have changed since you left. People are different. The island is divided after my dad's business fell apart. Ever since one of his own managers exposed the fraud, the business crumbled. And it got worse when they opened their own construction company and bought all the land my dad used to own. Anyone who moves into houses built by them is pretty much enemy number one now."

I stifle my laughter. Harper gives me her signature eye roll. "I know. Stupid, right? Rowan acts like they branded a red 'A' on his chest. But it's just business, and he can't seem to grasp that difference."

I know Rowan's always been a bit anal about the family business, but I never imagined he'd snap. And from what my best friend is telling me, it sounds like that's what he's done.

And that's so *not* hot.

"That's crazy that their adult lives are so boring they need to bully other adults," I say. Harper raises her brows in agreement.

"Rowan is the one leading the charge. He's the head bully. HBIC, if you will. B for bully," she explains, like I wasn't able to track, and I have to laugh at her new iteration of the acronym. "It's like he has a personal vendetta against every one of them, especially the Collins family."

"Who?" I ask.

"The Collinses. They're the ones who own the new construction company," Harper explains.

I nod, finally putting the pieces together. "Ah. I see. HBIC hates on the riff-raff bringer."

"Yep." Harper pops the 'p' and gives me a lazy smile. My mind is reeling with all the social hierarchy updates, so I force us to switch gears.

"So, while that sucks, tell me about this new man I've been seeing in all these pictures of you." I give her a wicked smile. She's told me all this before, but I have to hear it again to believe it.

A shy smile crosses Harper's face. "Kian."

"Ah! Kian! Tell me everything!" I can't hide my excitement. It's been ages since Harper had a boyfriend who made her smile like this.

"Oh my gosh, Bri. He's the best. I didn't ever think I could be this happy."

"Yeah. And…" I prompt her to continue.

"I met him last summer, and we were just friends until he finally worked up the nerve to ask me out a few weeks ago. He's one of the riffraff, but he's amazing. Like incredible. Very non-riff-raff-like." At this point, she does nothing to hide her beaming smile.

"I'm so happy for you. You deserve the world, Harper."

She's blushing but plays it off. "Stop it. But what about you? Any new guys in your life outside of my psycho brother?"

"Not really. Getting kicked out of university really kills any romance. And even before that, I didn't have anyone in the pipeline," I laugh, trying to gloss over the small fact that I've been suspended.

"You got expelled?" Harper shouts, stopping dead in her tracks.

I slow to a stop and hold my finger up to stop her. "Why does everyone keep assuming that? I'm just suspended. For now."

"What happened?"

I nod toward the road, and we resume a slower jog. "Long story short, they accused me of cheating, and it's not true. They're doing an investigation, but until they've done whatever they plan on doing, I'm suspended."

"You don't even have to cheat. You're a genius."

"That's what I tried to tell them, but they wouldn't listen." Harper snorts out a laugh. "I'm honestly so annoyed with the whole thing."

"I'm sorry. That sucks. I could be a character witness to your smartness if it helps," Harper jokingly offers.

"I'll mention that to my mom and see if she thinks that will help." I laugh as the diner comes into view.

Stepping inside, a kind older woman greets us as if we've known her our whole lives.

"Sit anywhere you'd like, girls." She calls from her spot behind the counter.

Harper offers her a smile and goes to our favorite booth by the windows.

"And when do I get to meet this boyfriend of yours?" I ask, pretending to read through the menu.

She looks at me with an awkward smile. "No time like the present."

I don't have time to question her before I hear a commotion behind me that sounds like a tornado tearing the front door off its hinges. Turning to look at what I'm sure should be wreckage, I'm greeted by two boys approaching our table.

The pair couldn't look more out of place. They both wear old T-shirts and look like they've been up since dawn. As they get closer, the realization sets in. One of these boys is Kian.

My answer comes quickly as the brown-haired boy leans over and gives Harper a quick peck on her cheek. The blond keeps his eyes on me, smiling devilishly.

Harper's boyfriend quickly introduces himself, extending his hand to me. "Hey. I'm Kian."

"Nice to meet you," I nod. "I'm Bri."

I feel the seat dip beside me as Kian slides into the booth beside Harper. Turning to face the blond-haired, brown-eyed delinquent, I raise my brows. "Oh, yeah. Please go ahead and have a seat."

"Thank you. I will. I'm Reece." He smiles, showing one adorable dimple on his left cheek.

"Good for you," I nod, turning back to stare Harper down as she sits across from me. Reece doesn't hesitate to get comfortable, resting his arm behind me on the backrest and leaning closer.

"You know, I'm a real sucker for blondes with green eyes," he says quietly, leaning in so only I can hear. I turn and look at him, stunned by his forwardness.

"Good thing I'm not a natural blonde, then," I quip, but I hear Kian snickering across the table.

"And she's quick. This one's a keeper," Reece says to Harper, not at all fazed by my rejection. He reaches across and picks up Harper's menu, and I feel a kick under the table.

I snap my gaze back to Harper. "Ouch."

She gives me her best be-nice-or-I'll-yell-at-you-later look. I throw my hands up in surrender and plaster on an annoyingly massive smile. I'd do anything for Harper—including playing nicely with her boyfriend's friend.

"Anyways, guys, I'd like you to meet Bri. She's been one of my best friends since we were practically toddlers," Harper says while gesturing to me across the table. "And Bri, this is my boyfriend Kian and the ever-so-lovely Reece," she continues as she points to each boy.

"It's great to meet you finally. Harper talks about you all the time. And don't worry about him. He flirts with anything that has a pulse." Kian nods toward his buddy, and I can't help but laugh.

"He's just mad I get all the attention now." Reece winks at me like it's some inside joke. My cheeks flush involuntarily, which only makes Reece's smile widen.

"I'm perfectly content," Kian says with a quick glance at Harper. "Anyways, we're going out on the boat today if you want to come with us."

His question is directed more to Harper, but she looks to me for confirmation.

"Sure, I'm down," I tell her because I'd do anything to keep my mind off the blue hair boy from last night.

"Great!" Reece's voice is louder than I expect, and I nearly jump out of my seat. "We'll see you guys at the docks later."

Then he turns his attention entirely to me. His arm is still splayed out behind me on the booth, leaving only a few inches between us. "I am looking forward to getting to know you."

With a wink, Reece stands and beckons for Kian to follow. I look at Harper, wide-eyed, as Kian stands to follow his friend.

"He's something," I tell her.

"That he is," she agrees. I laugh with her and glance over my shoulder to watch them go.

As they walk out of the diner, Reece looks back, and he's got a goofy smile on his face. He may be a flirt, but there's an odd kind of calm that accompanies his energy. And that calmness draws me in. I can't explain it, but there's some part of me that needs to know him.

I suck in a breath as I feel my cheeks flush as the realization crashes over me.

Reece is the kind of person who could easily derail my summer plans.

And with a face like his, I might let him.

Ten

Rowan

Today ranks among the top five worst workouts of my life. I can't focus, and my form is sloppy. All because of a girl. But she's not just any girl and the situation would be laughable if it weren't my life.

But even the cacophony around me isn't as loud as my mind. Nothing can shut out the thoughts of Briar, which won't stop looping in my head.

I barely notice as Darian struggles through his final rep of the set, his face a mix of determination and agony. "I hate leg day, man," he huffs, collapsing onto the bench to catch his breath.

I nod weakly, stepping up to the barbell. I push through three reps, and it's a push. Everything feels strained. My body, my mind, my patience for this. Halfway through my set, I can feel my grip slipping, so I rack the weight.

I can't do this today.

My muscles can handle more, but my head can't. Images of Briar, inches from me last night, crowd out everything else. It felt right. It felt good to have her there with me. Too good.

"I'm done for today, boys," I tell Nate and Darian, who have been watching me closely all day. It feels like they can read my thoughts, although I know they can't. Guilt gnaws at me anyway.

I can't even look at Nate right now. He'd kill me if he knew half the things running through my mind right now. And Darian, he'd just laugh at me.

She's Nate's little sister, which automatically puts her off limits. I shouldn't go there, no matter how much every part of me wants to.

So I have to ignore every part of me that wants her.

Without a second look, I head toward the front door and snag my keys on the way out. Nate and Darian are hot on my heels, but I ignore them.

"I think I would've passed out if we did another set," Darian says. He's trying to break the tension, but it doesn't work. The tension has set in like a bruise under the skin.

"I don't get why girls are obsessed with leg day. It's the worst day of the week," I mutter, trying to feign interest but failing miserably.

"I know, man. They're trying to build an ass, which I am grateful for, but I think my legs are about to fall off my body right now." Darian snickers at his joke, throwing an arm over my shoulder. I remain silent, my mind still trying to untangle the memory of Briar's soft skin against mine.

"Speaking of girls," Nate pipes up, his voice sharper than I expected. "You and my sister looked awfully comfortable last night, Rowan. Is there something I should know?"

My jaw tightens. I knew this was coming. I did my best to hide how much Briar affects me. But clearly that wasn't enough. Although, to be completely honest, there's absolutely nothing going on with Briar.

And that's the problem.

"You're kidding, right?" I shoot back. Nate raises his eyebrows and cocks his head like he knows I'm lying. "I can't help it that I'm just a fantastic actor. Besides, not only is she your sister, but she's not my type." The lie tastes bitter as soon as the words come out of my mouth.

"She's not your type?" Darian asks in disbelief, nearly choking on the words.

"Bri's got too much of an attitude problem for me." It's a lame excuse, but it's the only thing that comes to mind.

"Dude, girls with attitude are your exact type. What do you mean?" Darian laughs, giving me a knowing look. He knows that's a lie. He knows how long I've thought about Briar. But thankfully, he keeps that to himself.

"Not really," I mumble, shrugging like I don't care. "Anyway, Darian, where'd you run off to last night? You disappeared after we got there."

His eyes roll at my obvious deflection, but he allows it.

"I think you were too busy with my sister to notice much of anything," Nate mutters, just loud enough for me to hear. I ignore him and focus on Darian.

"Cut the guy some slack. He knows better than to hook up with your sister. But, me? I ran into a friend and bailed early." He wears a smug smile as Nate finally starts to relax.

"A friend? Is that what we're calling her these days?" Nate laughs.

"She's a friend." Darian doubles down on what I'm sure is an exaggerated truth. "But I gotta run home and help my mom with some things. Catch you guys at the bonfire later."

"His mom," I say, throwing air quotes around my words. Chances are, his friend is still in his bed from last night. But before we can get another word in, Darian walks across the parking lot toward his car.

We all know Amber is not just a friend. Then again, I'm pretty sure both Nate and Darian know Briar is one hundred percent my type. And if the smirk on Darian's face is anything to go by, he knows I'm in trouble because of it.

"Hey, I'll see you at the bonfire tonight, man. Do you know if…" I hesitate. "Think Bri's coming?" I try to sound nonchalant as I ask Nate, but I fail based on the frown that settles across his features.

"Why?"

"Just curious. She left some of her stuff in my cooler."

Another lie. But it disarms Nate just enough.

"I don't know. I told her about it the other day, but she didn't say one way or the other."

An awkward silence stretches between us. I have to know if I'll get to see her again, but I can't risk pushing it even further with Nate. He's already bent out of shape after last night.

"Have you heard from Calista?"

Nate's question catches me off guard. I'd nearly forgotten about Calista. I've been too wrapped up in how I want Briar.

I shake my head. "Nah, she hasn't called yet, but she will. Or maybe I'll get to see her at the bonfire tonight."

It's cheap talk. I don't want to see Calista at the bonfire, but if it keeps my mind occupied, then so be it. But I really don't care to see her. I only care about the next time I'll see Briar.

"Of course she'll call you, man." Nate claps me on the shoulder. "I mean, you're Rowan Callahan. How could she not?"

I force a laugh. "I'm heading to the pier for lunch."

"What time?"

"One." Another second of silence. I pause, then add, "Melissa might be there." Nate tries to hide his excitement with the mere mention of her name, but fails.

"I'll meet you there."

I nod as Nate gives me another pat on the back. Sitting in my car, I take a deep breath and prepare myself for the rest of the day. I give myself two minutes to think about Briar before forcing her from my mind.

The way her laugh makes my heart ache, the way her eyes sparkle when she's a little tipsy, and the way her hand felt in mine.
She's impossible to forget. And that's when I realize Briar is going to absolutely ruin me, and my summer.

Eleven

Briar

The sun beats down on my face, and I relish the feeling. Being back on the ocean is exactly what I needed.

"Guys, we've been out here for hours already," Reece whines. "Let's go to the beach and do some surfing!"

If there's one thing I've learned in the past two hours, it's that Reece can't sit still. He needs constant motion. The second thing I've learned? He's a shameless flirt. He really knows how to lay it on thick. And honestly, I don't mind either trait.

I glance to my right at Harper, who still has her eyes closed as we lie on the boat's stern. I'd think she was sleeping if it weren't for the slight smirk tugging at her lips. She's up to no good. I can feel it.

"I'm happy to relax on solid, dry land and watch you idiots wipe out. But count Bri out of the whole being in the ocean thing," she tells Reece and Kian.

My eyes widen at her comment.

"Oh, is Bri afraid of the ocean?" Reece teases, flashing a smug grin that makes me think he's planning something.

"I don't know what's in there, and I don't plan to find out," I reply, raising my hands in mock surrender. "Not afraid to admit that."

Kian laughs. "Oh, you've done it now."

I don't have time to question him before Reece lunges at me. He picks me up and cradles me against his very muscular chest as he stands on the edge of the boat. I might enjoy it if I weren't afraid of his plans.

"Reece, I swear. If you throw me in, I will rip your skin off and let you bleed to death on this deck," I growl. "I am not above committing homicide today."

He smirks as if he isn't afraid of my threat. I tighten my grip on him, half tempted to strangle him as I hold on for dear life. My mind races, trying to find another excuse to avoid being thrown in.

"I can't swim. Please," I lie.

His face falls, and he immediately steps back before placing me nicely on my feet.

"Sorry, Bri. I didn't know." Reece looks genuinely scared, and I feel bad for lying to him.

"It's fine. I'm fine," I assure him. "I just don't like the ocean." Technically true. It's just not the full truth.

Everyone nods in agreement, sitting in an uncomfortable silence as Reece gives me another apologetic look.

"I'm fine, Reece. I promise." I repeat my assurances, feeling bad for making him this worried. Reece gives me a quick nod before I sit beside Harper again.

She leans into my shoulder. "That's such a lie, Bri. You can swim."

"Shh." A guilty smile spreads across my face. "We can't let him know I didn't want my hair to get wet. Plus, it's not a total lie. I do hate the ocean."

We erupt into giggles as the boat lurches forward, taking off toward the docks.

Not ten minutes later, Harper and I are sunbathing on the beach and defending our snacks against the hungry seagulls. The grains of sand stick to my skin, and I couldn't be happier. The sweat, the sound of the waves, the people— it's perfect. Lying here, it feels like I'm exactly where I'm supposed to be.

Except if you ask the girls ten feet to our right, they'd rather I be anywhere but here. At least, that's what it feels like with how they're glaring daggers at me right now.

The boys surf, undoubtedly trying to show off for us, but Harper and I barely notice. We lay on the beach, chatting like we used to all those summers ago.

"How are you doing? You know, being back home and with everything in the air right now?" Harper asks, adjusting her sunglasses.

I shrug. "It is what it is."

"You're…" she presses, "Okay though, right?"

"Yeah. I'm all good."

There's a hint of uncertainty in her voice. "You're good because you're fine? Not because you're…"

I laugh at her inability to be subtle.

She wants to know if I've relapsed. Which I haven't. I haven't touched anything pill-related in two years, though I'd tell her it's been nearly six if she pushed me. And I hate how ready I am to lie about it, but it's the only thing that keeps everyone off my back.

But this is the same conversation I've had with my parents and Nate since returning home. Everyone's worried, and they have no reason to be.

Or maybe they do, since I've become a habitual liar.

"I'm not using again if that's what you're worried about, Harper."

"Okay." Her smile returns, and she's her happy, bubbly self again. "I just know you and uncertainty go together like oil and water. I just wanted to check in."

It's true. Uncertainty makes me more anxious than anything. But I've been managing. Without any kind of extra help.

"While I appreciate that, I am fine. By myself. This is all natural, baby!"

"Good." Her shoulders visibly relax. "So, what do you think of Reece?"

"He's okay."

Harper snorts. "Just okay?"

"Shut up," I nudge her shoulder, not willing to admit out loud how rattled he makes me. Everything about him is disarming in a way I'm not used to. But for now, my defenses have to stay up and at the ready.

Because he's not part of the plan either.

"He's cute, okay? Is that what you want me to say?"

"I was just asking." Harper throws her hands up in surrender. "He might seem like a player, but he's sweet."

"Is he single?"

Harper's face lights up. "He is. And I think he's got a thing for you."

"I feel bad lying to him earlier, though," I admit, hoping Harper can offer me some comfort and assure me that it isn't as big a deal as I think it is.

"Bri—"

"No, I know. " I cut her off. "He looked so concerned when I said I couldn't swim. Do you think he'll forgive me if I apologize?"

"Probably not."

I freeze. That voice is not Harper's.

I glance over my shoulder to see Reece looking at me with raised eyebrows. He does his best to look angry, but his dimpled smile fights to the surface. Reece is dripping wet, droplets of saltwater clinging to his fringe, and the way the sun dances across his tanned skin is distractingly beautiful.

And he's locked in on me. Reece shoves his board a few inches into the sand as he steps closer to me.

"Let's just talk about it, Reece."

Reece shakes his head. It's subtle, but there's a glint in his eyes. He lunges forward, wrapping his arms around me, lifting me from my spot, and carrying me into the ocean.

He holds me close, and I can feel his chest rumble as he laughs.

"Reece! Please!" I shriek between fits of laughter, kicking and squirming. I don't know what makes him pause, but he does and places me on my feet. I can feel the waves lap against my ankles when I turn to face him.

"Thank you, Reece. I'm sorry I lied—"

"Oh, you're going to be sorry," Reece says, bending down and throwing me over his shoulder. He continues into the ocean, my shrieking laughter wracking my body as I hold onto his arms for stability.

"I'm going to kill you," I tell him, laughing too hard to sound threatening.

"You're welcome to try. The last girl who lied to me got much worse, so you should be thanking me."

My heart clenches, but before I can ask him what he means by that, a loud whistle comes from the beach, and Reece turns to investigate. Whatever it is, he stops in his tracks, and my heart drops. I immediately think of the worst-case scenario—a shark in the water coming right for us, or worse, ten sharks.

"What's wrong?" My voice is tense, and there's no hiding my fear. Reece sighs, takes a few steps toward the beach, and puts me back on my feet. I immediately scan the water, looking for any sign of danger.

The water is calm, so I look back at Reece. His gaze is trained over my shoulder, and I shift to glance at the beach. That's where I find the real threat.

Nate and Rowan lean against the pier, watching us. The pair has their arms crossed, scowling as they pin us with a glare. Nate whistles again, making sure I see them. I roll my eyes, growing annoyed with my brother's new overprotective act. Nate doesn't seem to notice as he waves me over to him, and I give him a reluctant nod.

"Looks like the cavalry is here to collect you," Reece says, disappointed.

"My brother is a little protective on occasion." I have to fake a smile, but Reece studies my face with a frown.

"I see that. And I guess your boyfriend is the same way?"

"Boyfriend?" I nearly choke on the word.

"I heard you're with Rowan." He says it so calmly. So matter-of-fact.

I balk.

"Absolutely not. He's my brother's annoying friend who tags along wherever Nate goes."

The edges of Reece's lips tip up. "No boyfriend, then?"

"No boyfriend."

"Good."

I clear my throat and let out an awkward chuckle. Reece makes me silly in the head, and I'm scared by how easy things feel with him. I almost can't string together a coherent thought when he's looking at me.

"Well, I'd better get going before the cavalry gets upset with me."

Reece nods quickly as I turn and head back to shore. Before I get too far, Reece calls out, "Bri! There's this bonfire tonight. Will I see you there?"

He's got a shy smile that makes me melt.

"Yeah, I'll see you there." I turn away quickly, hiding a smile of my own. I give Harper a knowing look, not needing to confirm anything for her, as I gather my things and head toward the parking lot. My feet sink into the soft sand as I head further up the beach. The pier boards are rough underfoot, but they warm my feet as I approach Nate and Rowan.

"Was it truly necessary for you to come and collect me like this?" There's no hiding the annoyance in my tone.

They ignore my comment, walking toward the car on either side of me like bodyguards I don't need. Rowan opens the car door, gesturing for me to get in. I glare at him and wordlessly slide into the backseat, dragging my bag behind me.

It's not until we're back on the main road that any of us speak.

"Bri, what were you doing with them? You shouldn't be hanging around with that group. Harper is fine, but the others, especially Reece…" Rowan trails off, and his face contort in disgust in the rearview mirror.

"What's wrong with Reece? Why don't you like him?"

Rowan's eyes roll. "I never said I didn't like—"

"You didn't have to say; your tone said enough."

Rowan turns around in his seat, studying me. "Just be careful around him. He's not who you think he is."

I can't help but feel like his warning is skewed. He doesn't know that Harper told me what happened, but I suspect he assumes. And there's a small part of me that remembers that Rowan needs a warning label of his own.

"Noted." We stare at one another silently. I break our gaze and watch as the beach drops out of sight.

Twelve
Briar

The sun set hours ago, but the air is still warm with clear skies—perfect weather for a beach bonfire. Nate pulls into the parking lot, and we can already hear music and laughter.

"Sounds like the party has already started," Nate says, hopping out of the car as soon as he parks. I slide from the passenger seat and follow him. The beach comes into view, and there's ten or more kegs lined up in the sand.

"Oh, B. I almost forgot. Rowan told me he had something for you."

"What is it?"

"How would I know?"

"Rowan's your friend."

Nate rolls his eyes. "B, just go get whatever it is you left from Rowan."

I don't get a second to argue before Nate beelines toward the beach. I scowl at my brother's back, but it lessens as I watch him approach a petite girl. I smile, knowing she must be the reason for Nate's sudden lack of interest in flirty waitresses.

Scanning the beach, I spot Rowan sitting on a cooler, surrounded by a group of girls. His arm is around a brunette, pulling his sleeve tight against his biceps. The warm breeze tousles his hair, and I understand why the girls fall over him. He's good-looking but not worth the trouble. And that's something I have to remind myself of a lot lately.

Rowan glances up, catching my eye. He waves me over, then shoos the girls away. "What's up, Bri?" he says with a goofy smile, pulling me into a hug. I stand, frozen in shock. It takes a moment before my brain starts working again, and I lightly tap his back with one hand.

I pull away from the awkward hug. "Nate said you had something of mine?"

"Oh, yeah." He grins and opens his cooler. "I know how much you *love* keg beer," he says, pointing to the kegs lined up on the beach. "So I brought your bottle of tequila, so you'd have something to drink."

Once again, I'm left standing there looking dumb because of Rowan. He stands there with that smile again, watching me. "That's… uh, that was nice of you. Thanks."

"Here, I'll make you a drink," he says, already pulling a cup from his cooler. It's like he was hoping I'd show up tonight. And that makes the heat rise to my cheeks again. I'm tempted to read into this. To let my brain think something is happening here with us, but I know I shouldn't.

He's just being friendly.

Although this doesn't feel friendly.

"Well, we can't let a perfect bottle of tequila go to waste, can we?" I say, trying to act unfazed, and he hums in agreement, popping open the bottle. "And you know I love watching you make my drinks." It's a weak attempt at a joke, but it still earns a laugh.

Rowan hands me the cup, and I take a quick sip, nodding in appreciation.

"I'll keep the bottle in my cooler for you. Just come find me when you want a refill."

And suddenly, this feels like the only drink I'll be having tonight.

"Yes, sir," I salute before turning and searching the crowded beach for Harper. I'm hyper-aware of Rowan behind me, especially when he leans in and points over my shoulder.

"Harper's over there."

I mutter a quick thanks, unable to look at him. My feet move before I think, and I weave through the people to get to the other side of the beach.

I quickly put as much distance as I can between us, and as I push through the sweaty bodies, I glimpse Calista off to my right. The words "Lane Scholars Group" fall from her mouth, but I don't stick around to catch anything else.

I don't want to stir up more drama than I likely already have.

Harper's eyes light up when I approach. "Bri!" Her enthusiastic yell makes me laugh, and her smile is infectious.

"Hey, guys!" I hug Harper quickly and notice the same curly-haired girl from the diner. A look of recognition passes between us.

"Breakfast girl." It's more of a question, but I laugh at her nickname.

"Yes. Breakfast girl. Otherwise known as Bri." I give her another wave.

"Reece hasn't shut up about you," she gushes, giving me a sweet smile.

"Ah, good to know. I guess this means you're involved with this craziness, too?" I ask, pointing at the boys.

"I am. When I'm not stuck at the diner, that is. I'm Zara."

"Diner girl." I echo her nickname for me, and this draws a laugh out of everyone before I turn my attention back to the group to find Reece watching me. I ignore the flush of heat on my cheeks. "So, what did I interrupt?"

"Oh, nothing serious, you know. Just plotting world domination, the usual," Kian says, throwing his arm around Harper's shoulder.

"Wow, big goals," I joke back. "We should consider—"

A throat clears behind me, and I have to wonder who would be so bold as to interrupt someone like that. But my confusion melts away as I turn to find Calista standing behind me.

"I don't know what you think you're doing, but you need to stay away from Rowan." Her words are meant to be threatening, but I can't help but laugh. The way the shadow of the flames dances across her profile, she looks like some kind of errand boy for the Devil.

So *not* intimidating.

"No problem. I don't want him." I force the words out with as much certainty as I can. But she doesn't seem to believe me, her face falling into a deeper scowl.

There's a brief second of silence where the laughter from the beach trickles in around us, but we stay unmoving.

"He's mine, so just stay away," she repeats.

"Got it." I nod.

She looks so unsure of herself. And the cracks in her confident mask make my heart hurt for her. She's just another trophy for Rowan to add to his collection.

A collection we both want to be part of.

I try to offer her an olive branch, saying, "Did I hear you mention the Lane Scholars earlier?"

"I just sent in my application. But don't worry about it. They have a 'no slut' policy." She laughs with her friends. It's a cynical laugh that sets every hair on my body on end.

I click my tongue and smile at her. She deserves to be a trophy.

"Now that you mention it, my mom told me about that rule. You know she's on the board of directors for the Lane Scholars? I can put in a good word for you." I try to keep my tone light and friendly, but her face falls all the same.

"Your mom?" Calista's smile falls, and I feel a swell of satisfaction.

"Yep." I gloat, knowing that's knocked the wind out of her sails. "I'll be sure to point out your application to her when I get home."

The last ounce of determination evaporates, and Calista's shoulders drop. "Stay away from Rowan." Her tone is weaker now. Softer. And I almost feel bad for her. Almost.

She's just a girl going after what she wants. And I can't fault her for it. But she's nasty about it, and I hate that.

She turns and begins stomping away, and I can't help myself. "Oh, Calista!" I call out after her.

Her head snaps around, and she levels me with the meanest stare. "What?"

"Your insecurity's showing. You might want to fix that," I taunt, pointing to her outfit.

She groans and storms off into the crowd.

Turning back to my friends, I'm greeted with three shocked looks and Harper's disapproving glare. And that's when it hits me that I've gone too far.

She didn't need that, but it's like I couldn't help myself. I had to have the last word.

"Was that really necessary, Bri?" Harper asks.

"What? You just told me this morning how you didn't like her."

"That doesn't mean you should stoop to her level." I roll my eyes, knowing Harper is right. Before I have a chance to defend myself, an amused smile spreads across Kian's face as he wraps me in a bear hug.

"Oh my God, I love this girl!" he exclaims, spinning me around.

I laugh, mouthing, *he loves me*, as I look at Harper. It's her turn to roll her eyes as Kian puts me down.

"I didn't know your mom was on the board for the Lane Scholars," Reece says, drawing my attention.

"She's not. But Calista doesn't know that."

Thirteen
Briar

This summer is everything summer is supposed to be. The bonfire definitely lived up to my memories. The edges of the night are starting to blur, and I wouldn't have it any other way.

The five of us have settled into easy conversation, and it's like I've always been part of their little group. It's starting to feel like I never left. The kegs are nearly empty, and if I had any worries, the ocean has washed them away.

"Want to go for a walk and sober up a bit?" Reece asks, leaning into me.

I'm grateful for the darkness surrounding us to hide the blush on my cheeks. As much as I don't want to lose this buzz, I probably should before I go home. I nod, and he grabs my hand, interlocking our fingers. We walk silently for a moment, just listening to the sounds of the crashing waves.

"What's the deal with you and Rowan?" Reece's question comes out of left field.

And as shocked as I am, the denial falls from my mouth. "Nothing."

"Come on, Briar. You could have any guy on this island," he says, giving me a pointed look.

"I know." It might be true, but the edges of my mind are occupied with only one guy right now.

"So, why Rowan?"

"I'm not interested in Rowan." My voice sounds sure, even though I'm still trying to convince myself of that. "He needed me to be his date at a party last night to make Calista jealous. He's more like another older brother to me than anything. Rowan's been around since I was in diapers. It's strictly platonic."

Reece absorb the information, weighing the merit of my explanation. He nods, looking mostly satisfied, though there's still some hesitation. I don't have time to question it before he sits in the damp sand and lets out a relieved breath.

"Well, you two are selling it. You have the whole island convinced."

I drop into the spot beside him, not sure how to explain that.

"So, you're done with him now?" There's so much hope in his voice that I can't bring myself to deny it.

"I'd say so. I mean, you saw Calista earlier. She seems adequately jealous." I laugh at the memory of her face, but my chest hurts thinking about being done with Rowan.

"I can't blame her," Reece admits, making my heart skip a beat.

"What do you mean?"

"The two of you just seem to get on well."

"It's all just friendly banter. Doesn't mean anything. Rowan and I have known each other forever. I'm sure there are photos of him at my second birthday."

Reece's brows draw together like he's trying to picture it.

"And besides, Nate and Harper are the same way. It's almost… familial."

Even as I say it, something twists uncomfortably in my chest. Because what I feel for Rowan is anything but familial. But I don't want to have to explain the way it feels when he looks at me and my pulse races, or how he makes me feel like I'm the only one in the room.

That's not even something I understand myself.

Reece laughs, scooping sand into his hand and letting the grains fall through his fingers.

I nudge his shoulder with mine. "I mean, we're the same way. Friendly banter, right?"

"Something like that." Reece sneaks a glance at me, and my stomach flutters. "I had a great time with you today. I wish you had come home a little more often."

There's a part of me that wishes I had met Reece first. Sitting with him under the star-filled sky just feels right. Or that he'd been here before I left. Maybe then, I wouldn't be so caught up in a boy who uses me to make other girls jealous.

"Me too."

"If you're free on Monday, maybe I could teach you how to surf?"

"I'd love that."

The words hang in the air as we sit silently. I stare into the dark ocean and wonder what life would be like if I never had to move away. Maybe it wouldn't be such a mess. Maybe things would be easier. Maybe they'd be better.

The ocean breeze chills me, and I lean my head on Reece's shoulder as we settle into a compatible silence.

There's a prickling feeling on the back of my neck, like I'm being watched, but there's no one around besides Reece and me. And maybe a few beach creatures scurrying around in the dark.

"Well, my drink is empty, and I could use a refill. How about you, Bri?"

My cup is full of warm beer that I haven't touched since Kian poured it, but I dump the drink into the damp sand anyway. "Looks like I'm empty too."

Reece laughs before helping me walk back toward the party. He doesn't have to touch me or hold my hand to make me feel weak in the knees. He just exists. And I wish I could pause at this moment and live in it forever. Our small talk is easy; everything about Reece feels comforting and calm.

But just as quickly as the moment came, it's gone; blown away by the storm that is Rowan.

"Briar, where the hell have you been?"

His tone sends panic through me, making my blood chill. "Just down the beach. Why? Is everything okay? Is Nate okay?"

"Nate's fine."

I grow more frantic now and can feel the tension radiating from Reece. "Is it Harper?"

"She's fine."

I stare blankly at Rowan. "Then what's wrong?"

"Nothing, I guess." He exhales sharply, frustrated.

Relieved, I let out a breath. Reece pulls me an inch closer to him, his hand wrapped protectively around my waist. I swear I can feel his thundering pulse against my arm as Rowan watches us. His jaw ticks.

"Okay," I say, trying to cut the tension. "Well, thanks for checking in, Rowan. We're all safe."

Rowan's eyes stay locked on Reece, his fists clenched at his sides. "You're not safe with him." Rowan's voice has a deadly edge, making me go wide-eyed.

It's a side of him I haven't seen before. It's alarming how quickly he's flipped.

Reece tenses beside me, voice cool but edged with a warning tone. "Stop—"

"I wasn't talking to you, Collins." Rowan's words drip with venom. If I hadn't known Rowan for so long, I'd be scared.

"Reece, let's find the others," I say quickly, trying to lead him away from whatever fight is brewing. I know they hate each other, but I don't want a front-row seat to the fallout. Though a few kids have their phones out and are recording every second of this.

"Collins," Rowan snaps. "You always swoop in on my leftovers, don't you?" Then, Rowan turns his attention back to me.

Rowan's words feel like a gut punch. To him, I'm just his *leftovers.* I've officially been demoted from accessory to leftovers. I can feel the tears prick the back of my eyes, but I refuse to let them fall.

Not here.

Not in front of him.

The unspoken threats are thrown like silent daggers between the two. In the one day I've known Reece, nothing about him screams dangerous, not the way it does with Rowan. But their stare down has me reconsidering.

"I didn't take anything from you." Reece laughs bitterly. "If my memory serves, your dad's the one who pretty much handed it over."

Reece's words push Rowan over the edge. His face hardens as he takes a step closer. "You stole those contracts. And I plan on getting every single piece of that business back."

I feel helpless. I have no clue what they're arguing about. It's like they're speaking in some kind of code. My mind moves a hundred miles a minute as I struggle to put the pieces together.

Rowan's dad and stolen contracts…

Then it clicks.

The Collinses are the riff-raff bringers.

Looking around the beach, we've drawn quite a crowd. I hear a few gasps, and another person raises their cell phone.

"You think so?" Reece challenges, his voice equally as calm. "Tell me, now that Daddy's out of the picture, who's holding your leash?"

It's the first real metaphorical punch Reece has thrown, and I can see the anger flowing through Rowan.

He's there, fists clenched, and the veins in his arms are protruding further than I would consider safe.

"Please, stop," I beg, desperate to prevent a physical fight.

But it's too late.

Rowan's fist connects with Reece's jaw.

The sound makes me flinch. Then, silence descends on the beach—what feels like an hour's worth of silence before a few cheers from the crowd erupt into a frenzied cheer.

Reece rubs a hand over his chin, assessing the damage.

"Just like your dad. Resorting to violence when you don't get your way."

Without thinking, I step between them, desperate to break this up before anyone else gets hurt.

"Stop it. Both of you," I shout as I push against Rowan's chest to separate the boys.

Reece looks at me like I'm the one who punched him, but my gaze bounces between the pair. I feel helpless, but I have to try and get through to Rowan.

"Rowan, what are you doing?"

"I'm about to beat the shit out of this idiot," Rowan growls.

I take a step back, dropping my hand from his chest. "No, you aren't." I shake my head but see his glare still trained on my friend. I snap my fingers in front of Rowan's face twice before his eyes meet mine. "Stop it."

"No, Briar! I told you I'm going to—"

"What, Rowan?" I yell, cutting him off, not caring who hears. "What are you going to do? Huh? Go through me to get to him?"

I now have Rowan's full, undivided attention, and it's like he's just realizing what he's done. His face softens.

His brows pinch together. He searches my face, but I don't recognize the guy standing in front of me.

His voice drops. "No, Bri. I would never hurt you. You know—"

"I honestly don't care right now, Rowan. Just leave me alone."

His eyes don't leave mine. Rowan stands there looking dumbfounded. He sways a bit but takes a half-step back, scanning the crowd like he's finally snapped out of a trance.

"Bri, I'm sorry. I didn't mean it."

I shake my head, not sure if he even knows what he's apologizing for. "That's just not good enough."

Rowan's expression crumbles, and he looks utterly defeated. He takes a few shaky steps backward, and I finally turn to Reese.

"Reece, are you okay?" I reach for his chin to get a better look at the emerging bruise.

"I'm fine," he insists, brushing me off as Harper rushes over. His next words are to Harper, but they knock the wind out of my lungs.

"Tell her to leave me alone and go play girlfriend with the psychopath."

And for the second time tonight, the words land like a punch to my gut. The tears well in my eyes, threatening to spill over. This time, I don't wait around for him to change his mind.

I just run.

Fourteen
Rowan

I can't believe I did that.

I feel like the world's biggest idiot. I can't believe I let Reece Collins rile me up again. He just knows every button to push and everything to say to make me lose it. But he has such a punchable face that it's hard to contain myself. Especially with how smug he looks, knowing he stole my dad's business right from underneath us. And I hate him for that.

But I should've taken the high road, especially with Briar right there.

All I can think about is her face. The way she looked at me like she didn't even recognize me. I never wanted her to see that side of me. I try to calm myself with a deep breath, but it's useless. Everything about this night has gone to shit.

This was supposed to be our night. I had it all planned out—good food, easy conversation, maybe even a walk on the beach afterward. Instead, I let Reece Collins turn me back into the same angry kid who used to get suspended for fighting. The same kid whose father's arrest made headlines. Briar deserved better than watching me confirm every warning Nate's probably given her about me.

I abandon anything that's not already packed in my cooler and head toward my car. It's not until I'm in the lot when I see her. Briar's back is to me as she scans the parking area, likely searching for her brother's car. She drags the back of her hand across her cheek, and it guts me to know I'm the reason she's crying.

"He left already," I tell her, keeping a few feet between us. "I can take you home if you want."

"No." Her voice is sharp, ripping into me with all the turmoil I know I caused.

"Your other option is to walk. And I'm not letting that happen."

I hear her frustrated sigh, and she mumbles, "This must be a joke."

I stay still, the cooler handles digging into my palms as I wait for her to decide. She takes her time, but I'd stand here forever waiting for her. I glance at my car parked a few spaces over and silently beg her to give in.

"It's just a ride home. It's the least I can do."

"Fine," she huffs, stomping toward my car.

Relief floods through me, making me think there's a chance she might be able to forgive me. She grabs the door handle, but it doesn't budge. I take a few hesitant steps toward her, knowing it's locked and the keys are in my pocket.

"I already don't want to look at you. Don't make this harder than it has to be. Unlock the car, Rowan."

She sounds angry. Annoyed. But I cover the smile that spreads across my face. She's furious. And she has every right to be. But I'm just happy that she's here and is letting me drive her home. I place the cooler by the trunk. Taking a few cautious steps toward her, my heart sinks when she instinctively backs away.

I reach out, gently touching her arm. I have to make things right with Briar, no matter what it takes. "Hey, I'm sorry about that; I just—"

"I don't care, Rowan." She rips her arm out of my grasp. "Harper warned me about you, but I didn't listen. She told me you were like this, and you just proved her right. I don't want to talk. I want to go home. Unlock the car door."

I flinch at the sharp pain in my chest, hearing her say that. It feels like there's no air left in my lungs.

Harper had to warn her about me.

And I proved her right.

I lock my jaw and reach into my pocket. My fingers find the buttons on my fob, and the door unlocks with a click. Everything in me screams to open the door for her, but I know she'd hate that right now.

She *hates* everything about me right now.

So I step back and let her slide into the car on her own.

Briar slams the door closed and buckles herself into the seat with rushed, jerky movements.

Turning away from her feels like a sin, but I do it. With the cooler safely loaded into my trunk, I slide into the driver's seat beside her and stare at the steering wheel for a moment. My knuckles turn white from the anger still lingering inside me. But I'm more angry at myself. Angry for letting her get too close. Angry that I can't control myself. Angry that I hurt her.

Just being this close to her again is painful. Inhaling a quick breath, I turn the key in the ignition, and the car comes to life.

As I put the car in reverse, Briar stops me. "Wait, Rowan."

I turn my full attention back to her. Her eyes are rimmed in red like she's trying desperately to hold back from crying. "Yes?"

"Are you drunk?"

I want to laugh out loud. Have I been drinking? Yeah.

Am I drunk? Not even close.

Not after the way she looked at me tonight—like I was some monster.

That sobered me up in a heartbeat.

"I've only had a few drinks."

"That's not what I asked."

Her words are so sharp that I hesitate, unsure of what she wants me to say.

"Never mind. I'm walking."

She reaches for the car handle, and something inside me snaps. There's no way she's walking home. I reach across her and pull the door closed.

"You're not walking. I'm not drunk."

I lean back in my seat and drag my hand down my face, forcing a soft smile. I need to convince her of the truth, and try not to be the monster everyone's built me up to be.

The monster I am.

"I'm not drunk. I would never let you get in my car if I wasn't sober. I don't ever want to hurt you."

She sits there studying my face as if that will help her determine if I'm lying. Her shoulders sag as she gives in.

"Fine. Just remember, Nate will kill you if anything happens to me on your watch."

A smile barely crosses my face. "Oh, I know."

We ride in silence for the whole ten minutes to her house. I sneak glances at her during the drive, but her gaze remains fixated on whatever is outside the window. The drive ends sooner than I'd like, pulling into her driveway three minutes before ten o'clock.

I rack my brain for something to say to fix this.

"Look, Bri—"

But she's unbuckled and out of my car before I can finish my plea. I don't chase after her. I just sit and watch as she jogs up the stairs to the front door. As much as I want to punch something, I hold back.

I hold it all in and sit until Briar's safely inside. And even then, I can't do anything but just sit and stare at the closed door.

The weight of everything tonight is soul-crushing, and it feels like my one chance has slipped through my fingers.

Fifteen

Briar

As much as I need to run this morning to clear my head, I can't. It's raining. And not just a drizzle. It's raining like the bottom has fallen out of the sky.

So now, I'm stuck.

No running, and there's no one around to entertain me. Just me and my thoughts. And that's worse than having to relive whatever the hell happened last night.

None of it makes any sense. There's clearly more going on than I'm privy to, but I can't get over how Rowan lashed out. It was like he wanted to hurt me. And it seemed like he wanted Reece to fight back.

I hear Rowan's warning on repeat: *You're not safe with him.*

I don't want to believe Rowan, but… I don't know. I watched as Reece picked Rowan apart, seemingly just for fun. He *wanted* to get a rise out of Rowan, too. The whole thing has me spinning in circles. I'm caught in a web of confusion, unsure who to trust. And honestly, I'm tired of everything.

I can't do it anymore.

Staring out the back patio doors, wrapped in our thickest and fluffiest blanket, I stare out into the ocean as the waves rip apart the beach and the storm wages on. Dark clouds pass overhead, and a chill runs down my spine. All I've wanted for years was to be home: but now that I'm here, it still feels dark. And lonely.

A knock on the front door startles me as a flash of lightning dances across the sky. I can just make out a blurry silhouette through the glass, and I hope it's Harper finally coming to pick me up for our girls' day.

I open the front door and freeze.

Reece stands there, soaked from the rain, fist still poised mid-air. I'm lost for words. I don't know why he would be here.

I pull the blanket tighter around my shoulders and take a step back into our darkened foyer.

"Hi." It's a weak greeting, but nothing else feels appropriate.

"Hey." Reece smiles, but it doesn't reach his eyes. A nasty bruise shadows his jaw and stretches up toward his cheek. For a moment, I forget everything other than the purple mark that ruins his perfect complexion.

"Reece." I gasp, reaching for his face, but he moves away.

My heart drops. Then I remember his parting words. *Go play girlfriend to the psychopath.* He must hate me now.

"Can I come in?"

I blink, slow to register he's still on the porch. There's a sick feeling in my stomach, but I step aside, and he quickly steps into the house.

"Are you okay?" I ask, pushing the door closed behind him, taking my time to carefully secure it. I stare at the floor, where a growing puddle of water surrounds his shoes.

There's a beat of silence, permeated only by the crack of thunder outside.

"I'm fine." He laughs, and instead of being cold like last night, it's warm and inviting. I hesitantly look up and see him watching me.

"But your face…" I touch my own cheek, wincing.

"This is nothing. You should've seen what happened the last time we crossed paths."

The last time? My brain spirals. This has happened before? But I can't focus on that. All I can focus on is how my stomach twists, with Reece's harsh words repeating through my mind.

"What are you doing here? And why are you dripping on the floor? Did you walk here or something?"

"I just needed to clear my head. So I took a drive. Then I ended up here, at your house."

My mind struggles to piece together what he's just said.

I point to the rain falling in sheets outside the windows that bracket our front door. "You went for a drive in this?"

"Yeah."

"And you drove here?"

He shrugs. "Guess so."

"Why?"

"I wanted to apologize."

I open and close my mouth, still not knowing what to say to him. He turned on me last night, and now he's just… apologizing. I can't understand for the life of me what happened last night, and why he would drive here of all places. I blink a few times, taking in his words.

"You want to apologize?"

He nods. "I screwed up last night."

"Yeah." The shock must be evident on my face because Reece steps closer, but I mirror his motion and keep some space between us.

"I didn't mean what I said last night."

His words knock the wind out of my lungs. I didn't expect an apology from him, and I surely don't want him to know how much his words hurt, so I nod.

"I know."

"No. Don't do that." He shakes his head, and a few drops of water fall from his messy hair. "Don't just pretend it's fine. It wasn't. I shouldn't have said it. There's no excuse. I'm sorry, Bri." He sounds sad and genuinely upset about the whole thing.

I scan his face and finally see more than just the bruise. His eyes are red and puffy, like he's been crying.

My heart clenches.

"It's fine," I say, even though I don't know if it is.

"You don't have to forgive me. I just want you to know that I'm so sorry and that I won't ever say anything like that to you ever again. I promise."

His reassurance washes over me like sunlight breaking through the clouds. The words mend the broken pieces of last night, and it starts to feel okay again.

I suck in a breath. "All is forgiven. Thank you for apologizing."

He relaxes, and a soft smile spreads across his face. But my eyes linger on the swollen half of his jaw.

"I'm fine. I promise," he whispers, gently brushing his fingers across my cheek. I lean into the warmth without meaning to.

But part of last night nags at me, though maybe it shouldn't.

"Why did Rowan punch you last night?"

I search his face for answers. I need to know why things escalated and why he encouraged it.

Reece quickly drops his hand from my face. "I shouldn't have egged him on. But I didn't start hating Rowan and didn't intend to make enemies here. I can't speak for him, though."

"But clearly, you're not friends."

"No." He laughs. "It's not my place to rehash his family history."

I hesitate. "He said I wasn't safe with you." It comes out more like a question.

"I can promise you'll *always* be safe with me." There's no hesitation in his response.

A car horn blares from the driveway, tearing my attention away from Reece. I open the front door again and spot Harper in the driveway, waving her arms around wildly in the car, like a game of charades. She's pointing at Reece's car and shouting something, but it's lost to the cacophony of the storm.

Reece chuckles behind me.

I shake my head and yell, "One second" before turning toward Reece.

"Gotta love Harper," he says. "What's she got you roped into this time?"

"She convinced me to go shopping with her and Cora—or maybe it's Clara? Anyway, we absolutely *must* have new dresses for the Annual Charity Gala at the Vanderbilt house."

"Don't sound too excited," he jokes.

"I love Harper. She's great. But you know how she is. We'll probably end up with matching dresses." I frown at the thought.

"She's something, that's for sure," he mumbles.

I tilt my head, adding softly, "Thank you for coming by. Even in the rain."

"Even in the rain," he echoes.

Sixteen
Briar

We walk into the third shop of the day, and the rain has finally cleared. Cora trails behind me, her garment bag in tow.

"I'm so jealous you've already found a dress," I murmur to Cora. "I'd give anything to end this medieval torture Harper is dragging us through."

We laugh, and she helps as I rummage through the racks, searching for anything even remotely acceptable.

"Maybe you can go dressed as a sugar plum fairy," Cora teases, holding up a purple dress with a skirt that looks like a middle schooler made it... blindfolded. I stifle my laughter until Harper shoots us a death glare.

"Stop it." Her eyes look stern, but I can see the hint of a smile on her face.

"Can we at least get lunch after this? I don't want to kill one of you because I'm hungry. Cora doesn't deserve that."

Harper rolls her eyes at me. "Yes, Bri. After we find our dresses, we'll grab lunch."

I dive back into the racks. I pluck a few surprisingly good options and head to the dressing rooms.

I quickly learn the dresses are total duds. There's a pale-yellow frilly lace dress with no shape, a pink strapless dress that feels two sizes too small, and an odd-looking babydoll dress.

I'm starting to question if *I'm* the problem, then I step into the fourth one—a vibrant red with a slit that climbs high on my thigh. I bark out a laugh as I stare at my reflection. This couldn't be further from what I'm looking for.

It's stunning, just… not for this occasion.

"Bri, let me see!" Cora encourages me.

"Yeah, yeah," I call out, struggling with the zipper.

I open the door to see Harper in a beautiful sage green and cream slip dress that hugs her figure perfectly. She's beaming and it's like the dress was made for her.

"Harper, you look amazing," I say, momentarily forgetting about my revealing dress.

"You're practically glowing." Cora's agreement makes Harper's cheeks flush.

"Guys, you're too kind. But holy cow, Bri. Look at you!" Harper's excited squeal makes Cora whip her head in my direction.

"Don't look too hard. I might accidentally flash you with this dress." I'm laughing, but the girls stare at me all doe-eyed.

"Bri, the dress looks fantastic on you," Harper says more seriously.

Now, it's my turn to blush. I turn and stare at my reflection for a second. The warm tones of the red dress complement my skin and make every feature pop.

"That's the one." Harper's voice startles me.

"It's not," I argue. "The slit comes up too high for a family-friendly event."

Cora rolls her eyes. "Who cares? You'll be doing us all a favor showing up in that."

"I'm sure Reece would love to see you in that dress," Harper teases. And my cheeks flush an even deeper shade of red.

"No," I mumble, not allowing that to be why I get a dress. And besides, he's a guy. He won't even notice. Still, a small part of me wonders if being noticed by someone like

Reece or even Rowan might not be so terrible after all. Another moment passes, and I feel myself giving in.

"Fine. I'll get the dress, but it isn't for Reece." It's not a lie, but doesn't feel like the whole truth. But Harper doesn't need to know that.

"Yes!" Cora pumps a fist in celebration as Harper throws her arms around me.

I laugh along with them, but Rowan's image sneaks into my head. His eyes, the way they might inspect every inch of fabric that clings to me. His mouth, the way it might part slightly as if I've managed to take his breath away. His hands, the way they'll mess up his hair from running his hands through it, when I'd rather have them be on me.

I inhale sharply, coming out of the little daydream to refocus on the girls, still chatting away. I can't want him, not like that. So I'll have to forget, or at least distract myself. "But we need to get some lunch before I change my mind."

They agree, and soon, we're across the street in a charming little café. With its hand-painted signs and mismatched tables, it feels like we've left New York and have been transported to a spot in London. Thought this version of London doesn't have a headmistress who's trying to ruin my life. The school has yet to make a decision, and that's been enough to keep my anxiety at a level ten.

I shake the thought from my mind and try to focus on this moment. We order our snacks, and I devour mine before sitting at a corner table near the windows. Even with the threat of expulsion looming over me, I can't deny how much this whole place feels so much like home. I could just get lost in it.

"Um, hello? Earth to Briar?" Harper's teasing voice brings me back.

"Sorry, what?"

"I said, what went down between Reece and Rowan last night?" she repeats, but I don't have an answer.

Cora's eyes widen. "Oh, what happened last night?"

"There was a mild altercation on the beach." I try to sound unbothered, but Cora's eyes nearly bug out of her head.

"You call that mild?" Harper scoffs. "That was a full-on fight."

I hold up a finger to stop her. "I wouldn't call it a fight. Only one of them threw a punch."

"Technically, yes. You'd be correct," Harper concedes with a laugh.

"You skip one bonfire and miss a brawl," Cora whines, throwing her hands up. "What were they fighting about this time?"

I quirk a brow at her, but Harper beats me to the punch. "They were fighting over Bri."

"No. No, they weren't." I give Harper a playful glare. "They were fighting about…well, I don't know exactly what they were fighting about. But it wasn't over me."

"Someone's in denial," Cora sing-songs, a teasing smile on her face.

"Not you, too," I groan, looking at her in mock horror. "I don't know what happened. Reece and I were just talking, and then suddenly Rowan was there… then fists."

I don't miss the look that Harper and Cora share before they avert their eyes.

"Okay, you guys know something," I demand, pointing at them. "Spill."

"Bri, remember what I said the other day about Rowan hating the Collinses?" Harper asks. I nod. "He blames Reece's dad for what happened to our dad. He thinks if they hadn't shown up, Dad would still be around."

I shake my head. "He doesn't really believe that," I say, horrified. He can't be that dense to believe something so illogical.

"He does. I know Reece and his family had nothing to do with it. But you know Rowan. He's stuck in his ways."

"It's just boys being boys," Cora adds, shrugging like it's the most normal thing in the world for two boys to hate each other and end up trading blows.

"How childish. What is he, ten years old? He needs to get over it," I laugh, but I know it has to be more than just a family feud. And neither of them will give me a straight answer.

Harper cracks a smile, and her shoulders relax. "Honestly, yeah. He does need to get over it."

"That's lame. They're lame. Moving on," I say, turning my attention to Cora. "So, what's fun in your life right now?"

"Oh, not much. Compared to your life, my life's boring," she teases. "Sounds like you've been causing chaos since you got home."

"You have no idea," I mutter. I have just had one problem after another since the exams. The biggest problem is that I still can't get Rowan out of my head. Or Reece.

"You need a drama-free guy to get you back on track," Cora says, pointing a long, skinny finger at me.

I laugh, worried I admitted that out loud. "If you know one, let me know."

"Sorry, fresh out of drama-free boys around here. You'll have to check back next week," Harper plays along with Cora's joke.

"Wait. Hold on. There's Mateo. She should date Mateo." Cora suggests, and Harper quirks her brow.

"He is pretty drama-free," Harper agrees, but shoots me a you'll-hate-him warning look.

"I could set you guys up!"

I hesitate for a minute. "Uh, sure. A quick coffee wouldn't kill me."

I regret the words as soon as I say them. As much as I want a fun summer fling, Mateo isn't the one I want.

But it's too late.

"Great!" Cora lights up.

"Great," I repeat back, forcing a smile.

"Oh, shoot," Harper says, flashing the clock on her phone. "We've got to go if we're going to have any shot at make it back before Lucy's closes. I refuse to go another day without one of her lavender lattes."

"We can't forget about the lavender lattes," Cora teases.

"That would be a tragedy," I play into it, watching Harper roll her eyes as we pile back into her car.

With the windows down and our hair whipping through the breeze, we enjoy the July heat as Harper serenades us. Her voice carries with the wind, but we still hear every off-tune note she sings.

She only stops when we finally pull into her driveway, and my heart stops along with the song.

Rowan is there, shirtless, shooting a basketball like some damn model in a commercial for the latest sports drink. My stomach drops the second his eyes find mine.

"Hey, um, I'm going to head home," I say to Harper. "I'm not feeling great and want to take a nap."

"I'm sorry. Do you want me to drive you?" Harper offers, concern etched into her features.

"No. I'm fine," I assure her. "Maybe some fresh air will do me some good."

"Are you sure?"

"Positive."

"Okay. Text me when you get home."

"Promise."

I quickly wave to her and watch as the girls head inside. I can feel Rowan's eyes on me, and it takes some Herculean strength to avoid his gaze. By some miracle, I make it halfway down the drive before his hand touches my elbow.

"Hey, can I talk to you?" Rowan asks, looking more nervous than I've ever seen him.

I pull my elbow from his grasp and stare at him. I'm still livid, but the look on his face makes me pause. I want to pretend like last night never happened. I want to slip back into my delusion that he's perfect. And that we might work out someday.

But I can't.

I shouldn't.

Because I'm just *leftovers* to him.

I flinch just remembering the way he said that.

"About last night…" he trails off.

I cross my arms, waiting for him, but he says nothing. I look away, not wanting to get roped back into his current.

I wait another minute, though it feels like an hour, before giving up. "Pathetic."

I turn to head back down the drive, but Rowan begins pleading as he steps in front of me.

"Wait, Bri. Please. I don't know what happened. I couldn't find you, and then you were with Reece… I got mad, and I don't know…" he admits, almost embarrassed. "I wasn't thinking, Bri. I just wanted to make sure you were okay because I value you as a friend and—"

"We're not friends, Rowan."

The words hurt as soon as I say them and Rowan deflates. He stays there frozen, like a statue, his eyes boring into mine, emotionless.

"I did you one favor, one time. You're someone I tolerate because you're friends with my brother," I continue, because I know I should cut whatever this is off now, before it can ruin things.

Rowan stands there, unmoving.

"But us? We're not friends. Reece is my friend. You know, the guy you punched in the face last night?"

He flinches and steps back, like I've physically hit him. A flash of regret dances across his face before his mouth sets in a hard line, and every piece of the Rowan I know disappears.

"You're right. Whatever," he mutters before he turns and walks away angrily, grabbing the basketball and beginning to dribble it again.

I don't give either of us a chance to apologize and force myself to take calm, even steps away from him. I don't get far before there's a loud thud that echoes as I lose sight of the driveway. And that thud, it sounds a lot like a basketball colliding with the side of the house.

Seventeen
Briar

The longer I sit in Nate's car, the more I regret agreeing to this date with Mateo. I don't want to be here. I stare at the dashboard, fighting the urge to go home because nothing about this feels right. And I can't explain why.

Mateo sounds like a nice enough guy from what Harper and Cora have said. He looked like a model in the photos they showed me. But I'd much rather skip this and go to my surf lesson with Reece.

And a quick scan of the parking lot tells me Mateo is late. Strike one.

Every minute he's late is another minute for my mind to wander. And that's a dangerous thing since my mind always wanders to one person: Rowan.

I'm startled back to reality by a sharp knock on my window that nearly makes me jump out of my skin. I exhale in relief when I see Nate *and Rowan*. It's like the universe thinks tormenting me with his presence is funny.

But I'm not laughing.

Nate gives me a stupid wave as I get out of the car.

"You needed my car just to sit in a random parking lot this morning?"

I slam the car door shut. "No, I'm here to meet someone, but he's… late."

"Rookie mistake," Nate says, snickering with Rowan.

Before I can jab back at Nate, I hear the unmistakable slap of flip-flops against the asphalt. A tall guy with tanned skin and curly brown hair walks toward me.

"Yo, Bri!" he shouts. "It's, like, great to meet you, yeah?"

I tilt my head because he is nothing like I hoped he'd be. He's not disheveled, but he's not exactly polished either. It looks like he just rolled out of bed.

He moves in for a hug, but I pull back. I've never been one for hugs, especially not with someone I don't know. But it's too late—Mateo's already pulling me in.

He nods toward Nate and Rowan, "So, who are your friends?"

Nate takes a step forward, and there's amusement in his voice. "I'm her brother. Nate."

I glare at the back of Nate's head knowing that he's enjoying this far too much.

"Wow, mad formal out here. I like it," Mateo says, shaking Nate's hand.

Rowan doesn't budge from his spot but nods in Mateo's general direction. "Rowan."

"Well," I exclaim, cutting off the introductions. "Now that we're all acquainted, why don't we head inside, Mateo?" I gesture toward the café.

"Word, I could use some fuel for my body right now," Mateo says.

I stop mid-step. What? His words leave me speechless, so I plaster an awkward smile.

"Uh, yeah. Okay," I agree before turning to face Nate with a what-is-this-guy-on look. Nate does what he can to hide his laughter, but his shoulders are shaking as he turns away from me.

In a last attempt to escape the awkwardness, I mouth *please help me* at Nate before feeling Mateo link his hand in mine. It takes everything in me not to jerk away from Mateo, especially with Rowan watching me intently, so I let him lead me into the café.

The quaint space smells of freshly ground coffee, and the walls have little coffee cups painted across them. Sitting across from Mateo, I can't help but think this is a colossal waste of my time.

"Do you bring your brother and entourage to meet all your dates?"

I choke on my drink, coughing to cover it up. "Uh, no. I just happened to run into my brother before you walked up."

"Cool. I guess you and Rowan used to be a thing then, yeah?"

"Not at all." I can't keep the sharpness out of my voice. "Why?"

"You were with him at the party, and he didn't look thrilled to see me with you today. Just seemed like there was history. Ya feel?"

I shift in my seat as my mind does some mental gymnastics. I have no idea why everyone assumes we're together. We're not spending every day together… *are we?* But sometimes, it feels like he's always around, always on my mind.

But today, he seemed like he couldn't care less that I'm on a date. And I don't know why I care. It's not like he does. *Clearly.*

"He's my brother's friend. He's like another big brother to me. Just a little protective sometimes." The lie sounds hollow, even to me. But hopefully, Mateo is more inclined to believe me.

Desperate to shift the topic away from Rowan, I try to remember anything Cora or Harper told me about Mateo. But my mind draws a blank. "So, what do you like to do for fun?"

"I mix a lot of music."

I nod, feigning interest. "That's cool—"

"I get a lot of my inspiration from what's around me. You could be my muse," he continues.

I suck in a breath and fake a smile. Nothing gets under my skin like someone who cuts me off. And who uses the word muse anymore? Strike two.

"I just upgraded some of my gear and might redo my studio space soon."

I nod along, tuning him out as he continues to ramble and resign myself to sip on my drink and wonder if he'll pass out from talking without stopping to breathe. I have to stifle my laughter at the thought of his face turning red and him falling out of his chair as he loses consciousness.

"Bri," he says louder, dragging me back. He's staring at me expectantly, and I realize I have zero idea what he just said, too lost in the fantasy of him passing out.

"Hmm?"

"You think you can do that for me?" Mateo asks.

My eyes widen in panic. I don't have the desire to do anything for him. Let alone anything that was his idea.

"Uh, I mean… I don't know."

"Just put in a good word for me, will ya?"

I tilt my head, half curious and half worried.

"With Rowan." Wherever he's trying to lead me, I need a map.

I blink. "What?"

"I heard he's the best dealer in town, and he's mad exclusive. But you and I are tight now, so maybe he'd sell to me."

I stare at him, my mind reeling. *Dealer? Rowan?* He's never even smoked at a party. And he wouldn't be dumb enough to do so after what happened with his dad. But maybe that's why he snapped at the bonfire. Maybe he was on something.

Maybe he lied about being sober.

My heart drops.

"I don't think he—You must have the wrong person…" I trail off but realize Mateo might be right as Harper's warning comes back to me.

Rowan isn't the person I thought he was. And he's done nothing but proven that to me time and time again.

Mateo looks at me like he pities me. The way you might look at a kid who just realized that Santa isn't real.

And this version of Rowan I've built in my head, he isn't real either.

"Yeah. Must be the wrong person." His tone turns cold as he pushes back from the table. "Uh, well, this has been fun, but I've got other plans."

I don't have a chance to process what he says before he's gone. He's left me in the middle of this café, stunned and speechless. Strike three.

My chest tightens, and I feel like the world has flipped upside down. Not only did this DJ wanna-be just try to use me to get close to Rowan; he also just dropped the biggest bomb out of nowhere.

Rowan is a dealer, and he knows the consequences of those actions. But I guess he doesn't care. And it hurts my heart, but at the same time, I know I *shouldn't* care.

But just the idea of him being mixed up in that makes me feel sick to my stomach. I don't want to spend another second in this café, and I make a mental note to never speak to Mateo again as I push back from the table. In my rush, my chair hits against the one behind me. I curse myself as the guy sitting there nearly spills his coffee.

"Oh my gosh, I'm so sorry," I say, reaching for a stack of napkins. I move to clean up the mess, but stop before I can hand them over. Looking up, I lock eyes with the most handsome guy I've ever seen.

"I'm sorry," I repeat, softer this time.

"Don't worry about it…" he replies, no sign of anger in his tone.

"Briar. Uh, it's Bri." I stumble over my words as he laughs.

"You sure?" he teases.

"Yes. I'm Bri."

"Nice to meet you, Bri. I'm Cameron." He offers his hand, and it's like my brain has short-circuited. I stare blankly at him before it finally registers, and I shake his hand, embarrassed.

"I'm trying to play it cool here and not be wildly presumptuous, but you're gorgeous. I'd regret it forever if I didn't ask you out. Say you'll do dinner with me."

I blink a few times and nod, not trusting my words. It's a bad idea, but he could provide a good distraction. And he's the best-looking distraction I could have dreamed up.

"Could I get your number?"

"My number? Yes." I take the phone from his outstretched hands and try to dial the ten digits I should know by heart, but my mind is blank. Finally, my brain catches up, and I input my number.

"Great. I'll call you," Cameron says, taking his phone back, and I have to wonder if this is some kind of fever dream. He's polished and just the right amount of charming and flirtatious. Almost like he's the real-life version of the Rowan that exists in my mind. Which is nothing like the real Rowan.

Which is exactly why I've decided I like Cameron.

"Okay. Yeah." I can't help the smile that spreads as I leave the café.

I get halfway across the lot before feeling my phone vibrate, and an unknown number flashes across the screen. My heart beats nervously in my chest as I answer. "Hello?"

"Hey, Bri, it's Cameron. I was hoping you're free on Wednesday."

I glance back at the café and see him standing outside, smiling at me, all charm and suaveness. He's got the same dimples as Reece, but he lacks that boyish charm that I've grown to know.

"Hmm, Wednesday," I hum, pretending to think about it. "I might have to check my calendar. I'm just swamped, you know."

"Great. I'll pick you up at four." The line clicks off, and I stare at Cameron in amusement. He offers me a quick wave before ducking back into the café.

As I get back into Nate's car, Mateo is just a distant memory, but the sick feeling in my stomach lingers.

Rowan is the lesson I never seem to learn, and I'd be stupid not to stay away.

Eighteen
Briar

Rolling into Reece's driveway, I'm greeted by the sight of Reece doing push-ups in his backyard. And in the moment, I'm no better than any guy. I stop and watch, fully appreciating the view. Before I start drooling, I hop off my bike and prop it against the short fence that borders his backyard.

"I'm glad you're finally starting to work out," I call out. "Didn't want to be the one to say anything, but you're looking a little small."

He pauses mid-rep and looks up at me, smirking. Just the one look has a flush creeping up my cheeks. He slowly pushes up one last time before standing and stripping off his shirt.

"Oh, I've been looking small?" he jokes, flexing like he's trying to win a bodybuilding competition. And he's beautiful. I'm half tempted to trace my finger along each line of solid muscle. But I pull my eyes away and swallow the urge.

"Thanks so much for the show," I deadpan, gesturing at him. "My life is forever changed."

Reece's smile lights up his face as he walks over, opens the gate, and pulls me in for a hug.

"You ready for your lesson?" Reece asks, pointing to a surfboard he's laid out on the grass.

I shift my gaze between him and the board a few times. "I know I'm not the expert here, but I am pretty sure surfing happens in the water and not in the grass."

"You're correct. Look at you already learning; I must be a fantastic teacher," he teases.

I push him away. "Then what's the plan with this setup?"

"Well, it's a hundred times easier to learn how to stand on the board when you're not fighting waves."

"Right," I nod. "That makes total sense."

He raises an eyebrow. "You've never had a surfing lesson, have you?"

"Is it that obvious?"

Reece laughs and leads me over to the board. "Yes, but don't worry. We'll start you off with the basics."

"That's a great place for me. The basics." I punctuate my words with jazz hands.

He smiles, shifting his focus back to me. "Eventually, we'll get you out on some waves."

"Doubtful," I snort. Stepping onto the board, I strike a ridiculous surfer's pose and hear Reece's laughter.

"You're a natural!"

"Thanks. I'm kind of the best at everything."

Reece rolls his eyes and gestures for me to get off the board. "Uh-huh. Let's start by lying on your stomach."

I nod along with Reece's explanation, but don't hear a word he says. He still hasn't put his shirt back on, and the way his muscles move as he goes through the motions is dangerously distracting.

"All right. Let's see it," he says, gesturing to the board.

"See what?"

"I just showed you how to get into a standing position. Now it's your turn to try it."

I look at him and raise my eyebrows. There's no chance that I'll be able to remember even half of what he showed me. "Oh, right. Of course. I… I can do that."

I make a show of getting on the board and lying on my stomach. I pretend to paddle and see Reece trying to hold back his laughter.

"I'm paddling, I'm paddling… and now I stand," I say, narrating every wrong move I make for him.

"You were definitely not paying attention," he laughs.

"Oh, I was watching."

Reece chuckles and kneels beside the board. "Try it again, and I'll guide you so you know where to put your weight."

"Try it again," I mumble and lie down, a little disheartened I wasn't perfectly in form the first time.

He's patient with me as he re-explains the process, twice more. Then he places one hand on my lower back and the other on my shoulder, and my mind goes completely blank. Everything he just said goes out the window.

We struggle through a few attempts, me huffing in frustration, and Reece giving gentle directions. But I still can't do it. And that only seems to entertain him.

"No more," I plead, flopping onto the board. "I'm clearly destined for land-based sports. Surfing's just not in my DNA."

Reece barks out a laugh, eyes sparkling with amusement. "I thought you were good at everything?"

"Everything but surfing." I roll over onto the grass and stare at the clouds as they pass overhead. I watch from the corner of my eye as Reece finds his spot beside me, and we just lie still for a minute. We don't speak, we just bask in the warmth of the sun and listen to the waves breaking.

"You missing London yet?"

I laugh, weighing my answer.

"Honestly, a little. But it's nice to be home. Been a while since we've all been under the same roof, even if it's a little… complicated."

"Complicated how?" Reece asks, leaning up on his elbows to look at me.

His eyes scan my face, and his brows knit together like he's trying to read my thoughts. I don't talk about it much, but something about his gentleness makes me want to be truthful for once.

"Parents are separated, and I'm pretty sure it's because they hate each other." I laugh as I tell him this, but part of me knows it's true.

"Is that why you moved?" There's no judgment in Reece's voice, just curiosity.

"Yes. That, among other reasons." I lean up and stare into the ocean, and find myself questioning how much I should tell him about the move. The ugly truth is it was half for my reputation and half for my mom.

Reece nods in my peripheral vision, and I'm grateful he's not pushing. And that makes me trust him more. Then, before I can stop it, the words are falling out of my mouth.

"To make a long story short, my mom wanted some space. She wanted a fresh start somewhere where no one knew who we were. And I did, too. Now it just feels like we tried to escape our problems."

"But you came back," Reece says.

I laugh. "We did. Running from different problems this time, but yes. We did come back."

"I hear that. For the record, I'm happy you came home, even if it's just for the summer."

I glance over and there's a softness in his face that makes me think he actually means that.

"Me too."

For a moment, he looks at me like he's going to kiss me. I hold my breath, and my eyes bounce between his because now I'm the one trying to read his thoughts. His eyes flick down to my lips for just a second too long.

Then we hear the crunch of gravel from the driveway and turn our heads to find Kian's car. And just like that, we're pulled from whatever little bubble we're in as Kian, Zara, and Harper spill out of the car.

"We can save the rest for another day," Reece jokes, standing and offering me a hand.

"Another day," I agree.

Nineteen
Briar

Reece and Kian have endless energy. I didn't think I'd ever be more tired than I was after my half-marathon two years ago, but they proved me wrong.

"I need to go home before I pass away from exhaustion," I tell Kian as he tries to keep me from leaving. "Ask your girlfriend. She's going to be a nurse. That could happen if I don't get some sleep."

"I can confirm," Harper nods, stifling a yawn behind her hand.

"Thank you. I promise I'll see you later when I'm fully rested, but I have to go. Doctor's orders."

"Can't argue with that," Reece laughs, shooting a wink in Harper's direction.

"I'll see you guys later." I wave, heading down the steps of Harper's back porch with Reece hot on my heels. I turn to face him with an expectant smile. "Yes?"

"I can walk you home if you want," he offers.

"Oh," I breathe, surprised.

"I don't have to…" he trails off, his smile faltering.

"No. I was…" I pause. "I was honestly going to walk on the beach for a while." I study his face, not wanting to hurt his feelings, but wanting to go alone.

"I thought you were tired." There's a light teasing note in his voice.

"Being at home right now is just… a lot with both parents under one roof. I try to be there as little as possible. At least while they're awake. I don't want to hear them argue." I give him an embarrassed shrug.

"That makes sense." Reece nods, his words drawn out.

"Yeah." I wring my hands together, feeling like I might have been too honest.

"Would you mind if I walked with you? You know, just for safety reasons. It being nighttime and all."

His offer and consistency are unexpected, but it's comforting. It's like he doesn't mind how chaotic my life currently is. Reece just *wants* to be there.

"Sure. I'd like that," I nod, then quickly add, "For safety reasons."

He gives me a little smile as we walk a few blocks to the beach. His presence is calming, and while I don't *like him* like him, I do like him. Spending hours with him is easy. The streets are deserted, and most of the houses we pass are dark behind their windows.

Reece clears his throat after a few minutes of silence. "I, uh, I don't want to overstep, but earlier, you told me you felt like you were running away when you moved to London." He runs his hand through his hair. "What were you running from?"

I glance at him, once again unsure how to answer his questions. There are a lot of things I was running from. I was running from Natalie, someone I never want to be friends with again. My parents, who were constantly fighting behind closed doors, like they could hide it from Nate and me. From the pressure to be perfect. But when you boil it all down, it was-

"Myself."

The silence that follows is nearly deafening. That painful fact is something I've never admitted out loud, and it feels suffocating. The shame and guilt that have come with running away, it hasn't relented. It's just been pushed to the recesses of my mind as I try to ignore the unintended consequences of everything.

"And it hasn't worked out how I thought it would."

"Things rarely do."

Reece bumps my arm as we keep walking, and it feels like the weight of the world has been lifted off my shoulders. For once, it feels like someone actually sees *me*. Someone might actually care. Not because they want to fix me. Not because they want something from me. But because they care.

We continue walking the quiet streets, abandoning the trip to the beach as we explore. I point out a few local landmarks, like where I broke my arm when I was ten and where Harper had her first kiss. It's fun. It's easy. Reece listens intently to the town's local history, *our* history in the town, like it's his favorite story.

I don't know how long we walk, but we eventually end up back on my street, and I can see the house come into view. Like the other houses, it's dark, and I sigh in relief.

As we head up the stairs, neither of us makes a move toward the door. Reece follows my lead as I settle on the daybed swing that adorns our front porch. The blanket draped over the backrest falls into my lap, and I use it to cover up as Reece watches me.

"I used to sleep out here as a kid," I tell him. He raises his eyebrows in disbelief. "I used to call it camping."

"This is not camping," Reece snorts. "And you don't strike me as a big camper."

"Not at all. Sleeping out here is about as outdoorsy as I get. I can promise you that."

We fall into another comfortable silence, swinging as the soft breeze lulls me toward sleep. I let myself lean on Reece's shoulder and could let myself drift off. He brings an odd sense of comfort that feels like home.

"Thank you for everything." My voice is barely above a whisper. "Thank you."

"Always." My eyes start to flutter closed, and Reece nudges me softly.

I glance up at him, and his eyes are tender, almost pleading. But as quickly as the look appears, it's gone.

"Hey, you should go inside and get some sleep."

"I should," I nod lightly, but neither of us moves from our spot.

"Go inside, Bri. You need to go to sleep, and I don't want to be the one to keep you up any longer."

I force myself to sit up, and Reece helps me to stand. He pulls me into a hug, and I mumble into his chest, "Thank you for the surf lesson today, and I'm sorry I sucked."

I feel the vibrations from his laughter. "You did suck." I pull away and teasingly slap his shoulder.

"Rude."

"Go inside," he laughs and starts back down the stairs.

A part of me wishes he had tried to kiss me, but the other part, the larger part, is happy to have him as a friend, because he's a fantastic friend.

I watch him disappear into the dark before turning and going inside. The house is so quiet that it feels like I'm sneaking in. I make it up the stairs, ready to crawl into my bed and sleep forever.

I hear the floorboards creak behind me as I pass the media room. "Where were you all night, Briar?" I freeze hearing those words. I'd know his voice anywhere.

"I was with my friends, Rowan. Not that it's any of your business." I don't turn around and continue toward my room.

"Bri, hold on." Rowan's voice is so soft, almost desperate. I can't help but turn to look at him.

"What? What do you want?"

He stares at me silently before dragging in a breath. "I… I was just… I don't know. I guess I was worried. I'm sorry, okay?"

He looks concerned, and I want to ask what exactly he's apologizing for. But then I see flashes of him punching Reece, and I hear the bitterness in his words. And in an instant, my sympathy is soon replaced with anger.

"Well, I'm not yours to be worried about." I know my words hit home as he draws in a sharp breath. Guilt gnaws at my insides, but I try to push it aside.

He's not mine to be concerned about, either.

He made that perfectly clear.

"Briar…"

Before I have a chance to dig myself further into this grave and bury myself alive, I hurry toward the safety of my room.

The door clicks shut behind me, and for a moment, everything is still. Then, everything from the past few days comes crashing in.

Reece.

Rowan.

The chaos.

The confusion.

The ache that's worked its way into my ribs that refuses to leave.

And Rowan. Always Rowan.

His push and pull. His concern that feels like a trap. The way he says my name like it means something, like *I* mean something, when all he's ever done is prove I don't.

I press my back against the door, chest tight.

He's everywhere.

And the worst part?

I don't know if I want him gone.

Twenty
Briar

Cameron is, by definition, a perfect gentleman. He was right on time, as promised. When I came downstairs, he was talking happily with my father.

And I don't know what's more surprising – the fact I'm so excited to see him, or the fact that he's talking to my dad.

I'm not sure how he managed to steal any of my dad's attention. I can barely convince my dad to leave his home office. But here he is, with all his handsomeness, waiting outside my front door.

"Cameron, hi."

"Hi, Bri, you look fantastic," he says, flashing that gorgeous smile.

A flush colors my cheeks, and hiding it is useless. "Thank you."

"Make sure to have her home before midnight," my dad tells Cameron, laughing as if they have some inside joke.

My brows furrow in confusion. It's four in the afternoon. How long does he think we'd stay out? And why do his eyes sparkle like Cameron's said something funny?

"Yes, sir. I'll get her safely home in plenty of time."

My eyes dart between them, trying to figure out how they've built such a bond in the two minutes since the doorbell rang.

"Are you ready to head out?" Cameron looks at me, and I nod in agreement.

"You kids have fun!" My dad calls out after us as we head to Cameron's Jeep parked in the driveway.

Cameron gently guides me to the passenger side and reaches for the door handle. "You do look amazing, Bri," he whispers as he opens the door for me.

My cheeks keep their rosy hue as he closes my door and slides into the driver's seat. We pull onto the road, and I finally find my voice. "What exactly are we doing today?"

"Oh, it's a surprise," he says, his eyes never leaving the road. "So, Briar, sorry, Bri, what are three things I need to know about you?"

"Wow, very loaded question, Cameron," I say, trying to buy myself a few seconds to come up with three things that make me sound interesting. I quickly realize that I'm not interesting in the slightest. I've got nothing.

"Uh, well, I do live in London with my mom."

"What part of London?"

"West Central. Covent Garden specifically."

Cameron shakes his head. "I haven't spent much time in that area."

I look over at him, shocked. "You visit London often?"

"Here and there. We travel a bit as a family, and my dad used to travel for work. No big deal." Cameron is so nonchalant that it catches me off guard. And his familiarity with London makes me believe, for just a second, that this might not be just a summer fling.

"Right. What does your dad do?"

"He was a lawyer—international business law, but he's a senator now, so we travel less," Cameron says.

I force myself not to go slack-jawed. I try to mentally catalog our senators, and feel a little silly sitting here and not saying anything. But his dad is doing everything that I can only dream of doing. This, Cameron, could definitely be part of the plan.

I sit straighter in my seat, like that will help leave a good impression on someone who isn't even here.

"Wow," I breathe, trying to restructure my thoughts. "I… I'm looking to go into international law."

Cameron glances at me briefly, a slight smile on his face. "I could see you as a lawyer."

That simple phrase makes my heart flutter. Maybe he didn't mean it as a compliment, but that's how I take it. And it only makes me like him more. I regain my composure as we roll into the familiar parking lot.

"Roller skating?" I ask, excitement all but bubbling out of me.

"I haven't been since I was a kid, so I figured it might be fun," Cameron says, looking to me for approval.

"Absolutely! Growing up, I always came here, so hopefully, I still remember how to skate."

"Let's find out," he says, opening his door. I reach for my handle and tug at it, but nothing happens. Another pull, and it's stuck. Cameron rounds the car, a smirk on his face, and quickly opens my car door. He offers me a hand to help me out.

"Sorry. That handle always gets stuck from the inside, but at least I can open your car door for you."

"You don't have to do that," I say, trying to play it cool. But inside? I'm swooning. Trying to pretend this isn't the best date I've been on in over a year. He's a gentleman. He's polite, charming, and surprisingly very into manners.

We step inside, and a dingy-looking carpet that smells faintly of fried food and rubber greets us. The walls are still painted with a fun disco theme, and baby disco balls hang over the skating rink to my right.

It looks exactly as it did when I was eleven.

Cameron guides me to a bench and gestures for me to sit. "I'll grab our skates. What size are you?"

"A nine, please," I smile at him.

"Coming right up." He winks and strides off toward the counter. The place is relatively empty, but a few couples skate by while more people mill around the food court. But my eyes land on one person in particular.

Rowan.

He's standing there with an annoyed-looking Calista at his side, but his eyes are laser-focused on me. I give him an awkward wave before turning to watch Cameron at the counter. His forearms rest on the edge as he speaks to the girl working there, who looks about my age.

But I can't even focus on that.

Because of all the people to run into here, why did it have to be him? I take a few deep breaths and pretend this isn't happening, and when I glance back at the food court, he's gone.

Good.

Hopefully, he had the good sense to go somewhere, anywhere, else. I settle back into the bench and breathe a sigh of relief. Then, I feel it.

Two taps on my shoulder.

I turn and see Rowan leaning on the backrest.

"What do you want?"

"Just came to say hi." Rowan gives me a little shrug, like he's completely unaware of how awkward this is. His eyes shift to Cameron, then back to mine. "Who are you here with?"

"My date."

"Wow, a skating rink for the first date. Not very original, is he?"

I roll my eyes. "Says the one who's also here on a date right now. How is Calista, by the way?" He smiles, no doubt hearing the bite in my voice. But he doesn't push it any further.

We stay just like that for a moment, staring at one another like we're sizing up an opponent. His eyes soften just a touch, and he looks almost sad. Regretful. Then, in a flash, it's gone, and he takes a half-step back.

"Have a good night, Briar," he says, heading toward the girl he wants to date.

That thought stings more than it should.

She's who he wants.

I was just a pawn in his game.

And that reminder is enough to make me want to crawl into a very dark hole.

Even after everything he's said and done, I still can't hate him. I want to hate him, but there's the stupid part of my girly brain that makes it impossible. And I hate myself for that. I drag in a deep breath and watch him sling his arm around Calista. I force myself back to my own date.

Cameron picks up our skates from the counter and comes to sit with me. He places both pairs on the ground between us.

"Who was that?"

His question grates on my nerves just a touch. Because there's no way he doesn't know who Rowan is. But I reach for my skates and quickly slide them on, trying to feign indifference. "One of my brother's friends."

Cameron shifts, looking at Rowan, who is coincidentally still watching me. Not me. Us.

"He and my brother can both be a little overprotective at times," I say, trying to pretend that this is normal, but at this point, it feels normal. They're always around. Especially when I don't want them to be.

Cameron turns back to me. "Why don't you tell him to get lost?"

I'd say that would be ideal. But that'd be a lie.

I rack my brain for some way to answer the question, and not lie to him. "I usually try to pretend like he isn't here."

It's true. That's all I've been doing since I got home. Pretending like Rowan isn't real. Pretending like he's not constantly on my mind. "Seriously. Don't worry about him. He's harmless."

Cameron studies my face. "You sure about that?"

My hands turn clammy with the seriousness of his tone, like he knows something I don't, but he doesn't press. And I don't ask, although I want to. I've spent enough time thinking about Rowan over the past week.

He nudges my shoulder. "I'm kidding. The guy looks like he's ready to kill me."

I laugh in relief. "Yeah. He's got a wicked case of RBF."

"I'll say," Cameron agrees, putting his skates on with lightning speed. "Ready to skate?"

I smile, happy to have something else to focus on besides Rowan. Finally getting back to what's shaping up to be an excellent date.

"As ready as I'll ever be."

We head toward the rink. He interlocks our fingers, and I take a shaky step onto the rink floor. The tiles are so smooth, worn down from thousands of pairs of skates over the years, and it does nothing to help my balance.

Cameron must sense my hesitation, reaching out for me. "Do you trust me?"

"Should I? I just met you," I joke, but I don't hesitate to take his other hand. Anything to keep me from falling on my ass.

After just one lap around the skating rink, it's safe to say that I feel bamboozled. Cameron downplayed his skating skills. He's far better than I am. He holds my hands while skating backward and guides me around the outer edge. I'm sure to any onlookers, I look like a baby giraffe learning to walk for the first time. My balance is terrible, and I have a death grip on Cameron's hands.

None of this seems to bother him. He skates slowly, allowing me to set the pace. He checks in on me every so often, making sure I'm still okay. He's sweet, adding to my assumption that he's perfect, because he is.

"Looking good, Bri," he encourages me as he drops one of my hands.

I smile at him, starting to skate a little faster.

Until I slip and fall. I curse myself for looking like an idiot in front of this beautiful man. I burst into an uncontrollable fit of giggles.

Cameron immediately kneels beside me, concern etched into his features. "Are you okay?"

I nod. "Yeah, I'm fine, except my pride is bruised."

He cracks a smile and helps me to my feet. "I won't tell anyone if you won't."

"Deal."

He leads me to a bench along the rink's edge to take a break. And sitting down, I'm much more comfortable, not worrying about having to balance on these death contraptions they call skates. Cameron leans over and tightens the laces on my skates.

"It helps if they're tighter."

I don't know if that's true, but I'm inclined to believe anything from this man's mouth. He's pretty much an expert skater in my books, and I need all the help I can get.

"Okay," I huff, still slightly winded from my fall.

"You ready to try again?"

"Maybe a few more laps, but I must warn you, I might fall again."

"I won't let that happen."

Twenty-One
Rowan

The game plays loudly on the TV as Briar walks in with her date in tow. She's laughing at something he said as they disappear into the kitchen. I keep my eyes locked on the game, but the sound of countless drawers and cabinets opening and closing is annoying. And distracting.

Briar's infectious laugh floats into the living room, and I wish I were the one making her laugh like that. But right now, she won't even talk to me. I hear her giving gentle directions to what's-his-name, helping him find whatever he needs in the kitchen.

"Hey, B," Nate greets his sister absentmindedly, not taking his eyes away from the game.

"Hi!" Briar's voice is so soft it doesn't sound like her. It sounds polished and forced, and I have to wonder if she's putting on an act for this guy. Before I can question it, she's at the edge of the couch, looking at her brother doe-eyed. Her date is a few steps behind her, and I don't miss how his eyes roam her body when he thinks no one is watching.

As much as I want to look at Briar, I don't shift my gaze until his eyes find mine. I want him to know that he's been caught. I scowl at him in a poor attempt to dissuade him from continuing to leer at her like she's his next meal.

"Hey, Nate," she says again, this time even softer, getting his attention. Nate glances at her over his shoulder and immediately stands when he sees her date there, too.

With Nate's attention on Briar's date, I finally allow myself to look at her.

123

And she looks perfect.

She always does, but especially right now. She's glowing in the early evening sun, and everything about her looks relaxed.

But as perfect as she looks, her jean shorts suddenly look too short, and her tank top seems too fitted. She's showing too much skin, and I know her date is enjoying that fact a little too much.

Her date stands proudly with Briar, extending his hand toward Nate. "Hey, man, I'm Cameron."

"I'm Nate," he says, pausing and pointing lazily at me. "And that's Rowan."

I muster a head nod, not trusting myself not to insult the guy just for standing there with Briar. I hate him. And I don't have to know him to know I hate him. But I especially hate that Briar likes him.

The jealousy that bubbles up inside my stomach makes me feel sick. Cemeron's got everything I want, and now I'm forced to sit here while he rubs it in my face.

I had the opportunity to actually be with Briar, and I ruined it. I made her think she was nothing when in reality, she's everything. My grip on my beer can tightens, and I hear the unmistakable sound of the aluminum collapsing under my fingers.

"I was just telling Bri that I spoke with your dad earlier. I'm taking over the kitchen tonight to cook for her," Cameron explains. I snort at the idea. This guy looks like he's never even used a microwave. I doubt he knows how to cook a meal. Especially not one suitable for Briar.

I'm a second away from making a cruel joke about his probable lack of cooking experience, but I hold it back. For Briar's sake.

I discard my half-empty can on the coffee table, having lost any desire to drink.

"Have at it, man," Nate nods.

"Great to meet you," Cameron points at us before disappearing into the kitchen. Nate nods in approval as he sits back on the couch, and Briar has a shit-eating grin on her face.

"He's surprising me with dinner," she whispers to us, clearly awestruck. "He brought groceries over before we went skating and asked Dad about using the kitchen."

She looks genuinely excited about this, and that crushes me. My chest is tight, and I can feel my pulse hammering in my veins.

"Impressive," Nate says. He drops the volume two notches on the TV before looking back at his sister. "We'll try to keep quiet here. Have fun with your date."

Briar flushes a light pink, and she finally looks at me. Just for a second. But it's long enough to undo me.

I want to tell her to send the guy home and let me cook for her instead. I want to tell her I'm sorry. Sorry for everything I've said and done. I want to tell her that I'd give anything for one real shot with her.

But before I get the chance, she turns on her heels and retreats into the kitchen.

With the volume lower, I can hear Briar's conversation more clearly. I don't want to eavesdrop, but I can't help myself. I have to know what she and that Ken doll have to talk about. I can't make out every word, but whatever he's saying, Briar finds it incredibly funny.

I clench my fists, trying to focus on the game, but Briar's laughter makes me angrier. My eyes are on the TV, but my mind is still on Briar. And being in this house, which has traces of her everywhere, is painful.

A book that has to be hers is abandoned on the side table. Her worn Yale sweatshirt is tossed lazily over the back of the couch. And her senior portrait is framed and smiling down at me from just above the mantle.

She's everywhere.

Just when I thought it couldn't get any worse, the house starts to reek of fish. It's so pungent that it feels like the idiot burnt garlic and stuffed the cloves right down my throat. The smell alone turns my stomach. I can't help but laugh, hoping his culinary skills might drive Briar away.

"Man, that smells awful," I mutter, nearly choking on my words.

"That's coming from the kitchen? I thought you shit yourself," Nate jokes.

I scowl at him. "That smells so bad, I don't think you could pay me to eat whatever he's making. Hopefully, he doesn't try to kiss her after dinner."

This sobers Nate up immediately. "Don't talk about anyone kissing my sister."

Every nerve ending in my spine goes on high alert. I didn't mean to bring that up, but hopefully, he can't tell that's all I've thought about for days.

"Chill, it's a joke," I say, but I can tell Nate's unconvinced. So, I opt to leave instead of answer whatever question comes out of Nate. "I'm going to grab a pizza. The Bears have this locked in, and I don't want to torture myself with the smell of rotting sea creatures."

"You coming back for the Guardians game?" Nate asks, slipping back into his usual self again.

"Not if the house reeks like this," I joke, standing from the couch.

"Bring me back a pepperoni pizza."

"Pineapple-only pizza coming right up," I say, laughing as I head to the front door. I pass the opening to the kitchen, and against my better judgment, I stop for a second. One glance is enough to make my stomach drop.

Part of me wants to pop in and ask if she wants pizza too. But like a coward, I don't. I just stand there.

Briar leans against the kitchen counter, wrapped up in whatever Cameron's saying to her. Either she's doing a fantastic job of pretending the meal doesn't reek, or she's so interested in this guy that she doesn't care. Either way, the jealousy bubbles up inside me again before I force myself to look away.

She's not someone I can allow myself to want, but I don't care anymore. I don't care what the consequences are. I'm done sitting on the sidelines and letting the girl I've always wanted slip through my fingers.

And I'll be damned if I let anyone, including Nate or this bumbling idiot, get in my way.

Twenty-Two
Briar

This salmon tastes like it's been sunburnt and exiled from the ocean. It's overly charred, salty, and barely edible. It's a disgrace to seafood everywhere. But I take small bites anyway. I don't want to let on that it's awful, and it's sweet that he went through so much effort to make dinner for me. Besides, I'm equally bad in the kitchen, so who am I to judge anyone else?

I just won't agree to let him cook for me again.

"How's your fish?" Cameron asks, nearly finished with his.

"It's good. Thank you again for dinner. This was such a sweet surprise." I smile, hoping to sell my lies. "Do you cook a lot?"

"Never."

It's not a surprising answer.

I do my best to hide my shock, but now, his complete inability to cook makes sense. I'm lost for words with his admission, and the only thing I can come up with is, "Impressive."

"Enough about me. How about you? What's next for Bri?"

He leans forward on the patio table, focusing entirely on me. The gentle breeze lifts his hair, and the coolness raises goosebumps across my arms.

"Well, for me, the next thing is law school, then working for a firm doing international law," I explain.

"Law school is a beast. What makes you want to do that?"

I stare past him, watching the ocean view behind him. No one has ever asked me why. They always just nod and make some comment about how I must be in it for the money.

"It sounds dumb, but as a kid, my parents always told me that I was good at winning arguments and that I should be a lawyer one day. And it just stuck," I laugh at how silly that sounds. "I'm pretty sure I got my first Yale Law sweatshirt when I was eight."

"You want to go to Yale?" Cameron looks equally surprised and impressed.

"That's the goal."

Yale has always been the goal. I can't remember a time when it wasn't. One day, I was a happy-go-lucky kid, and the next, I told everyone I'd be going to Yale. No rhyme or reason, but that's the beauty of it.

"Plus, I like the idea of being able to help people. I think I'd want to do a lot of pro bono work to be a resource for people in our city."

"Right," Cameron's agreement isn't convincing, but I let it slide.

"What about you? What's your plan?" I chirp, hoping to move on to another topic.

"Oh, I'm just getting a business degree. My dad will just find me something when I graduate," he says.

"That's… nice." I drag the words out, not knowing how else to respond. I assumed he'd have higher aspirations than that. Cameron isn't like I expected him to be, but maybe that's exactly what I need—someone who can go with the flow and doesn't need every second of their life planned out.

"Yeah, he's got connections all over. One of his buddies' businesses will make a spot for me, and then I'm set."

"Do you know what you might want to do?" I ask.

"Whatever lets me do the least amount of work possible for the most money."

I stare at him wide-eyed, suddenly a lot less impressed with him.

"That's..." I pause, feeling the illusion of perfection slip as I try to find something nice to say to that.

"I'm kidding," he says, patting my arm.

I laugh. It's more like a snort of amusement, but I feel the relief flood my body. "You had me for a second. I really thought you meant that."

"Nah. I'm thinking logistics. I like making sure that things get to the right place on time," he explains, but he looks distant.

"Very nice," I nod, feeling myself relaxing with Cameron. Everything tonight has felt easy. Seamless.

"When are you headed back to London?" Cameron asks.

"Trying to get rid of me already?"

"No. I'm trying to see how much longer I get to keep you."

I raise my eyebrows in faux shock and bite the inside of my cheek to keep from smiling. "I don't have an official date for when I'm going home yet, but I'll have to be there before September when classes start."

"So, I have you for at least two more months? In that case, do you have any big plans this weekend?"

"Oh, do I. I'm getting my wisdom teeth out in a few days, so it will be Jell-O and a lot of naps this weekend." I laugh, but it's the truth.

It was supposed to be done in London, but my little detour forced us to reschedule with a surgeon here. Mom wasted no time getting it on the books, and we stocked up on soft snacks earlier this week, which consist mostly of Jell-O.

It's an easy snack, and I can even make it myself. No parental supervision is required. Which is good, seeing as my mom already has a return flight to London booked for Monday after my surgery.

"Fancy," Cameron nods with me. "Well, if you need anything, let me know."

"Will do. Although I think I'll just read and sleep for days."

"That's not a bad plan. I'm jealous," Cameron jokes before pointing to my half-eaten salmon. "Are you done with that?"

"Yeah, I had a big lunch." Another lie, but a small one, to spare his feelings.

Cameron grabs both plates, and we head back inside. We pass the boys, splayed out on the couch, eating pizza that smells mouth-wateringly divine. But I think a plain, uncooked potato would taste good after that meal. Dirt and all.

Back in the kitchen, Cameron immediately jumps in and begins cleaning up the mess from dinner. "No, sir," I shake my head, stepping into his path to the sink. "You cooked, so I clean up."

He places the dishes on the counter and leans down, eye-level with me. Our faces are inches apart, and I suck in a breath at our proximity.

"How about I wash, and you can dry?"

His words are soft, but they're dripping in heat and temptation. Almost like he's trying to draw me in. And it's working.

"Fine," I say, grabbing a dish towel from the drawer.

We finish all the dishes silently, his fingers brushing mine every so often as we pass the plates back and forth. But eventually, I can feel the night ending. I don't want it to, but it's inevitable. We can't stay here doing dishes forever.

"Hey, I have to ask you something," Cameron says as I put the last plate away.

"Ask away."

"It's kind of dumb," he says, looking at me nervously. "But… my family is hosting the Annual Charity Gala at the Vanderbilt house this year, and I need a date."

I had forgotten about the Gala, but it's always a fun time. I haven't been in years, and it might be a good distraction from everything else going on in my life right now.

"I see. Well, if I think of anyone, I'll let you know," I joke with him.

A smile spreads across his face. "Thank you. I was thinking of taking this girl, her name's Briar, but I don't think she even knows I exist," he shrugs playfully.

"Sounds like you have a tough decision to make."

Cameron makes a real show of looking flustered. "Any advice for me?"

"Maybe just ask her anyway. You might be surprised."

He flashes me that dazzling smile again. "Well, Bri, would you be my date to the Charity Gala?"

I pause. I want to go with him. But I don't know if it's because I want to go with Cameron, or because I know going with Cameron will spark that jealous glare Rowan had earlier.

Either way, I'm going with Cameron.

"Of course. I thought you'd never ask." I laugh, and Cameron wraps me in a hug.

"What a weight off my chest." He nods toward the entryway. "I should probably head out."

"I'll walk you out."

Opening the door, he leans against the frame, half inside, half outside. For a moment, I think he might kiss me, but he takes a step back onto the porch.

"I'll see you next Saturday," he says, his eyes dropping to my lips before finding mine again. "Wear something nice, okay?"

I laugh his comment off, hoping it's his attempt at a joke, and nod. "Yeah. Drive safe." I wave, slightly disappointed, as he jogs toward his Jeep and drives away.

Closing the front door, I beeline to the living room for the pizza. I could smell it the whole time we were doing dishes, and it's a miracle my stomach wasn't growling the entire time. There are still a few pieces left, so I grab one and take a massive bite, moaning dramatically.

Nate chuckles from his spot on the couch. "Oh, please. Help yourself."

I scowl at him as I swallow everything in my mouth. "I needed this more than you did."

"I guess the date didn't go well then?" Rowan asks, a smug look on his face. And the smugness just pisses me off. The fact that Rowan can sit here and make fun of my date, while he's probably never once tried to cook for a girl.

"It went just fine, thank you for asking." I take another bite of the pizza, not caring if I'm talking with my mouth full. "He asked me on another date, too."

"You can't actually like that guy, Bri?" Rowan scoffs without taking his gaze from the TV. "You could do better."

I snap. He doesn't get to sit here and comment on my dating life when he's clearly sad and alone. "I don't recall asking for your input, Rowan."

His jaw ticks, but he doesn't say anything. He just stares at the screen like it holds the answers to all his problems.

"Yeah, well," he mutters, his voice lower now, "Maybe I'm just tired of watching you pretend you're happy."

The silence that follows is sharp. Cutting.

I throw the crust of the pizza back into the box and stand. "Then stop watching."

Quickly standing, I brush past them and head back up the stairs; because that's easier than admitting he might be right.

Twenty-Three
Briar

The daybed is where I've always found solace. Today is no exception. Nothing beats a beautiful afternoon with a book that I know by heart. The quiet street is the perfect backdrop for an afternoon of doing nothing.

That is, until my peace is disturbed by the front door nearly flying off its hinges.

"B! Oh my gosh, there you are!" Nate shouts, coming at me like a bat out of hell. He stands there, beaming at me with a hopeful smile.

"Ah, yes, you've found my elusive hiding spot," I joke.

Not two seconds later, Nate drops to his knees.

"Will you please, please, please come and play water volleyball with us? We need a fourth, and we really need you," he begs, slurring his words a bit. He's wide-eyed as he clasps his hands together, literally begging me. "Please, B? I'll owe you big time."

I roll my eyes. But it's impossible to say no to Nate. He rarely asks for anything, even if it is just joining him in a silly volleyball game. And I'd still do anything for him.

"Fine. Can I at least have ten minutes to finish this chapter and change?" I ask him, waving my nearly finished book before his face.

"Yes!" He exclaims before getting up and hugging me. Then, he runs back into the house like a kid on Christmas.

Glancing back at my book, I laugh at my brother's stupidity. I love him, but sometimes he has the brain capacity of a twelve-year-old.

I turn my attention back to the book and know what's coming. The last ten pages are the most agonizing. Everything falls apart for everyone, and there's nothing they can do about it. Everything is out of control, and part of me breaks for these characters.

But I don't let myself dwell on that.

Instead, I force myself up, and with a quick change, I'm in the backyard. The boys have set up the net above the pool and are trying to hit each other with the volleyball.

"Children," I mutter before announcing my presence, "Okay, I'm as ready as I'll ever be."

The boys stop and look my way, with Nate and Darian letting out a drunken cheer. Rowan's eyes travel over my body, lingering for a second too long.

This isn't the first time I've caught him watching me, and I hate how it makes my heart race. His eyes find mine, finally, and his cheeks turn the lightest shade of pink.

"Took you long enough," he mutters, getting into the pool.

"Chill, man. She was reading her encyclopedia," Darian calls out, jumping into the pool after Rowan.

"I was not," I laugh. "But I wouldn't expect either of you to know what a book is, seeing as I'm not sure you can even read."

Nate snickers, beckoning me over to him. "You're with me, B. Let's go!"

"Of course I can read," Rowan scoffs.

"You read at a third-grade level, man," Darian says with a grin, winking at me.

I slide into the shallow end of our pool and glance at Nate over my shoulder in a silent assurance that I'm ready.

We start the game before they can bicker anymore, with Nate serving first. I'm not sure why the boys let us be on the same team. Nate and I have been playing volleyball together forever, and we look like Olympic athletes compared to Rowan and Darian.

Neither can reliably serve the ball over the net, and they're too slow to stop the ball when we return it. The pair looks more like two toddlers splashing around than two true competitors. So, it's not long until Nate and I are crushing the boys, and Rowan and Darian grow bored.

I get out of the pool after what might be the shortest game of water volleyball I've ever played, and can't help but laugh at them. But I didn't abandon my books for ten minutes of splashing around on this beautiful sunny day. So I dry off before lying on a lounge chair opposite the pool.

And like my shadow, Rowan follows me.

He takes the chair beside me, and I feel Rowan's eyes on me as I stare at the back of my eyelids. I want to relax, but I can't with him there.

"Bri," he pleads softly. "Can you please give me two minutes?"

Opening my eyes, I melt under his gaze. It's just like when we were kids and he'd bug me while I tried to lie in the sun. He looks so sad, almost broken. I steel myself knowing what's about to come out of his mouth. An apology that's somehow not a real apology but will make anyone forgive any of his indiscretions. Or maybe that's just the effect he has on me.

"What do you want?" I ask.

"I want to apologize," he breathes. "I don't know what came over me. I just… snapped at the bonfire."

I nod and avert my eyes back to the sky. Even looking at him makes my heart skip a beat. His wet hair clings to his face, and his lips are turned down in such a pouty frown that would look odd on anyone else. And every water droplet that slides down his body perfectly traces his muscles. I can't look for fear of gawking at him.

"There's something about Reece that gets under my skin. Seeing you with him messes with my head," he explains.

"Why do you care who I hang out with, Rowan?" My words are harsher than I intended, but maybe that's what he deserves.

We sit in another prolonged silence. The awkwardness spills over, making Nate and Darian retreat into the house, claiming they need snacks. But it's a sorry excuse to abandon the tension.

"Reece and his family," he pauses, "They take the things I care about. And I don't want to lose you. I know I overreacted, and I'm sorry. I didn't mean what I said about you. I… wanted you to know that."

I glance at Rowan, and he looks dejected, like part of him hated saying that, but the other part needed to. I watch him momentarily, sitting on the lounger with his elbows propped on his knees. He's studying my face, looking for any sign that might give away what I'm thinking. But I don't even know what I'm thinking. All I know is that I played a part in this, too.

"Thank you for apologizing. And I… I realize what I said to you the other day was a little harsh and—"

"You don't have to apologize. I know you didn't mean it. People say things they don't mean when they're upset. I get it more than most." He forces out a laugh, but it sounds flat.

"No. I do need to apologize. We are friends, and it wasn't fair for me to throw that back in your face." I sit there for a beat. "And you're not going to lose me."

"Thank you." A genuine smile touches his lips, and the pink shade returns to his cheeks.

And just like that, we're back to how we always are. Except, it's different this time.

I want to be more guarded around him, but he has this way of forcing me to dismantle my walls. He comes through and bulldozes his way into my heart every time. But I won't continue to excuse his bad habits.

"But, don't let it happen again. Because next time, I won't be so forgiving."

My warning hangs in the air before he nods.

Rowan stands, still dripping wet from the pool, and starts to towel off. And as much as I try to fight it, I can't help but watch him. And he's not shy about making sure I have the best view. He flexes his muscles as he lets the towel pass over them.

"Like what you see?" he teases.

This time, my cheeks go pink. I try to brush him off as I awkwardly put my sunglasses on.

"In your dreams, Callahan."

He looks at me with cloudy blue eyes and nods, "Oh, most definitely."

I won't dignify his flirting with a response, mostly because I don't trust that I won't drool all over him if I open my mouth. But seeing him stand there, I can't help but think about what it might be like to have his lips on mine.

"You ready for surgery tomorrow?" he asks, pulling me from my unrequited fantasy, relaxing back into his lounge chair.

I shake my head lightly. "As ready as I can be. I've met the surgeon a few times, and he's nice. I doubt I have anything to worry about."

"I guess Mr. Chef will be coming to check on you then?"

"Mr. Chef?" I ask and look at him over the rim of my sunglasses.

He tries to play it off, but his tone has a jealous edge. "Yeah. Your boyfriend. The salmon-slayer."

"Probably not." I smile, reveling in knowing that Rowan is bothered by my dating life. And not just bothered. But he reeks of jealousy. And I like it.

"What's the deal with him? Are you in love?"

"Oh, come on, like you care, Rowan."

Rowan places a hand over his heart. "His cooking was so awful that I had to leave. He interrupted a crucial baseball game for me the other day, which naturally means I care." I chuckle, ignoring him as I let the sun warm my body. "But seriously, Bri. If you need someone to talk to, I'm all ears."

I let my head fall to the side and scowl at him, but he lies there, arms propped behind his head with a stupid grin.

"I'm not in love," I say seriously.

Rowan turns his head and looks at me, raising his eyebrows and gesturing for me to continue. I take a breath. "I'm not in love. Really."

"I didn't say you were."

I sit up, take my glasses off, and play with them in my lap. "He's just really nice."

"Nice, huh?"

"Yeah." I nod, then the words are tumbling out of my mouth. "He's a perfect gentleman. He always opens my doors, even my car door, and I didn't even have to ask for that. He's attentive, and he's funny."

"Briar, that's the bare minimum that you deserve." Rowan looks at me sincerely, and it sets my skin on fire.

"I know, but—" I take a few breaths. "But ever since I moved, it seems like guys have been more interested in how I look than who I am," I admit quietly. "All they see is a blonde who looks like a good time, and that's it. It's one of the most frustrating things. But Cameron makes me feel like he sees me. He sees the parts of me that I want him to. Like, he respects that I have goals. I feel like he would still like me even if I didn't look like this."

"Does he make you feel safe?"

The question lodges in my chest as I take a few minutes to think. I wouldn't classify it as a feeling of safety, but more a feeling of contentment. "I don't know. I didn't feel unsafe."

Rowan gives me a sad smile. "Can I give you some advice my dad told Harper a while ago?"

I shift in my seat to sit more comfortably, looking at him. "Sure."

"He always used to tell Harper to go for someone who makes her feel safe. He said butterflies were the body's way of telling us something's off, like a built-in alarm system," he explains while looking at me. "I'm not saying it's true one hundred percent of the time, but I remember Harper telling him Kian was a feeling of safety and calm for her. Just something to think about."

I swallow hard, trying to think if Cameron makes me feel safe. And the worst part is, I don't know. Nothing felt inherently unsafe, but the fact that I can't answer this simple question outright has me questioning… everything.

Cameron wasn't shy about complimenting me, but now, I can't tell if they were sincere or not. Or if that perfect, gentlemanly idea I've cooked up for Cameron is just my brain looking at him through rose colored glasses.

"Well, you said yourself it isn't one hundred percent. But thanks for the advice, pal."

Rowan turns his head back to stare straight ahead. "No problem, pal."

I lean back onto my own lounge chair and stare into the bright sky, wishing I had the answers. But I don't.

All I have is this lingering feeling that Cameron isn't all I thought he was.

Twenty-Four
Briar

"Good morning, my lovely," my mom sings as she knocks on my door. She wastes no time, coming in and opening the blinds to allow the morning sunlight to pour in.

"Morning," I reply quietly.

"Have you been awake long?"

"Only a few hours, but I've just been lying here, relaxing before getting up," I tell her. She sits on the edge of my bed, looking at me softly. I can tell she's worried. And I don't blame her. I'm worried, too.

"Are you nervous, Briar?" There's a slight tremble in her voice.

"No." I lie. There's no need to worry her further. "I'm just hungry. Honestly, you look more nervous than I feel."

"I'm just worried about the pain medication…" she trails off. She doesn't have to explain. We both know the risks, but I've been fine for years. I haven't had a slip-up in two years. This surgery should be nothing.

"Mom, I told you. I'm past that. It was six years ago. I'll be fine. And besides, I'll only take the painkillers if I'm in agony. Otherwise, I plan on taking just regular over-the-counter stuff."

"I know. But I still worry. You're strong, Briar."

I smile at her, but I don't know if that's true.

"We leave in fifteen minutes, so let's get ready to head out," she says, patting the bed and standing before leaving my room without another look back.

It doesn't feel good to know that I scare her like that, but this could be a chance to prove myself.

Prove that I'm beyond the addiction.

Prove that I'm stronger now.

Prove it to her and to myself.

We begin the trek to the oral surgeon, and the tension in the car is thick. My mom and I sit silently, thinking about what's to come. I'm doing my best to focus on anything and everything besides the anxiety radiating from my mom. It's not long until my knee bounces uncontrollably, and I resort to picking at my nails.

The waiting room is no better. I feel like I'm under a microscope, with everyone just waiting for me to crumble. My mom's hand covers mine, and I realize I'm shaking.

"Sorry. I'm more nervous than I thought."

"You're going to be okay, sweetheart."

I don't even have a moment to protest. "Briar Abbott," a nurse calls, and I'm led into another room, which has become a makeshift operating room. It's a horrible combination of monitors covering an entire wall and a metal tray with horrendous instruments. I try not to look, but I'm my own worst enemy and can't help but take it all in.

The woman gestures for me to lie down in the chair and preps me for the procedure. She places a patch on my heart and then puts a hose of nitrous oxide over my nose.

"Just take deep breaths in and out through your nose," she instructs me kindly. I nod and begin to take deep breaths.

Everything around me feels fuzzy, a familiar haze I know too well. I start to relax into it, and my nerves ease instantly. It's welcoming, and I feel that craving tick in my brain.

I'm brought back as a cold alcohol wipe passes over the crook of my elbow, and then a pinch.

I lean my head back, knowing soon this will all be over.

***

After what feels like two seconds, I'm back, and every part of me feels heavy. Someone helps me stand, but I'm not sure I'm using my legs. Nothing makes sense, and everything is too much.

I close my eyes again and hear faint voices around me, but it all sounds far away.

"Hey, Briar. Sweetheart, are you ready to go home?" It sounds like my mom, but I can't find my voice to speak. I mumble something incoherent then I'm moved into a more comfortable chair and get to lie down this time. It feels like we're moving, but I can't be sure. The sound of some pop song filters in, and all I want is to sing along.

My mouth is dry, and I can't open it very wide. Everything I say is muffled, so I give up trying to communicate. I focus on my breathing and enjoy the stillness, the numbness.

For the first time in a while, my brain is quiet. It's not running through every possible scenario; I just exist. And it's pure bliss.

I hear quiet laughter beside me in no time, and I'm lifted from my comfortable chair. I try to fight, but there's no energy in me. I try to tell them to let me lie down, but nothing comprehensible comes out.

"B, you are down bad."

"Lie down," is my only response. I just want to lie down and sleep. Either this new person, who smells a lot like my brother, is a mind reader or a saint because they lay me down on the most comfortable bed I've ever been in. And I can finally sleep.

***

When I wake again everything is sore, especially my jaw. I feel like I've been chewing on rocks, and everything in my mouth tastes horrendously metallic. Bringing my hand to my face, I feel the swelling in my cheeks, and it all comes back to me. The surgery.

A light knock on my door forces me to open my eyes. Nate stands there with a cup of what I hope is water. "Hey, champ, welcome back to the land of the living."

"Water," I croak and reach for the glass in his hands. He rushes over, places the cup in my hands, and lets me take a big swig. It coats my throat, and I instantly feel better. "Thanks."

"Of course. How are you feeling?"

I take a quick inventory of everything. My jaw is sore, my head is foggy, and an ache deep in my brain is a loud reminder of what I'm craving. But nothing physically hurts.

"I'm okay."

"Good," Nate breathes a sigh of relief. "You had us worried."

"Why? Did something happen this morning?"

Nate stares at me blankly for a moment. "B, your surgery was yesterday morning. It's four in the afternoon right now. You had a bad reaction to the anesthesia or something and have been asleep since you got home yesterday. We've had to fight you to wake up and take your pain meds."

"Oh," I furrow my brows, and can't remember anything. Nate looks worried, so I try to make light of the situation. "That's weird. No wonder my mouth tastes horrible, and I smell bad."

This earns a small laugh from Nate. "You want anything? I've got some errands to run, but a friend's coming over to stay with you while I'm out."

"Maybe soup," I say weakly.

"Coming right up."

As soon as Nate leaves the room, I struggle to get out of bed. I'm desperate for a change of clothes and something for the pain in my jaw. It's slowly getting worse, and it feels like someone took an excavator to my jaw.

And maybe something to appease the craving that's only intensified the longer I'm awake. I glance around the room, but can't find the prescription I want. I only find Advil, but with the way the blood is pounding in my head, I know the pills are here somewhere.

I barely have enough energy to change before I crawl back under my covers. As badly as I want to tear this place apart, the only thing I can do is lie there until Nate comes back. Which, thankfully, doesn't take long.

"Hey, B. I brought some soup and a visitor," Nate says, knocking on the door frame again. Nate steps into my room, putting the soup on my nightstand. Behind him, Rowan's leaning against my door.

"Looks like I'm your designated babysitter for the evening," Rowan jokes, giving me a little smirk.

I glance over and see Nate sitting on the bed facing me. He helps me sit before handing me the bowl of soup. I give Nate a weak smile and take the bowl from him.

"Please be careful with this, B. And when you've eaten, Rowan will give you something for your pain, okay?"

I spoon the soup into my mouth, which might be the best thing I've ever tasted. I take a few more spoonfuls as Nate turns to Rowan and starts bombarding him with instructions for taking over my care. I laugh, seeing Rowan's eyes nearly bulge out of his head with all the directions he's being given.

Rowan looks past Nate's shoulder at me and gives me a slight shake of his head as if asking what Nate is on. I give a small shrug, but continue to take spoonfuls of soup and pour them into my mouth.

"Hey, man, I got it," Rowan reassures Nate, patting him on the back.

"Please just watch over her, man. She'll probably go back to sleep, but make sure she takes her meds," Nate breathes, looking over at me. I smile at him and make an exaggerated motion of bringing the soup to my mouth.

"Trust me, I'll make sure she eats and takes her meds, okay?"

"I'll be gone for four hours tops, okay? I have to do a few things in town—"

"Nate. I got it," Rowan says for what I assume to be the millionth time today.

"Okay." Nate puts his hands up in defeat. "I'll be back soon, B."

I nod and watch Nate hesitantly leave my room. As soon as he's gone, I extend the bowl of half-finished soup to Rowan.

"Princess, I just promised him you would eat."

"I don't want to," I say, and feel the bowl growing heavier in my hands.

"Please eat, even if it's just a few more mouthfuls."

"I did eat something. Technically." I drop my arms a bit. "It's heavy, please."

He laughs, coming over and taking the bowl from me. "How about I give you something for the pain now, and then you finish the soup?" He looks at me, raising his eyebrows. "Sounds like a pretty good deal to me."

"That feels like bribery."

"I like to think of it more like bartering," he says, grabbing the bottle of Advil from my dresser and shaking it.

I glare at the bottle as if the over-the-counter meds have personally victimized me. Which they haven't.

"I need the prescription ones," I tell him, pulling out the puppy dog eyes. I don't need them per se. But from Rowan's easy agreement, I can tell Nate hasn't told him about me. Which, at this moment, I'm grateful for.

"Fine, but more soup first," he says firmly, but his voice is still soft.

I nod, knowing I've won. I'd do anything as long as he gives me the medicine I so desperately need.

A proud smile crosses Rowan's face as he backs out of my room and reaches for something on the hall table. Two seconds later, he hands me a pill that I gladly take from him. He moves to sit on the edge of my bed and holds my soup bowl in one hand with the spoon in his other hand.

And suddenly, this all feels too intimate. How close he is. How willing he is to take care of me. How happy I am that it's him who's here right now.

I take the soup from him, and he chuckles.

Rowan wastes no time getting comfortable. He swings his legs up to rest on the bed, with his back relaxing against the headboard. I eat in silence and can feel him studying me as I do. But I do what he wants and take another few spoonfuls of soup, letting the warm broth give me an ounce of energy.

Rowan gently picks up the remote from my bedside and nudges me with his shoulder. "If you finish your soup, you can pick the movie."

"I forfeit that right," I say, passing off my bowl. I lean back into the pillows and close my eyes for a second. The pull of sleep is alluring, but I fight it and force my eyes open again. I want to stay in this moment. I want to stay here with Rowan.

Rowan scrolls through a few options before settling on one of my favorite shows.

"I love this one," I say quietly.

"I know."

I slump further into my bed, leaning against his shoulder. We sit like that for fifteen minutes, and my brain is quiet again. I think of nothing besides the show and the comforting way Rowan just sits beside me. And it's the first time I've been truly relaxed in years.

As I'm about to fall back asleep, I feel Rowan shift to pull me closer to him. I lay my head on his chest and can feel it rise and fall with his breathing. It's soothing, and exactly what I needed.

The TV plays in the background, but I can't focus on that. I'm more focused on the feeling of having Rowan so close to me. More focused on how his fingers drag across my skin and through my hair. Focused on how delicate his touch is, and how I could stay here forever.

"Thanks for being a halfway decent person today," I whisper.

"Oh, halfway decent?" His tone is light, and I can hear his smile. I hum in agreement. "I'll always be here for you. But if you tell anyone I said that, I'll deny it."

I close my eyes again as I take a few deep breaths and enjoy the feeling of numbness as the pain medication kicks in. Enjoy the feeling of being here with him.

"Don't worry. Wouldn't want to destroy your perfectly crafted facade."

"My facade?"

"Mm-hmm, do you need me to define that for you?" His laughter muffles my slow words.

"I know what it means, baby."

"Right. You pretend to be a grump. But I think it's an act," I mumble.

"Oh, yeah?" he asks, sounding amused.

"Yeah," I whisper, feeling reality slipping away.

"I like to think I have my moments, and some people see them more than others," he says just as quietly. "And I think you know I'll always be here for you."

He's right. I do know that. Somewhere deep down, I always have.

And that's all it takes to fall asleep in my Rowan-sized security blanket.

Twenty-Five
Briar

Mom is gone. She left earlier this morning, and it felt like she couldn't get out of the country fast enough.

Nate wasn't too far behind her. He's been spending every free moment he has with Melissa. While it's cute, it's also annoying. I haven't ever seen him like this. But he seems happy. So I'm happy for him.

Even if I'm stuck in the house, in agony, wishing I could have the same thing. I ignore that little fact and try to pretend it doesn't exist. Pretend like *he* doesn't exist. That's the only way I can go through my day.

I sit and stretch in the driveway, eager to literally and metaphorically try to escape every one of my problems. And if I can't outrun them, I'll at least be able to give my brain a few hours of rest from wanting everything I can't have.

Running is my escape. I don't need music or anything else. Just the open road and nothing to distract me.

But the blasting of a car radio breaks the silence as someone drives by. However, they don't pass our house. They pull right into our driveway, and I lock eyes with Rowan, the radio culprit and person I'm trying to avoid. He gives me a little wave before turning off the ignition.

He's out of the car and striding over to me a second later. "Well, if it isn't Briar. Finally risen from her four-day slumber."

I ignore his comment, hoping he'll leave, and continue my stretches. "You just missed Nate. He went to see Melissa for the afternoon."

Rowan stands there with his arms crossed for only a moment before sitting on the pavement beside me. "Well, what are you doing?"

I don't miss how he watches me with concern on his face. I do my best to ignore him, but he starts to copy my movements, stretching out his legs.

I glare at him. "I'm going on a solo run. Emphasis on the *solo* part."

"Are you sure you're up for that, Bri?" And there it is again. That look of concern with his brows drawn together. "Just after surgery, I don't know if you're fully recovered yet."

"I'm fine," I scoff. "Does Nate go around sharing everything about my life with you?"

Rowan laughs, and the sound is somehow both comforting and irritating. "That's funny," he muses, but the smile falls from his face as he studies me. "I… I stayed with you that night after your surgery."

Now, it's my turn to pause. I stare at him, stunned and silent. I can't tell if he's playing some joke or being serious.

"You don't remember?" The sincerity in his voice pulls me in.

I let us sit there in silence for another thirty seconds, hoping the awkwardness forces him to tell the truth. But he lets us sit. So I try to remember.

"I honestly don't remember much from the first few days," I admit, and my mind spins at the thought of him being there with me.

Rowan stands from his spot on the ground and extends his hand out to help me. "You were pretty out of it when I was there. I'm not surprised you don't." He's trying to play it off, but I can see the hurt in his eyes. And I desperately wish I could remember, but I don't.

"How many miles are we doing today?" Rowan asks. I scan his outfit and cross my arms.

"You're not dressed for a run," I tell him, eyeing the sweatpants that should be made illegal. I peel my eyes away from how the material clings to his muscular legs in just the right places.

"Since when did you become the expert on proper running attire?" he asks, teasing me.

"Since it's nearly eighty degrees out. You'll overheat in those sweats."

"Are you calling me hot?" A smirk pulls at his lips, and of course that's what he heard.

"No, Rowan," I start, but he's already returning to his car. Hopefully, to leave. Instead, he opens the door and kicks off his shoes in one quick move. Then he's stepping out of his sweats. In the driveway.

I squeal and turn around, not wanting to bear witness to this. I can hear his deep chuckle only a few feet behind me.

"Relax, Briar. I'm wearing underwear." The amusement in his voice is thick, and I have to dig my nails into my palm to refrain from thinking about Rowan in his underwear.

"I told you. I'm going on a solo run," I reiterate, nearly shouting even though his car is no more than ten feet away from me.

"How crazy! Me too," he says, standing in front of me again. He's now changed into shorts, short ones. My eyes trace his muscular frame, and my cheeks flush when my eyes meet his again.

"Shut up," I tell him, seeing his smug expression. He looks entirely too pleased with himself.

"Seriously," he says, looking at me. "I'm worried you're not fully recovered. My plans fell through with Nate, and I could use a good run. Just let me come with you."

"No, Rowan."

"You won't even notice I'm there. Please," he says, eyes soft as he looks at me. And that's all it takes.

"Fine," I give in to him again, and cross my arms. "My goal is five miles today."

"Five miles?" His brows rise in surprise. "Great." I can see him rethinking his decision to go with me, but I hold firm on that mileage, even though I don't know if I have five miles in me. We stand in silence before I turn and start toward the end of the driveway. I'm acutely aware of him, only a few steps behind me as we begin a slow jog.

The silence follows us for the first quarter mile, and I struggle to maintain a regular cadence with my breathing. It's ragged, and it feels like zero oxygen reaches my lungs. I don't know if it's the weakness from my surgery or the fact that Rowan is beside me that's leaving me breathless. As quiet as he's been, it would be impossible not to notice him.

Rowan steadily slows beside me, and I'm grateful to fall into an easier pace. I'm already tired, but I refuse to let on. It feels like we've already run a marathon, but we're less than a mile from the house. But I will finish these five miles, even if it kills me.

I can feel Rowan monitoring me as he slows to nearly a walk. "Do you mind if we walk for a second?" he asks. "I think I'm getting a stitch in my side."

I know he's lying. He runs at least three miles a day, rain or shine. He has since he was in junior high. But I take the out he's giving me.

"Yeah," I choke out and drag in a deep breath. Never in my life have I felt this out of shape, and if I had the energy, I might be embarrassed.

"I think I might need to sit," he feigns being breathless, pointing to a nearby curb.

My chest rises and falls rapidly as I finally meet Rowan's eyes. I want to fight, but he gives me a subtle shake of his head.

"Come on."

He leads me to the curb, and I all but collapse onto the ground. Every muscle screams at me as I let my head hang between my knees. Who knew being out for a week would ruin all my stamina?

"Hey, don't lean over like that," Rowan whispers, reaching for my hands and helping me sit tall before placing them on my head. I can feel the light-headedness subside, and the embarrassment sinks in. I never wanted anyone to have to take care of me, especially not Rowan.

We sit there another minute as I catch my breath. "Sorry," I mumble.

"For what?" he asks, confusion in his voice. I shake my head, unable to find the words to tell him how grateful I am that he's here.

"Come on. Let's head home. Are you okay to walk?" he continues.

"I'm just a little winded," I sigh, knowing this goes beyond just being winded. I'm tired. Exhausted. And embarrassed.

"I could run back and get my car, or I could carry you," he says, and I contemplate the offer for a second, feeling my muscles fighting me. "But I'm pretty sure you wouldn't want that. You tend to want to do things for yourself."

He pushes up from the curb and offers his hand. I let him pull me up, not having the energy to do it myself.

"You don't have to make excuses, Rowan. This is a safe space. You can be honest with me that you're too weak to carry me all the way home," I joke, my words breathy.

"Is it that obvious?" he asks, smiling at me as we walk home. He keeps pace with me, never more than a few inches away, acting like he's ready to catch me if I fall.

But Rowan keeps his promise, and he keeps quiet. But it's not awkward. It's comfortable. And it's not long until we turn onto our street, and I realize we didn't get far. Not even a mile.

We finally walk up my driveway, and Rowan bumps my shoulder lightly. "I'm going to grab my sweats, but I'll meet you inside."

I nod and slowly head up the front steps. Each step feels like dragging my feet through mud, but I somehow make it inside. I don't get far inside before allowing myself to slide down to sit on the floor. I let my back rest against the wall and close my eyes. Not a minute later, the front door opens, and I let out a frustrated breath.

"Briar?"

I open my eyes and give Rowan a soft smile. He crouches in front of me, and he gives me a once-over like he's looking to see if I'm injured.

"I'm fine, Rowan," I lie to him, hoping he can't see how weak I really am. His eyes stay locked on mine, unmoving and assessing me. There's a glint in his eyes that lets me know my lies are unconvincing, but he doesn't push.

"We can pretend that I believe you for the time being," he says. "But I'm ordering us some lunch because you need to eat. What are you in the mood for?"

"I can just make myself a sandwich or something in the kitchen," I argue, gesturing to the fully stocked kitchen behind him.

"Great. I'll order sandwiches. You like Lucy's, right?" he asks, but he's already pulling up their menu.

"You don't have to—"

"You'd be doing me a favor if you let me order your lunch," he smirks, barely glancing up from his phone. "They're having a buy one, get one delivery special."

"I'm sure," I mumble, but I can't hide the smile on my face. Lucy's never does a delivery special.

"What do you want?" he asks, still hovering right in front of me. I almost want to pull him to sit beside me, so he can't see the flush from exertion that I know still paints my face.

I run through the menu in my head, trying to think of something that I could easily eat. "I don't know. Maybe a BLT, I guess."

"Ah, yes. A classic. You want me to add avocado to it?"

"No, Rowan. I don't need you to add avocado," I huff.

"You love avocado, Briar."

"Yes, but that doesn't mean—"

"Okay, then I'm adding it," he says, cutting me off. "BLT on sourdough with avocado." He looks at me to confirm before tapping his screen several more times.

"You're ridiculous," I tell him.

"It will be here in thirty minutes, and I saved four dollars," he says excitedly as if this were something to celebrate.

"Thank you, Rowan."

"Of course."

I hold his gaze long enough for him to understand I'm thanking him for so much more than just lunch. It's for everything. For always being there for me. For always knowing what I need, sometimes before I even do. And that list seems to be growing longer by the day.

Though I hate looking so weak right now. I want him to see me and think I'm strong, but I'm sure that's the last thing he'd think.

I grab the wall and stand on shaky legs. "I'm going to shower quickly before it gets here."

Rowan gives me a look of hesitancy. "Are you sure that's a good idea before we get some food in you? I don't want you passing out in the shower."

"If it makes you feel better, you can join me in the shower, Rowan."

His eyebrows disappear into his hair, shocked by my brazen offer. And to be honest, I am too. But I don't let myself imagine a world where he'd take me up on it. So, I leave him there as I head to my room. But it only takes him a second until he trails behind me. I stop on the last stair and turn to face him.

"It was a joke, Rowan," I tell him.

He points to the guest room a few feet away from us. "I was going to take a quick shower, too. That is, if it's okay with you, Princess. Or do you prefer it when I'm a little sweaty?"

My face flushes as he smirks at me. "Right. Please, go shower."

"Thank you," he whispers, his voice going all husky. That's all it takes for me to reconsider my own offer for him to join me in the shower.

He steps aside and gestures to my bedroom door. "After you."

I give him a wide-eyed stare and question whether he can read minds. Taking a hesitant step toward my room, I glance at him over my shoulder, silently pleading for him to come with me.

"Try not to miss me," he taunts and winks.

I cough and try to force out a laugh. "Yeah, like I'd ever." I hear the tremble in my voice and hope he didn't catch it. But the way he chuckles and saunters into the guest room makes me think he knows exactly what I'm thinking.

The flush of embarrassment heats my cheeks as I hurry to my room and lock the door behind me. Only one thing might help me erase the thought of him from my mind. Only one thing is strong enough to make me forget.

It's on my nightstand, taunting me with its very existence. It's days later, but there's still pain. A different kind of pain, but it all feels the same to me right now.

It physically hurts to be this close to Rowan and have to restrain myself around him. I want, just once, for him to give in to my taunts and do something. To let me know this isn't all in my head.

I want him to tell me to forget about everyone else. But he won't. So, I'll settle for now.

My feet move by themselves now as I reach out for the bottle. I turn it over in my hand and read the label quietly to myself.

"Take one tablet by mouth every six hours as needed for pain."

I open the bottle and let one of the pills fall into my hand. Staring at it, I can already feel the guilt settling in. I told myself I wouldn't do this. I told my mom I wouldn't do this. But I can't help it. Desperate times call for desperate measures.

But I'm not that desperate, so I snap the pill in half and swallow it. And the countdown to numbness begins. Stripping down, I turn the water so it's nearly ice cold. And even that isn't enough.

Maybe it's the lack of food. Or the exhaustion. But at this moment, I desperately want Rowan in my shower.

Twenty-Six
Briar

I don't remember falling asleep. I barely remember eating my lunch. But judging by the empty wrapper on the coffee table, it must've been delicious.

The house is quiet and dark, the TV silently playing a sports show with subtitles running across the bottom of the screen. The door to the back patio is cracked, and Rowan paces while on the phone. He looks tense, even angry, but I can't make out much of what he's saying. I raise my eyebrows and watch him grip the railing so hard I'm sure his knuckles are white.

Whatever conversation he's having, it isn't a good one. And my gut tells me it's something I shouldn't be privy to.

Rowan finally hangs up the phone and releases his death grip on the railing. His jaw clenches and relaxes in rhythm, and the hatred in his eyes makes me think he's ready to kill someone.

He's silent as he comes back into the house and hasn't noticed me watching him as he moves around the back of the couch. Rowan finally glances over and sees I'm awake, and his frustrated expression evaporates as he sits across from me.

"Well, if it isn't Sleeping Beauty finally awake from her nap," he teases me.

My cheeks flush, but it's barely noticeable with the sunset painting the living room in oranges and pinks.

"How long did I sleep?"

"A couple of hours," he shrugs. "Did I wake you?"

"No." I shake my head. "Who were you on the phone with?"

"Just some business," he says casually, like he wasn't just pacing the patio and trying to strangle the railing. "Do you want to raid the kitchen with me and figure out something for dinner?"

"You don't have to stay for dinner. I'm feeling better after my nap, so if you have somewhere else you'd rather be..." I start, but the words die in my throat. I don't want him to agree, but I don't want him to feel like I'm holding him captive here, either.

"You're supposed to kick me out after I feed you," he says, a smile tugging the corner of his lips up. "Come on," he nods toward the kitchen, and I reluctantly follow him. He moves around effortlessly, opening the fridge and pantry as he takes stock of what's there. I hop on the counter to stay out of his way and observe as he collects ingredients.

"Don't tell me you think you can cook, too." It's mostly a joke, but I've never known Rowan to cook anything. I fear I'm in for another foul meal.

"I wouldn't say I fancy myself a chef, but I know how to cook," he says, his back still to me. The stack of ingredients grows beside me as he goes between the fridge and the pantry.

"We're having pasta?" I raise my eyebrows.

"Well, I know you like Italian food, and pasta is my specialty," he says proudly, finally turning to smile at me.

And I'm reminded why I've always liked Rowan. That relaxed and easy-going side of him that makes you feel at home. The side that remembers all the small details and never fails to make you feel special. That's how he reels you in.

"Your specialty?" I ask, leaning forward on the counter.

"Yes." I can hear his smile as he moves a pot filled with water to the stove.

"Is there anything I can do to help?"

"Absolutely not." His response comes so quickly that I'm surprised. Then, a teasing smile covers his face. "Briar, you need to learn to let someone do something for you. And besides, you're a terrible cook. I wouldn't want you to ruin the masterpiece."

I laugh at him. "Your masterpiece? It's spaghetti."

"And it will be the best spaghetti you've ever had."

Surprisingly, Rowan is the cleanest cook I've ever seen. I sit on the island counter for the next twenty minutes and watch as not even a drop of spaghetti water ends up on the stove . My constant questions don't even distract him as he works, so I switch gears.

"Why'd you seem so angry on the phone earlier?"

This one gets him. He pauses while stirring the sauce and stands silent for a moment. "You saw that?" he asks without turning around.

"I did."

"I told you, it's just business." Rowan's voice is calm, but I can see the tension in his back as he turns to face me. Leaning against the counter, he crosses his arms over his chest. He knows his vague answers won't get me to shut up, so I don't know why he doesn't just come clean.

"What kind of business makes you that tense?"

His jaw clenches, and he pushes away from the counter. "You're full of questions today," he chuckles as he steps closer.

"And you're full of non-answers."

He stops in front of me, just close enough to make my heart skip a beat. I want to reach out, touch him, and pull him closer, but I don't. He's just out of reach. Like always.

His smirk makes me wonder if he can hear my heart pounding in my chest. And I don't know if the dim light is making me see things or if his eyes are bouncing between mine and my lips.

"Why are you being so nice to me, Rowan?" The question slips out before I can stop it.

He chuckles and stands there contemplating his answer for a minute. "Nate would kill me if I let anything happen to you on my watch."

My heart sinks a little. He's only here because my brother expects him to be. The realization shouldn't hurt as much as it does, and I hate the part of me that wishes he were here because he wants to be.

"Dinner is ready," he says, backing away again and giving me space to breathe.

The distance between us hurts more than I expected. I nod and slide off the counter, moving silently to pull two plates from the cupboard. Placing them beside Rowan, I feel the heat radiating from his body and have to step away.

He carefully plates the food and carries it to the table for us. "C'mon, Bri. Let's eat."

I'm acutely aware of his eyes on me as I take the first bite, and I'm floored. This *is* some of the best spaghetti I've ever had. How he used only three ingredients and made this sauce, I'll never understand. But he swore it would be perfect. And lo and behold, he was right.

Rowan studies my face, looking for some reaction, and I take my time meeting his gaze. "So?" Rowan prompts me.

I swallow and try to put how good this is into words. "This is quite possibly," I point at the plate with my fork, "the best plate of spaghetti I've ever eaten."

A proud smile grows to cover Rowan's face, and there's a hint of a blush on his cheeks. "I did what I could with limited options and an annoying sous chef," he teases before taking a bite of his food.

"I didn't know you could cook, like at all," I tell him, a little surprised by how good he is.

"I don't cook for anyone but myself very often," he says, making my stomach flip. He doesn't cook often, but he cooks for me. "Is this better than whatever Cameron made for you?"

I cough, choking on my food. The thought of Rowan like this, jealous, is enough to make me second-guess him being here for me. "Not everything is a competition, Rowan."

"No. Of course not," he shakes his head. "But this is better, right?"

I laugh at him. "Speaking of Cameron, how is Calista?" Selfishly, I shift the conversation away from my love life, needing to know what's going on in his.

"Oh, now you remember her name?" he asks, a hint of amusement in his eyes. "She's all right."

"Trouble in paradise?"

"No. She's just okay. I feel like I can't ever have a real conversation with her. She's all about fashion, parties, and gossip. And it's boring."

"Ah, I see what's wrong," I laugh, covering my amusement with another bite.

"What?" Rowan asks.

"The newness has worn off. You got what you wanted, and now you're ready to move on," I say around a mouthful of food. "I'm not her biggest fan, but maybe give her some time."

"Oh, I heard about that." There's a sly smile on his face again.

"Heard about what?"

"She told me you called her insecure, then proceeded to explain to me for twenty minutes how you're the insecure one," he laughs loudly.

I blush, feeling stupid for thinking Calista wouldn't go crying to Rowan. Like I've gone crying to Rowan.

"That's not exactly what I said to her." I try to defend myself, but a laugh slips out.

"Oh, okay. Forgive me for spreading rumors. What did you say then?" He raises his eyebrows at me, leaning forward with that amused grin.

I pause, trying to remember what I did say. "It doesn't matter what exactly I did or did not say," I counter, scratching my head. "I just don't like mean girls, and I thought you didn't either."

He stares at me curiously for a moment, and there's a look on his face like he wants to say something. But he doesn't. We just continue silently eating. It's not awkward, but we exchange little glances the whole time.

And that's the part that kills me.

Rowan is an expert at whatever game we're playing. He knows exactly how much to give. Just when I think I'm over that little crush of mine, he does something that makes it impossible to forget the crush. And every time I doubt that we're just friends, he pulls back.

But then again, this might all be in my head.

Rowan clears our plates when we finish, placing them in the sink before cleaning up the rest of the dishes. We run like a well-oiled machine, even in silence. It's like he can sense my next move before I can. He passes the dishes to me as I rinse and load the dishwasher.

It doesn't take long until everything is put away, but I spend the time it takes us to clean up trying to think of some reason to ask Rowan to stay a little longer.

"So, what's next on the agenda tonight? Night swimming?" I ask.

He laughs but shakes his head. "I wish, but not tonight. I'm honestly a little tired. Not all of us took a four-hour nap this afternoon." His voice is teasing, but there's a part of me that feels like he wants to leave.

Because really, he's just here as a courtesy to Nate.

"Oh, okay. Yeah. Absolutely," I nod, trying to hide the disappointment in my voice.

Now, the silence feels awkward as it stretches between us. The only relief is when the garage door opens, and Nate comes in, looking startled to see Rowan and me together.

His brows pull in confusion. "Oh, hey, guys. What's up?"

"Hey man," Rowan slaps Nate's shoulder in greeting. "I stopped by earlier to see if you were around, and Bri was going for a run, so I stayed to make sure she was okay."

Nate's head whips around to look at me. "You did what?"

"I tried to go for a run today, and it didn't go well," I explain. "But I'm fine. Like Rowan said, he was just here to make sure I didn't hurt myself." There's a bite in my voice that's embarrassing. Like I'm mad at him for being a good guy.

"Bri," Rowan says pleadingly.

"It's fine. I'm actually headed to bed now. I'll see you around." My voice is clipped, and I rush out of the kitchen, ignoring both of their concerned looks. I get about halfway up the stairs before pausing to eavesdrop.

"Dude, after seeing her the other day, I didn't think her running was a good idea. I tagged along just in case, and about a mile in, she nearly collapsed. I made sure she got home and had something to eat," Rowan explains.

"She collapsed?" Nate's voice is strained with stress.

"No, but she almost did," Rowan sighs. "But she should be fine now. I was just headed out when you came in. I have to go meet up with Calista."

And those eight words drive a knife into my heart. He's going to see *her*. He's leaving me to go see her.

I can't help but feel like it's my fault. If I weren't so weak, if I weren't so needy, if I weren't so much, he might have stuck around. But no one wants to be with someone they're constantly having to babysit. Because that's all I am to him. Another responsibility.

I don't stick around to hear anything more. I want to hide in my room and never come out. All this time, I thought there might actually be something there with Rowan.

But there isn't. It's one-sided.

And it's devastating.

And I can't believe I was wishing for a reason for Rowan to stay.

He won't ever stay.

Not for me.

Twenty-Seven
Briar

It's been four days since I've seen Rowan, and he hasn't left my mind once. Not during my second surf lesson with Reece, or when I was on a run, or when I tried to fall asleep at night. He's like a parasite that's buried itself in my brain and made its home there.

I want to hate him, but I can't.

I can only think about what I might say when I do finally get to see him, which is hopefully tonight, though even the thought has my stomach in knots.

If I'm right, he'll be at the Gala, while I'm stuck there with Cameron. It's terrible, but I wish I'd never agreed to go with him in the first place. I'd rather go with Rowan, even after everything. And I know that makes me sound insane.

Yet here I am, pretending to enjoy being with Cameron's family as the numbness of the pain medication fades away, and the pain seeps back in. I regret only taking half a pill, as the insistent chorus of what-ifs comes flooding back, along with the nausea.

Now I'm left with this sinking feeling in my gut, Cameron's overly inquisitive family, and their judgmental stares. Every question they ask about me or my family, I can't help but think I'd never have to sit through something like this with Rowan.

Then again, it's not worth comparing Cameron to Rowan. It just makes me sad.

Cameron isn't Rowan and won't ever be—no one will. The sooner I get that into my head, the better. And the sooner I can get through today, the sooner I can get to the afterparty, kick off these heels, and finally relax.

A knock pulls me from my thoughts. Cameron peeks into the room, one hand covering his eyes. "Is everyone dressed in here?"

As much as I'm not thrilled to be here with him, I'm grateful he's here to finally rescue me. I've been trapped in this stuffy room with his family for three hours, and Cameron's face is a welcome sight.

Nearly all the women he's related to are here: his mom, three sisters, grandmother, six cousins, and an aunt. It's felt more like an interrogation than a pre-gala prep. Every one of them is all smiles to your face and whispers behind your back. I've heard them talking, but I pretend I haven't.

"We're all dressed," I say, playing along.

Cameron drops his hand and steps into the room, and he looks at me, a little slack-jawed. "Wow, Bri. You… you look incredible."

I blush at his words and let him pull me into a hug.

"You don't look so bad yourself," I reply, and it's true. He looks good in his suit.

But Rowan would look better.

"Are you ready?"

His question brings me back to our reality, and I smile as much as I can. I know how these things go. My family hosted the Gala when I was ten. It's boring and annoying, but as my parents always remind me, it's for a good cause.

"As ready as I'll ever be."

"Good, because the coordinator was hot on my heels," he chuckles as the door flies open behind him.

A slim woman steps in, dark hair pulled back so tightly I'd be surprised if she didn't have a headache. "Okay, everyone. We will go through the entry order and expectations for tonight. You're all seated at the first and second round tables to the right when you exit to the garden."

As she starts into her little speech, I tune her out. I know the drill. No one here cares about me. All they care about is Senator DuPont and his political pageantry. He'll make a speech, thank donors, and toss in a campaign plug. Then, we'll be forced to mingle. It's the same song and dance every year.

Although this time, I'm hoping the senator notices me. Knowing I might get the chance to speak with him long enough to get a recommendation letter for my Yale application is well worth being Cameron's date.

"This will be quick," Cameron leans in, reassuring me before any more doubt can trickle in. "We can grab a drink before we head to the table."

I nod along and follow his lead. He's the one everyone will be watching. At least, that's what I have to keep reminding myself. Taking a deep breath, I link my arm with Cameron's and let him lead me down the stairs.

From the gallery, I can see most of the tables as they wait for the senator's arrival. A few faces stick out, and most of them seem bored. And from what I can see, this event looks extravagant and overdone. The lush floral arrangements are nearly drowning the guests, and the tablescapes look more cluttered than classy, with the dozen pieces of silverware adorning the table.

But what do I know about class? I'm here with one guy thinking about another.

Finally, the announcement comes, and the Grand DuPont entrance begins. I have to fight the urge to roll my eyes at the whole thing, as I plaster on a practiced smile. Cameron's mother and father are the first out, and the crowd claps excitedly for them. Then it's our turn with his sisters not far behind us.

As we come into view of the tables, I try to remember everything I've ever learned about presentation. Head up, shoulders back, smile like you're thrilled to be here. Make eye contact. Look gracious.

And for the love of all things holy—don't trip.

The family waves at the attendees like some royal family, greeting their adoring subjects. I have to stifle my laughter because this whole event is gaudy at best.

On my right, I hear excited clapping and see my friends and brother giving me massive smiles and thumbs up. It brings a genuine smile to my face at their excitement, but it fades as I search their table and find no sign of Rowan.

As disappointed as I am, maybe that's for the best. Now I can focus on whatever is required of me from the DuPont family. But I can't pretend there isn't the nagging hope that he might be here soon.

Cameron puts his hand on my waist, bringing my attention back to him. He gives me a slight nod of assurance before we're forced to stand front and center for what feels like an hour as his dad's speech drags on.

Because it *drags* on.

Senator DuPont knows how to talk. And that's all he does. He talks about the event, his entire life, his career, his family, blah, blah, blah. If it weren't for Cameron holding me up, I might have collapsed from sheer boredom.

Once the monologue concludes, I let out a sigh of relief.

"Sorry, I should have warned you that my dad's a talker," Cameron chuckles beside me.

"No, it's fine," I lie as he guides me down a few stairs. As we start toward our table, I can't help but toss a glance over my shoulder, searching for Harper.

"I'm going to grab us a few drinks. Why don't you say hi to your friends? I'll come find you in a few." Cameron kisses my temple and nearly runs to the bar.

His sudden absence shocks me, but I'm alone for less than three seconds before Harper's excited squeals sound behind me.

"Bri!" She's waving like a mad person, and her smile has taken over her entire face.

"Harper!"

I throw my arms around her, grateful for a familiar face and one that doesn't look at me like something stuck to the bottom of their shoe.

"You. Look. Stunning. Right. Now!" She punctuates her words with claps, and I can't help but blush. She's always been my biggest supporter.

Zara and a few other girls follow her over, and I bring my new friend in for a hug.

"Girl! Look at you!" Zara says. "Face, body, dress— you're perfect! I'd skin you alive and wear you like a fur coat if it weren't legal, and bloody."

I laugh at her enthusiasm and twirl, basking in their compliments. "Thank you, thank you," I say, waving to them like I'm a royal princess.

"But you," I draw out my words and give my friends a once-over. "Harper! Kian's lucky he's not here, so I can pretend to be both of your boyfriend. I'll take care of my baby girls."

We erupt into more laughter, but we're silenced as I hear a slow clap behind me and look over my shoulder to see Nate and Rowan.

And I swear, in that moment, I forget how to breathe.

Rowan has abandoned his typical naturally wavy hair in favor of a shorter cut, nearly buzzed. His perfectly tailored suit fits him like I've never seen. And I was right.

He looks much better than Cameron. By miles.

If I thought he could be a Calvin Klein model before, I'm sure of it now. I look him up and down as he walks closer, and a flush heats my cheeks as he catches me. Our eyes lock for two seconds, before the concrete becomes the most interesting thing I've ever seen as I try to compose myself.

"That's my cue to leave," Harper says, exasperated and giving my arm a reassuring squeeze. "Bri, we'll find you in a bit."

I nod along, but my brain feels like mush as my friends nearly run away.

"B, you look beautiful. Although that was the longest speech I think I've ever sat through." Nate pulls me in for a bone-crushing hug as he laughs at his own joke.

I smile and can see Rowan watching me. "Thank you." I pull away from my brother and clear my throat, trying not to stumble over my next words.

"You both look good, too. You must be out here trying to impress someone with how you two clean up."

Nate laughs with me, brushing imaginary dust off his shoulder. "Maybe I am."

"You look great, Briar," Rowan says, his eyes never leaving mine as Cameron finds us in the crowd. He's holding two glasses of champagne, and I say a silent prayer of thanks. Now that the haze of the pills has faded, I am in desperate need of a drink. Maybe it will help stop my feet from hurting. And my heart.

"I didn't know what you liked, so I settled for champagne. I figured every girl likes champagne," he says before shaking Nate's hand.

My brother and Cameron make small talk while I stand there locked in a silent conversation with Rowan. My eyes trace every feature of him, trying to memorize this moment. But the feeling of Cameron's hand in mine pulls me back.

I try my best to keep my mask in place, not to let Rowan see just how badly I wish it were him. It's just a flash, barely there, but enough to make me think Rowan feels it too.

But it's not long until Cameron and I are pulled away to mingle. I give Nate one last pleading look, silently begging to be saved as I'm dragged into more forced conversations.

It's not terrible. Everyone I meet is friendly but boring. Terribly, terribly boring. It's like they're all the same person in different fonts. Cameron doesn't seem bothered by it, though he's had enough champagne to keep him laughing. We have the same conversation over and over for an hour before I finally have had enough.

"I'm going to the ladies' room," I tell Cameron as I escape into the crowd.

I'm thankful for a moment to breathe, and I immediately begin my search for Harper. I need to talk to a normal person before my brain explodes. One quick sweep of the area and I find she's by the bar, and I all but spring over to her.

"Finally, I found you," I say, throwing my arms around her shoulders and letting my head drop. "These people are so boring."

She laughs as she drapes an arm over my shoulders. "How is lover boy?"

"Fine," I shrug.

"Just fine?" Zara asks, her brow quirked.

"Yeah. I think the shine has worn off. He's just arm candy."

"Tragic," Harper pouts. "I thought this one had potential."

"Negative. I think getting ready with his mom and their entire family tree did him a disservice," I laugh.

"Yeah?" Zara asks.

"It was awful! They basically interrogated me and wanted to play dress-up together." I turn my nose up at the thought. "But they did have a snack table in there that made the whole thing worth it. There were all these little sandwiches and fruits and chocolate." Just the thought of that table has my mouth watering again. It was like heaven on Earth.

"Do you think we could sneak upstairs and see if it's still there?" Harper asks, her eyes nearly falling out of her head.

"They cleaned it up before we left." My news makes both girls frown. "I know. I know. Anyway, where are Kian and Reece?"

Both girls burst into fits of laughter. "You think either of them would be caught dead here? Besides, getting either of them in a tux is harder than getting a three-year-old to eat their vegetables," Zara chokes out.

I roll my eyes, but I know she's right. Besides, I'm fairly confident they'd rather eat their vegetables than be here. And I don't blame them.

"I'm sorry they couldn't make it," I tell Harper.

She shrugs while glaring at something behind me. "And as if tonight couldn't get any worse," she grumbles.

I glance over and see Rowan and Nate coming our way. It instantly gets ten degrees hotter, and my hands start to sweat just seeing him again.

Nate throws his hands in the air. "Relax, we come in peace."

"Yeah, right," Zara mutters and walks off.

I have to stifle my laughter with the look on Nate's face. It's like he's shocked that someone doesn't like him.

"What did I do?" He jokingly sniffs himself as if that's the issue here.

But we all know Nate isn't the problem. It's the guy he's with—the one with eyes like a Caribbean shore and a smile that melts away my inhibitions.

"I wanted to see if you fine ladies wanted to dance," Nate says, extending his hand to Harper. A flush paints her face, and she looks at me almost like she's asking for permission. I smile and raise my brows before shooing her off with my brother.

"Looks like you're stuck with me," Rowan says, extending his hand to me.

I hesitate, but only for a second, before my hand is in his and he's leading me to the dance floor.

"I thought you didn't dance, Rowan."

He pulls me in closer and rests his hand on my lower back. My skin instantly feels like it's on fire, and I'm very conscious of every move I make. I try to slow my heartbeat, but it's no use.

He flashes me his smile and leans in closer. "You do look amazing, Briar. How'd you know red is my favorite color?"

I laugh and have to remind myself to breathe before I pass out. It's a chore to pretend his proximity isn't affecting me, but it's my favorite chore. "Harper made me buy it."

He studies me, and I can't hold his gaze. Being this close to him is driving me crazy. The way he's leaning into me and guiding me. The way I want to melt into his touch. Everything about him is addictive, so I force myself to look at Harper and Nate instead. They look so happy together, as they laugh and dance.

I swallow down an odd sense of jealousy, wishing so desperately that Rowan could be my person like Kian is for Harper, or Melissa is for Nate.

I drag my eyes back to Rowan, who's still watching me intently. "Are you and Nate going to this afterparty tonight?"

"We are," Rowan whispers, dropping his hand from my waist. His movements are quick and effortless as he spins me out and pulls me back into him. He puts his hand back on my spine, and I laugh as he resumes our gentle waltz.

"Oh, you do dance!" I grin. "I'm impressed, Rowan."

He smiles, wide and real. "Good."

I want to ask what other tricks he's hiding from me, but I don't. I'd rather just live in this moment with him.

But like a mirage, the illusion shatters as Rowan drops his hand from my waist, as Cameron cuts in.

"I'll take it from here," he says, placing his hand firmly on my side as he pulls me to him. I can't help but wince as his fingers dig into my skin.

"Looks like she's in good hands then," Rowan says, seemingly unbothered. He takes a few steps away and winks at me before getting lost in the crowd. I suck in a breath and curse Cameron for interrupting. I just wanted five more minutes with Rowan. Maybe more.

Cameron leans in and whispers, "You look hot, Bri. You're amazing."

I try to smile, but I have to pull away from him with the stench of alcohol radiating off him.

"Thank you," I mumble, amused by how he looks the slightest bit lost.

"Why were you dancing with him?"

"Hmm?" I hum, looking at him confused. "What do you mean?"

"Why were you dancing with him, Briar?" Cameron questions me again, a note of jealousy in his voice.

"It was just a dance. Harper is right there with my brother," I point over his shoulder. "It wasn't anything serious."

"Right. Whatever." He rolls his eyes, and I can't help the small laugh that slips out.

"Are you jealous?" I tease him, but he doesn't seem to think it's funny. He doesn't even react.

"A few of us are getting ready to head to the afterparty. Are you coming?"

I pause, not sure I want to go anywhere with him if he's slurring his words like he is. "My brother is heading that way soon. I think he wants me to go with him," I lie, stepping away from Cameron. "I'll meet you there?"

He huffs in annoyance, but doesn't protest before he's stumbling away toward a few of his friends. I watch him go, wanting to make sure he's safe before heading to the bar to get a drink. I'll need one to make spending the rest of the night with him more tolerable.

"Done dancing already?" Rowan appears beside me.

"Yeah. He… uh," I hesitate, trying to find a nicer way to say he's a drunk idiot. "He was ready to go to the afterparty, and I'd rather go with Nate."

"He was drunk," Rowan laughs. "I'm impressed with your subtlety, though."

I nod, grateful I didn't have to be the one to say it. "Yes," I agree, thankful that Rowan gets it. "He was very drunk. I didn't want to get in the car with him."

"That's very responsible of you," he laughs, glancing off toward his sister on the dance floor.

"I do what I can these days," I say half-heartedly. I want to be anything but responsible when it comes to Rowan. But, for now, I have to pretend like I am. "But I am ready to get out of this dress and these heels."

Rowan chuckles and nods in understanding. "Go get Harper and change. Nate and I will meet you out front," he says, gesturing to the dance floor.

I look at Rowan, standing here in that suit, with that smile and that stupid charm that I can't seem to fight, and I wish for the millionth time that he had been my date.

"Go," he says again, with that unreadable look in his eye that makes me think he wants to say more.

I hesitate. Just for a breath. Hoping maybe he'll stop me. Maybe he'll finally say something that changes everything.

But he doesn't

And he won't.

So I turn away.

And as I walk back into the crowd, heels clicking against the faux-marble dance floor, I know the ache in my chest isn't just disappointment. It's something worse.

Hope.

Because deep down, I still want him to follow me.

And I always will.

Twenty-Eight
Briar

Harper and I ditch our brothers the second we arrive at the afterparty. I love them, and they're fun, but they'll only get in the way of a good time with all their brotherly protectiveness.

"Oh, there's Kian," Harper shouts, pointing into the crowd. I nod, though I don't see him, but I trust her ability to find him in any room. And the house is beyond crowded. The place already looks trashed, and it's only nine.

"I don't see Cameron," I shout over the music as she drags me through the crowd. Though I don't know why I'm looking. I don't particularly care to find him.

Kian finally comes into view, and, surprise, he's with Reece, who flashes that cheeky grin when he spots me.

"There she is!" Reece greets me with a hug.

"Hey! We missed you at the Gala," I say. He pulls away, screwing his brows up.

"No, you didn't."

I laugh. "I can confirm that you were missed."

Reece beams. "Bri, you're making me blush."

I glance at Harper, who's rocking the I-told-you-so look. She's been not so subtly trying to get me to consider dating Reece since I got home. Her persistence is something to admire, but she's fighting a losing battle. As I've told her many times, Reece is great.

But Reece is in New York.

And I'm not.

And he's not Rowan.

"I'm going to grab a drink," I say, heading back toward the kitchen.

"I'll come with," Reece says, earning a brow wiggle from Harper as we disappear into the crowd.

Shameless. But I love her.

The kitchen is significantly less crowded than the rest of this floor, and I get a chance to breathe. I grab a plastic cup and fill it with the red-colored liquid from the pitcher that smells like rubbing alcohol. Looking into the cup, I can't help but wrinkle my nose in disgust.

I turn to Reece but see someone else walking toward me.

Mateo.

And that's worse than whatever this drink will taste like.

"Well, look who it is. Never heard back from you, Bri," he slurs, barely able to stand.

"Is this your new boyfriend?"

Reece instantly tenses beside me, but I rest a hand on his arm to calm him.

"I don't have a boyfriend."

"I could be your boyfriend," he offers, not missing a beat before grabbing my hand and placing a sloppy kiss on my knuckles.

I can't choke down my laugh. "For so many reasons, no." I pull my hand out of his grasp and wipe the slobber off on a nearby towel, trying not to gag.

And just as quickly as he came, he's slinking off again to whatever hole he crawled out of.

"Thank goodness," I say to Reece. "I was not in the mood to deal with him."

"Is he always like that?" Reece asks.

"He's harmless," I assure him. "He just wants to get in good with me to get closer to Rowan. I've learned if you ignore him, he goes away."

"Like a weird rash," Reece nods.

"What?" I ask, tilting my head, not sure I heard him correctly. "Did you just compare Mateo to a rash?"

"Yeah," he shrugs. "If you ignore it long enough, it will go away. But let's go. Before the creepy rash boy returns," Reece laughs and grabs my hand, leading me back through the makeshift dance floor off the kitchen and toward the patio.

We find Harper, who has the biggest smile on her face, seeing Reece's hand in mine. She's so excited, I think her eyes might fall out of her head, so I let go.

"That took long enough! What happened to you guys? Where have you been?" Kian asks, elbowing Reece in his ribs.

"Well, Bri here was getting slobbered on," Reece says, laughing when he sees me gagging at the thought.

"Slobbered on?" Harper asks, her face a mix of confusion and disgust.

"Mateo," I say. "He's drunk and tried to kiss my hand, and…I really can't talk about it. I might throw up all over you if I have to relive that."

Kian shudders. "I'm sorry you had to go through that. The hardest battles go to the toughest soldiers."

"Shut up," I shove his shoulder as we migrate toward the backyard. The house itself is massive, and the backyard is no exception. It's got a pool that looks to be Olympic-sized, and it only covers half the yard. The other half is littered with plastic tables and chairs that are trying to look expensive.

And at one of those tables, my brother and Rowan sit with a group of girls. Six girls, to be exact. Nate has his arm around one with raven hair who leans into him when she laughs. And every other girl at that table has their eyes on Rowan.

But his are on me.

I can feel my cheeks flush, and I avert my gaze quickly, looking for anyone else I recognize. And the only other person is Cora.

She spots us, waving us down to join her, and Harper starts over before I can stop her. As we move across the yard, I'm acutely aware of Rowan's gaze on me, but I fight the urge to look at him.

There are a few other people with Cora, but I don't recognize anyone. Sitting down, Cora looks at me with a mischievous smile that makes my skin crawl.

"Hi, Cora. Have you seen Cameron?"

"Oh, he didn't tell you?"

I don't know whether she's mad it didn't go well with Mateo or what, but there's something in her tone that makes everyone go quiet.

"Tell me what?" I do my best to keep the bite out of my voice, but based on the way Reece gives me a once-over, I've failed.

"He's not coming. We had to drop him off on the way here," she says, smiling. Leaning in, she drops her voice to whisper, "Between us, I think he had one too many at the Gala."

I dig my nails into my palms to keep myself from saying something nasty. "Well, that is just too bad," I force out, keeping a smile on my face.

I can feel a knot forming in my stomach, but I don't know why. I don't think I even like Cameron, so I should be relieved he's not here. But there's no relief. Just a weird heaviness that sits in my stomach.

Conversation has picked up around us, but I'm barely listening. I'm barely even there, because my mind is somewhere else entirely.

"You okay?" Reece whispers, leaning into me. "You're quiet, and you seem off."

"I'm fine," I lie, bringing my cup to my lips and taking a sip that I have to force myself to swallow. The drink itself is awful, but it also burns like hell on the way down.

One look from Reece, and I can tell he knows I'm lying.

"I just feel sick. Might be something I ate at the Gala." Another lie, but this one must be more believable with the frown Reece is sporting.

"Anything I can do to help?"

I shake my head, right as Cora pipes up again. She's twirling a strand of hair around her finger as she nearly sings, "Guys, we should play a game. Like truth or dare!"

My stomach twists at the thought. I'd rather pluck out each individual eyelash of mine than play a silly high school game with Cora.

"I'm going to try to find some water. I'll be back," I say, already standing to leave.

As I weave through the backyard, I'm glad to see Nate and Rowan have abandoned their table. Now I can breathe a little easier. Hopefully, they left entirely, and I don't have to see either of them again tonight. I just want to be left alone to stew in this… something. I don't know if it's anger, or embarrassment, or irritation. But whatever it is, it's making my chest hurt.

I wander the house for ten minutes before finding the line for the bathroom. It's not much, but it should be enough to help me calm down.

The line moves slowly, but I don't mind so much. It gives me a chance to breathe, and the ache in my chest slowly begins to subside.

While I wait, I let my gaze drift over the people who pass by and see too many familiar faces.

Michael from high school chemistry.

Lucille from the cheer squad.

Mary Ann from French class.

And Rowan.

He stops when he sees me, a stupid grin spreading across his face as he comes to join me. "What's with the sour face?"

"I could sense you coming, and this is what my face does when I think about you," I taunt him.

"I'll work on correcting that."

My stomach flips. I know he doesn't mean it, but even him saying that feeds my hope.

"By the way, Nate left, and he asked me to make sure you get home."

"I can find my way home. Harper is here, and so is Reece. I'm sure one of them is more than capable of getting me home."

Rowan's jaw ticks. "No."

The bathroom door opens behind me, and a group of girls who look sixteen filter out.

"I'll find a way home, Rowan," I say, dismissing him as I step into the bathroom.

But when I try to close the door, it doesn't shut.

"What are you doing?" I ask as Rowan pushes his way into the bathroom with me. The click of the lock behind him sends my pulse skyrocketing.

This bathroom could easily fit ten people, but now, it feels entirely too small for just the two of us.

"You're not leaving with anyone else."

His words echo in my mind, but I can't understand them. All I know is he shouldn't be in here with me.

"Rowan, this is a bathroom."

"Tell me you understand."

"Okay, sure," I agree, hoping that's enough to satisfy him, and he'll leave.

But he doesn't budge. He stands there, staring at me like he's worried I'll disappear if he takes his eyes off me.

"This is a bathroom," I repeat. "I came here because I have to pee. Which means you have to leave."

He cracks a smile. "Yeah, me too. That's why I came in here."

"No," I laugh, thinking this must be a joke.

"Why not? Girls go to the bathroom all the time together. So, what's the big deal?"

"To state the obvious, you're not a girl."

"Oh, are you scared to be in here with me?"

I blink a few times, trying to understand what's happening. But it's impossible. At this point, Rowan's given me a severe case of whiplash with how hot and cold he is. I can't keep track of anything with him anymore.

"No," I breathe, but it's not a convincing answer.

"Come on. I'll turn around."

I huff out a frustrated breath and press my hands into my eyes until I'm seeing stars.

"Hey. Hey, Briar, what's wrong?"

Every ounce of charm is gone from his voice and replaced with concern as his hands find my wrists. He gently pulls my hands from my face while his eyes search mine.

"Nothing," I whisper. "Nothing."

"What's wrong? Talk to me."

And it's his voice, mixing with his touch, that makes me want to come clean.

"I don't," I hesitate. "I-I don't have to pee. I just… just wanted a few minutes alone. I-I was overwhelmed, and yeah."

I force in another ragged breath while my heart is hammering in my chest. He doesn't say anything, which makes it worse with how his electric blue eyes burn into mine with an intensity I haven't seen.

"I can… I can go," I offer, pointing over his shoulder to the locked door. "So you can… you know…"

"Don't go," he says, his words slow and measured. "I just wanted a few minutes alone with you."

I'm too stunned to speak as that admission hangs in the air. Because this time it feels real.

"Rowan. We shouldn't," I breathe out, but I don't have it in me to really fight him.

"You don't want to, or we shouldn't?" he whispers, stepping closer.

We both know that we shouldn't, not that I don't want to. But I won't let myself admit that to him. Not when I don't know what this is or what kind of game he's playing.

I force a laugh and put my hands on his chest to push him away. But he doesn't move.

Rowan chuckles, his eyes locked on mine.

"You can't push me away, Princess."

I hold his gaze for what feels like ten minutes before I pull my hands back from his chest. I've only seen this side of Rowan in fleeting moments, but he's locked in on me. Our proximity sets my body on fire, and I'm scared this time I'm going to get burned.

"Don't get quiet now, Briar." Leaning in, there's a cockiness to his tone as he asks, "What? Am I making you nervous?"

He knows he makes me nervous, and he's playing into that. But it's taking every fiber of my being to hold back from him. I flick my eyes up to meet his and instantly regret it.

He's watching me just as intently as he always has, but it's more.

Everything is always more with him.

"Rowan, that's cute. You think you make me nervous," I laugh, but it's hollow. Forced.

He smirks, and that warmth envelops me. "You think I'm cute?"

"Of course, that's all you heard." I roll my eyes, relief flooding me that the moment has passed.

"That's not a denial."

"I don't think you're cute," I tell him. That's mostly true because I wouldn't use the word cute to describe Rowan.

He's devastatingly handsome.

He's magnetic.

"Liar," he whispers, his breath fanning across my neck.

Everything about him makes my brain fuzzy. I take a deep breath and push him back a few inches. It takes more force than it should, but we separate just enough for me to slip around him and toward the door.

"I'm not lying," I say and reach for the lock. But I don't take more than two steps before he grabs my wrist and turns me so I'm pinned between him and the door.

And it feels like the Earth stops spinning.

There's still a centimeter of space between us, but I want it to disappear. Rowan's palms are flat on the door behind me as he leans in. His scent invades my nostrils, and it's overwhelmingly deep and rich, blurring the lines of what this is.

This is what I want. But he's not part of the plan.

He's my brother's best friend. But he's Rowan.

He moves a stray piece of hair from my face, dropping his voice and taunting me. "I think the only reason you're still fighting it is because you're scared."

He's right.

I *am* scared.

I stand there frozen, too stunned to protest his claims. My heart races, and I struggle to breathe, to think straight. But it's no use.

I'm scared of how this might ruin everything I've wanted. I'm afraid of what Nate would say. What Harper would say.

But I'm also scared of what might happen if I never get the opportunity to find out.

He's still right there, with his stupid blue eyes and kissable lips. They're so close. All I'd have to do is lean in.

"Now, Briar," Rowan whispers, cupping my face and gently tilting it up toward him. "Just tell me you don't want this. And I'll stop."

I can't.

I can't tell him that because it would be an absolute lie.

Because I don't want Cameron. And I don't want to keep comparing every man I meet to Rowan.

I just want him.

I want to give in and let him kiss me.

I open my mouth to do just that, but a pounding on the door startles me into silence.

"Hurry up! You're holding up the line!"

Rowan pulls back, unlocking the door with a satisfied smirk on his face as relief and regret settle into my stomach.

"Saved by the bell, Princess."

Twenty-Nine
Briar

My next three drinks go down much easier than the first. And much faster.

I left that bathroom with Rowan and have felt his eyes on me ever since. And if he's watching, then I'll put on a show. Everything Rowan does feels like a game, and I'm tired of it. It's time he realizes he's not the only one playing.

"Whoa, slow down there, Bri," Reece warns as I finish my fourth cup of whatever this punch is.

"I'm fine."

"Are you? Or do you want to tell me what happened between you going to get some water and right now? Because something had to happen to make you decide to drink the party out of booze," Reece says, taking my cup from my hands.

He levels me with a look that says he already knows what's sent me into a tailspin.

"Nothing happened," I repeat the lie I've been telling him for ten minutes. Though now, I'm questioning what happened—or if I imagined the whole thing. "I'm just annoyed with Cameron."

Reece quirks a brow in disbelief. "Bri."

"I'm fine! And honestly," I say, looking for an out. I spot the dance floor and point animatedly toward the living room. "I'm in the mood to dance."

"Dance?" he echoes, but before he can protest, I grab his hand and pull him into the crowd.

We push through the kitchen to the open living space, where people are half-dancing, half-grinding.

"Dance," I say again, laughing, but it's more of a demand. I need a distraction from the chaos in my brain. From Rowan.

And this is as good a distraction as any.

Because Reece has no rhythm. Absolutely none.

A toddler bouncing around has more rhythm than Reece.

But that doesn't stop him. He's in the middle of this crowded room, inventing moves that mostly consist of flailing his arms, like no one is watching.

"What on earth are you doing?" I ask, fighting to get the words out between laughs.

"I'm dancing," he replies, grabbing my hand and twirling me in a circle. "You wanted to dance. So I'm dancing."

And just like that, I'm smiling like an idiot. He's got this knack for worming his way into your heart and making you happy whether you want to be or not.

And I love him for that.

So I join in, nodding encouragingly as he keeps trying to find some rhythm. As we dance, I move closer until his hands find my waist. I let him pull me into his chest, and he lets me lead.

I swing my hips back and forth, but Reece's eyes stay locked on me.

"Are you using me as some kind of surrogate because Cameron's not here?"

"Maybe." It's not Cameron I'm trying to forget. "Do you want me to stop?"

Reece pulls me closer, an amused smirk tugging at his lips. "Nah, that's okay." He spins me again, and this time, I catch Rowan standing across the room.

Game on.

I have to stifle a laugh at how angry he looks.

"What's so funny?" Reece asks, his brows lifting.

"Nothing."

It's not nothing—it's Rowan. He's leaning against the wall, arms crossed. One of the girls from earlier is chattering beside him, but his eyes are glued to me. And judging by the scowl on his face, watching me dance with Reece is driving him insane.

Which is exactly what I wanted.

I keep a little space between Reece and me as I sway to the beat. I push my hair back and glance at Rowan, making sure he sees. Reece moves closer behind me, and I lean into him. I can feel his heartbeat against my shoulder, which only makes me laugh again.

"Oh, Cameron will not be happy with you," Reece whispers.

It's not Cameron I'm worried about.

It's Rowan.

It's always been Rowan. And Rowan's jaw tightens as I keep dancing.

"And I don't care."

I smile directly at Rowan, then turn to face Reece again. We dance, looser than before, and Reece pulls me closer. And I let him.

I don't stop him when he leads me deeper into the writhing crowd on the dance floor.

I don't stop him when his fingers press slightly into my waist.

And I don't stop him when his eyes flick down to my lips as he leans in.

"That's enough," a voice growls behind me. "Time to go home."

I turn to find Rowan looking infinitely more pissed than he was seconds ago.

"I don't want to leave. I'm having fun." I square my shoulders, but he doesn't flinch.

"No. Bri. We're leaving," Rowan repeats, voice sharp. "Now."

"Or what?"

He narrows his eyes at me, making my heart stutter. We both know he won't actually do anything. But I wish he would.

Reece is still behind me, his hand resting on my lower back, letting me know he's there. It's comforting, and I want to lean back into him. I don't, but I want to.

Rowan takes a few slow breaths, his chest rising and falling. "It's time to go," he says more quietly now. He's calmer. But it's only on the surface. I can still see the war in his eyes as he glares at Reece.

"She's not a dog. You can't order her around," Reece snaps.

Rowan's reply is quick and clipped. "She can speak for herself." His eyes find mine again, softening. Pleading. That familiar flutter wakes in my stomach, and I know I'd do anything he asked.

"Fine. We can go. But I have to say goodbye to my friends first."

Rowan does his best to keep his stone-faced expression, but I see the tiny signs of victory. The barely-there smirk. The light in his eyes. The way his shoulders ease. It's the slightest change that happens in a blink. But I catch every detail.

"Fine," Rowan agrees, and behind me, I hear Reece's sad sigh. I turn to find a sad smile to match.

"Come on," I say, tugging Reece's hand. "Help me find Zara, Kian, and Harper before I go."

Reece doesn't argue as we head out into the yard. We don't go far before we hear Zara's unmistakable laugh. It's warm, earthy, and contagious. Just like Reece's.

"There they are," Reece says, pointing toward the pool.

I nod along and follow him down the stairs. Rowan keeps his distance from us as we move through the crowd, but he's never too far out of sight. He hovers on the periphery of my vision, like how he lives in the periphery of my mind.

Reece and I make it halfway to the group before Kian finds us.

"Friends!" Kian yells and throws his hands in the air. He grips a can in each hand, and his tousled hair suggests someone's hands were just in it. I smile at Harper before hearing Kian call my name. As soon as my eyes meet his, his gaze flits to the pool, lifting a brow in a silent question.

I nod, and like an excited golden retriever, he drops his drinks and tackles Harper into the water.

The crowd freezes, stunned, then they lose their minds as Zara jumps in after them. It's not long until the pool is half filled with rowdy partygoers and their spilled drinks. Kian splashes around as Harper swims to the edge and spots me.

She knows instantly. "That was your idea," she shouts, smiling and pointing at me.

"Briar, don't you dare even think about it," I hear Rowan threaten.

But it's too late.

I glance at Reece with a mischievous smirk before he grabs my hand, and we take off running.

The water is colder than I expected for mid-summer, but it's too late to change anything now. Coming up for air, I wipe the water from my face and see Rowan pacing the pool's edge.

"Come on in, Rowan. The water's fine," I taunt him, knowing he'll never jump.

He drags his hand down his face, looking pained as he watches me swim. "Briar, get out of the pool. Right. Now," he grits out between clenched teeth.

"You'll have to come get me," I laugh, kicking away from the edge as I float on my back.

He hesitates, and he considers jumping in for a split second, and my heart stops. If he jumps in to get me, he'll have me. In every sense of the word, I'll be his. There won't be anything that can stop me from being his.

But he doesn't. He doesn't jump. He doesn't say anything else. He just walks away.

Rowan leaves me in the pool, and it takes everything in me not to shatter. He left me here to drown in what I started. He let me open that door, and now he's walking away.

Before I can let myself sink too far into this disappointment, I wade over to my friends, who look like they're having the time of their lives.

But I'm drowning in regret.

I should have kissed Rowan when he gave me the chance.

I should have left with Rowan when he gave me the chance.

Instead, I ruined my shot.

The tears start to fall before I can stop them. Then come the sobs. Ugly, body-wracking sobs.

"Oh my gosh. Bri, are you okay? Did you hit your head?" Harper asks, rushing over to me.

"I'm fine." I can barely get the words out between tears. I don't want to cry, but I can't figure out how to get the tears to stop.

"Collins," a rough voice calls out to Reece, and I turn to look at him. At Rowan. "Get her out of the pool."

"She's… fine," Reece tries to say, but there's hesitation in his voice.

"She's fine?" Rowan repeats, biting humor in his words. "She's soaking wet, and she's crying. It's clearly time for her to leave. Just let me get her home."

My chest heaves again.

Because he came back.

It might just be because he promised Nate that he'd get me home. But he came back.

"Hey," Reece's voice is soft. "Maybe you should head home and get some rest."

I nod and let Reece lead me out of the pool. Rowan stands waiting for me with a towel in his hands. He doesn't hesitate to wrap it around my body, and I hate how it brings me more comfort than it should.

I'm here, soaking wet and crying over him. Pool water saturates every piece of my clothing, and I'll reek of chlorine for the next week. But Rowan doesn't seem to notice any of that. At least, if he does, he doesn't let on. He just gives me that soft smile that makes me think everything will be okay.

As he leads me through the backyard, embarrassment crawls over me. My cheeks turn a deep shade of red as every pair of eyes follows us. Again.

I keep my head down as we go, hoping to spare myself the further embarrassment of seeing the pity on people's faces.

We find Rowan's car exactly where we left it an hour ago, parked a few streets over. Before I can open the door, Rowan leans against it and studies me. He looks equally worried and scared.

"Briar. Are you okay?" His voice is low.

I wipe away my remaining tears with my hand and nod. I can't do anything other than that. I'm too scared to speak, or the truth might come out.

Rowan looks at me like he doesn't believe me. And I don't blame him. I wouldn't even believe me.

"Briar," he says again, his voice breaking.

"I just want to go home," I say, but I can't quite get the words out right. Everything feels slow and fast all at once.

"What?" Rowan scrunches his eyebrows and leans in to look at me.

"Home," I repeat, and lean into the car for support to stay standing.

Rowan doesn't say a word as he opens my door. But he doesn't need to. I can see the worry and fear painted across his features as he watches me struggle to get into the seat.

He doesn't try to talk to me on the way home, so we ride in an odd silence. I don't know if he doesn't know what to say or doesn't want to speak to me.

After tonight, I wouldn't blame him either way. I want to explain why I was crying, but nothing I come up with sounds even remotely reasonable.

So I don't. I let us sit in the silence while I stay a crying, wet mess.

He pulls onto a familiar street, and his house comes into view.

"I thought you were taking me home."

Rowan backs into his driveway and parks the car in his usual spot. All the way forward, but not in the garage. Never in the garage.

He's out of his seat and rounding the car before I can get my seatbelt off. Rowan opens the door for me and extends a hand to help me.

"I would take you home, but you're drenched and smell like a distillery. I'll call Nate to come get you in the morning."

My pulse quickens with shame, and how he's still taking care of me when I don't deserve it.

"I'm not drunk," I mumble, then stumble into Rowan's arms.

"No?" He's got that annoyingly perfect smirk on his face as he holds me. I give him a death glare that makes him chuckle as he helps me into the house.

"This is your fault," I grumble, trying to shake him off.

"Oh, my fault?" He sounds genuinely surprised and amused. Like watching me struggle is funny to him. But he never let's go.

He keeps a firm hold on me all the way up the stairs, into the house, and up to his room.

His room isn't as messy as I expected it to be. There are a few piles of clothes on the floor, but otherwise, everything looks to be in place. The walls are plain aside from a dozen or so trophies lining his shelves. He made his bed, and the whole room smells like cedar and something smoky. It's clean. Like maybe he was expecting someone.

Rowan goes to his dresser, pulls out a faded blue shirt, and hands it to me. With how soft it is, it's clearly a favorite.

"You can sleep in this."

His voice is gentle as he backs up toward his door, "You can change, and I'll get you something to drink."

I glance over my shoulder and see the door to his bathroom cracked, and when I look back, Rowan's gone.

I stand there, looking like an idiot, clutching the towel in one hand and his shirt in the other. It takes a few seconds for me to get my feet to move, but when they do, I slip out of my clothes, grateful for something dry to wear.

I'm changed in a flash, then I crawl into Rowan's bed as quickly as possible. It smells like him, and I sink into his sheets. The warmth of everything makes it hard to keep my eyes open, but I fight it, waiting for Rowan. Like always.

He knocks lightly before cracking the door, and a smile spreads across his face as he sees me in bed.

"Comfortable?"

"I'm sleepy," I whisper, pulling the covers up to my chin. He tries to hide his amusement as he places a glass of water and some Tylenol on the table beside me.

"You'll need these in the morning," he says, moving back to his side of the bed. He pulls his phone from his pocket and plugs it in before turning to leave.

"Wait," I call after him. He pauses, looking at me expectantly. "Will you stay with me?" I don't mean to sound so desperate, but I can't help it anymore.

Rowan shakes his head. "I don't think that's a good idea, Briar."

He's right. It's not a good idea. But I don't care anymore.

"Please." It's nothing more than a whisper, but he sucks in a long breath. He glances at me quickly, and I see the turmoil in his eyes. "Please, Rowan."

He nods softly and switches off the lights, plunging us into darkness.

As he gets in, the bed dips beside me, and I roll over to face him.

"Thank you," I say, knowing this might be the last time I get to be near him like this. "And I'm sorry for tonight."

"You have nothing to be sorry for. I'd be there for you any day," he replies, but it's just as soft.

Thirty
Briar

World War Three may have started with how my head hurts. My body is sore, and everything feels heavy. I don't know who I thought I was last night, but this version of me is the one left to pay the price.

I groan, trying to stretch my aching body, but freeze when I hear a quiet rustling beside me. My eyes shoot open, and there's Rowan pulling a shirt over his head. My head spins as I watch him move, trying to piece everything together from the night before.

Because I shouldn't be here right now.

Of everyone I could have gone home with, Rowan didn't need to be a contender—let alone the winner. And the worst part is, I don't even remember hooking up with him.

"Oh, good. You're awake," he says, looking slightly surprised, flashing that smile.

I sit up and realize I'm wearing nothing but a T-shirt.

His T-shirt.

I suck in a breath and brace myself. "Did we…?" I can't bring myself to say the words out loud, but I need confirmation.

"No." He laughs. *He laughs.* Rowan thinks the whole thing is funny. "Nate left the party and asked me to take you home. But when it was time to go, you were too drunk, so you stayed here."

Part of me is glad to know that even in my drunken state, I didn't give in to the thoughts that have plagued my mind for weeks. But part of me hates that I wish something had happened. Wished that he had at least kissed me.

My cheeks heat at the thought, so much so that I can't look at Rowan.

"What do you remember from last night?" he asks, moving across his room.

I let my eyes follow him, trying to sort through the blur of the night. I remember most of it, and it's mostly embarrassing. The conversation in the bathroom and then my meltdown in the pool. It's too much for me to think about.

"Uh, not much," I lie. "I do remember dancing and vaguely remember jumping in the pool." I want to bury my face in my hands. Lying to Rowan is beyond mortifying. Because I can't tell him that I remember everything. And I know I'm not ready for the conversation we'd have to have afterward.

"There's some Tylenol on the nightstand," he says, clearing his throat and pointing to two little pills.

Rowan watches me intently as I take them, and his jaw tightens as I leave the bed. There's something oddly intimate about being in his shirt and his bed. And the way he's looking at me, it's like he feels it too. Or maybe I'm imagining things.

He checks his watch and sighs. "I have to head out, but Nate said he would pick you up. I dried your clothes after the pool," he smirks. "They're over on the chair. And your phone's plugged in on my nightstand, so don't forget that."

I nod and glance over at the chair pushed into the corner. My clothes are folded—not well, but folded. And my phone. It's resting on his nightstand, fully charged.

"Help yourself to anything downstairs. You know where everything is," he says, and an awkward silence stretches between us. "Okay. Well, I'll see you around."

Without another word, he slips into the hallway, and once again, I'm alone in his room. I can't help but wonder if this is how he treats every girl who spends the night; folding their clothes and giving them free rein of the house before he leaves.

A flash of jealousy crashes through me as I wonder how many girls have stayed the night this summer. Or even just this week.

I slip on my shorts, ready to leave. I don't want to stay in this room, where who knows how many others have been. The thought alone is enough to make my stomach churn.

I unplug my phone and see a few missed calls from my mom. I furrow my brow, wondering what she'd be calling about. No texts. No voicemails. And before I can think more about it, a loud honk sounds outside Rowan's window.

Now I have to face my brother as he picks me up from his best friend's house.

I sneak through the house, and just as I expected, Nate's car is in the driveway. I get in as quickly as possible, ignoring his suspicious stare.

"Hello, Nathaniel."

"Are you wearing Rowan's shirt?"

I laugh nervously. "Yeah." I try to be nonchalant, but my voice shakes. Even I would think something happened.

"Why?" Nate turns fully toward me, his tone more accusatory now.

"My clothes were wet." It sounds more like a question than an explanation, and there's disbelief written across every feature of Nate's face. I hold my now-dry shirt as proof, but I don't get time to add anything else before someone shouts from the backseat.

"Surprise!" I nearly jump out of my skin before recognizing the English beauty smiling at me.

"Faye?"

I blink a few times to make sure my mind isn't playing tricks on me. But no, my best friend is really here.

"Surprise," she repeats at a much more reasonable volume.

"What are you doing here?" I ask, jumping into the back seat for a hug.

"I wanted to come see where you're from," she laughs, eyeing my appearance. "I can't believe I had to ride along to pick you up from a hookup's house this morning. The Briar I know would never be so bad."

"That is not what this is," I correct quickly. I can't let Nate think anything happened with Rowan. And to be fair, nothing did happen. But the way Nate meets my eyes in the rearview mirror says he isn't convinced.

"What happened, or what I was told, is that I was a menace last night and was forcibly removed from a pool party."

"That wasn't a pool party," Nate says.

"It turned into one," I laugh. "Hence my wet clothes."

"Briar! That's my flat mate, the party animal!" Faye exclaims, smacking my shoulder playfully.

But if anyone is a party animal, it's Faye. She can dance for hours without breaking a sweat. Her energy is unreal.

"Yeah, Rowan told me this morning you were a real handful last night, B," Nate chuckles. "He mentioned he carried you out, but I thought he was kidding."

My heart drops at the mention of Nate and Rowan catching up on last night's events, and Faye must notice, considering how quickly she pivots.

"Clearly, we have so much to catch up on. Who knew so much could happen when we're apart?"

And that's exactly what we do. Within minutes of being home, we're poolside, talking each other's ears off.

"First things first," Faye says, popping a berry into her mouth. "I'm so glad we get to keep living together next year. My mom lost it because I refused to find a new flat mate."

I don't know if I'm still drunk, if she's not making any sense, or if she's just speaking another language at this point. She does know three.

I blink at her. "What?"

"Your mum didn't call?"

"I missed a few calls but haven't called her back. Why? Did she convince them to drop the stupid allegations against me?"

"Well, no. But Kent and I broke up," she shrugs, tossing another berry in her mouth.

My brain stalls. "Why? And what does that have to do with us living together? Well… besides the obvious?"

"He was the 'reliable source' who reported you to the headmistress," Faye says seriously. "He was jealous when the final grades came in and found out you beat him for top of the class. So he went to Feller and lied."

It takes a second to sink in. "That little rat! I knew he wanted first, but I didn't think he'd stoop so low."

"Yeah, he's the worst," Faye agrees.

"I can't believe Kent would do that. I can't believe I'm going back. This is the best news I've had all month." I grin, my voice rising with excitement. In two short minutes, Faye has managed to set my life is finally back on track.

"Yes! It's us again next semester. Back to cause more trouble," she giggles, wiggling her brows.

"I'm sorry about Kent. I know you liked him," I tell her with a sad smile."

"Oh, don't worry about me! I'm glad I had a reason to dump him. He wasn't great in bed anyway."

Her bluntness sends me into a fit of giggles. "In that case, I officially hate him," I say.

I lie back on the lounger and let the midday sun warm my skin. A huge weight lifts off my shoulders. Now, I can enjoy a fun summer with my best friends.

"I missed you," I admit softly, feeling the relief flood my body.

"I missed you, too. Who knew a few weeks could feel like ages?" she whines. "But I'd love to know what you've been up to. Looks like you've been busy. And for the record, I didn't buy any of that explanation you gave your brother in the car."

I scoff. "Everything I said was technically true."

"Technically true and conveniently vague. Spill it," Faye says, smirking.

"Nothing's going on, but there are a few guys I'm interested in…"

"I knew it!" Faye squeals, standing. "Details. Now."

I roll my eyes at her enthusiasm. "Like what? None of them is *that* interesting." I know what she wants to hear, but thinking about everything, truthfully, there isn't that much to share.

"Their names?"

"Well, there's this guy I met named Cameron. He was so charming, an absolute dream—" I begin.

"Hold on." She holds up a finger. "Was?"

"I meant he is," I correct, but even I hear the doubt in my voice. Even though he's done nothing wrong, there's just a bitter taste in my mouth after the party. And it just feels like the novelty has worn off.

"No. What changed?"

I sigh. "I don't know." But that's not entirely true. The way he was just gone and didn't so much as think to text me, that feels off.

Faye raises a brow, waiting. As much as I love her, I hate that she knows when I'm holding something back. Her sixth sense is annoying.

"Honestly, something just feels off, and I can't place it. He just leaves me unsettled more than anything these days."

"Bri, in all the time I've known you, your instincts have been solid. If it doesn't feel right, it's probably not."

We fall silent, and I'm forced to sit with my thoughts. And I'm slowly realizing that nothing about Cameron gives me the warm, fuzzy feeling I had when I first met him. Something happened last night, and I don't like it. He doesn't feel safe. It doesn't feel right.

"Tell me about this other guy!" Faye prompts.

I suck in a breath. "Technically, there are two more," I admit with a small smile before rushing to finish my thought. "But neither is particularly developed, just little crushes."

"I don't care how exciting you think it is. Friend code says you have to tell me. Best friend code says you have to tell me *everything*."

"Fine," I say. "One is in my little friend group, and the other isn't even worth mentioning."

Faye gives me a stern look. "Names."

I curse under my breath. Faye is persistent in the name of gossip. Given her tenacity, she'd be a great agent for the FBI or MI6.

"Reece. He's my friend, and absolutely adorable, but probably just a friend."

"We can work with that." She gives me a mischievous smile. "And boy number three?"

"Not going to happen, Sweet Pea," I shake my head and give her that sickeningly sweet sing-song voice she hates.

Faye sends me her death stare. "Just his name, that's all I'm asking for."

"He's off-limits. I don't even let myself think about it, so I definitely shouldn't talk about it and let you convince me it's worthwhile."

"How can a name be off-limits to your best friend?" she asks, brow quirked.

"It's Peter. And I'm choosing to ignore him, so maybe he'll go away."

"His name is *not* Peter," she rolls her eyes. "And babe, you know that's not how it works. But feel free to keep lying to yourself," she teases before lying back down.

And as much as I hate to admit it, she's right. It's not how it works.

But I'm still hoping. Just this once.

Because I know that if I fall for Rowan and he doesn't catch me, I won't survive the landing.

It won't just break my heart, he'll ruin every piece of it.

Thirty-One
Briar

Faye has never been on a speedboat before. I doubt she ever will again, at least not if Kian's driving. And I don't blame her.

We arrive back at Harper's family's dock, and Faye is out of the boat faster than I've ever seen her move.

"Thank every god that we're back on solid land!" she cries, pointing at Kian. "If it were up to me, you'd still be on your L's."

"My what? Elles?" Kian asks, laughing at the drama.

"Your L plate. It's like your learner's permit. She's calling you a bad driver," I explain, stifling my laughter.

"You'll get used to it," Harper assures Faye, ushering us toward her backyard.

The sun is setting, and the fire pit is prepped for an evening of carousing. We all fall into the cushioned couches around it while Kian and Reece stretch out in the pastel Adirondack chairs Harper begged her parents to buy when we were eight.

From their spot, I hear Reece laugh. "Looks like I have two reasons to visit London," he says, nudging Kian. He catches my eye and winks, completely unbothered by the fact that I was eavesdropping on their conversation. And knowing Reece, he's probably kidding because that boy isn't capable of being a player. He's too sweet.

Harper throws him a playful scowl and turns to Faye. "So, Faye, you live in London?"

My friends have been interrogating her all afternoon, but Faye doesn't seem to mind. I actually think she loves it.

"I live near the university with this one," she laughs, gesturing at me. "But yes, I've lived in London my whole life."

"That's amazing. What's it like?" Zara asks, starry-eyed.

"It's a lot like New York," Faye replies. "Just older. More chaotic. Fewer skyscrapers, more historic buildings. And walking is our way of life."

"Oh, but the streets are less organized. Like someone spilled a bowl of spaghetti and used it to create the layout," I point out.

"Hey!" Faye laughs, swatting my arm. "Our streets are wonderful!"

"Wonderful and confusing," I tease, and we all chuckle. "But they are beautiful."

Faye rolls her eyes. "So, are you all from New York, then?"

"Heck no. Just these two," Kian says, gesturing to Harper and me. "Reece and I moved up here from Georgia. Our families came a few years back when Reece's dad moved his business."

"And me," Zara adds, raising her hand.

"Yeah, Z moved here about five years ago," Reece says. "Her parents kept telling mine how great it was, and eventually, my dad caved. Wanted to be closer to his brother, I guess."

My eyes widen. This is new.

"Stepbrother," Zara clarifies. "We're barely related. I have to remind him of that often."

"You're related?" I ask, stunned. My mind races, trying to figure out how I missed that.

"Barely. I forget myself, honestly. But his dad and mine," Zara intertwines two fingers, "Like this. Always have been."

"Yeah, but you don't sound Southern," Faye says, face screwed up in confusion.

"Yes! Finally, someone who gets it!" Harper exclaims and nearly jumps out of her seat. "That's what I said when I met them. I expected movie-style 'yes, ma'am' and 'y'all' and that little twang."

Laughter bubbles through the group as Reece and Kian begin the most dramatic southern accents I've heard in my entire life, but I'm distracted as my phone vibrates in my pocket.

I'm still giggling as I check who's calling, but that's all it takes for my smile to fade.

Cameron.

"I-I'll be back," I say, standing and walking toward the deck stairs. The light from the fire pit fades out around me as I sit in the darkness and answer the phone.

"Hello?"

"Do you have anything you want to tell me?" Cameron's voice is sharp. Aggressive. So much so that I rear back.

"Who do you think you're talking to?"

"Briar. Stop playing dumb." He laughs, but it's humorless. I blink a few times, questioning if he's playing some kind of weird joke because there's no way he's actually speaking to me like that.

"I don't know what's wrong, but—"

"Oh, you don't know what's wrong? Cute. I know what happened at the party," he spits. The anger in his voice makes me pause, and I actually have to question if what I did with Rowan was wrong.

But then again, how does he even know?

I feel my pulse quicken, and I swallow down the fear that I can feel creeping in.

"You're dancing with other guys and jumping into pools like a lunatic. Do you have anything to say for yourself?"

I scoff, finally able to breathe, realizing he doesn't know. He doesn't know what *almost* happened. What I wish had happened.

"You mean the party you were too drunk to attend?"

"That's not the point, Briar," he nearly yells.

At this point, I really can't help but laugh. This guy had me completely fooled. "Then why don't you tell me what point you're trying to make, Cameron."

"I thought I was pretty clear. You're acting like trash. And that reflects badly on me."

I laugh in disbelief. He thinks I'm acting like trash? Maybe he should take a look in the mirror.

"You're out getting wasted and being carried out of parties—by Rowan, no less. Did you even think how that looks?"

His words bring a smile to my face. "Are you just mad about the fact that it was Rowan who carried me out?"

I know the answer, but I want to hear him admit that he's jealous. I want him to understand that he's acting like a seven-year-old who had his favorite toy taken from him.

I hear a few muffled profanities. "No. Are you crazy? Listen, Bri. You need to do better—"

"No, Cameron. I don't want a lecture on good behavior from you. You're clearly emotional, and this isn't productive. Why don't you just call me tomorrow?"

I hang up the phone, not giving him the opportunity to reply. He's becoming less and less appealing by the day. And he's not worth my time or energy.

I'm startled as I hear a slow clap begin from the porch.

"You handled that like a pro," I hear Rowan call down to me.

Of course.

I don't have the time or energy to deal with either of these boys.

I stand and head back toward the fire pit. "Don't you have someone else to annoy?"

"Only you, Princess."

I roll my eyes, and then my phone lights up again. Cameron. Again.

I send it to voicemail and reach the fire pit, slipping into a seat beside Zara. I feel Rowan's eyes on me from across the yard, but I refuse to give him the satisfaction of looking his way.

"What was that about?" Zara asks.

"Cameron called to lecture me about my behavior last night," I explain with a sarcastic edge to my voice. "He says my actions reflect poorly on him."

The girls all cringe like they've smelled something foul. And it's Cameron's shit attitude. "I know. I know," I say, hands raised.

I turn to Zara. "So—cousins?"

"More like half-cousins," she laughs. "But yeah."

"That's wild," I mumble, letting it sink in. But it makes sense. Their mannerisms. Their temperament. Their eyes. They have the same caramel-colored eyes. "That makes sense, but I wouldn't have guessed it."

"Most people think we're friends, or worse, dating," Zara says, feigning a gag.

"He's not all bad," I say.

"But he's not Rowan," she shoots back, just quiet enough that only I hear.

My cheeks flush, and I can't help but glance back up to the patio where Rowan still stands. I can only see the outline of him, but I'd know it's him without having to look twice. He's still leaning over the railing, drink in hand, and his gaze trained on me.

And she's right.

No one will ever be what Rowan is to me.

"Oh, come on, Bri. I see how you look at each other."

"No chance," I shake my head, forcing my eyes back to meet hers.

Her brows lift slightly. "No?"

"No. Believe me. I don't see him like that," I lie.

"Mm-hmm. Whatever helps you sleep," she teases, bumping my shoulder.

The others are still chatting, but I'm lost in thought, staring into the fire. Zara calling me out has me questioning everything. Is it ever going to not be Rowan? Or am I going to be forced to compare every man I ever meet to him? Because that's getting old.

I force a smile and glance back at my friend. "Anyways, how are you? You've been a bit MIA."

Zara sighs. "Yeah. Things have been weird." Her shoulders slump, and she looks about as off as I feel.

"What's wrong?" I ask, worried I've said something wrong.

"Money's tight at the diner. I've been missing out," she admits. "I've had to work more since my mom won't accept any help." Zara seems to struggle to get the words out, and I just want to squeeze her and tell her everything will be fine.

"Reece's dad has offered to help us, but my mom is too proud to let him. She's scared of failing."

"I'm sorry, Zara," I say, resting my head on her shoulder. "Is there anything I can do?"

"Not really. I appreciate the offer, but it's not all that bad. I'm just sad to be missing out, and it doesn't feel like I fit in with the rest of you... " Her voice drops off.

"What do you mean?"

"No flashy car, clothes, or giant house," she says, nodding toward Harper's house.

I crack a smile, knowing exactly what she means. Harper's house has four unoccupied bedrooms. The Callahan's have more money than they know what to do with. That's how most families are out here, and it's something I've never been blind to.

"If it makes you feel any better, I think you're too cool to fit in." Zara chuckles. "And besides, I wish I had the kind of style you have. I swear, anything looks good on you. I pretty sure you could wear my sixth-grade gym clothes and make them look like high fashion. It's those cheekbones," I laugh, gesturing to her insane bone structure. "And I wouldn't want you to be any other way."

"Thanks, Bri," she whispers, laying her head on mine.

"And just for the record, I'm not allowed to drive a car. In the States or in the UK. I failed both tests three times."

Zara bursts into laughter, barely able to get the words out between breaths, drawing attention from the group. "How do you fail three times?"

"It's not like I hit anything… hard." My explanation does nothing to quiet her fit of laughter. It only makes it worse, to the point where Zara is nearly keeled over and grabbing her sides.

"What?" Kian asks.

"Bri needs her L's too," she cackles, and Faye joins in instantly.

Kian and Reece give me bewildered looks.

"I'm as bad a driver as you," I tell Kian and a smug smile spreads across his face.

"Faye, got any other fun stories about Bri in London? Or just anything in general you feel you should share with the class?" Reece asks, giving me a heart-stoppingly wicked smile.

"Oh, she's a horrible influence," Faye jokes, and my jaw drops at her accusation.

"I am not! You're the one who dragged us to Prague, where we both lost our phones." I give her a pointed look, and then we both laugh.

"You lost your phones?" Harper half-laughs.

"They were stolen," Faye whispers, air-quoting. She tilts her head, thinking. "But I really can't think of anything crazy."

The group sits silently for a minute as Faye and I look at one another, trying desperately to come up with anything remotely fun that might be worth sharing. It's hard to remember anything with everything that's gone on recently.

"Oh, I know!" Faye lights up. "We used to double-date but never told the guys until they showed up."

I laugh at the memory. Those dates were always chaotic but fun, for us, at least. I can't speak for the unsuspecting men who were our victims. *Dates*. Not victims.

Laughter erupts.

"You did what?" Zara and Reece ask together.

"We would choose a day, time, and meeting place. Then we'd find a man to accompany us," Faye explains. "Sometimes, we'd tell them as soon as we met up that it was a double date, and other times, we'd just pretend to run into the other person."

Everyone looks at us slack-jawed.

"Diabolical," Harper says, shaking her head.

"What can I say? Faye's a bad influence."

I don't get the chance to regale the group with any other stories about Faye making poor choices before she launches into a story about sneaking into a West End show.

The group is laughing, but I'm too distracted by Rowan's silhouette, which still stands at the edge of the patio, watching me.

Our eyes lock. He's forty feet away, but it feels like only a few inches separate us.

It always feels like this with Rowan. Not even all the space in the world feels like enough to keep me away from him, not anymore. He's like gravity, pulling me in whether I want to or not. And that's what scares me the most.

Because I'm tired of fighting it, and I don't know how much fight I have left.

I break our gaze and fake a yawn. "It's getting late, guys, and Faye has an early flight in the morning."

She gives me a knowing look but doesn't argue. We say our goodbyes, and I feel Rowan's eyes on me the whole way out.

"He's boy number three, isn't he?" Faye whispers.

"Maybe," I admit, but my voice barely holds.

Because the truth is, he's more than that. He always has been.

I think some part of me has always known that he'd ruin me if I let him.

And I can't let that happen.

Thirty-Two
Briar

Less than forty-eight hours. That's all I get with my best friend. And that's all it took for her to pry the truth about Rowan out of me.

I sit on the bed as she pouts and packs her bag. "Do you have to go?" I already know the answer, but I ask anyway.

"I told you. My dad was only in town for a business meeting. I don't have much of a choice." Faye looks just as sad as I feel.

I give her a Cheshire cat grin. "You could just abandon your family and live with mine. I'll make sure you get back to London in time for the new semester."

"Ah, yes, I'll start a whole new life here with you," she laughs. "You'll see me in less than two months. And besides, they say distance makes the heart grow longer."

"Fonder," I correct her.

"It's longer. Like... a longer distance," she says, tilting her head.

"No, Faye. It's *fonder*. Like you miss me when I'm not around."

"Well, of course I do. You're my partner in crime."

"That's what it means..." I sigh.

Faye loves her sayings, but also loves to never quite get them right. One of her many quirks.

"Never mind. You and your long heart will miss me. But we still have a few precious hours. How do you want to spend them?"

"We could…" Faye pauses to think, but my phone rings before she can answer. I grimace at the screen.

Cameron.

It's the third time he's called today.

I stare at the phone while it rings and consider not answering the call at all. But I did tell him we could talk today. Faye's already shaking her head. I know I don't have much to say to him, and honestly, after the way he spoke to me last night, I'm not sure he deserves that chance. But against every fiber of my being, I answer.

"Hello."

"Hi, Bri." Cameron sounds remorseful. Hopeful. "How are you?"

"I'm fine." My voice is flat. Dull. I don't want to have this conversation right now. He should take the hint, but of course, he doesn't.

"Good. I'm glad. And I'm sorry. I shouldn't have said those things to you yesterday." There's a brief pause, and he sighs like the words are physically painful for him to say. "And you were right. I was just jealous, and I'm sorry."

I blink at Faye, silently asking her if she also heard him apologize just now, or if I'm hallucinating things. She just sits with her eyebrows raised in judgment.

"Bri? You there?"

"Uh, yeah. I'm still here. Uh, thank you for apologizing." It comes out like a question because I really don't know whether to believe him or not. I want to, but I have this sinking feeling in my stomach that I can't trust it.

"Yeah. Always. Despite our little argument, I'd love it if you'd let me take you out again. I swear I'll be on my best behavior."

He sounds more like he's pleading than asking, and I glance at Faye, who's still shaking her head. Her opinion of Cameron and his family is no secret. But despite everything, I can't fully convince myself he doesn't deserve one more chance.

"This is your last chance," I tell him.

"Absolutely," he agrees. "I know I messed up, but I promise I'll make it up to you, and it'll be a night you'll never forget."

I raise an eyebrow at Faye. Neither of us believes that, and the uneasiness is still there in my stomach.

Still, I don't hang up. Because a piece of me, albeit small, still *likes* him. And I want him to like me, too. I can't let one bad night get us off track.

"Tonight. You and me. Let's go to the drive-in. They're playing some of my favorite horror movies. Are you free around seven?"

I hate horror movies. More than anything. Well, maybe not more than *anything*, but it's a close second.

"Yeah. I'm free."

Cameron exhales with relief just as Faye groans in disgust.

"Perfect. Can't wait to see you."

"Yeah. I'll see you at seven." I hang up, and Faye gives me a look that could curdle milk.

"You're too easy on him, Bri." She doesn't even stop packing, which somehow makes her comment sting more.

"I know. But everyone deserves a second chance, right?"

"Not always. And not him." Her voice is flat, but her eyes are worried.

"What?"

She exhales and stares at me. "I'm worried about you. You seem… different."

"Different?" I scoff.

I'm exactly like I've always been. Maybe a little more forgiving. Maybe a little more distracted. But who wouldn't be with all this going on?

"I just have a lot on my mind. It's weird being home, under the same roof with both parents again," I admit. Which is true. School, the surgery, the weird tension between Mom and Dad—it's a lot. Honestly, my mom's leaving made things feel easier.

Faye studies me for several long seconds, then her shoulders drop.

"Okay. But if something's wrong, you know you can talk to me, right, Briar?"

I blink at the use of my full name. "I know, *Faye*."

She gives me a look like I'm a bird that's flown into a window. Like I'm broken. I steel myself, smile brightly, and change the subject because I hate that look. "Let's grab food before you leave."

She rolls her eyes but lets it go. "Fine. But only because I'm starving."

"Bless you," I grin, ushering her downstairs. I couldn't be happier to be out of that conversation and headed to the best sandwich shop in town.

Lucy's is a no-brainer. It's always been my favorite place. But lately, I think there's another reason I keep coming here, and it's not the food.

"So," Faye teases as we bike into town, "I know I said I'd drop it, but I have to ask a few things about boy number three."

I roll my eyes, but I can't deny the girl. She's my best friend, and she let me off earlier with the Cameron thing.

"What do you want to know?"

Her grin turns devious. "Why haven't you told Harper you're in love with her brother?"

I nearly fall off my bike.

I laugh, and I'm quick to correct her. "It's just a crush."

"Then why did Nate and I pick you up from a sleepover at his house?" Faye asks, slowing her pedaling.

"It wasn't my choice," I say, and it's true. It wasn't my choice. But I didn't mind it. Not one bit. "I told you. He took me home because Nate left with his girlfriend, and I was too drunk to get home by myself. You know my dad would've flipped if I'd come home alone that late."

"That's not what Nate told me." She gives me a knowing look. "But that *was* thoughtful of him."

"No. Nate asked him to. It's nothing special." I don't know who I'm trying to convince with that—Faye or me. But it's obvious that Faye doesn't believe it with how she's tilting her head and has that devil-may-care smile.

Even I don't believe that.

"Right," Faye says. "So, you're saying nothing fun happened?"

"Nothing fun," I repeat, though I remember how I *wanted* him to kiss me. How I *almost* let him. "He told me nothing happened, and I trust that."

"You trust him?" she asks gently.

"Yeah. Why wouldn't I? He's known me forever. And Nate would kill him if anything happened to me. So yes, I trust him."

"Then why are you working so hard to keep him at arm's length?"

I scoff. But the truth settles in.

She's right. She's always right.

If I don't let him get too close, he can't hurt me.

"I can't go there. He's Harper's brother. And having a boyfriend isn't part of my plan right now," I tell her. "I want to focus on my career and—"

"Yeah, yeah. Law school. Career. We've heard it all before. But what about what *you* want?" Faye presses. "You don't have to date him. It could just be a summer fling."

"I can't. Rowan's not the kind of guy you leave behind. And I don't think I *could* leave him."

Admitting that out loud doesn't help. If anything, it hurts more, like an anvil has been dropped on my chest.

"I need more distance from him. Especially after that party."

Faye beams. "So something *did* happen. I knew it!"

I laugh, this time genuinely. "Nothing happened," I say, unsure how to explain what did or didn't happen. I'm not even sure I know myself. "It almost did."

"What almost happened?"

I have one hundred percent of Faye's attention as we reach Lucy's and park the bikes.

"We almost kissed. I think," I admit, but the end of my sentence is drowned out by the sounds of Faye's excited cheering.

Faye gasps like a rom-com heroine. "Bri's in love!"

She's all but shouting, and I swear the entire town can hear her.

"My best friend is in love! Head over heels in love." Her voice continues to rise, and my cheeks flush. She's causing such a scene, but this is precisely how I knew she'd react.

Then she does the worst thing imaginable. She starts singing. "Bri and Rowan, sitting in a tree—"

"Shhh!" I slap a hand over her mouth. "If you don't stop, I'll poison your food."

"What a buzzkill," she mumbles into my hand.

"You ready to act like a normal person now?" I ask, a joking edge in my voice.

"Nope. But I'll stop saying you're in love. Starting… now." Faye starts walking toward the front door and tosses a smirk over her shoulder. "Peter, my ass."

I can't help but giggle as I follow her inside.

Then my stomach drops.

Rowan is here.

So is Nate.

And they're with two girls.

Faye gives me a cautious look, and my face must show every emotion I'm feeling. "We can leave, Bri."

I want to, but my feet feel like they're rooted to the spot. I know a date when I see one. And this looks like a date.

The girl looks so happy to be tucked into Rowan's side, and I can't blame her. That's exactly where I want to be. But I can't sit here and watch them without wanting to throw up.

"Let's just get it to go."

I force my feet toward the counter, hoping to keep a low profile and avoid being noticed. But just my luck, the universe has other plans.

"B!" Nate's voice carries across the restaurant just as my hands stop shaking. I swallow down every emotion and plaster a smile on my face, giving him a quick wave.

I avoid looking at Rowan, but my eyes betray me. He looks guilty. Busted. And it stings.

"B, come here for a sec," Nate says, beckoning me over.

I turn back to Faye, feeling nausea creep in. She watches me cautiously; all traces of our joking mood from two seconds ago are gone as she tries to assess what I might be thinking.

I swallow hard. "Can you order me the wrap?" There's no waver in my voice, and my muscles are tense as I try to force a calm facade.

"You want me to come with you?"

"I'm good," I lie. "I'm not special. Just proving it to myself."

I force a smile and head to their table. Each step closer feels like a stab to my chest, but I push forward and try not to think about the pretty brunette he just had his arm around.

The pretty brunette who's not Calista.

Rowan stands awkwardly as I approach, and even Nate looks confused. He glances around the table before sitting back down and staring at it.

"What's up, Nate?" I ask, opting to ignore the strange energy radiating from Rowan.

"Just wanted you to meet Melissa," he gestures to the familiar raven-haired girl beside him.

I smile at her, trying to hide my annoyance. Why now? I could have met her any other time.

But there's no reason to be mean to this girl. And there's no reason to look at Rowan, so I keep my eyes focused on Nate and Melissa.

I smile politely because this girl… she's not the enemy.

"Hey, Bri! It's so good to finally meet you! Nate talks about you constantly," Melissa gushes.

"You too! Nate said you're transferring to Columbia in the spring. Are you excited?"

She lights up. "So excited. Nate's going to show me around."

"He's a terrible tour guide, so I would recommend that you do your own research before you go," I joke.

"Rude." Nate feigns insult. "What are you and Faye up to?"

"We're just grabbing lunch before Faye leaves. We're meeting the gang at the beach for a picnic, and we're running a little late, so we'd better get going," I say, tossing my thumb over my shoulder. "But it was nice to meet you, Melissa."

"You too! Have fun today!"

Melissa is nice enough, but I don't have the energy to be nice anymore, especially not with Rowan so close. I want to run off and never see him again. But I don't. I keep up the happy illusion and walk back to Faye, pretending I'm fine.

"How was that?" She studies me and leans against the counter.

"Great," I say brightly, keeping the smile plastered across my face. "I'm going to wait outside if that's okay, so I can avoid strangling someone."

She frowns. "Of course. I'll be out soon."

"Thanks!" I say, my voice cracking so it sounds more like a squeal, before I turn toward the door.

The air outside is cooler, and I'm grateful to not feel so suffocated anymore. I start toward the bikes to collect myself, mumbling profanities under my breath.

Then I hear him.

"Briar."

I turn and Rowan's standing with his hands in his pockets, looking younger somehow.

"Can we talk for a second?"

"We're actually headed out. Can it wait?"

I say a silent prayer that it can wait. I don't want to do this, not here, and definitely not now.

"I'd rather not," he says, scratching the back of his neck. "It's about the party."

My stomach flips, and I have to remind myself not to go wide-eyed. "What about it?" I try to force an air of nonchalance into my tone. But with my luck, it probably sounds a lot more like desperation. Or worse, constipation.

"Don't you think we should talk about what happened, Bri?"

No.

Personally, I think we should bury it forever. At least, that's what I'll be doing for the foreseeable future. I roll my shoulders back, trying to mask any trace of embarrassment.

"Yeah, we should," I agree. "I wanted to apologize. I didn't mean to be such a handful. I'm sorry you had to deal with that."

He stands there, mouth agape for a second. "That's not what I'm talking about, Briar, and you know it."

I shrug, playing dumb and hoping he drops it.

"You've got to be kidding me," he mutters, running his fingers through his hair. "Just forget it."

He starts walking away, and the ache in my chest only gets stronger.

But I don't know why. This is what I wanted, right?

Then he turns around and comes storming back toward me. He doesn't stop until he's inches away, his eyes pleading. "Briar, please tell me you're joking. I can't go another day with you pretending like this."

I can't breathe.

I want to give in right now. But I can't. I keep everything hidden behind a wall and try to lock up my heart.

I can't admit what I'm sure we both know to be true because I can't handle the rejection right now.

"You don't remember," he whispers, eyes full of something that looks a lot like heartbreak. And that's when I feel the walls start to crack.

Because maybe he really does feel it too.

But I don't get the chance to find out before Faye comes into view. I clear my throat and take a step back from Rowan.

"We're friends, right?" I ask quietly, fighting to keep the longing out of my voice

Rowan stands there like he's debating what to do. Like he's questioning if he heard me right.

"I'll see you around," he says.

And just like that, he's gone.

I stand there, my turn to be frozen in the silence he leaves behind, pretending that the pain in my chest isn't new. The ache rushes in so fast, and suddenly I'm not sure if I'm heartbroken or just finally willing to accept the truth.

Because I wanted him to fight for me.

I wanted him to stay.

And now that he's gone, I don't even know who I'm more mad at—him or me.

Thirty-Three
Briar

Cameron pulls into the crowded drive-in. It's a sweet date, probably the best one for us after the Gala. We can sit in the dark and not talk, which might be exactly what Cameron needs if he wants a real shot with me. I'm still a little upset about everything he pulled that night, but he's back to his usual sweet self.

He's apologized, and I've forgiven him. But forgetting? That's harder.

Things are still awkward between us. So much so that we sat in silence for most of the drive. Even small talk feels hard now, which can't be a good sign.

"Do you watch a lot of horror movies?" I ask, trying to ease the tension. Cameron laughs while circling the lot for a spot.

"Yeah, definitely my most-watched category on Netflix," he says, pulling into a spot in the back row. We're nowhere near the other cars, and a pit forms in my stomach. I scan the lot. There are plenty of open spots closer to the screen, and it's hard to see from here.

My discomfort must be plain as day because Cameron gives me a small smile. "You don't like the spot?"

"Just thought we'd be closer… you know, to see the screen." I force a smile and try to put into words *why* I don't like the spot. But everything I think of just sounds paranoid.

"Trust me, baby. This is the best spot in the house." He says it with such confidence that it makes me think he's been here before. But I don't get a chance to question it before he's out of the car and setting up. He opens the trunk, folds the seats down, and arranges some blankets and pillows into a makeshift bed.

"Looks cozy," I hum, giving him a soft smile.

"I'm a little out of practice, but this will do," he says before helping me in and climbing in beside me. From his drawstring bag, he pulls out a mountain of candy: chocolates, sour sweets, hard candy. You name it, he's got it.

My eyes widen at the haul in front of me. He tunes the radio to the right station, and the opening soundtrack fills the car.

I hate horror movies. Always have. But they don't seem to bother Cameron. I cringe while he snacks through a gruesome torture scene. How he eats during this, I'll never understand. When the end credits finally roll, I'm horrified because he's unaffected.

"That's going to give me nightmares for a week," I mutter with a shiver. "If I'm ever held captive, I hope they kill me quickly."

"You're too pretty to kill," Cameron laughs and leans in to kiss me. It's fine. I'd just rather not be doing this, so I pull back.

"You're crazy, Bri," he murmurs before kissing me again. He pulls me into his lap with such force that I have to brace myself with my hands on his shoulders. He's doing all the right things, but I can't help but wish it wasn't him I was kissing.

And the only thing I can even think about right now is what it would be like to kiss Rowan like this.

Because I know it wouldn't be awkward like it is with Cameron. Rowan wouldn't push the limits. And it wouldn't just be… okay, I suspect.

Cameron's fingers trail along my arm, bringing me back to this moment when they stop at the hem of my tank top.

"What are you doing?" I ask, pulling back, my heart starting to race.

"Nothing," he says with a sly grin, pulling me back into the kiss. My stomach flips, but not in the butterflies kind of way. Before I can stop him, his hands slide under my shirt, and his fingers dig into my skin.

I pull away again. "Cameron, stop."

This time, I try to move off his lap, but he holds me firmly in place.

"Bri, I was just playing around. Come on," he whines. "Where are you going?"

He tries to pull me closer, back to him, but I'd rather be anywhere than here right now. His lips are on my neck, and I can feel the awkward tension growing. He's got one thing on his mind, and I want no part of it.

"I need to go to the bathroom before the next movie starts." The lie flies out of my mouth so fast I'm surprised he even understood what I said.

He eyes me but lets me go. "Don't be long," he calls after me as I rush out of the car.

I walk toward the bathroom and let out a frustrated sigh.

I enter the bathroom, duck into a stall, and exhale sharply. I didn't even realize how much panic had settled into my chest until now. I take deep breaths and try to ground myself.

I don't even remember why I thought he was worth a second chance, and if I'm honest, I think I'm still mad at him for what he said about my 'behavior' at the party.

I don't want Cameron, and I definitely don't want to be here.

I give myself a few more minutes, then move to the sink. My reflection stares back at me, disappointed.

And I don't blame her.

Before this summer, I wouldn't have settled for just any guy, and I won't start now.

"I'm done after tonight," I whisper.

Back at the Jeep, Cameron's on his phone. The opening credits of *Insidious 2* are playing. I don't want to sit through another movie, but I will if I have to.

I slide in, leaving a foot of space between us in the backseat bed setup. Cameron scoots closer and whispers an apology. I nod blankly, focusing on the screen.

He drapes his arm around my shoulder and pulls me into him as his other hand settles on my knee. I tense, realizing he doesn't notice, or doesn't care, that I don't want him touching me. And I hate that. Every muscle in my body is on high alert, and it's like he doesn't even register it.

Inhale. Hold. Exhale. Hold.

A jump scare makes me flinch, and Cameron snorts, pulling me closer.

"You're not scared, are you, Bri?" he whispers against my neck, trailing kisses down my shoulder.

I lean away from him and shift uncomfortably. Suddenly, this back seat is tiny, and there's nowhere to go that's far enough from this guy. It's my own horror movie.

"No, just an easy target for jump scares," I try to joke.

He grabs my face and tries to kiss me again.

"The movie," I say, pointing to the screen.

Cameron lets out a frustrated huff, looking at me like I've just slapped him.

"Why'd you even come with me, then?"

"What?" I blink.

"Bri. We're at a drive-in. Back row. Why do you think I wanted to come here?"

The truth burns worse than any flame ever could. He brought me here to hook up. That's all this was to him. Another notch on his bedpost. Without that, he's not interested in me. A sick feeling grows in my stomach, and I'm revolted.

"Wow," I breathe. "I thought… you know what? Never mind."

"No, Bri, that came out wrong. That's not what I meant."

He's trying to backpedal now… and failing. Because that's exactly what he meant. And we both know it.

"You know what, Cameron? I'm not feeling great. Can you take me home?"

The silence between us is loud as we pack up, and the drive back is just as awkward. My thoughts spiral because there were signs. I just didn't want to see them. I wanted to believe he liked me for me. I wanted him to be a distraction. I wanted him to prove I could be with someone who isn't Rowan.

But I'm such an idiot for not recognizing it sooner.

As soon as we pull into the driveway, I'm out of the car. I can't stand breathing the same air as him.

"Bri, come on," he begs, following me and grabbing my arm to stop me.

"Let go of me."

"I think we should talk," he says, his eyes pleading.

I glance at his hand on my elbow. "Let go." I don't have to shout. My tone is hard enough that he drops his hand.

"I'm sorry," he apologizes, stepping closer. "I think you might have taken what I said the wrong way."

I laugh bitterly. The more he talks, the angrier I get.

I don't mean to shout at him, but every ounce of frustration bubbles out of me. "You think I'm overreacting? You're insane if you think this is somehow my fault."

Silence falls between the two of us for a brief moment.

"Cameron, you're pathetic."

Cameron's lips set in a hard line, and I hear the front door open behind me, which can only mean one thing. Nate. I don't turn, but I know it's him.

"Bri, what's going on?" my brother asks.

"Please stay out of this," I plead, turning toward him. And there they are. Rowan and Darian behind him. Like Nate's little minions.

"Of course, the cavalry's here," I snap. "You're always here!"

I turn back to Cameron only because looking at him is easier than facing the others.

"You know what? Let's talk another time."

He pauses for a beat before shaking his head. "No. I'm done," Cameron says. "I heard the London party girl came back to New York and figured she'd be fun and easy. Boy, was I wrong."

His words land like a slap in the face. I knew what this was, but hearing it, especially in front of Nate and Rowan, breaks something in me.

"Why do you think I brought you to the drive-in?" he sneers.

I snort and shake my head, disgusted. I want to yell at him, say something that will make him feel just a fraction of the hurt and embarrassment that I feel. But before I can say anything, Nate is in front of him. He grabs Cameron, fists bunching his shirt with a look in his eyes I've never seen.

"The fuck did you just say about my sister?" Nate growls.

"Get off me, man!" Cameron shouts, shoving Nate, but he doesn't move.

I hold my breath. This is not good. It's a trainwreck in the making, angry and out of control. Yet I can't look away.

Nate slams my date against the car, and my eyes widen in shock as he does this a few more times. His fists clench tighter on Cameron's shirt, and he shows no signs of letting up.

I feel a gentle touch on my elbow as Rowan moves me closer to Darian before cautiously approaching Nate. The concern on Darian's face is enough to turn my blood to ice. I've never seen Nate like this, but something tells me the boys have.

I stand motionless, watching as Rowan tries to get through to my brother.

Nate slams Cameron again. "You keep my sister's name out of your fucking mouth. You got that, DuPont?" Nate shouts, punching him in the jaw.

There's blood pouring out of Cameron's nose, but Nate shows no sign of letting up.

"Nate, calm down, man," Rowan warns, grabbing Nate's shirt and pulling him back.

Cameron stumbles, wiping the blood from his mouth, glaring. Nate's chest heaves as he lets Rowan separate them. His eyes are filled with poison, and he's unrecognizable like this. But his eyes soften the second they turn to me. Everything stops as we both process what he's just done.

"My advice? Get in your car and leave," Rowan says to Cameron, but his words sound faint. "Don't come back. Or you'll deal with all three of us."

"Fuck all of you. You'll pay for this," Cameron shouts, spitting blood as he stands and points a broken finger at me. But he wastes no time getting back in his Jeep and hightailing it out of our driveway.

I watch his taillights disappear into the night, but his words twist in my gut. Everything in me knows that he meant that. He's not done with me.

The four of us stand in the dark driveway, everyone too afraid to speak. Nothing feels like the right thing to say. I keep my eyes on Nate. He's never lost it like that around me, but I'm not scared of him.

I'm scared for him.

I've struggled to understand the darkness I've carried for years, and I see it in him now. It's wrapping around him and suffocating him. It's anger. It's sorrow. And I know what it does to a person. It drives you to do stupid things just to feel something, and it is so easy to let that take over.

"Are you okay?" Nate whispers.

"I'm fine," I whisper back, reaching for his hand. "Come on. Let's get you some ice."

We turn toward the house, but Nate stops me.

"Be honest, B. Did he do anything? Because I swear—"

I don't doubt Nate's conviction, not after what he just did. But I stop him before he finishes the thought. "He's an ass, but nothing happened."

He doesn't seem convinced, but it's enough for now.

Inside, I grab an ice pack from the kitchen and gently place it on Nate's busted knuckles. The room is heavy with tension, and I can feel everyone's eyes on me.

"Bri, are you sure you're okay?" Darian asks, breaking the awkward silence.

"Yes, Darian. I'm fine." My voice is sharper now. "We had a disagreement. I was already done with him anyway."

Nate gives me a sad look. "We just want to make sure you're okay."

"I know, but I'm not a little girl anymore. I don't need you to hold my hand for everything. Stop treating me like I'm made of glass. I don't need to be wrapped in bubble wrap to keep me from breaking."

But it's too late. I've already broken.

I can feel the tears coming, and I don't want to let them see me cry. So, I run to the safety of my room, desperate to shut out everything, and everyone. I feel stupid. Everything's falling apart, and it's too much.

It's too much for me to handle on my own, and I just need everything to be quiet. Just once.

Without a second thought, I open my nightstand drawer and pull out the bottle of painkillers.

"Just one. It's been a long night."

The lie feels justified today, and I know it's what I need to make everything feel okay again.

So I open the bottle and let myself take one.

Thirty-Four
Rowan

"Bourbon, neat."

I don't need to tell the bartender my order; Juliana already knows. But it's a force of habit. And after last night, I need the drink. Watching Briar argue with that idiot who doesn't deserve her nearly made me sick. I'd do anything for her, and right now, I can't do a damn thing to make it better.

But I can't let myself think about her tonight. As much as I wish I could be with her instead of here, I can't.

I scan the upstairs lounge for my business partner, who's more like a child pretending to run a lemonade stand while I actually run the business. He puts on a good show but doesn't know half of what it takes to keep this club running. Keeping things stocked, getting our people paid, keeping it clean—it's like he thinks it's all magically done without us having to lift a finger.

"Here you are, Mr. Callahan," Juliana says, placing my drink on the bar top. I thank her quietly and move to the couch across the room. It's not as comfortable as the ones in the back rooms; it's just a wooden bench with a thin cushion, but it'll do for now.

I sit and wait for Kai, trying not to think about the girl who makes me stupid. She could ask me for anything, and I'd do it. And she has no clue.

Luckily, I'm not left alone with those thoughts for long. The lounge fills with a bachelorette party, a horde of barely legal girls who spent way too much money renting this place. They're decked out in themed costumes, throwing back tequila like it's water. And suddenly, I feel it.

That presence creeps in at the edge of my consciousness until she's everywhere. I see her in all of them. In the way they laugh, clutching each other for balance. In how they throw their heads back and sing off-key to whatever house track is playing.

There are pieces of her everywhere, and I've been collecting those things she thinks no one notices.

I take a slow sip and fight the urge to call her, like I do every time something reminds me of her. Like I do every time her brother catches me watching her.

Pulling my eyes away from the chaos, I finally spot Kai, who's just now decided to show up twenty minutes late.

As usual, he has a girl on his arm and looks completely unbothered that he's kept me waiting. He strolls over and drops onto the bench, scanning the lounge like it's his own personal buffet.

"Crowded tonight," he muses, skipping any introduction for his flavor of the night.

"Good for business," I say, lifting my glass. "We haven't been this busy in months."

"Ashton and his partner should be here soon," Kai adds like he's doing me a favor by passing along the intel.

I know already, but I nod anyway. After all, I'm the one who set the meeting with Ashton and am acutely aware of when he's planning to arrive.

"I want you to take the lead on this one. You've been on the sidelines long enough. Time to prove you're worth keeping around."

I scoff.

He wants me to take a more active role? I've been the one holding this place together since my dad left. Kai would've run it into the ground without me.

But I keep that to myself and agree with him. It's easier to let him think he's in charge. He causes fewer problems that way, and everyone already knows who really runs things. So I let him pretend as long as it doesn't get in the way of actual business.

"I got it," I assure him.

"Do you? Because this deal with Ashton… it's what takes us to the big leagues, kid." Kai challenges.

I take a breath to keep my temper in check. "Yeah, Kai. I got it."

"Okay. This is a big opportunity to expand into—"

"I know," I cut in, sharper than I meant to be. "I know what this is, and like I told you, I've got it."

Kai laughs because this is the reaction he wanted. "Damn. You need to get laid."

"Strictly business tonight," I say, steadying my voice though I know he's right. It's been weeks since I brought someone home, and I can't say it's from a lack of trying. Girls throw themselves at me all the time, but they're not *her*. "Not all of us mix business with pleasure."

I can't resist the jab. Kai laughs, knowing exactly what I'm referring to. There was a time when he used to take home any girl who worked here and demand that we fire them the next day.

Now, we pay a hundred-dollar bonus each week to any girl who doesn't sleep with him. Since then, his pool of options has dried up. He wasn't thrilled about having to find playthings elsewhere, but business comes first.

"There's always an exception," he says, waving down Juliana.

I roll my eyes and walk away. No matter how much he screws up, Kai never owns it. I cross the lounge to the DJ booth, needing space from his idiocy.

From here, I get a full view of the main floor. I let my eyes scan the crowd and spot a few regulars. Then I spot my sister and let out a frustrated sigh.

She's with her sorry excuse of a boyfriend and her friends, including Reece Collins. But no Briar. My jaw tightens just thinking about the stuff that idiot said to her last night. And seeing Reece's face pisses me off more than I can even put into words.

Without letting my eyes leave their little group, I call over one of our security guys.

"What can I do for you, Mr. Callahan?" Joe asks, all business.

"That group there," I say, pointing to my sister and her friends, "I want them gone."

I don't need to give him a reason, and he doesn't ask for one. "Yes, sir." He nods and disappears down the stairs.

Joe pushes through the crowd and starts ushering them out. They're pissed, but none of them fight it. I've kicked them out of the club dozens of times, so they had to at least expect it.

As they're leaving, Harper catches my eye. I give her a little wave and smirk as she's escorted out, with her underage friends in tow. Downing the rest of my drink, the empty glass is plucked from my hands by a passing bartender who gives me a little wink as she saunters off.

Shaking my head, I scan the crowd again, looking for any sign of Ashton or his little posse that follows him around like lost dogs. But I don't spot anyone from his team.

Instead, I find her.

Briar.

And my heart nearly leaps out of my chest.

Briar's the one I've been wanting to see all day, and now, like I've summoned her from the depths of my brain, she's here.

She's sitting at the bar in a short dress that makes it hard to breathe. She's beautiful—all legs and confidence. Like she doesn't have a care in the world.

I have to blink a few times to make sure it's her and that I haven't imagined her out of pure desperation.

But it's really her.

Seeing her, here in my bar, reignites that stupid protectiveness I've always felt for her. That instinctual need to make sure that she's taken care of, even if she won't admit that she needs it.

But she's not alone at the bar. Some regular is perched beside her, talking her ear off, and that jealous spark re-ignites like it did seeing her with Cameron at the Gala.

And just like that night I almost kissed her, I move on instinct. I need to be near her, but this time I don't intend to lie about it. This time, I won't blame Nate, pretending he's the reason I'm drawn to her. Pretending that the thought of her going home with anyone else, especially Reece, isn't nauseating.

Tonight, it's me and her, the way it's supposed to be. No lies, and no stupid half-truths.

I weave through the crowd and flag down a bartender a few feet from where she's sitting.

"Bourbon... and whatever she's having," I order, pointing at the girl I'd do anything for.

Thirty-Five
Briar

If there's one thing in life you need, it's a best friend like Harper. One word, Cameron, and she took the reins, planning a night out to get my mind off everything.

According to her, all I had to do was show up at her house and be ready for full glam. And, like always, a night out was exactly what I needed. Especially to help me forget about… well, everything. Including Rowan, Cameron, and Nate.

What I didn't need was to be separated from the group, all because I had to pee.

I insisted on going alone, which, in hindsight, wasn't the smartest choice. So now I'm stuck at the bar with some idiot rambling about his investments like that's supposed to impress me.

I sip from my glass and tug at the dress Harper insisted I wear. It's too short, but she promised it made my legs look good, so I let her dress me up like a Barbie. Though now, I regret it. I don't have long to stress about the shortness of my dress before someone clears their throat behind me.

"Thomas," a familiar voice says. I'd recognize it anywhere. "I appreciate you keeping her company, but I'll take it from here."

I roll my eyes as Rowan reaches out and shakes the man's hand. Thomas looks at me, baffled, but I shrug it off. He doesn't put up much of a fight but bolts with Rowan's dismissal.

I finish my drink, already preparing to track down my friends and get as far from Rowan as possible.

Last night was embarrassing enough. I don't need a repeat, and I surely don't need to relive it.

When I set my glass on the bar, it's not two seconds later before the bartender replaces it with a new one.

"I didn't order this," I tell her.

She smiles and nods toward Rowan. "He did."

"You," I say, forcing as much irritation into my voice as I can while turning to face him.

"What are you doing here?" His tone is sharp—and angry, for some reason.

"I'm here to enjoy myself, and you just scared away one of my prospects," I tease, pointing over my shoulder. I had zero intention of talking to what's-his-name, but Rowan doesn't need to know that.

"Why are you really here?" he asks, seeing right through me.

I clench my jaw. "I told you. I'm here to have fun."

"Briar, how did you even get in here? And what are you doing off by yourself?" His tone tightens, and this is quickly turning into a full-blown interrogation.

"Why do you care? I'm not a child. I don't have to explain everything I do."

Rowan chuckles, pointing over his shoulder. "Well, your friends just left. I mean, technically, they got kicked out for being underage, but... what's the difference?"

I stare at him, speechless. The smugness radiating from him makes me want to just scream.

"Briar, you shouldn't be here," he says, more somber now.

I scoff. "Yeah? Says who? You? Why don't you mind your own business and leave me alone?" This place has lost all appeal, and I'm ready to hightail it out of here.

"Bri, I'm sorry. Just wait." Rowan grabs my arm, stopping me.

"What? What do you want now?" I snap, surprising even myself. "I never know what to expect from you. One minute, you're pinning me to a door; the next, you're ruining my night out. You've robbed me of my sanity. What more do you want from me?"

His brow furrows as he pulls back just slightly. "You remember?"

I exhale. "Maybe I do. So what?" I throw up my hands in frustration. Even if everything he told me the other day was true, it wouldn't change anything. We're still stuck in the same push-and-pull we've been in all summer. "Just— never mind. I just want to go home and pretend like this never happened."

Rowan's grip slides down to my waist, pulling me into him. "No." His eyes search mine. "Please don't leave. We need to talk, but I've got some business to handle first."

I bark out a laugh. "Business? In a nightclub? What kind of business happens in a place like this?"

"Yes, Briar. Business in a nightclub. I do own the place, you know."

A wave of embarrassment hits me as Rowan's reminder lands. Because I had forgotten that this was his dad's club. The one we used to play hide-and-seek in when we were ten.

"Briar, please. Just stay."

"I-I can't," I say, stepping away. "I'm done playing your little game."

"This isn't a game," Rowan says, soft and desperate. "You're not a game to me."

His words hit me like a punch to the chest. That's what undoes me. He's chipped away at my defenses until there's nothing left. "And why should I stay?"

"Because I want you to."

Those five stupid words have every ounce of fight leaving my body. He wants me here. And it's enough to make me want to stay… because it's Rowan who's asking.

"I'll make sure you get home safely, but I want you to stay."

I huff a breath and search his face, looking for any sign that this might be just another move of his. But there's no hesitation, there's no reluctance. Just him looking at me like I've hung the moon.

"Okay." The word barely escapes my lips as my heart races. I've wanted to be close to him all summer, and now it's finally happening.

"And put this on," he says, shrugging off his jacket.

"Why?"

"Because I don't want anyone else looking at you when you're dressed like that."

There's a jealous edge to his voice that makes me not even question it as he holds his jacket open for me. I let it fall over my shoulders, and his scent envelops me. A part of me knows he's doing this to mark his territory, but I don't mind it. Because I think we both know that I'm his—whether he asks or not.

"Let's go," he says, placing a hand on my lower back to guide me through the crowd.

"Where are we going?"

"Over here," he says, pointing to a door guarded by security—the door we were never allowed through as kids. As we approach, the guard eyes me warily, and I instinctively move closer to Rowan, wishing I could sink into this jacket and disappear.

"Mr. Callahan," the bald man nods when he sees Rowan.

"Chris," Rowan says tightly, but I don't miss the warning in his tone. My eyes bounce between the pair while Chris takes his time opening the door for us.

"Have a good night, sir," Chris finally says, ushering us inside.

My eyes widen as we move down the dimly lit hall, taking in every inch of this forbidden section I've coveted for years. I glance at Rowan, hoping he'll offer some answers. But he doesn't.

He leads me down the corridor toward another door. My mind spins, trying to picture what Mr. Callahan kept back here. Maybe it's a cigar lounge, or a private office, or even a stock room with all the fancy bourbons he liked to collect.

But my stomach drops when I find out what's actually behind it.

A casino.

It's dim, but not as dark as the hallway we came from. And the smell. It's a strange mixture of sweat and smoke. There are a handful of slot machines and over twenty card tables dotted across the floor, and I can feel myself itching to sit at one.

I shouldn't be here, but I can't look away. I scan the crowd, hoping not to see any familiar faces. Luckily, I don't.

"Blackjack," Rowan whispers in my ear, making me jump.

I was so lost in this place that I nearly forgot he was beside me. His hand slides to my waist and draws me closer.

"Fun," I say, forcing a smile.

I know a blackjack table when I see one, and I've seen plenty of them. And have even been banned from enough casinos to know this setup well. Perfect memory and card counting? Not exactly welcomed skills.

"Do you play?" Rowan's question is entirely innocent, but I can't help the laugh that escapes me.

"No, not really."

There's a smug smile resting on his lips now that makes me feel a little guilty for misleading him. But it's true, I don't play. It's more like I cheat the system.

That is… until I get caught.

"I've got some clients at table fourteen," he says, pointing toward the center of the room, and I can feel the tension in my spine. The players there don't look like any competition, but I shouldn't be too quick to judge. I'm sure I don't look like I could take this place for all it's worth, but I could.

"Briar," Rowan lowers his voice, "I don't want you out of arm's reach. When I sit down, you're sitting with me, even if it's on my lap."

I nearly choke on his words. "Oh, on your lap?" I tease, but I don't actually mind the idea.

"Briar." His tone warns me. "I'm serious."

"Okay, okay." I raise my hands. "I won't cause any trouble. Promise."

"Thank you."

He exhales in relief, then gently guides me forward. We weave through the tables, and I study the dealers as we pass. They're slower than most I've seen, making them easier to read.

Rowan scans the area before sitting in the chair at the end of the table and pulls me down onto his lap in one fluid motion. I almost balk at the brazenness of his actions because I thought he was kidding about this seating arrangement, but apparently not.

His hand on my waist keeps me firmly in place, and I try to focus on the game to hide the blush on my cheeks. As much as I've wanted to be in this very spot all summer, now that I'm here, I can't help but feel a little out of my element. Even in a casino.

The group is in the middle of a hand. The dealer as he continues the game, his fingers moving quickly through the deck.

"You okay?" Rowan murmurs, tracing circles on my hip.

"Yeah. Just watching and learning." Another half-truth, but Rowan doesn't seem to catch on.

"It's easy," he says, quietly walking me through the basics.

I nod, listening intently, even though I already know the game inside and out. But it's nice to have him here, trying to include me. I keep my eyes on the table or on Rowan, and off the other men at this table who are not so subtly undressing me with their eyes.

Two of them, in particular, watch too closely.

They both look oddly out of place here. One has the brooding, tattooed look down to a science. The other looks like a nervous finance intern in a suit. Neither of them is shy about how they watch me, so I sink into Rowan and just focus on the table.

It doesn't take long to realize they're only using three decks, and it takes only a minute for me to start tracking the order of the cards with ease. I stifle a laugh as a few players get frustrated with their gameplay and watch as they continue to make horrible decisions.

"Who's your friend, Callahan?" the nervous finance guy asks, but I ignore him. I let my fingers trail up Rowan's neck, hoping he'll do the same. And he does.

He pulls me closer, his hand dropping to my leg, brushing against my bare skin. Everywhere he touches feels like fire. I try to control my breathing, not wanting to look like a stupid girl with a crush. But that's exactly what I am. And I think Rowan knows that based on how he lets his fingers trace my skin.

After a few more rounds, the finance guy finishes his drink and stands. "Well, shall we?" he asks, gesturing to me.

I freeze, stunned by his boldness. Rowan runs a calming hand along my leg before tapping it lightly and helping me stand.

"You okay?" he asks softly, never removing his hands from me.

"I don't want to go with him," I whisper.

"You're not going anywhere without me."

Rowan's assurance calms me, but only slightly, because the tension in his shoulders is new. But I nod, and he pulls me in tighter as the men rise from the table.

"We have a private room set up," Rowan says to them, his voice cool, professional.

His hand stays firm at my waist as he leads me away, but I can't help how my stomach drops. I can feel their eyes on me, and I know I'm not supposed to be here.

Whatever this is, I shouldn't be a part of it.

Thirty-Six
Briar

In this private room, it feels like the walls are caving in. I want to find somewhere to hide from all the eyes trained on me. I scan the room, looking for an escape, but there is none. We're so locked away that even the sound of the casino is muffled.

The room isn't large. It's barely big enough for the four of us. Two small sofas are tucked into the corner, and a fully stocked bar cart sits against the far wall that takes up most of the space. The moody green walls make the place feel even smaller than it is.

I want to walk over and pour a drink to calm my nerves, but I don't want to leave Rowan's side. He's got me tucked under his arm as he leads me to one of the couches, and I have to stop myself from collapsing into the cushions.

"You don't want to introduce us to your girl?" the finance guy asks.

Rowan scoffs and gestures for me to sit. I don't put up a fight. He takes a seat on the armrest beside me, letting his knee brush mine—a small reminder that he's right there.

"I didn't plan on it, Ashton," Rowan says with a shake of his head, and I'm relieved he's keeping me out of this. Rowan points to the tall, tattooed man on his left. "You know my partner, Kai."

Ashton nods like this is old news, but I flick my eyes to the tattooed man, apparently in business with Rowan. He's leaning against the wall, still watching me like a hawk.

His dark eyes search mine for something. It's unnerving being in the same room as him, especially with his eyes on me like he's hunting for weakness. I've overheard the crazy things Nate's said he's capable of, and I don't intend to find out if any of its actually true. And I prefer my scalp to stay intact.

"Oh, come on. You have to introduce us to a girl who looks like that," Ashton says, gesturing toward me. "And one who counts cards."

My stomach drops. I thought I had been careful, but clearly not if he noticed.

"What are you going on about?" Rowan asks, confusion laced in his words. I dig my nails into my palms, trying to keep calm.

"She can count cards," Ashton repeats, sprawling out on the opposite couch, all trace of nerves gone. "Your partner knows what I'm talking about."

"You've got the wrong girl," Rowan laughs but looks to Kai for confirmation. "I was just teaching her the rules of blackjack."

Ashton chuckles and shakes his head. But Kai is laser-focused on me, watching my every move. I'm sure he's checking for any sign of fear, so I try to sit taller. But I still feel like I could pass out.

"He has no idea, does he, doll?" Ashton grins.

I force myself to hold a neutral expression. One thing I've learned from playing cards—you need one hell of a poker face.

"Not sure I follow." My voice is calm and steady, and I almost believe it.

"She's a smart girl," Ashton chuckles, nodding toward Kai, who hasn't moved an inch since we entered the room. "She even knows better than to admit it in front of the owner."

If I weren't already freaking out, I am now. I've been in this position before, and I know how it ends. But I keep playing dumb.

"I was just trying to learn," I say, which isn't technically a lie. I clasp my hands tightly in my lap, trying not to fidget. Trying to look unbothered.

"Whatever you say," Ashton mutters, heading to the bar cart to pour himself a drink before turning to Kai.

"Kai, tell me something good about this next shipment," Ashton says, breezing past the accusations he just lobbed at me.

I let out a sigh of relief and pray they'll forget about me entirely.

"I'll be handling your shipments from now on," Rowan replies, stepping into Ashton's line of sight.

With him gone from my side, I'm as rigid as a pole. The tension in every muscle is enough to keep me from wilting under Kai's relentless stare, but it still feels like he's dissecting me with every passing second.

The only thing that calms me, even slightly, is when I focus entirely on Rowan. He looks unfairly good in his white button-down, the fabric pulling slightly across his shoulders as he moves. He's completely in his element, all confidence and control. I'm so locked in on him that I barely register as his conversation with the mousey guy concludes.

"She's a keeper, Callahan," Ashton says with a grin, shaking Rowan's hand. I give him a tight smile, even though I'd love to tell him to shut it. Rowan ignores the comment and extends a hand to me. I take it, grateful to be pulled back to his side.

"I'm ready to go home," I whisper. He nods in understanding.

"That's my cue, Ashton. The lady's ready to leave," he says, shaking hands again before leading us toward the door. With each step toward the exit, a little pressure lifts from my chest, and I'm one step closer to escape.

Kai's eyes track me until the door opens, and the casino noise crashes in. As overwhelming as it is, I'm grateful to disappear into the chaos. The crowd feels safer, like it offers some cloak of anonymity that lets your secrets stay your own.

As soon as we cross the threshold back into the club, pounding bass engulfs us. Sweaty bodies writhe on the dance floor to the awful house remix blasting through the speakers. Yet, as congested as it is, I can breathe easier here.

There are fewer eyes on me, and I feel more like a girl with a crush than a mouse in the viper's den.

"Chris, have them bring my car around," Rowan says, nearly shouting to be heard over the music. Chris nods and relays the message into his comms device, not sparing me a second glance.

"About five minutes, sir," Chris replies.

"Thanks," Rowan says, patting him on the shoulder before pulling me away. He leads me toward the front entrance, which is less crowded. I don't feel like I have to shout to be heard now. I lean against the wall, finally relaxing now that it's just us.

"I thought you didn't know how to play blackjack?" Rowan asks, leaning his hand against the wall, caging me in.

My heart stutters. I don't know if it's from his closeness or from being caught. But either way, it feels safe to be honest with Rowan. And the way he asks tells me he already knows.

I shake my head. "Technically, you asked if I played. Counting cards and playing aren't the same."

I watch his expression closely as it morphs from shock to amusement. He smiles faintly and rolls his head back to look at the ceiling.

"So it's true? You do count cards?" he asks quietly, but there's a gravelly undertone to his voice now that drives me wild.

I nod. "Yeah. That would explain why I'm banned from a few European casinos."

"A few?"

"Like ten or so," I laugh, realizing how ridiculous it sounds when I say it out loud.

"Briar. Ten?"

"Well, one guy owns all ten. He caught me in one and then banned me from the rest," I shrug. "It's not a big deal."

Rowan stares at me like he's trying to decide whether to be impressed or worried.

"And besides, this place only uses three decks. Makes the math easier. Once I figured out the dealer's shuffle pattern—"

"You're not helping yourself," Rowan says, chuckling.

"Right," I breathe, flushing with embarrassment and having to pretend like my shoes are suddenly the most interesting thing in the room. There's a brief moment that passes, with us just being together before he dives into what I've been avoiding for days.

"But I'm glad you brought that up," he continues, tipping my chin up. "With your near-perfect memory, you should have no problem telling me why you lied about not remembering our conversation the night of the Gala."

I hold his gaze for a beat, then break away. "I didn't want to talk about it. And after the pool, things got a little blurry, so technically, not a lie."

"You and your technicalities," he teases, the softness in his voice drawing me in further.

"I'm a future lawyer. What do you expect?"

"Okay, Ms. Future Lawyer. Why'd you lie about it?" Rowan steps closer to me, and I swear I feel my heart stop beating.

"Because I didn't want to talk about it." My voice shakes as I say this, knowing I still don't have any good reason for lying. I just didn't want to admit to what we both know is true. Having that conversation is a recipe for disaster. "And we were both with other people. I didn't see a reason to complicate things over one stupid moment."

"It wasn't stupid," he says, stepping closer. "And lucky for you, I'm not seeing anyone."

He's so close I can smell the whiskey on his breath. And I want to taste it. I want to lean into him and finally kiss him after all these years of wanting. But I place a hand on his chest and push him back slightly, needing that inch of space to think straight.

"That's not what it looked like earlier." The accusation is out before I can think twice.

He laughs. "Are you jealous, Briar?"

He's watching me with smoldering eyes and that little smirk because he knows I was. I don't have a real answer for him, and I have to look anywhere but at him so he doesn't see the truth in my eyes. But as soon as I pull away, I freeze as I lock eyes with Cameron.

My breath catches in my throat, and everything goes rigid. His nose is in the early stages of bruising , but I'm sure that's nothing compared to his ego. We lock eyes, and a sneer's plastered across his face, but Rowan steps into my line of sight.

"What's wrong?" The flirtatious tone that was there seconds before vanishes. I squeeze my eyes shut and breathe before looking back at Rowan.

"Nothing," I say too quickly.

"Briar, don't lie to me."

"Cameron's here, and he probably hates to see us here. H-he never really liked you," I admit.

Rowan glances over his shoulder. "Where is he? I'll get him kicked out."

"No. Just let him waste his money. I'll go. You can stay if you want—"

"No. I'm taking you home."

"You don't have to—"

"Briar. I said I'd get you home safely. And I will."

I nod, struck by the conviction in his voice. This side of Rowan—protective, steady—is disarming. The tension fades from Rowan's shoulders as he continues to block my view of Cameron.

"What do you mean he doesn't like me?"

I choke out a laugh. "I don't know. He asked about you a few times and got mad when you danced with me. He always assumed something was going on between us." I roll my eyes. "I told him it was nothing, but he never believed it."

"Do you believe that?"

I don't.

I shake my head, unable to say what I'm really thinking.

Rowan clears his throat and steps back slightly. I instantly miss how close he was, and I crave the feeling of his hands on me.

My thoughts spiral. I don't care what's smart or right. I don't care if I shouldn't. I just know that I want to. And I want to be able to go after the things I want without having to worry about the consequences or who's watching. I want Rowan, and if that's something that will wipe that smug look off Cameron's face, then that's just an added bonus.

"Kiss me."

The words are out of my mouth before I can stop them. Rowan's eyes widen, and I regret them immediately.

"It's just that he would… he'd hate that. It would make me feel better," I say quickly.

The muscle in Rowan's jaw tick. Once. Twice. And a third time, like he's actually considering it.

"Bri, I don't know…"

I flush with embarrassment. I shouldn't have done this. I curse myself and feel stupid. How could I have been so silly to think asking him to kiss me was a good idea? How desperate does that make me sound?

I force a smile. "I'm sorry. Forget I said anything."

But then Rowan shakes his head. "You might be sorry. But I'm not."

And before I know it, his lips are on mine.

Thirty-Seven
Briar

Last night was weird.

Rowan finally kissed me, and it was everything I needed. I asked him to, but I was still shocked when his lips met mine. And as perfect as the whole thing was, it was a mistake.

I still remember the stunned look on his face when he finally pulled away. We were both breathless, but reality came crashing in fast.

And that's when it got weird.

We drove home in silence. And as much as I'll never forget that kiss, I wish I could go back and stop it from happening.

Because now I feel guilty.

I should have told Harper about what's happening, or not happening, between us. I can't keep hiding this, especially not from her. Not now. It's time to bite the bullet and tell her everything. Even if that means potentially losing her.

When I head downstairs, I spot Nate on the couch, and my stomach sinks further. He's another person I've been hiding the truth from.

"Hey," he greets me, his voice sounding tired.

"Morning," I offer a weak smile.

We haven't talked in two days, not since the Cameron fiasco happened. I've done my best to avoid him, and maybe he's been avoiding me, too. But I can't deny that the tension between us has followed me around like a storm cloud waiting to break.

And now, we're at the breaking point.

"I'm sorry," I blurt out. There's so much I could apologize for, but I'm not ready to handle more than our fight the other day.

"No, B—"

"I'm sorry, Nate. I shouldn't have snapped at you the other day. And I appreciate you… for dealing with Cameron." I still remember the fury in his eyes. It haunts me, but it vanished so fast that I wonder if I imagined it, too.

After a pause, he gets up and hugs me. "I just wanted to make sure you were okay," he murmurs.

"I'm fine," I tell him. "We're fine."

He pulls back, eyes searching mine. "Where were you last night? I heard you come in late."

"I was out with Harper. I'm actually heading to her house now," I say.

"All night?" There's a hint of suspicion in his voice, but I'm sure I'm just paranoid.

"Yeah." It's a lie, and I hate how easy it's becoming to lie to the people I love when it comes to Rowan.

"Alright," he says, brows crinkled. "You'd tell me if something was wrong?"

"Of course."

Another lie. I don't want to burden him, of all people, with the stupid insecurities that float through my mind.

He exhales like he doesn't believe me but lets it go. "Have fun at Harper's."

I wave and head out, hating how much I left unsaid. But right now, I need to tell Harper.

Then maybe I can tell Nate.

Though there's not much to tell. It was just one kiss.

But nothing feels right. I'm torn between the ache to stay and the need to break free. But the harder I fight, the deeper I sink, drowning in everything I can't control. Drowning in Rowan.

Before I know it, I'm outside Harper's house, and I can't put it off any longer. Rowan's car isn't in the driveway, and that helps me breathe a little easier. As I cautiously open the front door, the house is quieter than usual as I start up the stairs.

"She's out back."

I freeze. Rowan's voice follows me up the stairs.

My heart jumps in my chest as I face him. He looks exhausted but still... perfect. Tousled hair. Circles under his eyes. Like he got as little sleep as I did.

"Cool. Thanks," I mumble, brushing past him, leaving a few feet between us as I do. I can't even look at him as I pass.

I silently open the back door and breathe in relief when I slip outside. Harper's lounging on a chair, flipping through a magazine like she hasn't got a care in the world. I take a few tentative steps toward her before she looks up and sees me.

"Bri, there you are!" Her voice is a mix of relief and confusion. "What happened to you last night? We tried calling, but you never picked up."

I force a laugh. I saw the messages after I got home. I'm not sure how to tell her it was because I was too distracted by her brother. So I give her a half-truth.

"My phone's been acting weird."

She hums, twirling her hair, and the guilt gnaws at me.

"I lied. I was with someone," I blurt out.

Her eyes widen. "With someone?" Her expression holds a mix of surprise and intrigue, making what I have to say next even worse. I wring my hands, trying to calm my nerves.

"I was with your brother."

Her face falls. "Rowan?"

"Yes." I barely whisper the admission. She stares at me, silent. I can feel the pressure building in my chest until I can't take it.

"I didn't know he'd be there. We got separated, and then... he was just there. I tried to leave, but he asked me to stay. And I don't know why I did, I just... everything with Cameron, and coming home…it was a lot. I'm sorry I didn't tell you sooner."

The truth pours out of me like floodwaters breaking through the dam. Tears threaten, but Harper's empathy steadies me.

"I should have told you sooner. I'm sorry," I repeat. And I know that I'll keep saying it as long as it takes to make her forgive me.

She nods. "I know."

Relief crashes over me. Harper doesn't seem mad. She actually doesn't even seem surprised. She looks… like she gets it.

Now I'm speechless.

"You know?" I struggle to breathe, imagining the worst, and not daring to let myself hope for her approval. "How long have you known?"

"Well, I didn't know, not until now. But I had my suspicions."

A sob nearly escapes. "Do you hate me?" I ask, tears welling in my eyes.

"Gosh, Bri. No." She stands and hugs me. "I couldn't hate you."

Her words wash over me like a tidal wave of relief. She doesn't hate me. I wrap my arms around her shoulders and drag in a long breath.

"I couldn't hate you…especially not when I think I'm in the exact same position."

I freeze, my mind reeling. She's in the same position?

"You?" I pull back. Then it sinks in. The guilt that's written across her face is a familiar look. One I know too well. Because it's the same one I've seen reflected back in the mirror all summer.

"I didn't think it was anything, and then it just... crept up on me," she admits.

"You and Nate," I say, stunned, trying to connect the dots.

"Are you mad?" Harper's expression flashes with apprehension.

"No," I rush to assure her. "I'm more... surprised. I thought you and Kian were good?"

"We are," she assures me. "But Nate. We ran into each other a few times before you came home, but it was always casual. Then, at the Gala... we talked. It was easy. He's just easy to be with."

I nod. I get it. I know exactly what it feels like to be that torn.

"And Kian's amazing, but last night, when we ran into Nate, I wanted to be with him more."

I pause, taking in her admission; then it hits me.

Harper was with Nate last night.

And I wasn't with Harper.

"You were with Nate last night?" I ask her, hoping that I've misunderstood her somehow. I need her to tell me I didn't just lie to my brother's face this morning, while he knew it was a lie.

"Yeah. Why?"

"All night?"

"Yes," Harper repeats, more confused now than before. "I told him we got kicked out of the club and that you were right behind us. But then you didn't answer your phone... because you were with my brother."

"And you were with mine."

The weight of everything falls right back onto my shoulders. My brother knows. He knows I lied about where I was last night, and I'm sure he's smart enough to figure out why I lied.

"I'm sorry," I sigh.

We stand there awkwardly, each trying to figure out where we go from here.

"No, I should have asked you about it. Instead, I just pretended I didn't have eyes and tried to push you toward Reece," Harper finally says, sitting down. "But I don't want some boy to come between us—even if it's our brothers."

"Me either," I agree, sitting beside her. "I'll always be your best friend. No matter what. I just want you to be happy."

"And I want you to be happy, Bri. But do you really think that's Rowan?"

Her words sting, though I know she doesn't mean them to. Even after everything Rowan's done, he's still the only person I think about.

"I don't know," I tell her honestly. I don't know what this is with Rowan, but I can't sit around and keep fighting the idea of him. "Everything you told me about him just doesn't add up. I don't see that side of him."

"Just because he's nice to you doesn't discount all the bad things he's done." Her tone is serious, and I don't disagree with her.

"Harper, I know," I say, barely above a whisper. "But I also know that he's shown me that he's not all bad. It's hard to describe, but he feels like home somehow. I have to trust what he's shown me, and I trust him."

Harper bites the inside of her cheek, taking in what I've said. "You know, he even apologized to Reece for hitting him at the bonfire?"

Her question hits me straight in the chest, and for a second, I forget how to breathe. I had no idea he'd done that, but my heart swells thinking about how hard that probably was for Rowan.

"Ah, no. I-I didn't know that," I say, trying to hide the smile that I can feel creeping in.

A strained silence falls at my admission. I have to question if I said something wrong or even if it was too much. But I can't pretend anymore that I don't want to know what comes of this. Of us.

"He feels like home, huh?" Harper looks at me more seriously than before.

I suck in a breath and nod. But I can't help but question if she believes it. Or if she already knows everything I can't figure out how to say, everything I'm too scared to admit.

"Yeah, he does," I say, not looking away from her. It might be hard for her to hear, but it's true. My truth.

Harper lets out a strangled laugh. "You know my dad used to say to find someone who made you feel safe. Who felt like home."

I can see the tears in her eyes, and I have to swallow back my sadness for her. "I really thought that was Kian. But Nate..."

She doesn't need to finish. I get it.

Nate is the kindest person I know. He's always willing to lend a helping hand, an ear, or whatever you need. He's incredible, and I couldn't imagine anyone *not* liking him. I just never thought that someone would be Harper.

"You don't realize someone is that person until it's too late," I say. "It sneaks up on you."

"Yeah," she agrees and smiles.

The silence that follows isn't heavy. Just thoughtful. We've both just broken the door off its hinges, but it feels good in a way. I don't feel like I have to run from the truth anymore. And I can finally admit what I've always wanted.

"How are you doing with your dad?" I ask.

"It's been rough. Sometimes, I visit him. Makes it a little easier. But if I don't have the time, I listen to a voicemail he left me."

"I'm sorry," I say, voice cracking.

She wipes her eyes and flashes a wry smile. "This feels like a moment for a drink."

As soon as she says it, I'm grateful for the distraction. "You can say that again," I mumble as she pulls a few cans out of the cooler beside her chair.

I take one of the two seltzers from her and open it. The first sip burns, but it instantly relaxes me as I lie back on the lounger and kick up my feet.

"Last thing, then we drop it," I say, turning to her.

"Okay," she nods.

"I'm truly okay with you and Nate. If that's what you want, I'm here for you. Whatever fallout comes of it."

It's true. She deserves the world, and someone on her side. And I'll always be on her side until the end of time. No matter what.

Her smile is genuine. "As much as I never thought I'd say this… I'm okay with you and Rowan. You guys are actually so cute. I watched you together at the Gala, and just seeing how he looks at you… You're good for him."

My cheeks flush, and I try to hide it behind my drink. But before I can revel in the thought, Harper holds out her can to me.

"Here's to dating each other's brothers."

"Dating each other's brothers," I repeat, clinking cans.

And I can't help but laugh—because this might just go down as one of the stupidest things we've ever done.

But now that I have Harper's blessing, now that nothing is standing in the way… I don't know what scares me more.

Starting something with Rowan, or the chance that it might actually mean something.

Thirty-Eight
Briar

Talking with Harper helped ease a lot of the anxiety I'm feeling. It's not gone entirely, but it's lessened. At least I could be honest with her, even if I don't know how to be fully honest with myself. One thing I do know is that I need to go home and figure out what I want. Figure out what this thing with Rowan actually is.

I stand from my spot on the lounger, wobbling a bit. "I should head home before I turn into a tomato." I laugh, noticing the pink tint on my skin. We stayed out longer than we should have, but we needed it.

"You're right. I should shower and go see Kian."

I nod and help Harper pack up. The air is thicker now, either from the humidity or the thin layer of tension still hanging between Harper and me. She pulls a T-shirt over her head and then stares at me.

"We're going to be okay, Bri."

I can't tell if she's reassuring me or herself, but either way, it's exactly what I needed. We will be okay—her and me, the boys, everything.

"Yeah, we are," I agree, pulling her in for a hug.

We part with awkward smiles, trying to reassure each other.

"I'll see you later," Harper says with a wave, retreating into her house. The sliding door closes, and I stand rooted in place. I have to force my feet toward the front of the house and away from Rowan, who I assume is still inside. As much as I want to see him, I'm not sure I can handle it right now. At least not until I know what I want.

My feet hit the paved driveway, and my stomach drops. Rowan leans against the house, seemingly waiting for me. I curse silently and plaster on a fake smile.

"You again," I mumble.

"Me again." He steps toward me, scratching the back of his neck. "I want to talk to you, Briar. I just need five minutes."

My stomach twists. There's no way I can spend five minutes with him after everything that happened last night. The kiss has played on a constant loop in my head, and I can't bear to hear that he regrets it.

I cross my arms and weigh my options. I could run away and hope never to see him again, but with how often he's around, that seems not even remotely possible. Or I could hear him out and let him break my heart sooner rather than later.

"You have two minutes."

Rowan studies me for a few seconds, weighing his next move. I stay rooted in place, happy to let him waste time. And he does. He's quiet for what feels like an entire two minutes. I try to hold my ground, seeming unfazed.

But it's Rowan. He's always had that heart-skipping effect, and that's hard to hide.

"I wanted to talk to you about last night," he finally says, stepping back slightly.

My heart sinks, but I knew this was coming. "Yeah, we should probably talk about that."

He doesn't respond right away. He's watching me too closely. I sway a little, wishing I hadn't spent the last hour roasting in the sun with my best friend. I wanted to be clear-headed and not exhausted for this conversation, but luck isn't on my side today.

"Great. I'll go first," I say, trying to get it over with. "I'm sorry for putting you in that situation. I didn't mean to cause trouble, and I really should've just left with Harper.

But I appreciate you helping me, and you don't have to worry about me. I know that kiss didn't mean anything."

The words taste bitter, but I'd rather lie and make him feel less guilty about what he's about to say. At least one of us should leave this conversation feeling fine.

He crosses his arms and scans my face. "Briar, you're kidding, right?"

"No, it was a mistake to ask you to kiss me. It just makes everything complicated, and I don't have time for complicated. Do you?" The forced calm is evident in my voice, but I don't care.

He clears his throat, clearly shocked as his eyes search mine. "No. No, I don't. But I don't think it was a mistake either."

His words hit me like a ton of bricks. Never in a hundred years did I think he'd say that—that he doesn't think it was a mistake. And the sheer thought of that makes my heart race.

Could he actually want this? Want *us*?

"You don't mean that," I say, giving him one more opportunity to back out before we go running toward an inevitable collision.

Part of me hopes he'll agree and spare me the future heartbreak. But the other part wants him to throw caution to the wind and fight for it. For me.

He lets out a soft, disbelieving chuckle that only adds more fuel to my fire. "You have no idea, do you?"

I run my fingers through my hair, frustrated that he's dragging this out. At this point, I'm more inclined to run for the hills before he has the opportunity to ruin me.

"No idea about what, Rowan?"

There's a harsh bite to my words, but I can't keep it tamped down any longer. I've already mentally prepared myself for him to twist the knife in further and create a hole in my heart that I can't repair.

Now, Rowan has a stupid, smug look on his face that makes me hate him for finding this whole situation funny. Because nothing about this is funny.

Other than the fact that despite everything that's happened, I'm still desperate for him to kiss me again.

And that's dangerous.

"You have no idea that I'm crazy about you. And that I have been for as long as I've known you."

His admission knocks every bit of air from my lungs. I'm rooted to the spot, scared that if I move, this beautiful hallucination in front of me will come to a screeching halt.

"You're everywhere I look, and I can't get you out of my head. Everything about you, Briar, drives me crazy. I can't eat or sleep—I can't do anything without thinking about you."

He runs his fingers through his hair, and he looks at me so intently I'm scared to blink. Like if I take my eyes off him for one second, he'll realize how absurd this is and rush to take it all back.

Because this can't be real.

Everything he's saying hurts my heart more. I want to give in, but I can't. I know there's a catch somewhere.

Nothing ever works out like this.

Not for girls like me.

There has to be something that I'm missing, something that will come back to bite me. And I can't let myself fall and get hurt.

"Stop."

I hear myself say the word, but it lacks any sense of conviction.

"No, Briar. You need to know." He's flushed now, like keeping this in has been so physically hard for him that he might combust if he can't get the words out.

"I don't know about you, but I haven't been able to think about anything other than kissing you since last night.

It's driving me fucking crazy. You're acting like it's impossible that someone could actually like you—*love* you—while I'm standing here, completely in love with you, and you won't even give me a chance."

Everything around me stops, and I forget how to breathe.

Rowan starts pacing the driveway, and I hear the words he's saying, but I can't process anything other than what he's just told me.

He loves me.

He's in *love* with me.

He finally stops and looks at me, and he looks just as lost as I feel, but the second our eyes lock, his entire body relaxes.

"I'm sorry, Briar—"

"You're in love with me?" My question comes out so soft that I'm not even sure I said it out loud.

He sighs, laughing under his breath. "Yeah. Briar, I'm in love with you. How do you not see that?"

My heart skips a beat.

No one's ever said that to me before. But I've never wanted anyone to—until now.

I swallow, letting everything from the past five minutes sink in. My legs feel weak, but I don't care anymore. Nothing else in the world matters because Rowan *loves* me.

But his love, as exciting as it is, is equally as dangerous. I've seen how quickly his feelings can fade. They come and go like the tides, and he's never there to pick up the pieces. It's like now we're in the eye of the storm, and this is the calm before the real chaos ensues.

Still, right now, he's looking at me like I'm the center of his universe, and I can't be bothered to think about anything other than him.

We stand there, silently assessing each other.

"Briar, please, tell me what you're thinking."

The desperate edge in Rowan's voice could bring me to my knees, and I can feel the final piece of whatever was holding me back snap.

I have nothing left in me to keep fighting this losing battle.

I want Rowan. Complications and all.

I don't care anymore.

My legs move before I can second-guess myself, shaking and sure all at once.

I don't know if I'm running toward something or falling into it. Still, either way, I'm ready for whatever consequences this brings.

I run to him, free to finally stop pretending that I don't want this. Want us. But everything else fades away as he pulls me into him.

Our lips move in sync, and this kiss is better than the first.

Better than I ever imagined.

And he's mine. Finally.

Thirty-Nine
Rowan

"I didn't know you were hitting it with his sister," Darian chuckles. He raises a hand for a high five, but I ignore him and focus on Nate. "Aw, don't leave me hanging, Rowan."

I don't move. Nate's shooting daggers at me with his eyes. "He better not be."

Darian drops his hand and sinks an easy layup, leaving the two of us in a staring contest.

Briar and I have both talked to Nate over the past twenty-four hours, and I can only hope he's not icing his sister out the same way he is with me.

"It's not like that with Briar," I tell Nate for what feels like the hundredth time. And it's the honest-to-God truth. She's different. I wouldn't risk losing her for anything.

"Not yet, he isn't!" Darian calls out, laughing at his own joke. He's funny, to the point where I'm fighting the smile threatening to discredit my whole argument. I clear my throat as Darian misses a shot from laughing too hard, but Nate still doesn't crack.

"How would you like it if I hit it with your sister?" Nate taunts Darian. "You've got three for me to choose from, and I have to say, Maddie's been looking really good—"

"Okay, okay. I get it. I'll let up," Darian groans, dropping the ball and raising his hands in surrender.

"Here's an idea. How about we forget I said anything in the first place," I suggest, taking the ball and watching as my shot bounces off the rim.

"That's arguably the best idea you've ever had," Nate agrees, jogging to grab the ball and sinking a three-pointer.

"I would've paid good money to see the look on your face, Nate, when he first told you," Darian laughs. He passes the ball back to me as I shoot again, ignoring him.

"I can just picture it," he drawls, scrunching his face into mock rage. "Yo, man, that's my sister. I'll kill you if you mess with her."

I have to stifle my laughter because his impression of Nate's reaction isn't that far off.

"Darian," Nate warns.

"Sorry," he mumbles, and we fall into a weird silence. The only sounds are the ball smacking the pavement and the occasional bounce off the backboard as we continue to shoot around.

"So, how long has this been going on?" Darian asks, like he can't help himself.

I pause mid-shot and turn toward him with the ball still poised in the air. Of course, he can't let it go. "I'm going to kill you if you keep this up."

"Dude, I'm just curious," he shrugs, swatting the ball from my hands and dribbling off with it.

"Haven't you heard the phrase 'curiosity killed the cat'? Right now, Darian, you're the cat." Nate's voice is calm, but there's irritation behind his vague threat. As awkward as this whole thing is, I'm over Nate's little possessive act. He acts like I'm setting out to ruin his sister's life.

I want to tell Nate to get over it already, but the guy's only had an hour to process. And I'd be just as pissed if the roles were reversed.

Before I can throw in another insult, my phone starts buzzing with notifications.

"Is that her?" Darian smirks, dodging the ball Nate chucks at him.

"Bro, be so for real right now," I mutter, grabbing my phone from the planter but finding humor in the fact that Darian just continues to add further insult to injury.

I scan the notifications, and they're just more messages from Mateo. That makes four today. The kid is relentless, but he's got the wrong idea. I'm not interested in selling to him. Never have been, never will be.

I roll my eyes and put the phone down. Darian's watching me, but I clap my hands in a silent request for the ball. Nate eyes me down expectantly, but I say nothing and gesture for the ball again before he passes it over.

"Not going to tell us who it was?" Nate asks, humor creeping into his voice for the first time this afternoon.

"Not your sister, if that's what you're asking." I jab back.

"So, who was it then?" Darian pushes.

"Mateo," I say flatly as I make a clean shot.

Nate raises an eyebrow. "Mateo?"

"What's he want?" Darian asks, passing the ball back to me.

"He's been harassing me all week. Thinks I'll sell to him. Keeps blowing up my phone and even tried stopping by the house a few times."

That gets Nate's attention. "Whoa, what?"

"Yeah. It's getting to the point where it feels like harassment."

"Are you seriously still dealing?" Nate looks like he's about to explode, and the glare he's worn for the past hour is back squarely on his face. His eyes narrow and start that weird flutter that happens when he gets mad. "You expect me to be okay with you and Briar when you're still out here doing this shit?"

"I'm gonna grab some water," Darian mutters, backing away toward the house.

"You better not expose Briar to this," Nate says, but it sounds more like a threat. His eyes lose some of that dangerous heat as he runs a hand through his hair. "We can't have a repeat of her freshman year."

"What do you mean by a repeat of her freshman year?" I narrow my eyes at him as he begins to pace back and forth. Nate shakes his head like the words won't come out.

I stand as patiently as I can for a few beats before demanding, "Tell me."

He stops pacing and stares at me like he's sizing me up. But finally, he releases a long breath and gives in.

"There was this girl Briar was friends with back in high school. Got her into pills and shit. It got pretty bad. Briar had to go through a ton of therapy. Honestly, I didn't think she'd recover from it," he admits, refusing to make eye contact with me.

That hits me harder than I expect. I've never known the part of Briar that isn't striving for perfection, so this feels wrong. Part of me knows Nate wouldn't lie about this, but I can't help but hope he is.

"Oh." It's the only thing I can say. I let the ball slip through my hands as I try to process his words.

"I swear if you're still dealing while you're with her... You may be one of my oldest friends, but I will murder you, Rowan," he threatens. I barely register it. I'm still stuck on Briar.

How she never told me.

How she pretends nothing's wrong.

She's always focused on the future and terrified of messing it up.

And now I know why.

I can't help but feel like I should have been there for her then, too. But if I couldn't be there for her then, I'll do everything in my power to be there for her now.

Because she's my entire world, and I can't imagine a life where she's not in it.

Shaking my head, I look at him. "I had no idea that happened." I'm sure that does little to quell his fear, but it's all I can offer. "If it helps, I've only been selling to a few regulars recently. But I've been thinking about getting out for a while... and I will. For Briar."

Nate clenches his jaw. It's clear he doesn't believe me. I don't blame him. I've said this before, but I never had a reason to give it up. But Briar's more than enough to make me leave this behind.

I turn back to the makeshift court and take another shot. It misses, and the ball bounces across the driveway. I jog after it, miss another shot, too distracted by my thoughts and the feel of Nate's eyes drilling into me.

"I can't concentrate with you staring at me like that," I snap.

"Do you talk to Briar like that?" Nate huffs angrily.

I pull my focus away from the basket and glare at him. "Man, fuck off with that. I would never snap at Briar. You know I'd never treat her like that."

I take a step toward my friend, anger building in my chest.

"If you ever lay a hand on her, I swear... there's an unmarked grave out there with your name on it."

I drop my scowl. I'd like to punch or threaten him back, but I can't. I know he's just protecting her, and I'd do the same. "I know."

He takes a few deep breaths, working to calm himself down, and the anger starts to recede.

"Listen, I'm going to take care of this and keep Briar out of it."

My assurance doesn't help, based on how quickly his head snaps back in my direction.

"What does that mean?" Suspicion creeps into his tone, but if I had to guess, he probably already knows what I'm talking about.

Nate's met Kai.

I've never spelled out what kind of business we're in, but he's been around long enough to know where the cash comes from. The life we live didn't come from the success of one bar. It's from the shit that happens behind closed doors, with private security and collateral collected before the deals.

It's messy, but the lifestyle it affords is picturesque.

I leave out the critical details with Nate because, as much as I don't want Briar getting caught up in this, I don't want Nate to either. Because if something ever happens to me, Nate's the one who has to look out for her.

"I need you to trust that I've got this."

He laughs. "You should know I don't trust you for shit when it comes to Briar."

I nod. Because that's fair.

The garage door closes as Darian returns. "Did you ladies kiss and make up?"

"No," Nate says, scooping up the ball and laying it in. Then, he starts dribbling around the driveway further away from the basket.

"What'd you do this time?" Darian lowers his voice, glancing at me.

I shrug. "He's sensitive today."

"I'm not sensitive. You're just an idiot," Nate shouts.

I laugh and watch as he nails a shot from halfway down the drive.

"I've got some calls to make," I tell Darian, patting his back.

"Hey, man," he says, stopping me. "Don't push him. He's your oldest friend. And you're dating his sister. Just take it easy. He needs time."

His advice makes me roll my eyes. "*Me?* You're telling me to take it easy when you're the one out here poking the bear. Funny."

But I nod along because he's right. For all his jokes, Darian's one of the smartest people I know. "We'll work it out eventually."

With one clap on Darian's shoulder, I head into the house and hope that's true.

I can't lose Nate as a friend. But I can't lose Briar either. And it feels like we're on a collision course where I'm bound to lose something. Because, as much as I will get out for Briar, there are a few things I have to handle first.

I move through the house, grab my burner phone from my room, then head toward the back room and settle onto one of the couches. I soak in the air conditioning before firing off a text to Kane. Two names.

Cameron DuPont.
Mateo Flores.

Kane replies almost instantly with his usual questions: *What's the timeline? What's the job? Client request or something personal?*

I never expected someone known for his muscles to be so damn efficient. But that's why Kai keeps him around.

And speaking of Kai, it's not even two minutes later that my phone rings.

"Kai," I answer.

"What are you doing? You can't just pull Kane whenever you want." His tone is clipped, controlled. Classic Kai. He hates not calling the shots.

I let his annoyance roll off me. "Was he busy?"

"He might have been."

I roll my eyes. "He wasn't. And besides, this won't take long."

I can practically hear his teeth grinding. "Which is?"

"I've got two guys. One won't stop blowing up my phone, the other's spreading shit. I just need Kane to put the fear of God in them."

"Why are you bothering Kane for this? Just kill them."

I laugh. Kai's humor is dark, but usually not during business talk.

"I can't kill a senator's son. That creates more problems than it solves. You know that better than anyone."

"Why do I feel like this has to do with that cute blonde on your arm the other night?" There's a taunting edge to his voice now, and I laugh. Because these are precisely the games Kai likes to play. But I won't let him drag Briar into this. Not now, and not ever.

"Didn't you once lecture me about keeping business and personal separate?"

I let my head roll back on the backrest and stare blankly at the ceiling. I did say that, but a hell of a lot has changed in two days.

"You also said there's an exception to every rule."

Kai barks out a laugh before he falls silent, and I can sense his wheels turning.

"You get my message about Chicago?" he asks suddenly.

"Yeah. What's in Chicago?"

"More like *who*. Ashton connected me to a potential buyer."

I inhale slowly. I know this means trouble, but I let him continue.

"We leave in two days. Be at the hangar by eight. And Callahan, don't screw this up. Got it?"

I clench my jaw to keep from snapping back. I want to remind Kai that he's the one who goes around ruining our business.

I clear my throat. "Got it."

Kai hangs up the line, and a weight settles in my chest. I'm supposed to be getting out of this, but I know I can't. I'm too far in, and Kai will do anything to drag me back, even if I'm kicking and screaming.

The best I can do is put distance between myself and anything Kai touches. As much as I hate to admit it, I need this business. I need this partnership.

But if I want any chance at keeping Briar, I have to keep her as far away from it as possible.

From him.

Even if it means lying to her to protect her from herself. Protect her from me.

Forty
Rowan

I don't have to open my eyes to know it's early. Really fucking early. I can all but sense the sun pouring in from every window of the house through my eyelids. It feels like I just went to sleep a few hours ago, and that's probably true. The game dragged on last night, and with each extra inning, we kept drinking.

A loud knock echoes through the house, dragging me out of my thoughts. I squint in the morning light, trying to pinpoint the source.

But I don't see anything other than Nate and Darian passed out on the sectional, completely unbothered by the pounding. Maybe I imagined it, or maybe that's just my brain punishing me for the twelve-pack I downed. The knocking would go hand-in-hand with the splitting headache I'm developing.

But there it is again, and it's louder this time.

I sit up and take a second to assess my surroundings. Only then do I realize the knocking is coming from the front door, and not my brain. Though knocking is generous. It sounds more like someone's trying to break down the door.

Groaning, I shift my weight to stand from my spot on the couch. I'm wobbly, but I manage. The guys stir from my movement, rubbing the sleep from their eyes as they try to adjust to the light.

They both look worse than I feel, and Darian goes green the second he sits up, and he bolts toward the bathroom.

I glance out the front window and spot Sheriff Clarke on the porch, which makes me a little sick to my stomach. I can't see the man's face without remembering the day he came to the house about my dad.

Two police cars are parked in the driveway, and judging by the look on Clarke's face, he's just as thrilled to be here as I am.

"Open up, Callahan. We have a warrant," he says, holding up a paper for me to see through the window.

I heave a sigh and move toward the door. I stretch my limbs, still stiff from sleep, then slowly open the door. "Clarke, I didn't realize you made house calls this early."

He crosses his arms, frowning hard.

"What's this even about?"

Clarke hands over the warrant, and I skim it. It's for my car, nothing else, which is the best-case scenario. I don't keep anything at the house. Not anymore. The texts to Kane are long gone from the burner phone. My car is clean. I'm clean.

But it still makes me nervous.

"We got an anonymous tip that you're in possession of drug paraphernalia," Clarke says, all bravado, puffing his chest out.

Clarke and my dad had a sort of understanding. He gave us more information than he should, and we kept our business off the island. A win-win.

But that was with my dad.

And I don't know if Clarke is just testing the waters with me, or if that's a courtesy he plans to extend my way as well.

"Then Mr. DuPont and Mr. Flores were beaten pretty badly after talking to us."

I glance up, pleasantly surprised by how forthcoming he is. "Not so anonymous if we're dropping names," I say with a smile. "But, that's too bad. I hope you catch the guy."

"Would you know anything about that?"

"Clarke, I respect you, buddy, but this is a waste of time. I was here all night with the guys. We were celebrating a Bombers win." I tuck the warrant into the pocket of my sweats and watch him as he paces back and forth, peeking in through the windows.

His jaw ticks, revealing his frustration. We've been playing this cat-and-mouse game for a year. He knows something's up, but I'm not stupid enough to get caught. Or give him a reason to look any harder than he already is.

"Right," Clarke huffs. "Well, given the tip and the boys' condition, we had to come out here and look. You understand how these things work."

"Just doing your job," I say with a smirk, but there's still an edge of paranoia that lives on the outskirts of my brain. I know there isn't anything in my car. But I don't know whether those two idiots planted something there.

Despite it all, there's nothing I can do but watch and wait. Which would be a lot more entertaining if I weren't so hungover. The sooner they leave, the sooner I can get back to bed.

"Search away, Clarke. We both know you won't find anything in my car."

"I don't have time for this, Callahan," he waves me off, stomping down the porch steps toward my car.

"At least let me unlock it so you guys don't mess up the paint job," I call after him, feigning a nonchalance I don't possess. But I do manage to keep a smile on my face just to piss him off.

"That'd be the first helpful thing you've done in your life, kid," he mutters as his deputies circle my car like vultures.

I nod and head to the entryway table, grabbing my keys. Darian and Nate are watching me like I've grown a second head, but I ignore them.

I raise my arm and click the unlock button. "I'll be inside if you need me, Sheriff."

Back in the kitchen, I drop the keys and fill a glass with water. If I'm going to survive this morning, I need to hydrate before I hurl.

"Dude, what's going on?" Nate asks, joining me in the kitchen. He watches the deputies through the window that overlooks our driveway, eyes sharp. "Why are the police here?"

"They're searching my car. They got some anonymous tip about me. This is pretty routine." I wave it off.

"Yeah, I can see that. I do have eyes," Nate snaps.

"Then why'd you ask?"

"I heard what Clarke said about Cameron and Mateo. Did you do that?" Nate asks, staring at me.

I want to kick him for asking, but his eyes tell me he already knows.

"He was being dramatic. If they really thought I had something to do with it, they'd have come last night."

A beat passes.

"That's not a denial," Nate mutters.

He's right. It's not a denial, but I'm not dumb enough to tell a lie that I can get caught in. And the less Nate knows, the better. It's bad enough he's here to witness it, but I'd do anything to keep him out of it.

"I was here the entire night," I remind him, crossing my arms across my chest. "Besides, this is par for the course with Clarke. After everything with my dad, he started showing up with some new bullshit warrant every week. Today, it's the car. Next week, it'll be the shed. But they're not going to find anything."

"He's here once a week?"

I sip my water to keep myself occupied while I try to come up with something to get Nate off this topic. "Yeah. Same song and dance every time. He leaves empty-handed."

"Let's not pretend those warrants are baseless. I know what you and Kai are capable of—"

"Whoa." I cut him off, worried that he's connecting the dots. "Who said anything about Kai? And what exactly do you think I did? Do I need to remind you *I'm* the one who pulled *you* off Cameron the other day?"

Nate stiffens, and I regret it instantly. That might have been just a step too far.

"That was different, and you know it."

"You think the cops will see it that way?" I nod toward the deputies just outside the window.

Nate freezes. He knows even a whisper about that fight, and he'll be stuck answering questions until next week. I almost feel guilty for bringing it up, but sometimes he needs a reminder.

He's got a record, too. It's not hard to imagine him as a suspect. I'd never throw him to the wolves like that, but I need him to keep his distance from this.

For my sake. For Briar's sake.

"Just do me a favor and stay out of my business. You'll have to trust that I know what I'm doing, and that Briar won't be involved. Now, if you'll excuse me, I've got cop cars in my driveway that I need to deal with."

I turn on my heel and step back onto the porch, that sick feeling churning in my stomach. I hate using Briar against Nate, but if it keeps them both out of it, I'd do it again.

"You find anything, Clarke?" I call, leaning against the siding.

"Not yet, Callahan. Care to help us look?"

I shake my head and lean over the railing. "I'll pass. But it's funny, two idiots manipulate the island's finest, and suddenly, my driveway's the one full of patrol cars."

The deputies pause their search, giving me their full attention. "What?"

"Come on, Clarke. Cameron and Mateo are the problem. They've been harassing me and my girlfriend for weeks. I tried to let it go, but look where that got me. Mateo's been showing up at my house all week, and I watched Cameron verbally assault Briar just days ago."

My selective truth-telling hits its mark like I knew it would. Clarke's got a soft spot for Briar after she got lost for a few hours when she was twelve. She had half the island looking for her, but the girl was just off behind the old water tower, pretending to be in some fantasy world where the trees were her castle.

Clarke looks at me, assessing my every word. "They did what?"

"They're wasting your time, is what they're doing, Sheriff. I wouldn't be surprised if they're the ones supplying kids around here. I told Briar and her friends to stay away from them. Total lowlifes."

Clarke nods slowly, then calls out, "Anderson. Parker. Come here."

The three of them huddle around my car, whispering angrily to one another about who knows what. I pretend not to strain to hear every word, but catch pieces that sound a. lot like they're believing me.

New warrant.

DuPont house.

Pack this up.

Finally, Clarke shakes his head. "Wrap it up, boys."

I smile as the deputies pack up and return to their cruisers. Clarke starts down the drive but pauses at the bottom of the porch steps.

"Why didn't you mention any of this before?"

A heavy sigh escapes me as I try to come up with something believable. "Briar. She begged me not to," I say smoothly. It's the simplest lie, and my first real one to Clarke today. I don't want to see her dragged into this, and I know Clarke won't go questioning Briar if he thinks it will make her upset. "I didn't think it would come to this."

"Well, let me know if they keep coming around. And sorry for the disturbance this morning," he nods, the words stiff in his throat.

"Tell Maggie I said hello." I wave casually.

His jaw tightens at the mention of his wife, but he lets it go and returns to his car.

I stay on the porch, watching him pull away. I don't move until his taillights disappear down the road, and only then do I let out a breath that's been stuck in my chest.

There's nothing worse than having to deal with Clarke first thing in the morning, and his presence still fries my nerves.

But he's gone now. And if I'm lucky, that's the last I'll see of Cameron and his little minion.

Just the thought of their plan backfiring has a slow, satisfied smile creeping across my face.

Some people dig their own graves.

I'm just here to sell them the shovel.

Forty-One
Briar

This dinner is vastly different from the last one with Rowan. Instead of dancing around each other, he pulls me in and kisses me. There's no holding back and no hesitation as he interlaces our fingers and leads me to a beautifully set table on the back porch.

I raise a brow, surprised, and can't hide the smile in my voice. "What's the occasion?"

"I can't do something nice for my girlfriend?"

"Your *girlfriend*?" I choke on my laugh, caught off guard by his use of the word. "I didn't realize we had someone else joining us."

"That's not funny, Briar." He walks over and pulls out my chair, gesturing for me to sit. I do and cross my arms as he takes his seat directly across from me.

"I must've missed the conversation where I agreed to be exclusive." I give him a teasing smile, but Rowan doesn't budge.

"Baby, I'm working on it," he says, gesturing to the table between us. "What do you think all this is?"

I scan the table and can't help but smile. He's lit candles around the balcony and placed a fresh bouquet on the table. The warm glow wraps around us like our own little corner of the world, making it feel like we're untouchable.

"Go on." I eye him, noting how his black T-shirt pulls taut across his chest as he pours us each a glass of wine. He doesn't have to ask for me to be his girlfriend, but I can't deny the giddiness in my stomach at the thought.

"I want all the cards on the table," he says hesitantly. "I want you to know exactly what you're getting into."

I nod because I think I know exactly where this is going. And I want him to know that doesn't scare me. Nothing about him scares me. Except for the way he makes me feel.

"I've heard things… and I was at The Lounge. I know what this is."

He chuckles and leans back in his chair, arms crossed. "I know. But I don't want you to have any doubts or reservations."

I don't have any reservations, but I appreciate the effort he's making to make me feel secure. I give him a soft smile of assurance.

"So I made us dinner. We'll eat, and I'll answer whatever questions you have."

I study him. Rowan's elbows rest on the table, and he's leaning toward me, sincere and unguarded. It warms my heart that he's willing to be this open, and I can't lie, my interest is piqued.

"I can ask anything I want?"

He nods.

"Is there a limit to how many questions I get?"

"No. Ask anything and everything."

I swallow and pick up my fork, eyeing the meal. A million questions are swimming in my brain, but just one that needs to be answered immediately.

"What's in this?" I ask, pointing to my plate. It looks like a stuffed meat pinwheel, and I can't decide if it looks trustworthy or sketchy.

He laughs. "It's braciole. You'll like it; it's steak, prosciutto, and cheese. That's all."

I take a tentative bite, and he's right. The steak practically melts in my mouth. The cheese is soft and warm, and the whole thing couldn't be more delicious if it wanted to be.

"Do you like it?"

"Holy crap. Yes! How have I gone my whole life without this?" I take another bite, and it's just as mouthwatering as the first.

"Good. I'm glad you like it."

"No. I love it."

He grins, taking a bite for himself. "Is that the only question you have for me?"

He sounds hopeful, but there's still so much I don't know. And I want to know everything. I want to know about his business, which he keeps so hidden from me. I want to know what his plans for the future are. I want to know it all, but there's only one place to start.

"No. I want to know what happened with you and Reece."

Rowan's jaw tightens, and he drains half his wine in a single go. I know he doesn't want to talk about it, but I need to know. His hand finds my leg under the table, and he strokes his thumb gently across my knee, almost like he's reassuring himself that I'm still here.

"It's not really about me and Reece. It's more about my dad and his dad."

"You blame his dad?" I ask, though it sounds more like a statement.

"Yes and no. I blame Reece's dad, but it's ultimately my dad's fault."

I sit in stunned silence. He's never admitted that out loud before, at least not to my knowledge. I know he apologized to Reece, but I never thought that would lead to him being so honest about his dad in this moment.

"Briar, I know I've done some horrible things because my dad asked me to. I want to believe it was because

I didn't know any better… but that doesn't change the fact that I still did them."

"Like what?" I can't help myself. My mind spins faster, creating scenarios out of thin air that set my nerves on fire. Everyone, including Rowan, has told me he's done terrible things. But no one has ever gone further than a warning.

"Well, for starters, there's the dealing on the side. And there were a couple of alleged assaults. But no formal charges were ever filed against me. That all kind of comes with the territory of owning a nightclub, I think."

I nod along. None of it is surprising. I've seen how he's always guarded with Mateo. I saw him hit Reece. But he sits there now, haunted. And I know there's more. Maybe he's not ready to share it, but I need to know.

"Anything else?"

He takes a deep breath and looks away like he can't bear to see my reaction.

"It's not like you killed anyone, right?" I laugh lightly, trying to make it easier, trying to ease the tension. But Rowan drops his hand from my leg, and my breath catches.

"Rowan?" This time, it's barely a whisper as he hangs his head. Another silence engulfs us as my mind runs wild with the possibility.

"Well, not directly, no," he finally admits.

My eyes widen, and I lean back. I've seen him get violent, but never expected anything to this level. He's always gotten himself in trouble, even from a young age, but this feels completely out of the realm of possibility.

"What do you mean, not directly?"

He shakes his head and meets my gaze. He looks like he could shatter, and that only makes my chest squeeze tighter.

"You know. Sometimes, my dad needed someone to disappear."

I inhale sharply as the pieces fall into place. The words between what he's telling me are loud and clear. That responsibility fell to Rowan.

I sit, mouth slightly open, trying to wrap my head around that fact. So much always fell on him, being the oldest, but this is more than I ever imagined. It makes me hate Mr. Callahan more than I can put into words for what he's put Rowan through. There's nothing I can say that would make this better.

Rowan shifts in his seat, then stands and walks to the edge of the deck before I can reach out for him. He grips the railing so hard his knuckles turn white.

"I was honestly kind of glad when he got locked up. Meant I didn't have to do that shit anymore… You know, I haven't spoken to him since the arrest?" He glances at me briefly over his shoulder. "When the heat came down on us, we decided no contact would be safer. He just wanted to keep me out of it."

The pain in his voice cuts deep. He seems almost fragile now, like a boy who just needs someone to be there for him. A boy who needs his dad.

"Rowan," I whisper, rising from the table, dinner all but forgotten now. I go to him and wrap my arms around his torso, holding him tightly. "I didn't know."

His hand covers mine, our fingers interlacing.

"My dad might've made bad choices, but he wasn't bad. He didn't want this life. He just couldn't give it up once he had it. And I thought he had it all figured out. At one point, I wanted to be just like him," he says, voice rough.

He squeezes my hand like he's trying to stay grounded, and I understand that feeling all too well. I want to tell him everything will be okay, but that feels like a promise I can't keep.

"But then the Collins family came to town and ruined everything. They came in and blew up the entire operation. My dad tried to get Graham to drop it and not go to the police. When he couldn't pay Graham off, he threatened him. I don't even know half of it, but I know my dad had Reece and Molly followed. He wanted Graham to know he could get to his family."

I can't hide the shock on my face with the anger that's laced in Rowan's every word. I'm glad he can't see me right now, but I'm sure he can feel the tension I'm trying so desperately to hide.

"Graham went to the cops. I guess they were already collecting evidence against my dad or something. Who knows what they found when they really started digging." Rowan's shoulders slump forward like he's bearing the weight of all these secrets, so I hold him tighter.

"Then, one morning, out of nowhere, it was like every cop in New York was on our lawn, and Clarke was leading the charge. And before I could do anything, they put my dad in cuffs and took him away."

I shudder at the thought. I can't imagine what it must be like seeing your dad carted away in handcuffs. I've envisioned it before, but now it's more than that. It feels real hearing it from him.

"Rowan, you don't have to—"

"I do," he cuts me off, turning to face me. "I have to tell you this."

I want to tell him he doesn't. That I wish I hadn't asked. But I just keep holding him like my life depends on it. We stand like that, silently, both afraid to let go.

"He left me with this mess to clean up," he says hoarsely. "Now I'm the one who has to keep things going. For my mom. For Harper. I can't just leave them like he did."

"He didn't want to leave you," I whisper against his chest.

"I know. It still feels like everything can be taken away from me in an instant. I can't lose anything else. I can't lose you."

Rowan kisses the top of my head, and his words shatter me.

"I've never told anyone about the things I've done. I didn't want you to know either. But I had to tell you."

I pull back and look at him, reaching up to wipe a single tear from his cheek. He looks so broken as my thumb drags across his face.

His blue eyes are darker than I've ever seen, and his brows draw together in a frown. As much as I want to know more, how many people he's hurt, I can't bring myself to ask him anything else.

"Well… thank you for telling me," I say softly. "You didn't have to, but you did. That means a lot."

"I'm going to get out of all of it for you, Briar," he says, eyes searching mine in the dim candlelight of the patio. He pulls away and starts pacing again, like it's a nervous tic of his.

I lean against the railing, watching and waiting for him to need me to step in.

"I never want you involved. I won't let you get caught up in any of this. I'm going to tell Kai I want out. I'll tell him I'm done."

He runs his fingers through his hair. "Kai needs me for one more thing. One trip. Then I'll tell him I'm done."

"Okay." I nod, and he drops into the chair, head in his hands. He sits there for a long moment, then looks up at me, eyes full of worry.

"Does this change anything for you?"

The pain in his voice hurts my heart. Because I don't think there's anything in this world Rowan could tell me that would change how I feel about him.

I smile softly and walk over, standing between his legs just to be close to him. He reaches for me, pulling me closer, his thumbs tracing circles on the backs of my thighs.

"No. It changes nothing," I say, settling on his lap. "I knew you'd made some bad choices. That doesn't change how I feel. The details are unimportant, and they don't change how I feel. I don't think anything could."

His shoulders ease, and he lets out a quiet sigh before he kisses me gently.

"Are you sure? I don't want you to feel like you're in the dark, but I can't always tell you everything. I just… don't want to lose you," he murmurs against my lips.

I don't even have to think about my answer. Not for a second. "I'm positive." Rowan chuckles and pulls me to his chest.

"You're everything to me, Briar. I can't lose you. I won't. I'm always yours. Always."

His words make my cheeks flush, and he presses a kiss to my temple.

"Always," I whisper, more to myself than him.

"And now there are no secrets between us. You know everything," Rowan says, sounding relieved.

My breath catches, and I force a smile because that's not true.

I have secrets.

But I can't expect him to be honest with me if I'm not honest with him.

So I breathe out and say, "There's one thing."

The words hang between us like a heavy, dangerous breath. His smile falters, just slightly, and I know once I say this, nothing will be the same.

But I owe him the truth.

Even if it breaks me to admit it and ruins everything we've just started to build.

Forty-Two
Briar

This isn't at all how I imagined tonight going. Rowan's been nothing but honest with me all night, yet every part of my brain screams to run and hide. My hands are shaking, but Rowan keeps his eyes on me. He's calmer now after shedding the weight that sat on his shoulders for so long, but it doesn't give me hope that I'll feel any better once I do the same.

I take a long breath. "You have to promise not to say anything to anyone."

I've spent four years keeping this a secret, and I'm still not sure it's a good idea to come clean now. But I've already started, so it feels like I can't back out now.

"Of course. I promise."

I shift in his lap, not wanting to look directly at him. I can already feel the weight of everything pressing in around me. I don't need the added pressure of watching Rowan watch me. Sitting silently, trying to figure out how to put this into words, I tug at a loose thread on my shirt. I've never told anyone, and I never thought I'd have to. But I can't hide from this anymore.

"Not many people know this about me, but when I was fourteen, I made some pretty stupid choices. A girl at school introduced me to pills. It was during a time when my parents were fighting almost every day, and everything was just kind of crappy. It was a nice escape from it all. It got pretty bad for a while. Then I had to go to therapy, which was even worse."

I can't help but laugh at the memory. Hours were spent sitting with a stranger, pretending I was getting better, pretending there wasn't an underlying itch that reminded me every day that it wasn't over. Always pretending.

"Eventually, I did start to feel better. But that's when my parents split, and my mom and I moved to London. I thought getting away would help. But it didn't. I went through a kind of party-girl era where I went out *every* night. It was all glamorous and fun until I went on a trip for what I guess might pass as spring break."

I risk glancing at Rowan, trying to sense what he's thinking, questioning if I should keep going. But he stares at me, his face giving nothing away. He's just patiently waiting for me to continue.

"We went everywhere—Paris, Rome, Barcelona, Milan; you name it, we were there. Every city started to blur together after a while. We'd drink on a boat, in a bar, or in a club, anywhere we could really. Then rinse and repeat in the next city. It was a girl's trip for the books. But the girls didn't know I was also popping pills in every city.

"If someone offered me something, I wouldn't turn it down… And that's how we met Isabella. She was a local and wanted to take us to the most exclusive club in Italy. She said it's where all the celebrities and high rollers hung out. So, in my mind, I knew that's where the good stuff would be, and off we went."

Looking off into the backyard, I close my eyes. The shame and embarrassment rush back like it happened yesterday. If I had the opportunity, I'd go back and never step foot in that place, but what's done is done, and I'm left to suffer those consequences.

Rowan places his hand on mine, pulling my attention back to him. I can feel the tears welling, but I push them back.

"I was stupid."

"Briar, it's okay."

His assurance feels good, but I shake my head. "It's not. I don't know what I was thinking, but I knew I could play blackjack and make real money for the next leg of our trip. So I did. And the drinks were flowing, and the next thing I know, I was injecting who knows what in the bathroom. I was already on such a high from winning and felt unbeatable, but that's when it all started to go downhill. Whatever it was felt like ten pounds of syrup had been injected into my bloodstream. I was slow, and everything started to blur around me. I could barely function, so I had to go back to the hotel and sleep it off for two days."

"Briar," Rowan breathes, shock etched into every feature.

I let out a hoarse laugh, ignoring his surprise. "I went back a few days later, wanting to continue the party, like an idiot. I was greeted by security at the door. I guess they suspected I was counting cards, and the casino's owner, Marc, wasn't too happy. Rightfully so," I grimace, remembering the look on his face.

"Before he could say anything, I collapsed right there in the lobby. I don't remember much of anything, but from what I was told, I got rushed to the hospital, and after dozens of tests, they told me I had a weak and inflamed heart. It was the scariest moment of my life. I didn't know what to do. I was practically alone in a foreign country, finding out I had a heart condition. I didn't want to call my mom because I didn't want to admit what happened. I couldn't even tell my friends what happened."

Rowan draws little circles on my leg with his thumb, trying to offer comfort.

"Marc came to my hospital room before I was discharged. I thought it was to check on me, but he banned me from all ten of his casinos and said they'd escort me out if I ever showed up. He let me keep the money I won, but he made me promise that I wouldn't tell anyone what happened. He claimed it was because he didn't want his casino to be known for being lenient with card counters. I think he didn't want it getting out that a girl almost died there."

"He didn't want the wrong people asking the right questions," Rowan says, almost out of reflex, like he knows the feeling.

"Right. Now I get regular checkups for my heart and try to avoid taking drugs from strangers." I force some lightness into my voice, but it doesn't seem to ease the heavy tension that's surrounding us.

Rowan's arms wrap around me, pulling me into him. "But you're okay now, and there are no more drugs, right?" he asks, his voice cracking slightly.

I let him hold me, weighing what answer to give him. Because the truth isn't what he wants to hear; it's not what anyone wants to hear. Even after everything, I haven't been able to give it up. And since I can't give him the whole truth, I won't. I'll give him as much as possible.

"It doesn't go away. I get to live with this for the rest of my life because of that one dumb decision. But I haven't had a flare-up in six months, which is good. And last time, it was just a little chest pain."

"You were having chest pain six months ago?" He stares at me in disbelief, and almost fearful.

"I was only in the hospital for a night. It was to monitor me and make sure it wasn't anything more serious. Which it wasn't. But we missed Christmas because of it. My mom found out I'd been in the hospital, and I lied, telling her it was something with my spleen. When she heard that, she canceled our trip home."

He sighs and pulls me closer, hugging me tightly to his chest, like that will magically fix everything. Like it will fix me. "Briar, you should tell your parents. They'd want to know," he whispers.

I pull away, fear worming its way back into my gut.

"You can't tell anyone, Rowan." The words tumble out of my mouth, sharp. "I can't admit it to them, and I don't want them to worry or be disappointed. They would overreact, and I don't want that. You have to promise."

He furrows his brows, clearly torn, but finally exhales. "Briar, I promise. I just want you to be okay."

"I am okay."

I'm not, but what he doesn't know won't hurt him. He already knows more than I ever wanted to share with anyone, and I fear that might be the thing to ruin me. I never wanted to burden anyone with that secret. It was mine, and mine alone. But Rowan pulled it from me like a storm tearing away the shutters, leaving nothing to hide behind.

"I didn't mean to ruin our night."

Rowan pulls away, looking at me with so much softness and care. "You didn't ruin anything. Any night with you is a perfect one."

"I mean, we let our dinner go cold," I say, glancing at the half-eaten meals on the table.

He huffs, like that's the last thing on his mind. "I'm more worried about you than our dinner."

I can't stand the idea of him worrying or having to keep talking about this. I'd rather talk about dinner, or him, or literally anything else—anything easier.

"It was fantastic. If things with Kai don't work out, you'd have a pretty decent shot at being a shirtless bartender and chef," I say. "I know I'd pay top dollar for that service."

"Briar." He says my name more like a whispered prayer than with disappointment, but I feel it nonetheless.

I'd give anything for us to fall back into our easy rhythm, but we're emotionally exposed here, and it's scary to think there's no remedy for it. Rowan managed to sneak into my heart in a few short weeks, and it's an odd invasion.

I want to trust him with every fiber of my being, but it feels somehow wrong. Then again, maybe it's too late.

Rowan's the first to break the uncomfortable silence. "Well, I know this might not be the best moment to bring this up again, but this is something I've been wanting for a while."

My heart stops. I can't imagine what's left to confess, but I try to hide my growing anxiety.

I swallow my fear. "Okay…"

"It's more of a question."

I hold my breath, not knowing what to anticipate. If he wants to know about my continued drug use, I might have to lie. I don't want to, but I don't want to admit anything more. Not to him. And not now, when it's all been so recent.

Rowan places his hands on my hips and guides me to stand in front of him. He's wearing a goofy little smile that instantly puts me at ease.

"Briar May Abbott…"

I snort at his use of my full name, but nod along as he continues.

"Will you be my girlfriend?"

I pause and tap my finger on my chin a few times, pretending this isn't something I've always wanted. Pretending this isn't a scenario my mind has played a million times over. Pretending his name isn't the one I would doodle in my notebook surrounded by hearts.

"I mean, I guess," I say quietly, fighting a smile.

"If you're not sure about the long-distance thing, we don't have to be that serious," he assures me with a playful edge in his voice.

"No, I think we could make it work."

"Good. And you're staying here tonight," he says quickly, leaving no room for argument.

Not that I would. I don't want to be without him tonight. Or ever.

He grins, pulling me in and kissing me. The second our lips connect, he wraps his arms around me and lifts me off the ground. It's exactly how you'd imagine it in a fairytale. He spins me in a circle, and I can feel his smile. He holds me close like it's the most natural thing in the world, and I feel like the luckiest girl in the world.

Kissing Rowan leaves me breathless. His touch drives me crazy. He's intoxicating, and it's better than any drug. I feel lighter with him, and I think I'd do anything he asked.

I'm at the mercy of Rowan Callahan.

And I think I love that.

And as dangerous as it all feels, I think I might love him, too.

Forty-Three
Briar

The backseat feels lonely, even with Rowan sitting beside me. I can feel the emotional distance growing between us by the second. I'm not sure if it's out of fear or necessity, but he's almost restrained. I finally got him, and I was happy, but now it feels like everything might slip through my fingers. I'm stuck in this strange state of limbo. I can't tell what Rowan's thinking, which leaves me unsure of what to think or feel.

And I don't want to do either of those things.

I don't want to wonder what Rowan is doing in Chicago. I don't want to think about the fact that he can't tell me where he's going. Or how I won't be able to talk to him until he's back. Or that I'm stuck in this car with Nate on the way home.

He was mad enough at Rowan for even suggesting that I come with them.

"You said you'd keep her out of this."

"Nate. It's just the airport. Relax, man."

I'm sure Nate will have an earful for me on the way home, but the only thing I can worry about right now is Rowan.

He's told me it's just a business trip, but that's all he can tell me. And I don't know if knowing the details of it all would make this better or worse.

Rowan intertwines our fingers and gives my hand a gentle squeeze. "You okay?"

"Yeah."

We both know it's a lie. I never imagined I could be this uncertain about something. About a *business trip*. I force a smile to ease his worry because he doesn't seem concerned for himself, only for me.

I stare straight ahead, trying to figure out how I'll get through the next few days. The answer feels obvious, even though I know I shouldn't rely on the pills. But this has been the summer of breaking my own rules. What's one more time?

Nate catches my eye in the rearview mirror as we stop at the intersection before heading toward the city. He's wearing his best concerned big brother scowl, and tears prick my eyes. I want to tell him I'll be okay, and mean it, but I don't know if I will. The cravings are getting louder. I try to resist, but the numbness is easier than the anxiety.

We drive in silence. Even the radio doesn't dare break the tension. I let Rowan hold my hand and watch the last light of sunset disappear beyond the horizon. He traces circles on my skin, trying to keep me calm, but even that's not enough.

Nate pulls up to the gate that protects the hangar, and it feels like we don't belong here. Rowan leans forward, giving directions. "Just around there and to the back."

My heart pounds as we roll to a stop. A few people loiter nearby, and Kai stands below the wing of the plane, arms crossed, surveying everything. Rowan climbs out, grabs his bag, and helps me out of the car.

"Thanks for driving me, man," Rowan says, giving Nate a grateful pat on the shoulder.

"Yeah," Nate replies, but my focus is locked on Kai. As soon as the car doors opened, his eyes were glued to us.

I glare at him until Rowan touches my back. "Hey, why don't you get back in the car?" he suggests gently.

"No, I want to talk to him." I jut my chin toward Kai. As much as he has every hair of mine standing at attention,

I want to make sure he knows what's at stake here. I'll ruin his life if anything happens to Rowan.

"Kai?" Rowan asks, confused.

"Yeah." I don't budge.

"Why?"

I shrug, trying to feign that nonchalance I know it will take to sell this. "We weren't properly introduced last time."

"I think this is one person you can skip meeting," Rowan jokes, but there is the briefest flash of fear cross his features.

"Rowan, please. I just want to feel like I'm part of your life, and less like your friend's sister who follows you around."

My words land, and I can all but feel the heavy sigh he huffs out. "Okay," he says, waving Kai over. "This should be interesting."

Kai hesitates for a second but covers the distance with long strides. The corners of his lips tip up as he approaches us, and the sick feeling from the other night washes over me again. "Well, if it isn't my partner who's," he checks his watch, "twenty minutes late. And my favorite card-counting blonde."

"Play nice," Rowan warns, shaking his hand.

"I heard you took him off the market."

"I heard you cried when he told you." I snap back, trying to sound as innocently playful as I can.

Kai blinks, clearly thrown by my bite. Rowan gently grabs my elbow in a silent warning, but I won't back down with someone like Kai. He's all bravado. All bark and no bite.

"Been to any more blackjack games lately?" he taunts.

I smile, knowing my presence gets under his skin.

"Been back to your illegal little club recently?"

"Everything I do is perfectly legal."

"Except for the unlicensed casino in New York. That why it's behind closed doors?"

He narrows his eyes and crosses his arms. It's a guess, but judging by Kai's reaction, his tenseness, and how his eyes narrow. I know I've hit my mark.

"Briar, calm down," Rowan murmurs, pulling me closer, and that's all the confirmation I need to know I'm right.

"Ashton was right. She is feisty," Kai chuckles, but he's watching me with more attention.

I glance at Rowan. "Can I have a second alone with him?"

"Why?" He scans my face, and I can all but see him running through possible reasons in his mind.

"Please."

Rowan exhales and shakes his head. I know my words from earlier will likely haunt him, but hopefully, I'll have all the time in the world to make it up to him.

"Good luck, man." Rowan nods, patting Kai's shoulder as he hesitantly walks to the other side of the car with my brother.

Kai's eyes gleam. "What can I do for you, sweetheart?" His tone is syrupy. Flirtatious. Gross.

"Don't call me sweetheart," I snap. "I don't want any trouble, for Rowan's sake. But don't think I won't ruin you if something happens to him."

"Rowan's a big boy. He can take care of himself."

"I don't know what you're doing in Chicago, but he'd better come back unharmed."

"Or what?" he laughs, stepping closer.

"I'll shut down your club. One call. That's all it will take to shut you down. And I bet there's more to find if the right people start digging, I'm sure they'll find plenty."

A vein pulses at his temple.

"You wouldn't do that. Because it's not just my club. It's also *Rowan's* club." The way he emphasizes Rowan's name has my stomach curdling. "And if you do the same thing to him, that the Collinses did to his dad… I don't think there's any coming back from that, sweetheart."

Kai's words sting, but I know he's right.

"Rowan said he's done with that."

The words aren't even out of my mouth before Kai lets out a throaty, amused laugh. "Is that what he told you?"

It feels like a slap in the face.

Because Rowan did tell me that, and I believed it. I still want to believe it. But now I don't know.

"Let me tell you something," he draws out. Gesturing to the plane and hangar around us, "This… this thing we have going, it isn't something you just drop for some flavor of the week."

As much as I know what he's saying is true, Kai's little business is chump change compared to what I know Marc has.

With my silence, it's clear that Kai thinks he's won, leaning against Nate's car, pulling out a pocketknife, and cleaning under his nails. "But you're hot when you're threatening me. I see why Rowan has a thing for you."

"It's not just a threat. I'll do what I have to do to protect Rowan."

Kai takes a step closer, eyeing me warily. Once again, it's like he's trying to peer into my soul, but this time, I don't back down.

"That's cute. But we both know you don't have it in you," he laughs lowly.

"You don't know anything about me, Kai," I warn him.

We stand there for a second, neither of us moving a muscle, before he finally gives in.

"You've got balls, blondie. I like that. I get why Rowan likes you. Let me know if you ever get bored with him and want a real man." Kai stares at me with a sleazy grin.

"Not a chance," I tell him over my shoulder as I start back to Rowan and slip my arms around him.

"Done already?" he asks, kissing my head.

"Yeah." I pout, clinging to him. "Do you have to go?"

"Yes. But then, no more trips. I promise."

Suddenly, I can't breathe.

Thoughts race through my mind, and I can feel the anxiety creeping back in as I have to wonder if Kai meant what he said.

Rowan stands there, holding me and swaying back and forth, and I have to force myself not to question him about it now. He's been so honest with me so far that I have to choose to believe him.

With all those worries, still the thought that he might not know how much he means to me makes me breathless.

He needs to know.

"I love you, Rowan," I whisper into his chest.

"What?" He pulls back, startled. His mouth hangs slightly open, like he's trying to process what I've just said and doesn't trust he heard me correctly.

"I love you. So please, be careful." I pull him back to me and soak in his presence.

He holds me tighter now, and he plants a few soft kisses on the crown of my head. We stand there for a few minutes before he finds his voice again.

"I promise, Princess. When I come back, I'll take you anywhere you want, Madrid, Paris, or wherever. Just us."

"Let's go, Callahan," Kai calls from across the hangar, forcing Rowan to pull away.

I don't want him to let go, but I know he has to. And I hate Kai for reminding me of that, but I know he's right. We can't stand here forever. They have to get going.

I turn to Rowan, tears brimming in my eyes. He offers me a soft smile, then leans in and kisses me. It's so soft and tender, and I let myself linger there for a second longer.

Then, without another word, he walks me to the car and opens the door, helping me in like he always does.

"I love you, Briar," he murmurs.

"I love you," I whisper as he closes the door and walks away.

Two seconds later, we're being directed back toward the main gate and pulling onto the main road. As Nate drives off, it feels like I'm leaving a piece of myself behind. The piece that held everything together. My brother watches me from the corner of his eye, concern etched into every line on his face, but he lets me sit in the silence.

A few minutes later, Nate finally asks, "You love him?" I look at him, hesitating momentarily as I see the worry etched deeply into his features. He looks physically pained to be asking that question, like me answering it might shatter the very ground we're on.

"I love him," I finally breathe in confirmation as Nate pulls into the driveway. We sit in silence for a while, neither of us knowing where to go from here. I can't move, frozen by the fear of every what-if scenario playing through my mind, and I feel like I'm unraveling.

"Try not to worry about him, B." Nate's words do nothing to quiet my mind.

"I know. But I'm tired. I'm going to bed." I lie more to myself than to Nate, but I need the quiet. Even with Rowan, my mind has been louder the past few weeks than it has in the past two years. And now, without him, it's the loudest it's ever been. Nothing can help quiet it like the solace of what I have tucked in the drawer beside my bed.

It's the only thing that will be able to make the night more bearable.

Closing the door to my room, I go to my nightstand and quietly open the drawer. The pill bottle is still there. It's been there ever since my surgery, and has been quietly tempting me every night.

But now I don't have the willpower to keep ignoring its draw.

Unscrewing the cap, I pour one pill into my palm and swallow it.

"It'll help me sleep."

It's a lie that's all too familiar to me, but I don't have the energy to come up with anything else today.

I climb into bed, not bothering to change, and curl into a ball. I stare blankly at the wall and let the sadness engulf me.

I want to cry, but no tears come.

I want to scream, but it feels like it's stuck in my throat.

But soon, the familiar haze settles over me, and I let it take me.

Forty-Four
Briar

The past forty-eight hours have gone by in a blur. The steady flow of pain medication has kept me in a hazy state, halfway between sleep and consciousness. I sleep more than I'm awake, and when I am awake, I barely feel anything.

Nate has tried to check on me a few times, but I tune him out. Mostly because of the guilt—about Rowan, the pills, all of it. I can't bring myself to face him. And I don't want to have to answer any of his questions. Because I don't even know how to explain the gaping hole I feel whenever Rowan's not here.

But Nate's persistent. Like clockwork, he knocks on my door. Once an hour, every hour.

"Hi," I mumble, not bothering to look away from the ceiling.

"Let's go for a ride," he offers.

I don't want to go anywhere. I want to lie here and rot. But Nate doesn't move.

"B, I'm not taking no for an answer. You haven't eaten or left your bed all day."

I lift my head just enough to glare at him with whatever energy I can muster.

"You can hate me all you want," he says, "but I'm worried about you. I'm worried you're on something."

The knot in my chest tightens.

I can see the stress etched into his face; the deep lines in his forehead, the tired eyes. It's probably been there for days. I just hadn't noticed.

"I'm not on anything," I lie. A white lie. Sort of. I haven't taken anything in the past four hours, so it's probably out of my system. It's a technicality, but it's more about easing his pain than easing mine.

"What'd you do with those pills from your surgery?"

The question hits harder than it should. I didn't expect him to even remember that, or follow up about it. But now, it sounds like an accusation—because it is. And he's not wrong.

"I flushed them after the surgery."

Another lie. They're still in the drawer next to me. The few pills that I haven't taken.

But what's one more lie to add to the pile? And the relief that washes over him makes the lie feel worth it.

"Good," he exhales. "I know we never talked about it, but you scared me last time. I don't want to get to that place again."

His admission breaks something inside me. We never talked about it for exactly this reason. Because I didn't want to scare him. And now, I know that was the right call. He doesn't need the weight I carry.

I stay quiet. I can't tell him another lie.

"I think you should at least get out for a bit," he says. "I was thinking about fishing. It's beautiful out. Want to come?"

It's been forever since we went fishing, and Nate looks so hopeful. I don't want to risk scaring him anymore, and for once, the idea doesn't sound awful. Maybe being out for an hour will feel better than lying here, drowning in my own thoughts.

"Fine. I'll go, but I don't want to be out too long," I say. "My bed might miss me."

"Perfect. I'll prep the boat. Half an hour."

"Sure."

Nate vanishes from the doorway like he's afraid I'll change my mind if he lingers, and I can hear him rushing out through the back sliding glass doors.

I exhale a long breath and tilt my head back to stare at the ceiling again. I don't want to keep lying to Nate, but I don't want to burden him either. If going for a boat ride makes him think I'm okay, then that's what I'll do.

It takes more effort than expected to force myself up, but once I'm moving, I'm fine. I pull on a sweatshirt and step out of my room for the first time today. My bare feet make no sound against the cool hardwood floor as I trek down the stairs.

As I move, I can't help but notice how the house is quiet. Peaceful.

Not like the quiet that lives in my head.

That quiet drives me mad. The silence that settles in when there's nothing to focus on but my thoughts. The thoughts that won't leave me alone. That reminds me I'm not enough. That I'm screwing something up. That I won't get where I want to go.

But when I'm with Rowan, those thoughts fade. That's why I miss him so much.

That's why I *need* him.

I find Nate in the kitchen, cutting the crusts off a sandwich and making a mess of the counter.

"What are you doing?" I ask.

"Making a sandwich," he says. Then, seeing my face, he adds, "It's for you. You haven't eaten."

I have no appetite. But I can't tell him that. "Thanks."

I pause as Nate packs up, and we walk to the boat in silence. Nate carries the sandwich and keeps glancing at me like I might disappear. It feels like I'm being watched, studied; like one wrong move will send me bolting.

I climb into the boat with him behind me. The seat covers are folded and off to the side, and the engine roars to life as Nate starts it.

As we pull away from the dock, a calm washes over me. I lie back on a cushioned bench, watching clouds drift by while Nate heads toward our favorite spot: Silverfin Cove.

The fish here are tiny, technically bluefish, but their silver sheen gives the cove its name. Or maybe it's just a coincidence. Or maybe someone just made it up, and then the fish came.

Either way, this is our place. Mine and Nate's.

We've never caught anything bigger than a palm-sized fish, but that's not the point. It never has been about the fishing here.

Nate docks the boat, and we thread bits of breadcrust onto our hooks before casting our lines into the shimmering water. We sit and sit, but nothing bites. Though I don't know what we expected. It's mid-afternoon, not the best time to fish.

I can feel Nate watching me as I watch for any movement on our lines.

"Thanks for bringing me out here," I tell him, my gaze never leaving the water. This place has always been my happy place. It's the same place that helped me get over my seventh-grade breakup with Cody Howell. Nothing else matters when I'm here; I think Nate knows that.

"Of course. Rule number four," he replies, and I smile at the thought.

We made a list of rules when we were kids that had to be followed while we were here. Rule Four came after Nate dropped his sandwich in the water: *No pouting at Silverfin Cove.*

"Rule number four," I repeat, letting the quiet settle over me again. For a moment, it helps.

But my brain never lets the peace last. It fills the space with what-ifs and worst-case scenarios, and today, my brain is feeling particularly dramatic.

"Are you not worried about him?" I finally ask.

Nate lounges in the captain's chair, feet kicked up, hands behind his head. He seems almost too relaxed, but then again, maybe I'm just too tense.

He doesn't say anything for a moment and watches the horizon, taking a few exaggerated breaths. "Rowan can take care of himself," he finally says, which does nothing to calm my mind.

We sit there for a long time. Or at least it feels long, with everything running through my head. And that's enough to make me want to crawl into bed and never come out.

"I'm ready to go home," I say.

"Okay. Let's reel in."

We pack up quickly. I curl up on the floor against the bow seats with a clear view of Nate, who returns to the captain's chair, checking every dial and gauge before the boat roars to life. Tucking my knees into my chest, I silently count the minutes until I'm back in bed, pills in hand.

The boat lurches forward. I close my eyes, holding everything in. The fear, the tears, the nausea—everything. Swallowing the lump in my throat just keeps getting harder. The breeze whips through my hair, grounding me and keeping me from breaking down into tears.

When I open my eyes, Nate is smiling. It looks so out of place for him to be smiling so hard, when I feel so broken, that I snap.

"What's wrong with you?"

"Don't say I never did anything for you, B," he laughs.

"What?" I ask, feeling the boat slow down, and the frustration growing inside of me. If he just brought me out here to laugh at how down I feel, I might kill him.

"Look," he says, pointing out past the front of the boat.

I turn and instantly recognize the Callahan dock.

My head snaps back to Nate. "Why'd you bring me here? I don't want to be near that house," I tell him, my voice breaking.

"Are you sure about that? Look again," Nate says, gesturing toward the house.

I don't want to be in this place, at the reminder he's not here, but something in my gut forces me to look again.

This time, I see it; someone leans over the railing.

But not just anyone.

Rowan.

"He's back," I whisper.

My pulse stutters. For a second, I can't move. Can't breathe. It doesn't feel real.

But it is.

He's standing there like he never left. Like I didn't watch him climb into that plane two days ago, my heart unraveling with every step he took.

I missed him.

More than I should've in just forty-eight hours. More than I wanted to admit even to myself.

I press a hand to my chest, like I can hold it all in; every ache, every hope, every piece of me that only ever settled when he was near.

Nate doesn't say a word. He doesn't have to.

Because Rowan's here. And somehow, the moment our eyes meet, I know.

He missed me, too.

Forty-Five
Rowan

If you'd told me a month ago that I'd be counting down the minutes until I saw this girl again, I would've said you were crazy. Yet here I am, leaning against the deck railing, waiting for her.

I scan the entrance of the inlet, searching for any sign of movement in the water, anything to prove she's almost here. I hear the boat engine before I see it. Then come the ripples. Then the boat.

Nate waves as he comes into view, and my pulse kicks up a notch. It's not chaotic, just sharper. Steady. Expectant.

Then I see her.

And suddenly, the pain of the last few days disappears. All I care about is how good it'll feel to have her in my arms again. She looks like she's been crying, and I hate that she's been crying over me. I never want to make that girl cry, and I'll do everything in my power to make sure it never happens again.

I push off the railing and jog down the stairs as the boat nears the dock. The second it's close enough, Briar jumps off and starts running—straight to me.

I can't help the grin that breaks across my face. She's everything I've ever wanted. And now, she's mine.

She slows just before she reaches me, and I open my arms, allowing her to crash into me, breathless.

"You're back," she gasps.

I hold her close and inhale her sweet saltwater and wildflower scent. She feels lighter, smaller somehow, like the worry has been weighing her down.

"I told you I'd come back to you, Princess," I whisper into her hair. I could hold onto her forever, but I'm acutely aware of her brother, my best friend, still at the docks.

I gently set her back on her feet and glance over her shoulder to wave at Nate, who is already backing the boat away. Briar's eyes dart between us.

"He knew?" she asks, still in shock as her eyes bounce around my face. I suck in a breath and know she's memorizing every bruise and cut.

"I asked him to help me surprise you," I say, watching her face light up like the sun breaking through the clouds. Before she can say a word, I pull her into me and press my lips to hers.

It's rushed and needy, and I don't know if that's from me or her, but we're both desperate for this moment. Her hands thread through my hair, keeping me here in this moment. It's perfect.

Her lips are soft, and I never want to stop kissing her. Ever.

When I finally pull back, it's only because I need to see her face again, to look in her eyes. To know she's really here.

"You're back and breathing, and in one piece," she says, her voice cracking as silent tears fall. Like she's not sure I'm real.

I laugh and brush a tear from her cheek.

"I'm back," I tell her. I'll say it as many times as it takes her to believe it. I'll repeat it for her forever.

Her eyes linger on the stitches above my eyebrow, and I can see the questions turning over in her mind.

"Rowan, what happened?" she whispers, fingers grazing the raised skin. She holds her breath, like she's bracing herself for the worst.

"Hey. Breathe," I tell her gently. She takes a shaky breath, her eyes still asking me the same questions. "It's just a few cuts and bruises. I'm fine."

She still looks unsure, like she can't find the words for anything she's feeling. But that's okay. I'll spend as long as it takes showing her that I'll always find my way back to her.

"I was beyond worried, Rowan," she says, wrapping her arms around my neck again.

I hold her to my chest and start walking us back toward the house, keeping her as close as she'll let me. If I get my way, I'll never let her out of arm's reach again.

"Come on. Let's go inside."

She doesn't let go, just lets me carry her along, so I duck under her arms and toss her over my shoulder.

"Rowan!" she shrieks. "I am perfectly capable of walking."

"Sure," I drawl. "Like you actually wanted to."

Walking up the stairs, I feel the vibrations of Briar's laugh in my own body, and the sound of her amusement warms my heart. I keep my hand firmly on her thigh and finally put her down only once we're on the deck. She looks at me like she's still searching for something, her eyes scanning every inch of my face again. Then, she smiles—a real one.

"I missed you," she says softly.

"I missed you, too, baby." I kiss her again. It's short. It has to be. Otherwise, I'll never be able to stop.

"You want something to drink?"

She hesitates at my offer, lost in thought, and doesn't answer until I'm two steps from the bar.

"I'll just have water."

I nod, not pushing. She's clearly been through a lot the past few days, and I don't want to make anything worse for her.

At the bar, I pour myself a generous bourbon, but I need it. Anyone would need it after dealing with Kai for two days straight. Then, for Briar, I mix a little cranberry juice with sparkling water in the second glass. She might not want anything, but I know she'll like this.

When I return, she's curled up on the couch, legs tucked under her. I hand her the drink and sit beside her, pulling her close.

She rests her head on my shoulder, and for a minute, everything feels exactly how it should. The two of us sitting here, and reveling in the other's presence.

"Where are the cuts and bruises from?" she asks so quietly that I almost don't hear her.

I can't tell her the truth, that they came from Kai's stupidity. I could pretend not to hear, but with the way she's looking at me, I can't lie. Not again.

"We ran into a few minor complications," I tell her, but that's really all I'll be able to say, and I hate that. Because if I tell her about how we were ambushed, she'll worry. And I don't want her to keep worrying about me.

However, I wouldn't classify Sal as a *minor* complication. He's the competition, but she doesn't need to know that. Because, as much as I don't want to admit it, things with Sal and his family are far from settled, and I know this peace won't last. Right now, I don't want to think about what might come next.

"But I don't want to talk about Chicago. I'd rather talk about you, about Paris."

It's a deflection. But a good one.

"You were serious?" Her eyes go wide with excitement, and she scoots to the edge of the couch.

"Absolutely." I tuck a strand of hair behind her ear. "I'll need you to be my tour guide while we're there."

She has a sparkle in her eyes as she looks at me like that's the best thing she's ever heard.

"There's this cute little hotel in the heart of Paris that has this incredible rooftop," she says, reaching for my hand. I lace our fingers together as she keeps talking.

"You can see the Eiffel Tower, Montmartre, and the Sacré-Cœur Basilica all from the rooftop pool," she explains in wonder. "We could stay there, and I could show you the views. It's the best spot in Paris for a midnight swim."

Her voice has a hint of mischief while she stands and pulls me along with her toward the pool deck. As soon as our feet hit the concrete, she peels off her sweatshirt and lets it fall. "Briar," I say, as she moves closer and her hands find the hem of my shirt. My breath catches because this girl is going to absolutely ruin me.

But I don't mind letting her ruin me, and she doesn't hesitate to pull my shirt off.

"What?" she says, all innocence and fire.

"What are you doing?"

"I'm having some fun, Rowan," she teases, unbuttoning her jean shorts. I clench my fists in a failed attempt to restrain the rampant thoughts. She's perfect.

I already knew that, but damn, if it isn't hard to keep myself from losing myself in her. Every part of me is screaming to grab her and kiss her, but the other part of me, the rational part, knows I have to take it slow with her. And if I have to be the one to hold back, so be it.

I drag my hand down my face, watching her step out of her shorts, knowing there isn't anything I wouldn't do for this girl. Briar raises her eyebrows with a wicked grin like she knows.

"It's not like we're skinny dipping. We're still wearing our underwear."

I bark out a laugh at her logic. She's technically right, but that isn't doing much for my dwindling willpower.

"It's practically the same as a bathing suit," she says before diving into the pool without a second thought. Watching her prop her elbows up on the edge, I get a sense of déjà vu.

We were in this exact spot less than a month ago. A month ago, I could only hope to be in this spot with her. I truly thought I'd be just a blip on her radar, someone she barely noticed, barely remembered. But I've never been more wrong. And I've never felt so lucky to have been wrong.

Because she's the only one I want. The only one I've ever wanted.

"Come on in, Rowan. The water's great."

I curse under my breath. I know I shouldn't get in, but I want to be close to her in any way possible. I'd follow her to the ends of the Earth if she asked me to.

The buttons of my pants are undone, and I let them slide down my legs. "You're going to kill me one day, Briar."

I dive in after her, and in two strokes, I've got her in my arms again. Her legs wrap around my waist, and every rational thought leaves me.

"I know," she laughs before leaning in and kissing me again. It feels so good to have her here with me, and my resolve weakens even further, feeling her rock her hips into mine.

I pull her closer to me, walking us backward until her back is flush with the side of the pool. There isn't anything I wouldn't do to get closer to her. A little moan escapes her, and it dies in my throat.

She has no idea what she's doing to me right now. Or maybe she does.

"Briar," I groan. "We should take things slow."

"This is slow," she whispers, forehead against mine. I feel every movement she makes.

It's torture.

She's here, touching me, but something still feels out of reach. Her fingers trail down my chest, but she avoids my eyes.

"What are you thinking about?"

"Hm?" She looks up, blinking like she's trying to find the words. "Are we… dating?"

The question stuns me. I've never had to define things before because it was never real before. Or the girls knew it would never be anything serious.

But Briar is different.

She's always been different; I don't want to risk jeopardizing that.

"Is that what you want?"

"Yes," she breathes.

"Then we're dating." I grin and kiss her again. No hesitation this time. I've waited long enough to be able to call this girl mine, and I can't wait another second. She's mine.

She pulls away from me. "There is one other thing," she says, biting her lip.

"What's that?"

"There's this party tomorrow…" she says, trailing off, and I can't fight the smile that finds its home on my face.

"There's always a party," I say, quoting her.

"I know you don't love my friends, but they're throwing it, and I'd like you to go with me. It would mean a lot. You don't have to agree now, but can you promise to think about it?"

There's nothing to think about.

"No," I say, and she starts to roll her eyes before I stop her, pinning her gently in place. "No, I don't need to think about it. I'd do anything to make you happy. Including going to this party with you."

Forty-Six
Briar

I've never had a hangover like this in my life. Everything hurts—my muscles ache, my head feels like a construction crew is working overtime inside it, and my mouth is as dry as the Sahara. I barely have the strength to open my eyes, let alone get up.

I let myself lie still for another minute before necessity overrides the pain. I need water before I swallow my tongue. My eyelids are heavy, but I force them open and freeze.

This isn't my room. And it's not one I recognize. A well-loved lacrosse stick hangs on the wall, and the bed sheets smell like sea salt and something almost citrusy.

My mind spins as I try to place where I am and why. Why I'm in a bed that's not mine. A quick glance around reveals Reece sleeping on the floor, and my heart drops into my stomach.

The wave of anxiety that hits me is so strong, I'm worried my heart will give out here and now.

I can't be here. I shouldn't be here.

My eyes land on my phone on his bedside table, sitting face down. I don't know what happened last night, but I know one thing: I have to get out of here.

I need to find Rowan.

I need him to make this make sense.

I crawl to the edge of the bed and spot my shoes across the room. Every movement feels like I'm dragging anchors behind me, but I force myself to keep moving. It takes everything I have to stumble outside.

The sunlight is blinding, and I nearly fall down the front steps, but I regain my balance on shaky legs. I don't make it far before I have to sit and rest. My head is spinning, and I think it'd hurt less if I got run over by a semi-truck. I rack my brain for any memory, any detail about how I ended up here.

But there's nothing.

It's like someone wiped my memory clean.

I fumble for my phone, hoping for a clue about what happened last night. But when I unlock it, I'm met with more questions than answers. Dozens of missed calls and texts from Rowan, Harper, Reece, and Kian.

I tap Rowan's name, desperate to hear his voice. The call rings once, then goes to voicemail. I try again. Same result.

"Stupid phone," I mutter.

With no other option, I force myself to my feet. I have to find Rowan. He'll make this all make sense. He always does.

The ringing in my ears grows louder as I stumble through the streets. When I think I might lose my bearings, Rowan's house comes into view, and I sigh in relief.

My breathing is ragged, and I feel like I might collapse. I want to, but putting one foot in front of the other, I climb the stairs and knock weakly on the front door. There's no answer, so I knock again.

"Rowan," I croak, not able to handle this anymore. My muscles are weakening with every movement, and the nauseous feeling in my stomach grows every second that passes. I'm desperate now, knocking on a door that's never locked. Never.

The door finally swings open, and Rowan stands there, looking furious.

"Rowan," I breathe, taking a step toward him.

He raises a hand, stopping me from getting any closer. "Don't."

I flinch. The harshness in his tone makes it feel like he's punched me in the gut. "I don't want to see you right now, Briar."

"What?" My voice cracks. I don't know if it's from fear or sadness, but I can feel the cracks setting into my heart.

"Leave me alone." His eyes flick up and down my body with disgust. I blink a few times, questioning if my mind is playing tricks on me or if he really hates me.

"Can we just talk? Rowan, please. I don't understand."

"Just stop. I'm not in the mood to talk." His voice is cold. Distant. Pained.

My throat tightens, and if I weren't so dehydrated, I'm sure I'd be crying already.

"Rowan, please. I don't—I don't remember. Did we fight? Did I do something?"

He barks a bitter laugh. "Did you do something? Where did you wake up this morning, huh, Briar?"

I shake my head, not understanding why he's yelling at me. I can't piece anything together, and I just don't understand. I don't want to understand.

"Darian said he saw you leave the party with Reece. You were all over him."

"No," I whisper, like saying it will make it not true. I don't want this to be true.

"Yeah. You left with him. And I'm sure you woke up in his bed." His voice rises, loud enough to send a spark of fear through me.

Before I can say anything else, I glimpse a quick movement upstairs from the corner of my eye. I'm praying Harper is here to save me from whatever I must have done, but when I glance up, it's not Harper.

It's Calista.

She's standing at the top of the stairs, wearing nothing but one of Rowan's shirts, smirking at me. My blood turns to ice at the sight. I don't have any words as I look back at Rowan searching for an explanation. But he stands there, completely unmoving.

The only logical explanation my brain can muster is that I must be in some nightmare, some kind of walking, talking night terror that I'll wake up from any minute.

"I think you should go," he says, closing the door just enough to block the sight of *her*. The girl he's obviously always wanted.

I don't have words.

After everything, he still chose her.

And that hurts worse than any physical pain I'm feeling.

He made me believe I was different. But I wasn't enough. I never was.

Not for Rowan.

I take a step back. My legs wobble. The weight of it all—his anger, the confusion, the betrayal—comes crashing down around me.

I can't breathe.

The hurt bombards me, coming from every direction, and it's suffocating.

Things with Rowan have changed so quickly, like a rip current dragging me out into the open sea and leaving me there to drown. I don't know which way is up anymore. All I know is I have to get away from this.

From him.

With the realization setting in, there's nothing left to say. I shut down. The walls go back up, and I back away from the boy I thought I knew.

Everyone warned me about Rowan.

And it turns out they were right.

He took everything I had to give, and threw me away in the process.

My brain shuts off, and I let autopilot take me home. The only thing driving me is the welcome escape that waits for me there.

I take the stairs to my room two at a time, the itch consuming my mind. I need to numb the pain, numb how deeply my heart hurts. Every inch of this island is covered in the memory of Rowan, a memory I can't run from. My throat feels like sandpaper, but I force the pills down.

One. Then two. Then three.

I want to forget everything that's happened. I want to erase this entire train wreck of a night, of a summer.

I stagger downstairs, searching for something to take the edge off. The pills haven't kicked in yet, and I need something, anything, to numb the pain faster.

I find a half-empty bottle of wine in the fridge, and decide that will have to be good enough.

I collapse on the couch, bottle in hand, but can't force myself to take a drink. This is the bottle I opened with Rowan, and the thought rips my heart from my chest. The blank television stares back at me as my mind replays the mess of my life; every mistake and misstep is there, sharp and grueling.

Time seems to stop as I think about everything I've ruined.

Eventually, the numbness starts to take over. The edges blur. The constant noise in my head finally fades into silence. I finally have some semblance of peace.

Then, someone calls out, pulling me back from the haze.

"Bri?"

I blink. Nate and Harper stand in front of me, their faces blurry.

"Bri, what happened last night? Are you okay?"

"Don't know. Don't care." My words come out slow and slurred.

Harper vanishes into the kitchen while Nate sits beside me, taking my chin in his hand.

"B, are you on something?"

"I was in pain." I laugh, and it shakes my entire body as Nate takes the wine bottle from my hand. "Now I'm not."

"Did you get hurt?" Harper reappears, scanning me and trying to hand me a glass of water.

I don't want it, so I swat it away.

"Yeah. You were right." I slur. "He chose her."

"B, you're not making sense. Drink this." Nate tries to force the water toward me.

"Rowan," I say. "He chose her. Calista."

They both still. The room is so silent I can hear my heart beating.

"I saw them together this morning. She was in his shirt. You were right, Harper. They're perfect for each other."

I try to stand but stumble, nearly falling.

"What are you talking about?" Nate asks, his voice sharp with concern.

"He chose her," I repeat and sway.

My vision blurs, so much so that I can't see Nate's face anymore. Their voices fade like someone stuffed cotton in my ears. Then blackness creeps in.

"Nate," I whisper, reaching for him.

Then everything goes dark.

The End.

Read On for a Sneak Peek of What's Next
Escaping the Maelstroms — Coming October 3rd

The storm may have calmed, but their story is far from over.

Turn the page for Chapter One of *Escaping the Maelstroms*—and step back into a world where love is tested, secrets surface, and nothing is ever simple.

Now available for pre-order wherever books are sold.

Escaping the Maelstroms

Her plan was simple. Until it cost her everything.

Hanna Grace

One
Nate

Never in my life did I think I'd see my sister like this—broken in a way she couldn't fix. I've seen her fall apart before, but never like this. Never in front of me. Never so completely. Two days ago, everything was fine. My sister was happy and in love. And now, she's lying on the floor, unresponsive.

The sound of wailing sirens grows louder, slicing through the early morning quiet as they approach the house. I cradle my sister's limp body in my lap, my tears blurring the flashing lights that reflect off the walls. She looks so fragile, like someone I should have protected—even if that meant protecting her from herself.

I barely notice the EMTs rushing into the living room, surrounding us as we're sprawled across the floor. My heart breaks as they attend to Briar, my brain barely able to process the instructions passing between them.

"Is she breathing?"

"Yes."

"Great. Let's get a set of vitals."

A soft touch lands on my shoulder and urges me to move. Harper's voice, barely a whisper, takes a moment to register as I lean on her for support.

"Come on, Nate. Let's give them space."

Numbly, I allow her to guide me to the couch. Harper's so calm. Like she didn't just stand beside me and watch her best friend collapse on the floor. Or maybe this is all some kind of nightmare that I'll wake up from.

The room spins as I collapse into the cushions, watching helplessly while the paramedics work. My vision blurs again, but Harper's firm grip on my forearm keeps me grounded. Keeps me from losing it.

One of the EMTs, a middle-aged woman with kind but focused eyes, signals to her partner, a younger man, briefing him on Briar's condition. "I have a weak pulse, sluggish pupils, shallow breathing. Prep her for transport while I speak with those two." Her eyes dart over to Harper and me on the couch before she stands, her features softening.

"Hey, guys. My name is Linda, and I want to take the best care of your friend. But I need one of you to tell me what happened. Can you do that?" She looks between us kindly, unsure who will be most helpful. I stare blankly at the woman.

I open my mouth, but nothing comes out. It feels like my throat is swollen shut, suffocating me.

Harper's voice pulls me out of the haze as she jumps in. "We don't know."

Linda nods. "Okay. Let's start simple. What's her name?"

"Briar," I manage to choke out.

"And what happened with Briar?" Linda encourages us.

"Um," Harper takes a shaky breath. "One minute, Bri was sitting here, drinking and rambling. She wasn't making sense. Then she stood up and… I don't know. She just… collapsed." Her voice cracks as tears well in her eyes.

Interlocking my fingers, I rest my hands on my head, trying to force oxygen into my lungs.

"Did you see if she hit her head when she passed out?" Linda asks Harper calmly.

"I don't know, I don't think so," Harper shakes her head.

"You said she was drinking." Linda glances at the wine bottle on the coffee table. "Was she drinking that?"

I drop my hands from my head and have to lean forward to prevent myself from passing out or throwing up. Or both. My forearms rest on my knees, yet I still struggle for breath. This can't be happening. This can't be real.

"Yes." My voice is barely audible. "Yes," I repeat, louder this time.

"When did she last eat or drink anything besides the wine?"

"I don't know."

"Does she have anything in her system other than alcohol?" Linda keeps her focus on our conversation but moves back to my sister on the ground. Crouching beside Briar, she opens her eyes and shines a penlight into them.

"Yes," Harper answers. "She said she was on something but didn't tell us what it was."

Linda glances back at Briar, checking her eyes again. "Does she have a history of drug use?"

I swallow hard. "She does," I confirm. "Pills."

Linda nods, her expression neutral. "Possible overdose. I need an IV drip, NARCAN and immediate transport," she tells her partner.

The words hit like a gut punch. Overdose. I sit frozen with fear coursing through my body as the man leans over Briar and administers an odd nasal spray. An overdose? *No. She wouldn't.*

I stare at her body, wishing for Briar to come to, but she doesn't.

"Nate." Harper's voice snaps me back to reality. I lift my head and find Linda crouched in front of me.

"This is important," she says gently. "Do you know what she took?"

I'm shocked by her calm demeanor. She and Harper both—they're just calm. I swallow and shake my head, trying to think as I rub my palm over my face. "She likes pain pills. She had oral surgery a few weeks ago, and they prescribed something, but she told me she threw them out. I didn't check. I should have checked."

"Do you know the name of what they prescribed to her?"

"No. I don't."

Harper stands abruptly. "I'll check her room to try and find something."

Linda nods and turns back to me.

"You didn't do anything wrong," she says. "We're going to take good care of your friend and get her to the hospital," Linda assures me.

"My sister," I whisper. "She's my sister." I swallow back the lump in my throat.

Linda's eyes soften. "We're going to take good care of your sister," Linda corrects herself as she stands. She moves to Briar's side and silently helps her partner load my sister onto the stretcher. They start toward the door and that's all it takes for me to push myself off the couch.

"I'm coming with you. I'm not letting her go alone."

"Of course." Linda's agreement is all I need to force myself to move toward the door.

Before I can reach it, Harper returns with a prescription bottle clutched in her hand. She presses it into Linda's palm before pulling me into a quick hug. Wrapping my arms around her, I relish her touch before she pulls away with a pained smile.

"Go. I'll meet you there."

The pressure builds in my chest as the fear takes hold of my body again. All I can do is offer her a quick nod, unable to form words, and follow Linda outside.

She and her partner load Briar into the back of the ambulance, and I collapse onto the bench.

My gaze lands on Briar's pale face, and a strangled gasp escapes me, seeing her strapped onto the stretcher. I clutch my chest, struggling to take a deep breath or calm my racing heart.

"Are you okay, Nate?" Linda's soft voice draws my attention.

"No."

"Can you take a few deep breaths with me?" she asks as she begins to breathe, continuing to monitor Briar's vitals as she does. I try to imitate her breathing cadence, but I feel strangled by the sound of the sirens that pierce through the back cabin.

"Nate," Linda's voice is steady. "Breathe with me."

I try, but the sirens feel like they're crushing me.

"Good, that's good," she encourages.

She turns to her partner. "Call ahead and let them know we'll need her stomach pumped. We don't know what all she has in there and she's not responding to the NARCAN. I'll go ahead and get a blood draw. Vitals are low. BP eighty over sixty, heart rate fifty-five, thready pulse, slow breathing," Linda relays to the man, who documents everything on a tablet before closing us in. I lean back against the wall, steadying myself as we lurch forward.

After confirming her vitals, Linda turns to me with a smile. "Now I have a few questions about your sister, okay?"

I remain motionless as I stare at Briar, still unable to process seeing her so pale yet so peaceful. I force a nod.

"Okay, great. How old is Briar?"

"She goes by Bri." It's the only thing I can say.

"Bri," Linda repeats gently. "Good. Now, how old is she?"

"Twenty. Turns twenty-one in March. March twenty-sixth."

I tear my gaze from Briar and really look at Linda. There are fine lines around her eyes and mouth, and they're the only signs of how worried she is. "She's going to be okay, right?"

"We're doing everything we can, Nate," she continues to reassure me. I watch them draw blood from Briar's arm, the sight causing me to feel lightheaded. I concentrate on my breathing, trying to collect myself.

Calm down. It's just a little blood.

"Nate, you told me earlier that Briar has a history with prescription pills. Can you tell me more about that?" Linda prompts me, dragging my attention away from the needle currently in my sister's arm.

Focusing on her words, I swallow my nausea. "She had a problem at fourteen but went to therapy. We thought she was okay."

"Do you know what she took when she was fourteen?"

"No. My parents kept it under wraps, and B never talked about it with me," I admit, my voice barely audible above the siren's wailing.

"Okay. Do you know anything else about Briar's medical history? Surgeries? Hospitalizations?" she rattles things off as she rechecks Briar's eyes.

"I think she's missing her spleen. She had something wrong with it last Christmas. I think they took it out." My eyes refocus on her hands as she works. "What are you doing?"

"I'm monitoring her pupillary response to ensure she's remaining stable," she explains calmly. "Are there any medications she takes regularly?"

"I don't know." I run my hands through my hair, desperate to have an answer to these simple questions. I should be able to answer questions about my own sister.

"That's okay. You did a great job and gave me a lot," she offers a small smile. "We're about twenty minutes from the hospital. Do you need to call anyone to meet you there?"

Her question knocks the air from my lungs. "I should call my parents."

Hands trembling, I pull my phone out of my pocket and scroll through the notifications. There are too many to count. From Harper. From my friends. From him. The whole thing is too much. Maybe Harper has already called my parents. At least I hope she has. I flip the phone over, resigning to call my parents once we arrive at the hospital.

Looking at Briar—so still, so pale—I lean forward, resting my elbows on my knees as I stare blankly at the floor between my feet. The weight of it all crashes down. This isn't a nightmare.

This is real.

About the Author

Hanna Grace writes stories for anyone who's ever felt stuck between who they are and who they want to be. Her books blend women's fiction and romance, following characters who are messy, resilient, and trying, just like the rest of us, to figure it all out. If you love complicated relationships, deep feelings, and a little swoon along the way, her stories are right up your alley.

Hanna is so grateful for every reader who picks up her work. You can find her online to stay in the loop on new releases, behind-the-scenes peeks, and all things bookish!

Stay connected here:
TikTok: @theotherhannagrace
Instagram: @theotherhannagrace
GoodReads: @theotherhannagrace

www.ingramcontent.com/pod-product-compliance
Lightning Source LLC
Chambersburg PA
CBHW071749110726
47908CB00006B/1742